THE HARROWING OF GWYNEDD

Volume I of *The Heirs of Saint Camber*

By Katherine Kurtz
Published by Ballantine Books:

THE LEGENDS OF CAMBER OF CULDI

CAMBER OF CULDI
SAINT CAMBER
CAMBER THE HERETIC

THE CHRONICLES OF THE DERYNI

DERYNI RISING
DERYNI CHECKMATE
HIGH DERYNI

THE HISTORIES OF KING KELSON

THE BISHOP'S HEIR
THE KING'S JUSTICE
THE QUEST FOR SAINT CAMBER

THE HEIRS OF SAINT CAMBER

THE HARROWING OF GWYNEDD

THE DERYNI ARCHIVES

LAMMAS NIGHT

THE HARROWING OF GWYNEDD

Volume I of *The Heirs of Saint Camber*

Katherine Kurtz

A Del Rey Book
Ballantine Books • New York

A Del Rey Book
Published by Ballantine Books

Copyright © 1989 by Katherine Kurtz
Map by Shelly Shapiro

Manufactured in the United States of America

For
Anne McCaffrey,
who saved our sanity, if not our lives,
too many times to count
during that incredible first year in Ireland!

CONTENTS

CONTENTS

CONTENTS

CONTENTS

THE HARROWING OF GWYNEDD

Volume I of *The Heirs of Saint Camber*

PROLOGUE

*Let us now praise famous men, and our fathers
that begat us.*
—Ecclesiasticus 44:1

Silvery handfire preceded Evaine MacRorie down the narrow, cut-stone passageway. It lit the subterranean darkness ahead and glinted the gold of her coiled and braided hair to tarnished silver, but the dusty black of her gown swallowed up most of the remaining light.

The close darkness fitted her mood—bleak and weary, especially this early in the morning. She had slept but little after she and Joram finished their work of the night before. Only the two of them knew what lay this deep beneath the Michaeline haven that they once again called home, as they had some twelve years before, when upholding the rights of a now-dead king. The secret of that knowledge would be guarded by every resource at their disposal—and the resources of Evaine and her kin were by no means inconsiderable, as the regents of the present king had cause to know full well. Still, caution mingled with uneasiness as Evaine quietly rounded the last corner.

Different light shimmered cool and opalescent across the doorway she approached, parting like a curtain at her gesture, but she allowed herself only the faintest of smiles as she pushed at the narrow door beyond and felt it move beneath her hand—acknowledgment of a thing working as it should, rather than any real satisfaction, for what lay within the tiny cell was a source both of hope and of dread.

I'm here, Father, she whispered, though she would not look at him until she had closed the door behind her. She had not been

1

alone with him since she and Joram brought him from Saint Mary's, two days before.

She crossed herself as she turned, still wrenched anew to see him laid out thus, the blue-clad body shrouded from head to toe with a veil of white samite. Her hands shook as she lifted the part of the veil covering his own dear face and carefully folded it back. She did not cry, though. She had no tears left for crying.

Camber. Camber Kyriell MacRorie. Father Camber. Father.

Lovingly Evaine recited his true names in her mind as she sank to her knees beside his body, the fingertips of folded hands pressed hard against her lips to stop their trembling.

Oh, Father, do you know what they've done? They called you Alister Cullen, and bishop, for these last twelve years—and Saint Camber, for more than a decade. Now there are those who want to ruin both good names. They're calling you traitor and heretic, using our young king's regency to enrich their own coffers.

She shook her head as she gazed at him, finding but little comfort in the knowledge that he no longer need play at anyone's conception of who or what he ought to be. He had worn the Alister Cullen identity for the last twelve years and more of his life, and vestiges of it remained—and would, even to the grave. The fine, silver-gilt hair capped close to his head was tonsured in the manner his alter-ego had favored, but both men had loved the white-sashed cassock of rich Michaeline blue. And the smooth, roundish face now dimly illuminated by her handfire was wholly his own.

He looked more austere in death than he had seemed in life, even as Alister, but the well-loved face was peaceful in its repose, the agonies of those final moments all but erased by some small, secret satisfaction evinced in a gentle upturn of lip discernible only to close intimates.

Well, the regents shall have their reward in the end, God willing, she mused. *What do they know of truth, who twist and mold it to their own ends? Traitor and heretic you are none, nor ever were, for all that such declaration serves their evil purposes. Alister Cullen you are no more, though remaining priest forever. Saint, I know not. But you were and are my father, my teacher, my friend.*

She bowed her head at that, closing her eyes against the sight of him dead, and wished she could close her mind to memory as well—of finding him in the snow, nearly a week before, his own shape upon him, his quicksilver head pillowed on the breast of the dead Jebediah, their life's blood mingled and frozen on the icy crusts surrounding them.

But though "Alister Cullen" appeared to be as dead as Jebediah,

Evaine had come to believe he had not died at all, but lay bound in a deep and powerful spell, thought by most magical practitioners to be only the stuff of legends. The coolly polished Deryni adept part of her warned that such speculation might be mere denial, an unrealistic refusal on her part to accept the inevitability of his death; but the loving daughter, so recently bereft of husband and first-born son as well as father, kept whispering seductively, *What if? What if?*

Help me know what to do, Father, she breathed, raising her head to look at him again after a few seconds. *I don't know where you are now. If you really are—gone beyond my reach—then it is my fervent prayer that you abide in the Blessed Presence, as your beautiful soul most certainly must merit.*

But what if you aren't really dead? Is that only my loving wish, to keep you with me a little longer, or does some part of you truly cling to life as we mortals know it, so that we really could somehow bring you back to us?

She felt a fluctuation in the shields behind her and then the soft breath of the door opening and closing for another presence. Joram set his hand on her shoulder as he knelt beside her for a moment, golden head bowing in a brief prayer for the man who had sired both of them. Then he crossed himself in a brisk, automatic gesture and turned his gaze full upon her, grey eyes meeting blue.

"Ansel is waiting for you to relieve him," he said quietly. "The others will be expecting us at Dhassa."

Sighing, Evaine gave him a nod and rose as he, too, got to his feet.

"I suppose it *is* time we began picking up the pieces," she murmured. "I've indulged my grief quite long enough."

Joram managed a taut smile. "Don't be too harsh with yourself. You've lost a husband and a first-born son as well as a father. I'd be the first to agree that grieving overlong begins to be self-indulgent to the point of selfishness, but the loss does need to be acknowledged."

"Yes, well, I think I've done that rather thoroughly. Now it's time to make plans for the future. I can't do anything about Rhys or Aidan, but Father . . ."

"I wish you wouldn't."

"Joram, we've had this discussion before."

"That doesn't mean I have to like your conclusion." He sighed and set his hands on his hips.

"Look. He lived a long, full life in his own right. By taking on Alister's identity twelve years ago, he had another full, productive life, at an age when most men are about ready to meet their Maker. He was seventy-one, for God's sake, Evaine. Why can't you just let him be dead?"

"But what if he wasn't ready to die?" she retorted.

Joram snorted, shaking his head bitterly as he turned his gaze to the shrouded body.

"How like Father, to presume to take that decision out of God's hands!"

"How is it presumption, if God gave him the means to continue, and it harms no one? His work was unfinished."

"All men leave work unfinished when they die. Why should he be any different?"

She grinned, despite the weight of their conversation. "Are you going to tell me that he *wasn't* different?"

"We both know that he was," Joram breathed. "That isn't the question."

"Then, what *is* the question?"

He sighed. "It's the same question he asked himself, when Rhys was dying. By then, he was fairly confident that he could work the spell—and it *might* have spared Rhys until a Healer could be brought. But he also feared that a spell powerful enough to hold back Death might have its own terrible cost, to the subject as well as the operator. He would have been willing to accept the risk to himself; but he decided that no one has the right to make that decision for another soul."

"But no one else was involved in Father's spell," Evaine reminded him.

Joram nodded. "That's true. But again, the spell is powerful. If Father is still alive in some strange, mysterious way, who's to say he wouldn't rather stay that way? Who are we to try to bring him back?"

She glanced down at the body before them, then drew the veil of samite over his face once more. Farther down the veil, she could still see the slight bulge of the hands—not just folded peacefully on his breast, the way they had folded Jebediah's, but slightly curved— just—so. That he had *tried* to work the spell to hold back Death, she had no doubt. Whether or not he had succeeded, they would not know until they attempted to reverse it and bring him back. But she believed he would want them to try.

"Joram, I know this isn't an easy question," she said quietly, not looking at him. "But when have we ever expected easy answers? Actually, we aren't considering one question at all, but several. First of all, if he tried the spell and failed, then he's merely dead, and nothing we do will make any difference—so it doesn't hurt to try.

"But if he *is* under the spell, then there are three distinct possibilities. Either we bring him out of it and restore him—which, presumably, is what he would have wanted, so he can carry on his work. Or we bring him out of it and he dies anyway—which at least releases him to the normal cycle of life and death. Or we *can't* bring him out of it, and things stay the same.

"But we can't just leave him here, in limbo, not knowing whether we could have made a difference. And what if he's somehow trapped in his body? We certainly couldn't bury him, not knowing."

Joram nodded grimly, unable to refute that argument, at least. "The last is certainly a factor," he agreed. "I can't imagine anything much more terrifying than regaining consciousness in a tomb and realizing you'd been buried alive."

"I can," Evaine murmured, not looking at him. "Being bound to a body that really, truly, *is* dead—decaying."

Joram shook his head and suppressed a shiver. "There's no sign of *that*, at least. It's something more than just the cold, too. Almost as if Rhys—as if one of the Healers had put a preservation spell on it," he amended awkwardly. "Jebediah's body—isn't in this condition."

"No, and the real Alister's body isn't in this condition, and there *was* a preservation spell on *him*," she said quietly. "But Death-Readings were done on Alister and Jebediah. We *know* they're dead."

Sighing, Joram nodded. "And we couldn't Read Father," he murmured. "*Ergo*, he isn't dead. Or it *could* just be the blocks he would have set, to preserve the identity of his alter-ego—"

"From us?" Evaine interjected. "Joram, it isn't that there's nothing to Read. It's that something won't *let* us Read. He knew we would be there soon. Do you really think he would have cut us off that way?"

"No."

"Neither do I." She looked at him oddly. "Something else is bothering you, though."

Joram cleared his throat, looking decidedly uncomfortable—but in a different manner than before.

"Well, yes. How can I explain this to you without sounding as if I think it's true?" He cocked his head at her, searching for just the right words.

"Do you remember how, when everyone thought Father had been killed and they wanted to canonize him, we didn't dare produce his body, for fear it would be discovered that Alister had died instead of him? The bishops said he had been 'bodily assumed into heaven,' and used that as part of the rationale for declaring him a saint. But if saints aren't taken directly into heaven, what other thing sometimes happens to their bodies?"

"They don't decay," Evaine breathed. "They remain incorruptible."

"Exactly. And right now, his body is incorruptible—for no logical reason that we can offer." Joram glanced at the shrouded body with a mixture of disbelief and awe.

"Evaine, what if he really *is* a saint?"

CHAPTER ONE

Every purpose is established by counsel.
—Proverbs 22:18

"I have to tell you that burying those three men was one of the most difficult things I've ever had to do," Joram confessed to their Dhassa compatriots an hour later—though he tried not to think about that fourth body he had just left, hidden beneath the chapel where the other three lay. "I know we must put our grief and outrage behind us now, and move on to the more constructive measures we all know they would have wished, but I won't even pretend that can happen overnight. For now, we're going to have to take it a day at a time—and maybe even hour by hour, when things get particularly difficult."

He was pacing back and forth beside a table in Bishop Niallan's private quarters in besieged Dhassa, drawn and gaunt-looking in monkish black instead of the now-dangerous blue of the Michaelines—though he had worn his former habit the day before, to honor two of the three men he buried. The pale cap of his hair, tonsured now in the manner of any ordinary priest, shone like a halo as he paused where a beam of weak winter sunlight filtered through an east window. Niallan, seated at the head of the long table, resisted the urge to cross himself in awe at the pent-up power smoldering in Saint Camber's son, though he, like Joram, was Deryni and fully capable of not a little power himself.

So were most of the other men ranged around the bishop's table—all, in fact, save the younger man at Niallan's immediate left, who also wore episcopal purple. Dermot O'Beirne, the deposed Bishop of

Cashien, had thrown in his lot with Niallan on that fatal Christmas Day a fortnight before, when everything else seemed to fall apart. The regents' assault on Valoret Cathedral, given color of authority by the young king's active presence and participation, had put an end to Alister Cullen's brief tenure as Archbishop of Valoret. It had also put an end to any subsequent hope of tempering the regents' increasingly anti-Deryni policies via the established Church hierarchy. Indeed, one of the most notorious of the regents now occupied the primatial throne, and had suspended and excommunicated both bishops at Dhassa as one of his first official acts.

The rest of Niallan's now-renegade household were under similar bans, for standing by their master and refusing to surrender his See of Dhassa to his designated successor. At Niallan's right sat his chaplain and personal Healer of many years' standing, Dom Rickart, the Gabrilite priest's white robes a startling contrast to the bishops' purple and the shades of mourning that everyone else wore. Rickart was of an age with Niallan, but the long hair drawn back in the tight, single braid of his Order was glossy chestnut, where Niallan's hair and neatly trimmed beard were steely grey.

Another, younger Healer sat across from Rickart, next to Dermot, though nothing in his demeanor or dress declared his Healer's calling today. Both his tunic and his nubbly wool mantle were a dull dust-umber, the color of weathered stone. Nor did he look old enough to be a Healer, though up until a few weeks ago, he had been personal Healer and tutor to young Prince Javan, the king's clubfooted twin brother and heir. The talented and sometimes head-strong Tavis O'Neill was not exactly a member of the bishop's household, but Niallan had given him refuge when he was forced to quit Valoret. He remained their one reliable contact with the prince.

Tavis was also, so far as they knew, the sole possessor of an apparently unique Deryni talent that held up some hope of preserving their Deryni race against evil times to come—though the ultimate cost of such salvation might be dire, indeed. His dark red head tipped downward in close-shielded reverie, the pale eyes moody and unreadable as his right hand absent-mindedly massaged a hand-less left wrist.

And at the far end of the table, looking gloomily preoccupied, the seventeen-year-old Ansel MacRorie turned a dagger over and over in his hands, his pale golden hair proclaiming him close kin to Joram, even if all in the room had not already been aware that he was Joram's nephew. Though Ansel should have been Earl of Culdi by right of his birth, as heir to Camber's eldest son, he, like Joram and everyone else in the room, was an outlaw in the eyes of the established government.

The rest of Niallan's principal household officers and functionaries occupied stools set along the rest of the table, two men to a side, his chancellor, comptroller, provisioner, and garrison commander, the latter still wearing the dark blue tunic and white sash of a Michaeline knight.

Sighing, Niallan slowly shook his head, not in negation of anything Joram had said, but in grim resignation.

"Aye, 'tis an incalculable loss," he murmured. "Alister, Jebediah, and Rhys. And unfortunately, I'm afraid we have to expect that things may get worse before they get better. To assume anything less would be to leave ourselves open to even greater disaster than we've already suffered."

"Which is precisely why I want you safely out of Dhassa, sir," Joram said quietly.

"I will not even try to gainsay you," Niallan agreed, "but do try to accept my position. When I became Bishop of Dhassa, I was made shepherd of *all* her people, human as well as Deryni. I have Deryni responsibilities, that is true; but I cannot desert my human flock when they need me most."

"No, but you must not wait so long that you let yourself be taken," Joram retorted, setting his hands on the back of Ansel's chair. "That does no one any service except the regents, who you *know* seek your death."

Niallan smiled, toying with the bishop's amethyst on his right hand. "Then, I am in good company," he said lightly, "for you and Ansel have even higher prices on your heads than I. But don't worry, my friend. There is no martyr's blood in these veins. I shall stay here in Dhassa as long as I may, but only to ensure that nothing will fall into the regents' hands that ought not."

"Including Dhassa's bishop?" Ansel said archly.

"Including Dhassa's bishop," Niallan repeated, favoring the boy with a fond smile. "But you must remember, dear Ansel, that such title applied to my person no longer means what it once did, now that one of the regents is our new archbishop."

"Hubert MacInnis will never be *my* archbishop," Joram stated flatly, as he started pacing again.

"No, nor mine," Niallan agreed. "But in the eyes of those who do not know that his election required deception, slander, and murder, he is senior archbishop and Primate—and woe be unto the people of Gwynedd, in the hands of such a shepherd."

"If I'm given the chance," said Tavis O'Neill, speaking for the first time, "I shall kill him!"

"And betray your Healer's oath?" Dom Rickart gasped, obviously putting into words what several of the others also felt.

"Healer's oaths be hanged, if they protect a man like Hubert MacInnis!" Tavis snapped, the pale aquamarine eyes blazing as he glared across at the other Healer. "I am no Gabrilite, to submit meekly to the slaughter. I will not offer my throat to the regents like some silly sheep, as your brethren did at Saint Neot's. Nor will I allow Prince Javan to become their victim—not while there is breath in my body to prevent it!"

"Easy, Tavis, *easy!*" Joram murmured, jerking out a stool beside Rickart and straddling it as Niallan and Dermot also made soothing noises and gestures. "No one's asking you to sacrifice yourself—or faulting your defense of the prince."

"Certainly not," Rickart hastily agreed. "Prince Javan is our major hope that something eventually may be done to reverse what the regents have set in motion. But I beg you, Tavis, do not deliberately seek out MacInnis' life."

"Shall your brethren die unavenged, then?" Tavis demanded.

As Ansel and the Michaeline Knight at the end of the table muttered something between them about divine retribution, Rickart gently shook his head.

"My dear young friend, Hubert MacInnis shall pay for what he has done—never fear. Not only to my Gabrilite brethren but to all innocent folk who have become victims of his avarice. But it is not our place to seek vengeance. 'Vengeance is mine, saith—' "

"Yes, yes, but the Lord generally works through mortal agents," Joram interjected, raising a hand in a fending-off gesture. "Please, Rickart, let's not start a theological debate. Tavis is not a Gabrilite or a Michaeline, so he's not arguing from the same assumptions. If the two of you want to take up this discussion privately, at a later date, that's another matter. Right now, however, I have more important things on my mind, the chief of which is the prince we're all trying to protect, in our own ways. Which leads me to ask, Tavis, is it tonight you're to see him again?"

Tavis sighed, a little subdued. "Aye. He doesn't yet know about Alister and Jebediah, either. At least *I* haven't told him. We'd just had a meeting when I found out, and I didn't want to increase the already considerable risk he runs every time I go there, by going back too soon."

"I don't envy you the telling," Niallan said quietly.

Shrugging, Tavis shook his head. "Someone else may already

have told him, by now. That kind of news travels fast. If it *has* reached Valoret, you can bet the regents won't keep it a secret."

"*I'll* say!" Ansel snorted. "There'll be dancing in the streets."

Joram, hushing Ansel with a hand signal, returned his attention to Tavis.

"Naturally, the regents' reaction will be of great interest to us," he said quietly, "but Javan's safety is our most important concern. I take it that we can expect a full report in the morning, provided all goes well?"

Tavis nodded, but said nothing.

"Well, then," Niallan said with a sigh. "I suppose we'll have to wait until then. But you've done right, not to endanger the prince unnecessarily. Whatever else happens, he must be protected. I wonder, though, if it will make the regents more or less vindictive to learn that two of their most bitter enemies are dead."

Dermot managed a sickly grin. "They'll probably use it as justification to step up their campaign against two more troublesome priests. I suppose we should be flattered that Rhun and his men are giving us so much attention, camped right outside Dhassa's gates."

"Which is precisely why I do not intend us to stay in Dhassa any longer than we must," Niallan replied. "And that brings us back to the subject of Saint Mary's. Joram, I know you've abandoned it for the time being. How long do you think we must wait before it's safe again? When I *am* ready to vacate Dhassa, I must have places to send my people."

"Then you'll do better to funnel them through Gregory's new Portal at Trevalga," Joram replied. "I'll have him show you the coordinates in the next week or so. From there, it's a relatively simple matter to disperse through the Connait, where folk are a little more sane about Deryni these days."

"Then for now, you feel that Saint Mary's is out of the question?" asked the Michaeline Knight.

Joram sighed. "If Alister and Jebediah hadn't been killed so close to there, we'd be fine. I think I told you all that one of their killers got away. The latest we hear is that Manfred MacInnis' men have been scouring the area, looking for some trace of the bodies—which makes it a less than desirable place for Deryni. Frankly, I'm not even happy that Queron is on his way there."

"You expect him soon?" Rickart asked.

Joram nodded. "Any day now, provided nothing else has gone wrong. The brothers know he's coming, but none of them can speak of it to anyone but him or one of us. Evaine and I made sure of that before we left. The compulsion won't stand up against anything stronger than a very cursory Truth-Read, but we're gambling on the probability that Manfred doesn't have a Deryni working for him yet—and that no one will have cause to suspect that our monks have anything to hide."

Niallan snorted. "Poor Queron, walking into the lion's den. Do you think he knows?"

Ansel chuckled mirthlessly. "Well, if he doesn't, I suspect he'll find out, soon enough."

Indeed, Queron Kinevan certainly knew that soldiers were looking for Deryni by then, even if he did not know the particular reason. He had been dodging mounted patrols for days. The night before Joram made his report to his Dhassa confederates, Queron had taken refuge from soldiers and a gathering snowstorm by hiding in a rickety barn, burrowed deep inside a haystack. He was still there, curled in a tight, miserable ball, as dawn lightened a slate-colored winter sky.

He knew he was dreaming, but he could not wake himself to stop it. In the fortnight since the nightmare's first occurrence, he had never yet succeeded in doing so. Fueled by his own memories, the dream seemed to have lost none of its potency. And whether he tried to sleep by day or by night, some part of it always found him, always in heart-gripping detail.

It was dusk in the dream—a haunting dusk, two weeks before, as the fires finally died down in the yard at Dolban. From where Queron crouched to watch in disbelieving horror, just at the crest of a hill overlooking the abbey, he could almost imagine that none of it had happened—for the soldiers had spared the buildings.

But not its brethren. And therein lay the basis for the quarrel that, for a time, had set Queron at odds with the younger man hunkered at his side. The first flames already had been licking skyward on that cold December afternoon when he and Revan scrambled to the top of the rise above the abbey, in the wake of an excited band of Willimite brethren from the campsite the two had just left. Partway down the slope on the other side, some of the Willimites had started singing a militant, off-key hymn whose major theme was hatred of magic, exhorting God's faithful to be His scourge to rid the land of the undoubtedly evil magic of the Deryni. And in the yard beyond—

"*Jesu Christe*, what are they *doing*?" Queron had gasped, stumbling to his knees in the snow—though at least he had had the presence of mind to keep his voice down.

For the soldiers in the yard below seemed to have taken the Willimites' hymn very much to heart. Dozens of stakes had been erected in Dolban's yard, most of them unwillingly embraced by men and women in blood-soaked grey habits—for the soldiers had bound their wrists above their heads and were scourging them with weighted whips that rent mere cloth and laid open the victims' backs with each new stroke. Queron quailed at the spectacle, hardly able to believe his eyes, for he had been abbot to these innocent folk—the Order he himself had founded, to honor the blessed Saint Camber. Only by chance had he not been among them on this Childermas of 917, three days past Christmas—fittingly called the Feast of the Holy Innocents, he had realized, days later.

Knives and pincers figured in the treatment of some of the prisoners, and a great deal of blood, but Queron mercifully was too far away to see exactly what was being done. However, there was no mistaking the bundles of faggots the soldiers had begun piling around the base of many of the stakes. A few already sprouted flames among the kindling, and rising shrieks of agony began to float up on the cold winter air.

"My God, this can't be happening," Queron sobbed. "Revan, we must stop it!"

But young Revan, not Deryni or highly trained or even of noble birth, had shaken his head and set his heart, knowing with that certainty of common sense so often lost or buried in those of more formal erudition that any intervention by just the two of them was futile.

"There's nothing we can do, sir," Revan had whispered. "If we go down there, we'd only be throwing our lives away. *You* may be ready to die, but I have a responsibility to Lord Rhys and Lady Evaine. I'm willing to die for *them*, but I don't think they mean it to be at Dolban."

Queron had refused to let the words make sense, something akin to madness seizing him as the outrage unfolded below.

"*I* can do something!" he had whispered. "I'll blast them with magic! I shall make them taste the wrath of Saint Camber, through *his* Servant. Magic can be woven—"

"And if you do weave magic against them, what then?" Revan said, grasping Queron's sleeve and jerking his face closer. "Can't you see that you'd be doing exactly the thing that the regents say Deryni do? Is that what you want?"

"How dare you presume to instruct *me*?" Queron snapped, icy anger keeping his words all but inaudible. "Take your hands off me and stay out of my way. Do it *now*, Revan!"

Wordlessly Revan had released him, apparently cowed. But as Queron sank back on his heels, preparing to unleash magical retribution, Revan had shifted the olivewood staff hitherto nestled in the crook of his arm and cudgeled Queron smartly behind the left ear. Queron crumpled into the snow without a sound, his vision going black, and Revan's voice had seemed to come from a long way off.

"Sorry, m'lord, but throwing your life away is *stupid*!" Revan had murmured, as he rooted in Queron's scrip for a Healer's drug kit. "Gabrilite or not, I can't let you do that."

That had been the end of their quarrel. With the sedative Revan gave him in melted snow, Queron had drowsed the afternoon through, never quite unconscious, but too groggy to offer further resistance of any kind. He had dreamed then, too, haunted by the images of his brethren being tortured and killed, the nightmare embellished and intensified by the sounds that floated up from the yard beyond.

Gradually, the winter shadows lengthened. Slowly the heart-wrenching screams and the gabble and gurgle of dying gave way to the hungry crackle of the flames and then the softer whisper of a rising wind and the feather of new snow falling, mercifully muffling some of the horror.

More wind wailed somewhere outside Queron's present dream, and he bit back a groan as he stirred in his haystack hollow. Again he tried to claw his way up to consciousness, out of the nightmare, but still it held him fast. He whimpered a little as it dragged him into its depths again, not wanting to remember what he had learned from Revan when he woke that other time, there on the slope above Dolban.

"It's over now," Revan had said softly, leaning heavily on his olivewood staff and looking for all the world like some latter-day John the Baptist—which was precisely what Revan intended. Suddenly Queron had found himself wondering whether that made any more sense than what the men below had done.

"I know it doesn't make any sense," Revan had said, when Queron did not speak—as if he somehow had caught Queron's very thought, though the Healer knew that was impossible. "What possible sense could there be, much less any modicum of justice, to burn to death more than three-score men and women simply because they chose to honor and revere the memory of a man they believed holy?"

"Is *that* why they did it?" Queron had whispered, his vision blurring anew as he gazed down at the blackened stakes in the yard, and the soldiers moving among them.

"More or less." Revan had turned his head to look Queron in the eye. "I spoke with several of my Willimite 'brethren' while you were asleep," he said quietly. "They, in turn, had spoken with several of the soldiers down below. Apparently, the orders came directly from the bishops in council at Ramos. Go ahead and read the details for yourself. I'm not afraid."

And Revan was *not* afraid, though a lesser man might have had ample reason to be, after physically assaulting a Deryni of Queron's ability. As Queron lightly touched the younger man's wrist and began to focus, trying not to make the physical contact too obvious to anyone watching, he was surprised and humbled by the younger man's fearless trust. Though Revan could not have stopped his doing anything he wanted, Reading was always easier with the subject's active cooperation.

But the wonder of that discovery was blunted almost immediately by what Queron had learned—that the abbey's own patron saint was at least indirectly responsible for the attack. The men now gaining ascendancy in Gwynedd, regents for the twelve-year-old King Alroy, had declared Dolban's patron, the Deryni Saint Camber, to be no saint at all, but a heretic and traitor—and therein lay Dolban's fate.

Nevermore was the name of Camber MacRorie to be spoken in Gwynedd, on pain of consequences almost too terrible to comprehend. Henceforth, a first offense would merit public flogging, with the offender's tongue forfeit for a second utterance—which accounted for the pincers and knives Queron had seen. And only that special death reserved for heretics would answer for further intransigence.

Not that Saint Camber's Servants at Dolban could have known in time how they transgressed the law—or would have cared, had they known, for their devotion to the Deryni saint had been unswerving for more than a decade. The edict rescinding Camber's sainthood and declaring the penalties for defying that edict had only been promulgated the day before, many miles away in Ramos. Their enemies had never intended to give them any advance warning. The first inkling of their plight would have been when the regents' soldiers—episcopal troops, at that—swarmed into the abbey yard and began taking prisoners.

All surely had heard the edict read as the floggings began, however, and had ample time to contemplate the full measure of the edict's horror as the executioners began their grisly work with pincers and knives. Tongueless, the condemned could not even plead ignorance of the law, or recant, or beg for mercy, as the soldiers piled the kindling high around the rows of stakes and passed among them with their torches.

Stunned at the legalism behind the savagery he had witnessed, tears streaming down his cheeks, Queron had withdrawn from Revan's mind, burying his face in his hands to weep silently.

"Forgive me for my earlier lapse," he finally had whispered, mindful that the breeze had shifted upwind of them and would carry sound down to the guards below—though at least it no longer brought them the stench of burned flesh. "You were entirely correct that magic would not have been the answer."

Wiping at his tears with the back of his hands, he had summoned the courage to look up at Revan humbly.

"Rhys taught you well," he went on quietly. "If I'd been thinking clearly, I suppose I should have expected you might hit me over the head. But I never thought to be drugged from my own Healer's kit."

Revan managed a hint of a bitter smile, turning his light brown eyes on Queron only briefly. "Be thankful I didn't dose you with *merasha*. You'd still be out of action. I couldn't let you go to certain death, though, now could I?"

"I suppose not."

Sighing, Queron fingered the end of his grey-streaked Gabrilite braid where it had escaped from under his hood, knowing that a painful decision was approaching.

"I think I've been away from my Gabrilite Order far too long," he had whispered. "It becomes all too easy to forget that I swore never to kill. I suppose that goes for killing myself as well as other men—though there are a few down below who could do with killing."

He glanced at the dimming yard below, at the torches moving among the burned-out stakes as the guards patrolled the last of the dying fires, then looked back at Revan thoughtfully.

"It will be dark soon. I think it might be healthiest for both of us if I went on alone."

"Why?" Revan had asked. "No one suspects who you are."

"Not *who*, no." He held up the end of his braid. "But if anyone were to see this, they might suspect *what*. It isn't necessarily true that only Gabrilites and the Servants of Saint Camber wear braids more or less like this, but in this vicinity, given what's just happened down there, it strikes me that such a symbol might cause—ah—dangerous questions to be asked. I wonder, are your barbering skills as good as your medical ones?"

Revan had blinked and looked at him strangely.

"Beg pardon, sir?"

"I want you to cut it off for me, Revan." Queron pulled the braid over his shoulder. "I've had this a long time, and losing it will not be without cost, but I'm afraid it's become more of a liability than an asset. Our founders never meant it to be a betrayal unto death—mine or yours."

Revan shifted uneasily, but he pulled from his belt the little knife he used for cutting bread and cheese, fingering its edge uncertainly as Queron turned his back.

"Go ahead," the Healer murmured. "Don't worry about finesse. Just hack it off. We haven't got all night."

He tried to make himself relax as Revan gingerly took hold of the braid and worked his fingers up toward the base of Queron's neck where the plaiting began, sensing Revan's surprise and curiosity when he discovered that the braid was composed of four strands rather than the more common three—though Revan did not ask about it.

"We call the braid a *g'dula*," Queron said quietly, taut as a catapult as Revan began sawing across the wiry mass with his knife. "The four strands have a special symbolism for us. I mayn't tell you what it is, beyond the obvious connection with the four Archangels and the four Quarters, but since I'm sure you noticed, it seemed only fair to tell you." He sighed heavily and suppressed a shudder. "No blade has touched my hair since I took my first vows—it's been nearly twenty-five years ago now. The braid will have to be ritually burned, when time and place permit."

Cutting the braid had been a psychic wrench as well as a physical one, and Queron, reliving the trauma in his dream, twitched in his sleep and startled awake at last, all at once, one hand automatically groping toward the scrip at his waist. His heart was pounding, his breathing rapid and alarmed, but the braid was still there, wound in a tight coil the size of his fist.

Thank God!

Gradually, the panic past, his heart rate and breathing returned to normal. After a while, very cautiously, he began burrowing out of his haystack, squinting increasingly against the glare of the early morning sun on snowdrifts, for the "barn" sheltering the hay was a roof only, supported by four stout posts, and the roof itself was none too sound. He knew he must deal with the *g'dula* soon—which probably would stop the nightmares—but right now, his first priority was to find Saint Mary's Abbey. The goodwife who had given him beggar's fare of bread and hot, thick stew, the previous noon, had said she *thought* there was a small monastery in the hills not far from here, but she had not known its name. It *might* be Saint Mary's.

God willing, it would be the *right* Saint Mary's this time, Queron thought, as he emerged stiffly from his fragrant cocoon, pulling his mantle more closely around himself and brushing off bits of hay. The name seemed all too popular in this part of the world, notwithstanding Queron's personal devotion to the Blessed Virgin. He had had enough of false alarms since arriving in these hills above Culdi, several days before—and of dodging mounted patrols of the new Earl of Culdi's men. Far more often than he had hoped, in the two weeks since leaving Dolban, he had had to abandon perfectly good lodgings to avoid a possibly fatal confrontation with men sympathetic to the regents' most recent atrocities.

Nor had he dared to be too blatant in the use of his powers to improve the situations. In these troubled times, simply *being* Deryni seemed likely to bring about one's death, whether or not one actually used his or her magical powers.

But perhaps today would be different. At least the storm seemed to have blown itself out. His hood had slipped back from his head while he fretted and squirmed in the grip of his nightmare, and he combed stiff fingers through his shorn hair as he surveyed the morning. Nothing stirred to break the pristine silence of the new snowfall on this cold winter's morn.

So then, briefly lamenting the past month's lack of a razor, he covered his head again and knelt to make his morning offering of praise and thanksgiving, as he did each day on rising. And today, as always, he raised defiant prayers to Camber of Culdi, whose lands these once had been, and who was and would remain a saint, so far as Queron Kinevan was concerned.

CHAPTER TWO

They were killed, but by accursed men, and such as had taken up an unjust envy against them.

—I Clement 20:7

Snow began to fall again by midafternoon, but the sky stayed bright. Queron drew his hood closer as he approached the gate of yet another tiny abbey, raising a numb, mittened hand to shade his eyes against the snow glare and study the thin curls of smoke eddying upward from several sets of chimneys.

At least no horses appeared to have been this way today—a fair indication that he would find no soldiers about. And the smoke meant that he might hope for a hot meal and a chance to warm himself in the abbey's parlor. His booted feet were near frozen after another day's trudging through the snow, his cloak and hood rimed with ice. With any luck, this might even turn out to be the Saint Mary's he was looking for—though he had had enough disappointments in the last few days not to expect too much.

No horses stood in the yard of this new abbey, either—another good sign that the place was safe. As Queron paused at the open gate, cautiously casting out with his mind for danger, a middle-aged monk in a black habit and mantle came down off the catwalk over the gate arch and made him a deferential bow, hands tucked into sleeve openings, as was seemly.

"The blessings of God Almighty be upon you, good traveler," the monk said. "May I offer you the humble hospitality of Saint Mary's?"

Mentally allowing himself a tiny sigh of relief—for at least this was *one* of the local Saint Mary's—Queron swept back his hood and returned the man's bow, hoping his tonsure had not grown out so far as to be totally unrecognizable.

"Thank you, brother," he murmured. "Who gives charity unasked gives twice. God will surely bless this house. May I ask the name of your abbot?"

With a gesture for Queron to accompany him, the monk turned to lead him across the yard toward the chapel.

"Our abbot is Brother Cronin," he said easily. "I am Brother Tiernan. And you are—?"

Truth-Reading to confirm, for he had been given the names of several of the brethren of the House, Queron let himself relax a little more, stomping snow from his boots as they mounted wooden steps to the chapel door.

"My name is Kinevan. Queron Kinevan. I believe you've been expecting me."

The monk turned and set his back against the chapel door, eying Queron speculatively.

"Ah, we *were* told we might expect a Gabrilite by that name," he said softly, "but I see no Gabrilite before me."

"I have lately been abbot of—another Order," Queron murmured, not wanting to mention Saint Camber's name until he knew for certain that all was well. "I have not worn Gabrilite habit for many years."

"It is my understanding that Gabrilite habit does not consist solely of the garment," the monk insisted, "and that its putting off is no light matter. Is there not some further proof you might offer, that you are what and who you say you are?"

Queron allowed himself a wry smile. This Brother Tiernan was a bold one. Not all humans would dare to make such a demand of an unknown Deryni. The fellow wanted to know about his braid—not normally a topic of discussion outside the Order, but perhaps it was necessary.

"I think you wish no graphic demonstration of *what* I am," Queron said quietly, digging in his scrip for the coil of plaited hair, "but I suspect that this should prove adequately that I am *who* I claim to be." He displayed the coil on his open palm. "Is this what you expected to see? I fear it became a liability, attached to my head. I advise you not to touch it, but I assure you, it *is* mine."

Tiernan glanced a little nervously at the braid, as if a bit taken aback by his own effrontery, but shook his head and swallowed when Queron would have lifted it nearer.

"Please come inside, out of the cold, Dom Queron," he murmured, averting his eyes as he turned to open the door. "Instructions have been left for you."

The inside of the chapel was little warmer than outside. Queron could see his breath pluming on the air before him as he followed Tiernan down the center aisle, tucking the braid back in its place in his scrip. Shadows wreathed the open beams of the simple ceiling, but the walls were whitewashed and made the little building seem lighter and more airy than it actually was. He could hear the sounds of construction going on behind a wooden screen that closed off the north transept, but they gradually ceased as Tiernan led him past the simple transept crossing and toward the altar, where a red lamp burned above the tabernacle.

"Wait here, please," Tiernan said, when the two of them paused at the foot of the altar steps to reverence the Presence signified by that lamp.

Mystified, Queron watched the monk continue on alone to the tabernacle and fit a key to its lock. From behind several veiled ciboria, Tiernan removed what appeared to be a small, suede leather pouch, no bigger than the palm of his hand. This he tucked into the front of his habit, signing for Queron to rise and come with him toward the screened-off northern transept.

As Queron followed his guide through a doorway in the screen, several more black-robed monks backed off skittishly from a bare patch of earth in front of the transept altar, bowing cowled heads over folded hands as they pressed against the far wall. They had been shifting heavy flagstones back into position to cover the bare patch—which might pass as a grave, to the uninitiated; but Queron recognized it instantly as the probable site of the Portal he knew Evaine and Joram had planned to construct.

"God bless the work," Queron murmured, declining to speak more specifically until he knew the exact status of the men watching him.

His quick mental cast locked on the Portal's distinctive tingle almost immediately. Cautiously he moved the few steps necessary to center himself within it—to the apparent consternation of several of the watchers. And to his own consternation, a quick stretching of his powers failed to touch any other Portal. Either he was out of range, or all the others he knew about had been destroyed or blocked.

"Interesting," he murmured under his breath. "Brother Tiernan, I don't suppose anyone left me any more explicit instructions?"

With a quiet hand sign, Tiernan signalled the other monks to depart. Only when they had gone did he move close enough to Queron to hand him the brown suede pouch.

"The Lady Evaine asked that I give this into your keeping only when you had placed yourself where you now stand. I—do not know what it contains or what will happen when you take it out."

"But I am to open it here," Queron said, gingerly feeling at the contents of the pouch through the leather. It seemed to be something flat and round, perhaps of metal, possibly a medallion of some sort.

"Curious," he murmured. "Did she give you any other caution?"

Tiernan shook his head. "No, my lord. I watched them all leave through this Portal, though. I know what happens, and I am not afraid."

"And you are rare among humans for that," Queron replied. "Did you know that, Brother Tiernan?"

Tiernan shrugged. "I am only an ignorant monk, Domine. But I trust the Lady Evaine and Father Joram. Ah—he said that you would recognize what lies inside and that you would know what to do."

"Father Joram said that?"

"Aye, Domine."

"Then, we must not make a liar of him, must we?" Queron loosened the strings of the pouch and peered inside.

"Well, what's this?" he said, beginning to pull out part of a narrow, green silk cord, along with what was attached to it. "It's—a Healer's seal. It's Rhys' Healer's seal!" he breathed, as he caught the dull, silvery medallion in the palm of his hand.

Rhys' name and the year of his matriculation from Saint Neot's were cut into the side facing Queron; and if he turned it over, he knew it would bear Rhys' personal coat of arms augmented with the star-pierced hand that was a Healer's badge of vocation.

"But—Rhys would never give this up. Not to anyone. Not unless—"

Convulsively he clutched the medal harder in his hand as the implication registered. Now he thought he knew why Evaine had wanted him to stand precisely here, in the center of the new Portal, before he opened the pouch. For something had happened to Rhys—he feared the younger Healer was dead—and reading that tragic message here, in this place, would send up a psychic beacon for one of them to come back to get him.

He had to blink back tears as he tucked the empty pouch into the top of his scrip and then smoothed the silk cord over the back of his hand, trying not to look at the medal, now that he had an inkling of what it bore. Just in time, he realized that Tiernan was still watching, awed even by Queron's reaction thus far; and he signalled with an impatient gesture that Tiernan should leave.

The monk backed out without demur, quietly closing the door

through the screen before padding off through another door that probably led to the sacristy. Only when Queron was certain he was alone did he allow himself to look at the medallion again.

Rhys Thuryn's Healer's medallion. This time, the arms and badge were uppermost, but that did not change the foreboding now lurking all around Queron's consciousness. Nor would further delay soften the medal's message.

Drawing a deep, centering breath as he laid his hand over the silver, Queron closed his eyes and triggered the spell set there. It was even worse than he had dreamed. Briefly, he sensed the psychic signatures imprinted there at the time Rhys received it—Dom Emrys and another, unknown to Queron.

But then, all the psychic impact of Rhys' death—plus the slaughter at Trurill and the slaying of Alister Cullen and Jebediah—came punching through any resistance he might have tried to raise, relentless in all the detail he must know, in order to survive.

Evaine nibbled at the end of her quill and glanced aside as the infant sleeping in the basket at her elbow stirred. The list she had been working on all afternoon was mostly complete—well, it was a good working draft—but she wished again that Rhys were here to help her. She missed him more and more with every day that passed.

God, what a splendid team they had made! Looking across the table to the chair that once had been his, she could almost see him gazing back at her, the amber eyes a little amused at her acclaim, the fingers of one tapered Healer's hand lifting in a light-hearted gesture of self-deprecation. The scholar's training and the eye for detail had been hers—and the skill with languages—but it was he who had brought that unique gift of intuitive logic, that knack that often cut through layers of artifice that might have taken her weeks or even months to fathom. Sifting through the ancient records on her list would have been a joy, with Rhys at her side.

But Rhys was not at her side; nor would he ever be again, except in her dreams. The little daughter beginning to squirm and coo in the basket would never know her father, for he had died a week before her birth. Though he had been among the greatest Healers of his age, Rhys Thuryn had died for no better reason than any of the others they had laid away last night in the Michaeline chapel, fated never to see the daughter who, like his younger son, bore the sacred gift of Healing. Nor, in his final moments, had his gift been able to save *him*.

He had not even *looked* dead, Evaine recalled, angrily casting down her quill and turning tear-brimmed eyes to the dome of dull amethyst above her head, trying *not* to remember. Preserved under a stasis spell set shortly after he died, he might merely have been asleep—though he had been dead for a fortnight by the time she actually saw his body. Not a mark or wound had he borne upon him—only a faint indentation at the back of his skull, padded by the wiry, reddish hair—surely not enough to kill a man such as he!

But it *had* killed him—had killed his body, at any rate, though Rhys himself no longer resided there. That some eternal part of him still survived elsewhere was a firm cornerstone of her belief, too profoundly affirmed by what her father had told her of others' passing ever to be questioned. The body was a temple of the soul during life, but no more than an empty shell, once the soul passed on.

Still, she had loved the body as well as the soul and the brilliant mind it housed; so before consigning that body to its cold and lonely tomb, she had covered him tenderly with the cope her father had wrapped around him where he first fell—a princely vestment of ivory silk and rich embroidery work, stiff with bullion, fit for a king. In fact, it had been the gift of a king—Cinhil Haldane, for whom most of the suffering of the past decade and more had been endured.

Now Cinhil was nearly a year dead himself, along with the others who had joined him since: Archbishop Jaffray, and Bishops Davet Nevan and Kai Descantor, and Jebediah—and Rhys. Evaine had not cried as they laid him away, but she cried now. She told herself that crying did no good, that she but squandered energy better hoarded for the living, but the tears still came, runneling silently down her cheeks to drip off her chin and splash on the list she had written, blurring the ink.

The destruction brought her back to reason, though, for in the words she had written lay hope for at least one of the men she mourned.

The Annales of Sulien, she read. *The Protocols of Orin. The Liber Sancti Ruadan. Tomes by Leutiern and Jorevin of Cashel.* And she knew that Camber himself had written commentaries on some of the texts. She even knew where some of them were.

Wiping her tears on the edge of her sleeve, Evaine picked up her quill again and dipped it, making several more notations. When the tiny Jerusha stirred and began to fuss a little, demanding to be held, Evaine gathered her to her breast, continuing to tick off items on the list.

All of the texts were likely sources of information. Copies of a few of the documents lay hidden beneath the flooring in the Portal at her and Rhys' former manor house of Sheele, where she had left them for safe-keeping when she and Ansel fled with the children. Some of the rarer texts might be available through the Varnarite library at Grecotha—though gaining access to the library might be a problem, since the nephew of one of the regents was now Grecotha's new bishop.

Other clues perhaps lay in the ancient ruins underneath Grecotha itself. She had never been there personally, but Joram had. Perhaps the ancient Deryni who built and then abandoned the site had left information. The chamber where she now sat was their work—though she suspected that she and her family had hardly begun to plumb the depths of the secrets hidden just in this one place.

One other consideration must come before even these, however—and that was one of the reasons she kept watch now in this chamber. The Healer Queron Kinevan was expected—an odd ally, he, for it had been Queron who pressed so earnestly and so effectively for Camber's canonization, so many years before, to Joram's enduring dismay. What irony that they now should be considering Queron for a rôle that would surely shatter his faith in the cause to which he had devoted this latter part of his life.

Sighing, Evaine put her list aside and pushed her chair back from the table, laying little Jerusha in her lap, head on knees, and echoing the baby's smile as she ran a gentle fingertip along the downy cheek.

"How are you, little darling?" she whispered to the child, slipping a hand under layers of blanket to check the diaper. "Shall Mummy feed you some more before the others come back? You seem to be dry enough."

But she had no more than started to pick the baby up again when she was nearly staggered by a wave of grief and shock—not her own, this time, but someone else's.

Queron, she confirmed, as she raised her eyes to the great crystal sphere suspended above the table, locking through it to the ripple that continued to reverberate through the link she had set. "And about time, too," she breathed, shifting her focus to Call the others.

Queron trembled near collapse on the Portal at Saint Mary's. The knowledge imparted by the medal throbbing in his hand had staggered him, leaving him psychically as well as physically devastated. He had no idea how long he stood there, reeling in the aftershock of what he had just learned; only that, the next thing he knew, he was not alone on the Portal.

He sensed Evaine's presence before she could even touch him, before he opened his eyes to see her standing before him, all in black, her two hands catching up his wrists, her blue eyes snaring his as she softly commanded him to relax, to release the medal that was biting into his clenched fist.

"You've cut yourself," she murmured, as he numbly opened his palm to blood. "I'm sorry. It was harsh to tell you that way, but I thought that getting it over all at once would be kindest, in the end. I'm all right," she added, as she sensed his concern shifting to *her* grief.

He blinked, forcing himself to draw a slow, stabilizing breath, then let it out in a whoosh as he absently wiped his blood off the medal and handed it back to her.

"I am so sorry, child," he whispered. "I wish I could say that I brought better news—though at least it is no worse than yours."

"Revan?" she asked, with dread in her tone.

He shook his head, not yet ready to contend with his own grief again.

"No, Revan was well, when I left him a fortnight ago. This is other news. But, let us go wherever it is you are to take me, before our presence puts the good brothers of Saint Mary's more at risk." The wound in his hand was slight, he discovered as he spoke, and he cupped his hand over it and Healed it with hardly a further thought.

"Very well," she whispered. Drawing a deep breath, she took his free hand and moved closer beside him.

I'm taking you to the Camberian Council chamber, she went on, in his mind. *In light of what's happened, you're certain to become a full member, so I'll give you the Portal location as we make the jump. Ready?*

He had been ready for *that* for as long as he had known of the Camberian Council's existence, though he had never dreamed that so many violent deaths might open the way. But Evaine's instruction had not invited further speculation at this moment. Best that they be on their way, as he had already urged. Closing his eyes, he dropped his shields and opened to her, feeling the fine controls surround his, balancing all in readiness. In less than the space of an indrawn breath, they were elsewhere.

The great, octagonal council chamber was essentially as Queron remembered it, from his several visits there as an unofficial observer, but the people were not the same, even the ones who were left. As he and Evaine entered through the great, hammered bronze doors in the north facet, Joram rose to give him silent greeting from across the ivory table; but it was a quiet and subdued Joram, showing every one of his thirty-nine years. Part of it was the dull, dusty black of the monk's robe he wore, instead of the customary blue of a Michaeline cassock, but the lines on his handsome face had not come from a mere change of habit. Nor could Queron remember the silver dulling Joram's coin-bright head at the temples.

And Gregory, rising more slowly in the place to Joram's left, had weathered the past few months even less well. Though Queron knew that the former Earl of Ebor had moved physically out of harm's reach the previous October, when he abandoned his Ebor estates and took his family westward to a new, hidden stronghold in the Connait, the forty-two-year-old Gregory looked old. To Queron's practiced Healer's eye, Gregory appeared to have dropped perhaps a quarter of his weight from a frame that already had been lean. Now he looked gaunt. His thinning hair, far less of it than Queron remembered, had gone from reddish blond to nearly colorless, and the pale blue eyes burned with an almost feverish brightness beneath the high, noble brow. Queron made a mental note to make Healer's Reading later on, for Gregory did not look well.

Gregory's son Jesse, bending over a cooing basket set on the table at the eastern quarter, also looked up as Queron and Evaine entered. Jesse, too, had changed, from stripling lad to hard, seasoned warrior, though Queron was sure he was barely seventeen. The fingers grasped by the tiny personage in the basket were calloused and still burned nut-brown from the previous summer's campaigning, the face no longer rounded with the curves of youth. Queron remembered Jesse as husky, still a little gangling, but this young man was trim and muscled, holding himself with the feline grace and precision of an experienced fighting man as he gave Queron a respectful nod and then stepped sideways a few paces to stand between Evaine's chair and the next—the one that had been Alister Cullen's.

"Welcome, Dom Queron," Joram said, gesturing toward a stool set next to Rhys' old place in the eastern quarter. "Please join us."

Only then did Queron notice Ansel MacRorie, Joram's and Evaine's nephew, watching from the shadows to the left of the doorway. His hair gleamed fair again in the light from the cresset set on the wall behind him—it had been dyed a nondescript brown the last time Queron saw him—but otherwise he looked much the same, clad in worn brown riding leathers and with a sword strapped at his hip. Ansel nodded as Queron caught his eye, moving behind him to close the great bronze doors as Evaine also indicated that Queron should sit in the eastern quarter.

"All's well at Saint Mary's?" Joram asked, as all of them sat down.

Evaine nodded, sliding the baby's basket a little closer on the ivory table.

"Yes. However, Dom Queron has other news that he wished not to convey until he could tell it only once. It isn't about Revan," she added, forcing herself to glance at the Healer, "but that's all I know."

Queron, intensely occupied with staring at his hands folded on the table before him, uttered but one word: "Dolban."

"Dolban?" Joram murmured.

"Sweet *Jesu*," Gregory breathed. "Not the Servants of Saint Camber?"

Queron shrugged, his vision blurring, and tried to distance himself a little from what he must tell as he raised his eyes to the blessed darkness of the great amethyst dome arching above them.

"I'm afraid so," he said steadily. "Oh, the buildings still exist. I don't suppose you've heard yet, but Saint Camber had his sainthood rescinded at Ramos a few weeks ago. Not only that, they declared him heretic and traitor. On an individual level, that means that all his lands and holdings would be forfeit to the Crown—which hardly makes much difference now, since that already happened when Ansel was outlawed and deprived of his Culdi inheritance.

"On a wider scope, however, the regents apparently extended their earlier interpretation to include forfeiture of the lands and holdings of those who supported Camber's sainthood—to wit, the Servants of Saint Camber. So they did spare the buildings and the fields for the next tenants."

"But not the people," Evaine murmured dully. "Well, go on. It can be no worse than Trurill."

"No, but no better." Queron closed his eyes briefly. "Let's see. I don't think it's necessary to go into needless detail. Not counting what I'm about to say, I have now uttered Saint Camber's name three times. According to the new law recently enacted by the regents, my first offense would merit a public flogging. The second would require my tongue as payment. *Writing* his name risks the loss of the hand involved.

"Any further defiance of the new law—and in a religious house dedicated to him, you can imagine how often his name was invoked, in word and in script—places the violator in the same category as our heretical ex-saint—who would have burned, if they'd been able to lay their hands on his body. Fortunately, where Camber was concerned, God took that possibility out of their hands, by bodily assuming him into heaven. The good men and women of Saint Camber's at Dolban were not so fortunate."

"So they—*burned* them at Dolban," Gregory muttered. "God help them—all of them!"

Queron scowled. "Amen—but I pray He also helps the perpetrators swiftly to His justice. I have no fear for those who died, for I know that they reside now in the fullness of His glory, but I pray that those who did this thing may be made to suffer. They were episcopal troops, by the way—not just regents' men. I hold Hubert MacInnis personally responsible for this one."

"*He deserves to burn in hell!*" Ansel whispered bitterly.

"Aye, he does," Queron replied. "And there's worse yet to tell."

"*Worse?*" Gregory gasped. "What can be worse?"

"It wasn't just the fires," Queron murmured, closing his eyes against the memory. "Simple burning at the stake was not sufficient for Hubert's men. Before enacting the ultimate punishment, for heresy, they—imposed the first two penalties as well."

Young Jesse gasped, going a little white beneath his olive tan. "You mean, they—beat them and—cut out their tongues, and—and *then* burned them?"

"*No one* could be that monstrous!" Ansel stated flatly.

"Those men were," Queron whispered, brushing a trembling hand across his eyes. "And I might have ended up the same, had it not been for Revan." He glanced up at Evaine. "Your young man has guts, I'll say that for him. He knocked me out, then dosed me with my own drugs to prevent me going down there to try to stop it—as if I could have made any difference, other than maybe to prove that Deryni do, indeed, use their magic to harm humans—even humans who deserve to come to harm. I don't think I've ever felt so helpless."

As Ansel and Jesse continued to mutter, exchanging glances across the empty chair of Saint Camber's Siege between them, Joram said nothing, and Gregory only buried his face in long, trembling fingers. Evaine, tight-lipped and pale, finally glanced over at Joram and stared at him until he looked up, exchanging her recommendation in the blink of an eye.

Nodding, Joram drew a deep breath and sat back in his chair.

"Thank you for telling us, Queron," he said softly. "We realize how difficult it must have been. However, I think little purpose can be served by dwelling on this any longer. All of this will be filed away for further action, as such becomes possible, but for now, I fear that mere survival remains our overwhelming priority.

"To that end, I note that only four of us present are sworn members of this Council. That must be remedied. Evaine, Gregory, Ansel, are we still in agreement?" At their affirming nods, Joram went on. "Excellent. We've agreed on two additions, then. Jesse, your father has already briefed you on what that involves. Queron, I'll speak with you privately, but I suspect that, like Jaffray before you, you'll require time to make additional preparations before taking our oath, to avoid conflict with your Gabrilite vows. Or, are you still bound by them? I know you left active service to the Order some years ago, but I see you've also cut your braid now."

In an almost reflex gesture, Queron's hand went to his shorn hair, and he smiled.

"The braid still would have bound me—yes," he replied. "But in itself, it is only a symbol, albeit a powerful one. When a symbol becomes a liability, it is time to retire it. So I had Revan cut it off. It—*will* need to be dealt with in an appropriate manner, in private. I'm sure you understand."

Joram nodded. "Of course. We'll proceed with Jesse's swearing-in this evening, then, as planned, and hope to do yours tomorrow night. It's best they were done separately anyway. Jesse, is that agreeable to you?"

Jesse, following the exchange with keen interest, made Joram a ritual bow of his head.

"I will place myself at the Council's disposal, as always, Father Joram," he said carefully.

"Thank you. In a sense, this is all a formality now, since the Council as such is hardly what it was, but in these times, we can't be too careful. After we've gotten both of you properly installed, we'll think more about whether we still want to elect Tavis O'Neill as our seventh member. We do have at least one other option, now that Bishop Niallan is firmly in our camp. But in Tavis' favor is the point that he managed to learn Rhys' power-blocking trick before Rhys died—which I don't believe you knew, Queron."

"*Did* he?" Queron murmured. "I freely confess my envy. I shall have to question him about it."

Joram smiled. "I'm sure you will. I think you'll find he's done a bit of maturing, too."

Queron snorted good-naturedly. "A stubborn young man, last time I saw him. Where is he now?"

"Preparing to make contact with Prince Javan—after which he'll return to our sanctuary at Saint Michael's," Joram said, rising. "I'll take you there now, if you wish, and explain what will be involved for tomorrow night. You may have the use of the chapel for the rest of the evening, for—whatever you need to do."

"Saint Michael's—ah," Queron said with a nod. "Is that where the children ended up?" he said, glancing at Evaine as he also rose.

She nodded. "And my men at arms and the Trurill survivors, such as they are," she murmured. "Eventually, we'll be taking in part of Niallan's party as well, along with Bishop O'Beirne and a few more Gabrilites and Michaelines who've been sheltering at Dhassa."

"Other Gabrilites," Queron said. "Do you know who?"

"Dom Rickart, for one," she said. "I believe that Dom Kenric and Dom Juris passed through as well, but I don't know whether they're still there."

"A good start, at least," Queron agreed, moving with Joram toward the doors which Ansel rose to open for them. "And what about Prince Javan, if Tavis is working with us now?"

"Oh, he's still at Valoret, being a prince," Joram said smoothly. "However, you'll be surprised when next you see him, too. Not only is he actively supporting us, Queron, but he's functioning practically like a Deryni."

"Indeed?" was all Queron said, as he and Joram stepped into the Portal outside.

CHAPTER THREE

For they speak not peace: but they devise
deceitful matters against them that are quiet in
the land.

—Psalms 35:20

Valoret, at that moment, was a scene of triumph for the regents—not for Prince Javan, who dared act nothing like a Deryni if he hoped to survive. The royal stewards at Valoret had turned the castle's great hall into a gala banquet room for the new Earl of Sheele's wedding feast, for the earl was one of those regents. That noon, the former Baron Horthness, sometimes called Rhun the Ruthless, had exchanged nuptial vows with the only daughter of Murdoch of Carthane, another of the regents—whose elder son Richard had wed Lady Lirin of Udaut, the Constable's daughter, in a double ceremony. The two couples now sat at the high table to either side of young King Alroy, resplendent in wedding finery no less sumptuous than his own—royalty themselves, were one to judge only by their appearance. Rhun and his bride wore coronets more costly than those worn by the king's own brothers.

Not that *everything* was exactly as the nuptial couples would have wished, Prince Javan thought, as he studied the other occupants of the high table while pretending to listen to a minstrel troupe performing in the center of the hall. The randy young Richard Murdoch would not even be permitted to bed his bride tonight—a circumstance for which he probably had found scant cause to thank his father. Lirin Udaut was only twelve, even younger than Javan and the king. For several more years, young Lirin would continue to live in the Udaut nursery, under the watchful eyes of her mother, her marriage a matter of form and financial alliance only—much to

Richard's annoyance, though he doubtless would find other willing partners eager to share his bed.

Unfortunately—for Javan hated Rhun of Horthness *quite* thoroughly—the youngest of King Alroy's five regents had fared far better than his new brother-in-law in the marriage market. Rhun's countess, glorying in her new place at the king's high table, there between him and her husband of four hours, would not be going back to the nursery with *her* mother when the feast was over. At eighteen, Agnes Murdoch was more than ripe for marriage. The king's twin, though hardly an initiate himself into the mysteries of bridal chambers, had seen that look on enough maids at court to know that Agnes could hardly wait for the bedding ceremony. For that matter, Javan doubted she was even still a maid!

Snorting softly to himself, for he knew that the alliances made today had been largely those of politics, to cement firmer ties among the regents' families and their allies, Prince Javan Haldane raised his cup to his lips with exaggerated care and pretended to gulp deeply. He let his eyelids droop as he set the cup down, feigning wine-fogged sleepiness as he let his gaze drift idly over the rest of the hall.

He was not drunk, though. In fact, he had managed to drink very little today, though wine had been flowing freely in the hall since the feast began, early in the afternoon, and he was sure that anyone bothering to notice him assumed otherwise. He wished it were later, though, because he was eager to take his leave of this mockery of the marriage sacrament. Tavis was coming tonight!

But Vespers had only rung a short while before, the bell sounds drifting with the dusk and the falling snow, and he dared not seek out the renegade Deryni until after Compline—which was probably just as well, since most of the wedding guests would be too drunk to notice his departure by then. Or so he hoped.

Meanwhile, he must keep up his façade of an amiable if lonely drunk. At least it got easier, as the evening deepened along with the guests' cups. The darkness outside had dulled the glazing of the hall's clerestory ranges and window embrasures, making the glass mirror back the light of the torches in their cressets and the dozens of good beeswax candles ranged down the long, food-laden tables. The firelight made the silver and pewter glow golden, and gilded the increasingly florid faces of the revellers. Had Javan not loathed his immediate company so, he might have managed at least a grudging acknowledgment of the beauty of the setting.

Not that *everyone* was terrible, of course. He loved his brothers, though he did not think either of them was having a good time. He knew that Alroy was not. Trapped at the center of the high table between the two brides, Alroy looked bored but resigned—and tired, *too* tired—tugging irritably at the collar of his stiffly embroidered state tunic—though at least he had set aside his crown a little while earlier, so it did not threaten to tumble into his plate every time he tried to eat something.

Poor Alroy. He had never been physically robust. Javan, clubfoot and all, had always been the healthiest of the three boys. Of late, Alroy seemed almost fragile—though Earl Tammaron, the least odious of the regents, had assured Javan that his brother was in fine health, the one time Javan dared to inquire.

But Javan hardly ever got an opportunity to speak privately with his twin these days—and when he did, it was increasingly obvious that they were drifting apart. Nor was it just the weight of kingship that kept widening the gap—or if it was, it was isolating Alroy from everyone else as well. Between the physical sequestering, couched in a new set of protocols and etiquettes for keeping the king apart from common people and things, and the insidious medication that Javan felt *sure* was being slipped to the king on a regular basis, Alroy was an extremely lonely boy, growing ever more dependent upon his regents.

And then there was Rhys Michael, who was eleven and well on the way to being drunk tonight—not that it probably mattered. More and more, of late, wine seemed to be Rhys Michael's recourse. At the other end of the table, the youngest prince was chatting very animatedly with Lady Nieve Fitz-Arthur, Earl Tammaron's countess. The earl himself had gone to exchange some ribald anecdote with Archbishop Hubert, seated at Alroy's right hand, next to Rhun and his bride.

Whatever he told Hubert was uproariously funny. Tears streamed down the archbishop's face as he listened, the rows of extra chins quivering beneath the deceptively cherubic face, with its blond-fringed pate and pale blue gaze and rosebud pout. Capping it all, the flat golden links of Tammaron's chancellor's collar of Haldane *H*'s had gone askew over one shoulder, so that the pendant seal dangled in a dish of gravy as Tammaron gesticulated—something Bishop Cullen *never* would have allowed when he was chancellor! Javan loathed both men, and wondered how Tammaron's wife could put up with him. She had always made a point of being kind to Javan and his brothers.

Not that *she* could be trusted any more than *they* could. One of her sons by her marriage to the late Earl of Tarleton was Paulin of Ramos, the newly created Bishop of Stavenham, who had spearheaded much of the anti-Deryni legislation enacted in the past three weeks at Ramos. And Peter Sinclair, the present Earl of Tarleton, was touted to be a rising star in the new army of Gwynedd. He had been with Rhun at the sack of Saint Neot's—at the express behest of his brother Paulin.

Nor was the countess' eldest son by Tammaron much better. Two years ago, while still inveigling a position for himself as a future regent, Tammaron had arranged a brilliant political match between his eldest son, Fane Fitz-Arthur, and one of his wife's cousins by her first marriage—the Princess Anne Quinnell of Cassan. Young Fane stood to inherit most of Cassan when his father-in-law died, for Prince Ambert had no sons. Cassan would become a duchy in the holding of Gwynedd, and Fane its first duke. Naturally, the new duke would be his father's man in all things. No, with entanglements like that, Javan did not think it wise at all to trust the Lady Nieve.

Nor was Gwynedd's only other duke to be trusted, sitting with his pretty wife to Javan's left, listening to Tammaron's anecdote along with Hubert. Oh, the noble Sighere's son Ewan might be Duke of Claibourne now and apparently in the process of establishing a new dynasty in the person of his ten-year-old son, young Graham MacEwan, who had been one of the pages at the wedding earlier, but Ewan was proving himself an opportunist of the worst sort. Ewan shared blame with Tammaron, Murdoch, and Hubert for giving the orders to sack Saint Neot's and two former Michaeline establishments on Christmas Eve—unforgivable, as far as Javan was concerned, even if the deed itself had actually been carried out by the elder of today's bridegrooms.

And then there was Murdoch of Carthane and his bitch of a wife, over between their newly married son and Lady Nieve. God, how Javan hated Murdoch, with his whiney voice and his pious mouthings and his hypocritical heart! It was Murdoch who had actually come up with the idea to strike at the former Deryni houses on Christmas Eve, and Javan *knew* that the smarmy little weasel followed Archbishop Hubert's fanatical philosophy.

But, if Javan let himself dwell too long on the despicable Murdoch, he knew he was going to start showing his anger and ruin everything. For nearly a year now, since his father's death, Javan had tried to keep a very low profile, cultivating the outward mannerisms of an immature and almost simple-minded child, uninterested in politics or the machinations of the regents—and staying out of the regents' way. People who wanted to believe that the deficiency of his clubbed foot was indicative of deficiencies in his mind seemed ready to accept that he was harmless—though he knew the act might prove a double-edged weapon, if something should happen to Alroy and Javan must try to assume the crown, especially if he was still underage and must satisfy the regents.

Usually, however, the regents left him alone these days, especially since the beginning of the year, when Tavis had fled court on the very day that the Council of Ramos promulgated its new anti-Deryni statutes. Javan had feigned a childishly single-minded indignation that stood up even to the casual scrutiny of Lord Oriel, the Deryni Healer forced to use his talents for the regents. And since then, Javan had made it increasingly clear that he regarded Tavis' defection as a personal betrayal, perhaps extending to a growing distrust of all Deryni. It galled Javan to have to play that part, but Tavis had assured him since that the lie was permissable, under the circumstances. It was certainly safer that way, for now.

So Gwynedd's heir presumptive consoled himself with thoughts of future restitution as he dreamed over his cup, running an idle finger around the rim and letting the din of the banquet continue to wash over him like a mind-numbing wave, details of sight and sound receding as he retreated into his own mind. Another course was served—roast swan stuffed with chestnuts and wheatberries, presented with the plummage still in place—and he picked at his portion despondently, wishing for escape. The escape that came, however, boded ill by its very appearance, even as the chamberlain's iron-shod staff rapped on the flagstones to command attention to an eminent new arrival.

"My Lord King, Your Royal Highnesses, my lords and ladies," the chamberlain intoned, "The Lord Manfred MacInnis, Earl of Culdi and Baron Marlor."

Good God! Javan thought, as his eyes, like everyone else's in the hall, darted to the cloaked and capped form of the archbishop's elder brother just entering the room. *What's* he *doing here?*

Manfred was smiling as he swept off his cap and strode down the hall, but it was not a smile that Javan liked. A seedy-looking knight in Manfred's livery followed at his master's heels, a helmet tucked under his left arm, and *he* looked pleased with himself. Manfred's son Iver brought up the rear—a pimply-faced boy in his early twenties whom Javan had abhored on sight, when he came to court the previous season. Javan noted with disgust that Iver had donned the white belt and gilt spurs of knighthood since his last appearance at court.

Conversation died as Manfred and his party approached the dais. Hubert had stood as his brother entered the hall, easing to his left

until he stood beside Alroy's chair, a beringed hand resting on the
finial by Alroy's ear, and it was to the archbishop that Manfred
bowed when he reached the high table—not to the king.

"I bring news that will cause joy within this assemblage, my
Lord Archbishop, Sire," Manfred said, brandishing something small
and shiny gold as he straightened from his bow. "Consider it a wedding present to Lord Rhun and his bride, and to Lord Richard and
his." He included both couples in his expansive gesture. "I bring
you a cross lately worn by the renegade Alister Cullen, and am happy
to report that both he and the outlawed Jebediah of Alcara are dead!"

In the eruption of whooping and shouts of relief and pleasure
that followed, Javan was just barely able to temper his own shock
and horror, though it took every jot of his will and self-control to
do so. Alroy's control was not as good, and he looked appalled. Rhys
Michael, who had idolized Jebediah before his resignation as earl
marshal, appeared to be close to tears. The two *could* not be dead!
It was impossible! Surely Manfred must be lying.

But as the new earl sketched his account of the slaying, giving
due credit to the fawning knight beside him, Javan very much feared
that Manfred was not lying. Nor was the knight, supplying details
on demand. Javan even dared, after brief consideration, to try using
his growing ability to tell whether a person was telling the truth—
a Deryni ability, Tavis had told him, though Alister Cullen had
hinted that it was much, much more, somehow tied in with the
succession and with what he and Javan's father had done to him the
night Cinhil died. Whatever its source, Javan seemed to be able to
do it. Tonight, he wished he could not.

"They slew three other of my knights before they fell, and the
good Sir Rondel was knocked senseless for a time," Manfred was
saying, "but he saw the bishop's ring on Cullen's finger. His de-
scriptions of both men leave little doubt as to their identities."

"Then, why did he not bring back the ring?" Hubert demanded,
turning suspicious eyes on Rondel. "For that matter, why did you
not bring back the bodies, man?"

Rondel, immediately all deference and obsequious charm, could
only make Hubert a bow of his own, gloved right hand to his breast
in abject apology.

"I had planned to do that, your Grace, but it was getting dark,
and I was dazed and alone, far from known friends. As I began trying
to load the first body on a horse—which I had to *catch* first, your
Grace, and the animals were crazed with the smell of blood— As I
began trying to load the first body, I could see torches approaching—
nearly a dozen. With night falling, not knowing exactly where I was

or who they might be—well, it seemed the better part of valor to get away, to at least report what I'd seen. I couldn't get the ring off Cullen's hand, and there wasn't time to cut off the finger to get it, so I settled for the cross he was wearing." He gestured with his chin toward the item Manfred was handing to his brother. "I had to break the chain to do that."

Snorting, Rhun rose lazily and leaned across his bride to take the cross from Hubert, turning it impatiently in his hand.

"Manfred, this could be anyone's cross. How do you know he's telling the truth?"

"Well, there's a very quick and reliable way to find out, isn't there?" Manfred replied, without hesitation or resentment. "Have him Truth-Read. Hubert, haven't you got a tame Healer named Oriens, or something like that?"

"It's Oriel," Rhun said. The cross chimed against the wood as he tossed it onto the table in front of Alroy, who stared at it as if transfixed. "But why not try *my* Truth-Reader?" the regent went on smoothly. "He isn't a Healer, but he doesn't have to be, to Truth-Read. I campaigned him hard at Saint Neot's. Perhaps it's time he confirmed his worth by performing in front of an audience. My lords, what say you?" he asked, glancing casually at his fellow regents.

Seeing no objection, he signalled a guard who snapped to attention in a side doorway.

"Fetch Declan Carmody. And don't tell him what this is all about."

Javan almost groaned aloud as the guard went to do Rhun's bidding, for Carmody, like Oriel, was a collaborator, albeit an unwilling one—a "Deryni sniffer," in the vernacular—forced by threat of harm to his hostage wife and two small sons to use his powers at the regents' bidding, even to the detriment of others of his race. For Oriel, the incentive was a wife and infant daughter. Unlike Oriel, however, Carmody still went about in chains. Rhun apparently still did not entirely trust his drafted "pet" Deryni.

Carmody certainly did not look like much of a threat, however, as he was ushered in a few minutes later, light shackles hanging from his wrists. Though he was a man obviously in his vigorous prime, perhaps thirty or so, he looked cowed, weary and sick at heart—which was exactly how Javan felt. When the captive Deryni saw who had summoned him, he glanced only fleetingly at Manfred and the two knights standing with him, immediately dismissing them as threats.

For it was Rhun who was the ever present danger—Rhun, who held the lives of a woman and two small children at his whim and had snuffed out the lives of others' wives and children, even infants, without a twinge of remorse. In the early days of his captivity, Carmody had been forced to watch the slaughter of innocents more than once, and knew Rhun's threat was not an idle one.

So he dipped his head obediently in Rhun's direction as the regent moved around behind Alroy's chair to stand opposite Hubert, masking his hate, his plain face bland and attentive. Rhun, for his part, smiled mirthlessly and leaned an elbow languidly along the back of Alroy's chair.

"That knight says that he saw two dead men," Rhun said, gesturing toward Rondel with a negligent wave of his hand. "Do not harm him, for I believe Lord Manfred values his services, but we wish to know the names of those dead men."

As Carmody drew a resigned breath, lips set in a grim line, Javan had to admire the way Rhun had set it up to be certain the man did not just repeat what they wanted to hear. And since Rondel was telling the truth, he was in no danger whatever.

Still, the knight did not look happy as Rhun crooked a finger for him to come closer to the Deryni—though he obeyed. He was trembling as Carmody lifted a manacled hand and laid it on his forehead. He closed his eyes tightly as the hand touched.

"Think about the men," Carmody was heard to murmur, also closing his eyes. "Picture them as clearly as you can."

Rondel apparently complied, for almost immediately Carmody gasped and drew back his hand as if stung, his eyes opening in shock.

"Whom did you see?" Hubert demanded, leaning forward eagerly. "I can tell that you knew them, Carmody. Who were they?"

With a little shudder, quickly controlled, Carmody dropped his hands back to his sides, manacles jingling discordantly.

"Alister Cullen and Jebediah of Alcara, your Grace," he said without emotion.

Carmody was allowed to leave after that, and Rondel as well, the latter for a much appreciated hot meal and a bed, for he and his MacInnis masters, father and son, had been riding for three days. Manfred himself, though travel-stained and weary, took a place of honor between Rhun and his brother, for he was clearly the hero of the evening. Cups were raised often in the next few hours to toast his accomplishment—for the credit was his, since his man had achieved it—and the mood in the hall quickly returned to an even more riotous level of celebration.

But Manfred's news had plunged Javan into new depression, and watching an increasingly drunken Iver MacInnis leer and paw at the younger ladies of the court nearly made the prince physically ill. He tried to ignore Iver, but so blatant a display of lechery was hard to ignore. Eventually, Javan could not help noticing that Iver seemed to be concentrating most of his attentions on two surprisingly plain young girls who hardly could have been older than himself. Neither looked pleased at his attentions, especially the middle-aged woman sitting with them—who was Ansel MacRorie's mother, Javan suddenly realized!

Which meant that the girls must be the famous MacLean heiresses, much the topic of court gossip since the reported slaughter of their cousin Adrian MacLean and his son at Trurill. Adrian's father, Iain, the sixth Earl of Kierney, was still alive; but with the death of his son and grandson, his dead brother's children now became his heirs—these two young girls.

No wonder Iver MacInnis was interested—though how he would choose one, Javan had no idea. The girls were co-heiresses, so would inherit the Kierney lands jointly, on their uncle's eventual death, but the title would remain in abeyance until one of them died, the survivor then becoming Countess of Kierney. What if Iver picked the wrong one?

But Javan did not think Iver would move *too* quickly in choosing his bride—though Ansel certainly should be told that Hubert's nephew was courting them. Javan wondered whether Ansel even knew his MacLean cousins were at court.

And so, as the next course was announced, to fanfares of trumpets and a jaunty little pipe tune as the servants brought it in, Javan resolved to convey that bit of information as well as his more tragic news, and wondered how he could bear to stay in the hall until it was time to go and meet Tavis.

Tavis had known of the tragedy for days, of course. In fact, he had attended the Requiem Mass that Joram and Bishops Niallan and Dermot celebrated in the little Michaeline chapel for Alister, Jebediah, and Rhys, and he had watched the bodies laid to rest in the chapel's vaults.

He had planned to stop in that chapel to meditate for a few minutes, as he usually did before going on to the sanctuary's Portal to meet Javan, but he recalled that Queron had reserved the little chamber for some mysterious Gabrilite ritual that he needed to perform. So he was surprised to see the door standing ajar as he came abreast of the chapel doorway. Curious, he paused to push it further in and peer inside.

"Ah, Tavis, I had hoped you might drop by, before I got started,"

Queron said, turning away from a small table he had set up in front of the altar and lifting a hand in invitation. "Please, come in and close the door. I wanted to ask you something."

Surprised, for he and the former Gabrilite had never spoken privately, Tavis entered and pulled the door shut behind him. He also was surprised to see that Queron had donned Gabrilite habit again, the fine, snow-white wool badged at the left shoulder with the green, star-pierced hand of an ecclesiastical Healer.

" 'Tis Gabrilite work I do tonight," Queron explained, noting Tavis' look of question, though he was careful to keep his body between Tavis and whatever lay on the little table. "Once a Gabrilite—" He shrugged. "But, I did not ask you in to discuss that. I—gather that you were able to learn from Rhys what I was never able. I hoped that perhaps you might teach me."

"Teach you to block Deryni powers?" Tavis replied, getting right to the point. "I don't know if that's possible, if Rhys couldn't teach you. He was far, far more adept than I."

"And more adept than I, at least in that respect," Queron murmured. "But I *would* learn it, Tavis. It's important. A few weeks ago, I left a very brave but helpless man out in the hills near Dolban. I left him in the midst of a band of Willimite extremists who are beginning to look to him as some sort of prophet or savior—which could save hundreds of our race, if they come truly to believe in him. But in order to succeed, he has to have someone to work with him who can do what Rhys could do. If *I* could do it, it might help him enormously. And I'm willing to make the sacrifice."

"Are you suggesting that I am not?" Tavis said quietly.

"Of course not." Queron shook his head. "But you do present—problems. Aside from the mere physical stigma of your lost hand, your former close association with Prince Javan may make it more difficult for you to build a convincing cover."

"I'm aware of that," Tavis said, crossing his arms on his chest a little self-consciously to hide his empty sleeve, irritated with himself that he had allowed Queron to let the reminder bother him. "With all due respect, however, I don't think you're going to be able to learn the procedure."

"Will you let me try?" Queron persisted.

"Here? Now?"

Queron shrugged. "No time like the present—unless I'm keeping you from Javan."

"No, I have a few minutes," Tavis murmured, "but—"

With a sigh almost of exasperation, he suddenly stepped closer to Queron and brushed his hand across the other Healer's forehead, at the same time reaching out with his mind to trigger the block he had learned from Rhys. Queron recoiled instinctively, but not quickly enough. The older Healer staggered a little as his loss registered, unable to resist as Tavis caught him by a wrist and pulled him closer, holding him with his hand while he lightly laid the end of his stump against the right side of Queron's neck.

"You know, I could leave you this way," Tavis whispered, engaging Queron's gaze and snaring the wide, frightened brown eyes with water-blue ones. "I wouldn't, of course—and I won't invade your privacy by probing for the reason you pushed me to this—but you took a big risk. You hardly know me."

"Yet, you could do this to me without any preparation," Queron breathed, recovering his composure even in this vulnerable state. "It was the same with Rhys. And even once I knew what to watch out for, resisting did no good. Did he ever tell you how Emrys and I put him through his paces, that first time he and Alister came to tell us what he'd learned to do? It's a terrible gift, Tavis. God help us, that we must learn to use it against our own kind."

"Yes. God help us," Tavis said, breathing out with a loud sigh. With a downward flick of his gaze, he restored Queron's powers and disengaged his control, though he did not release Queron's arm or pull back from physical contact.

"Forgive me. I shouldn't have done that. Would you like to have a look at where I think it happens?" he went on, returning his gaze to Queron's. "Not that I think it will make any difference."

Smiling wanly, Queron lifted his hands to clasp lightly around Tavis' wrists.

"At least I'll know, won't I?" he whispered. "If I can't learn it from you either, maybe I can let go of the notion and get on to more productive things. May I?"

Relaxing a little, Tavis closed his eyes and began lowering his shields, aware of Queron doing the same. He had been afraid of Queron before, fearful of the powers of this highly trained and almost legendary Gabrilite, but knowing the vulnerability of just about any other Deryni now, Tavis no longer feared him. He let the other Healer wander in his mind for some little while, poking and sniffing at the area where the blocking function took place, then triggered it on and off several times in Queron—to the other Healer's utter dismay and mystification.

Queron was shaking his head as he dismantled the contact, physical as well as mental, and Tavis knew that the older man was finally convinced.

"Thank you," Queron whispered, lowering his eyes. "I shan't bother you again, Tavis."

"It was no bother, sir," Tavis murmured, a little sorry for Queron. "I only hope that you'll prove better at teaching me than I have at teaching you. Father Alister told me that my Varnarite training was sadly deficient in some areas, when compared to Michaeline or Gabrilite."

He had to admire the way the older man rallied, once more the assured and confident Healer-priest.

"We all have our uses, I suppose," Queron replied, hardly wistful at all. "Sometimes God does not give us the talents we think we should have, but we must trust in His greater wisdom. I believe that Alister always wished he had been a Healer. One is rarely satisfied."

"No." Tavis smiled sympathetically and held out his hand in a gesture of peace. "Well, I'd best go on to my meeting with Prince Javan. And I believe you had important work to do, before I interrupted you. I shall look forward to studying with you further."

"And I shall look forward to having such an apt pupil," Queron replied, clasping Tavis' hand briefly but warmly. "God bless you and keep you safe, my son."

Grateful, Tavis crossed himself in echo of the Healer-priest's blessing, then turned and went out of the chapel, closing the door behind him. And Queron, when he had gone, barred the door and then returned thoughtfully to the table before the altar, where a charcoal brazier, a small, razor-sharp knife, and a coiled Gabrilite g'dula awaited his attentions.

CHAPTER FOUR

Shall not they teach thee, and tell thee, and
utter words out of their hearts?

—Job 8:10

At least an hour had passed since Compline, by the time Javan finally
was able to slip away safely and head for the Portal secreted beneath
the King's Tower. As he left the turnpike stair and headed along the
curve of a final, dimly lighted corridor, he reflected that Tavis probably had come and gone several times by now, checking periodically
for either Javan's presence or some message that the prince was not
coming. Since royal princes had little business in this part of the
castle, especially at this hour, Javan hoped he would not have to
wait too long for the Healer's next appearance, for guards did patrol
these corridors.

But he was nearly there now, and thus far he had not been challenged. He tried to tread very quietly as he approached the shadow
of the Portal cubicle, but his pace quickened with anticipation as
he sensed a whisper of movement inside. Just as he came abreast of
it, however, some sixth sense cautioned him not to speak. To his
utter horror, he found a guard using it for the garderobe it appeared
to be.

More than a little rattled, Javan started to ease on past, hoping
he would not be noticed, but the guard finished and turned at that
moment, as startled as Javan.

"Your Highness," the man murmured, hurriedly adjusting his
clothing before sketching Javan a sheepish salute. "An' am I glad ye
weren't the officer of the watch. Ye took me totally by surprise.
Anything I can do for yer?"

The man was big, armed and lightly armored, the red ram's head badge of Rhun of Horthness on the shoulder of his cloak and on his breast. He did not look or sound suspicious—yet—but Javan knew that what the man was really asking, as he got his wits together, was: What the devil are *you* doing down here? Fortunately, Javan had already thought of a plausible excuse.

"No, I—ah—was just stretching my legs," he improvised. "It's snowing like sin outside, but I thought I'd better walk a little before going to bed—clear my head." He raised a hand to his forehead in what he hoped was a gesture of faint dismay. "I—ahem—had a little too much wine at the wedding feast."

"Ah, well then," the guard replied, apparently satisfied. "That's what a wedding feast is all about, ain't it, sir? I mean, even them of us as drew guard duty tonight got our extra wine rations, for when we go off watch. The Lord Rhun's a generous master, he is."

"Aye, he is that," Javan murmured, mentally cursing the man for a loquacious fool and wondering whether he dared try his developing powers on the man, in an attempt to discourage him. He had an idea . . .

"Well, I don't suppose I should keep you from your—oh, damn, I've got something in my eye," he muttered, knuckling at his right eye and wincing, blinking rapidly, pretending distress. "It's probably just an eyelash, but—damn, it feels like a rock!"

Apparently taking the bait, the man moved in amiably and set his hand under Javan's elbow to draw him under a nearby torch, taking off his gloves and tucking them into his ample belt.

"Here now, sir. Ye want t' pull the lid down a few times an' wash it out with tears. Let's have a look. My little lads get things in their eyes all the time."

As he tipped Javan's face up toward the light, peering intently into the grey Haldane eyes, Javan knew he had him. He was amazed at how easy it was to stretch out his powers and take control, so that all at once the man was simply—*his.*

"What's your name, soldier?" he asked softly, raising his hands quietly to take the man's hands from his face and retain them for physical contact.

"Norris, sir," the man whispered.

"Excellent. Go to sleep, then, Norris, and remember nothing of this."

Somewhat to Javan's dismay, the guard's eyes immediately rolled upward and disappeared under the lids and he buckled at the knees. Javan gasped and managed to ease him to the floor without too much of a clash of armor, but the effect was not exactly what he had planned. He was trying to decide how to get the man on his feet and on his way again when he suddenly became aware of another presence behind him.

He whirled on his heels in alarm, utterly panic-stricken until he saw that it was Tavis stepping from the Portal cubicle.

"Sweet *Jesu*, don't *do* that!" he whispered. "You nearly gave me heart failure!"

"Imagine how your friend would feel, if he woke up and remembered what you just did to *him*." Tavis glided to Javan's side and knelt beside the unconscious guard, laying his hand lightly on the man's forehead. "Fortunately, you'd got that part right. He wouldn't have remembered your involvement in all of this. But he would have had a hard time explaining why he fell asleep on watch down here. No point drawing any more attention to this area than we must." He paused briefly, apparently working his own magic on the sleeping Norris.

"All right, then," he murmured after a few seconds, shifting his hand to the guard's shoulder. "Let's have you up, old chap, and back on duty. That's the lad."

Javan stood back as the man roused and, with Tavis' help, got nimbly to his feet, apparently no longer even noticing Javan's presence. Without further instruction or even a backward glance, he turned and headed down the corridor in a slow, casual guard pace. Tavis was grinning as Javan turned to stare at him in question.

"I just finished up what you'd started," the Healer said with an amused shrug, gesturing toward the Portal cubicle. "Now let's get out of here before any of Norris' chums come along. I've told him to make whatever excuses he needs to, to be sure they don't, but we wouldn't want to push our luck."

Nodding, Javan let himself be ushered into the Portal cubicle, his mind churning with a dozen unasked questions. He forced himself to still them as Tavis stepped into place behind him, though, for he knew he must clear his mind for the Healer to take him wherever they were going tonight.

"It's the Michaeline sanctuary, this time," Tavis whispered in his left ear, answering that question, at least. He set the end of his stump just beneath that ear as his other arm encircled Javan's shoulders, the *vee* of his thumb and fingers lightly bracketing Javan's throat over the pressure points at the carotid arteries. "Now, am I going to have to *take* control, or can you give it up this time?"

Closing his eyes, Javan took a long, deep breath and let it out softly, ignoring the sour stench of urine, feeling himself begin to center. He still had not learned to like Portal travel, especially from *this* Portal.

"I think I can do it, but I'm not proud. Help me out, if you need to."

Tavis' answering breath, in and out, helped Javan go deeper as well, and he felt his link with Tavis open even wider, faintly sensed the tingle of the Portal under their feet; but he knew he was still too slow for Tavis.

Just a little help, this time, came Tavis' thought, softly flowing into his mind. *We mustn't be here too long.*

Resigned, Javan gave up trying and bowed his head a little, welcoming the blacker darkness that rose behind his eyes as Tavis compressed the pressure points. A ghost of awareness still played at the edges of his mind as Tavis wrenched the energies, though, and Javan recovered almost immediately as the Healer released him in another Portal chamber that did not reek of the garderobe.

"Well done," the other murmured, pushing open a panel that opened into a dimly lit corridor. "If you hadn't still been a bit shaken up from tackling the good Norris, I think you could have done it on your own that time. What *am* I going to do with you?"

Javan grinned as he followed the Healer into the corridor.

"Keep teaching me how to do better, I hope," he said. He sobered quickly, however, as he remembered the ill news he had brought. "I—don't think I'll be much use as a student tonight, though. Did you know that the regents—that they've killed Father Alister and Jebediah?"

Tavis stopped stock-still in the corridor and threw back his head to take a deep breath and let it out explosively.

"So, the news has finally reached Valoret, has it? I'll bet the regents loved *that*!"

"Oh. You already knew."

Sighing, Tavis nodded, not looking at the prince.

"We buried them with Rhys, a few days ago. Evaine and Joram brought the bodies through, after they got the Portal at Saint Mary's working." He glanced aside at Javan, still bitter in his own sense of loss. "Would you like to pay your respects?"

"Yes, I would," Javan said in a small, quiet voice.

"All right. We'll have to see if Queron's finished in the chapel, first. He was working a ritual in there, earlier, but I don't think he meant to be long."

The chapel door was standing open when they reached it, however, and Queron nowhere to be seen, though the small table Tavis had noticed earlier was still there, empty now. A Presence Lamp above the altar and a rack of votives to the left were the only light.

Standing aside for Javan to enter, Tavis directed him across the Kheldish carpet to a row of three marble plaques set into the wall to the right of the altar. A strip of parchment had been wedged into the crack at the top joining of each, and Javan's eyes blurred with tears for the second time that night as he laid a reverent finger under the nearest one and tilted it toward the light of silvery handfire that Tavis conjured.

Rhys Malachy Thuryn, Healer, 877–917. "For of the Most High Cometh Healing," Javan read.

The second slip was Jebediah's: *Lord Jebediah of Alcara, Knight and Grand Master of the Order of Saint Michael, 861–918. "With the blessed Archangel, he shall stand at the right side of the altar of incense, defending the Light".*

"There hasn't been time yet to have the markers carved," Tavis said quietly, nudging his handfire to follow as Javan moved to the third strip of parchment. "Nor are the texts completely decided yet."

Alister Kyriell Cullen, Archbishop of Valoret, Bishop of Grecotha, Chancellor of Gwynedd, Vicar General of the Order of Saint Michael, Priest and Knight, 838–918. "Nunc dimittis, Domine . . ."

"*Nunc dimittis,*" Javan read aloud, recognizing the quotation. "Lord, now lettest Thou Thy servant depart in peace."

Tavis nodded. "Bishop Niallan suggested the texts. Evaine isn't entirely happy with them, though, so she's looking for some better ones." He glanced at his feet. "I'll—leave you with them for a few minutes, if you wish."

He moved silently toward the door at Javan's stricken nod, quenching the still-hovering handfire as an afterthought, but the prince paid it and him no further mind. Sinking heavily to his knees, Javan buried his face in his hands and began to weep, thin shoulders shaking silently. Tavis paused uneasily in the doorway and watched for a few seconds, debating whether he really ought to leave Javan totally alone, then turned to see Queron watching both him and Javan.

He's only just learned, has he? Queron sent, laying a sympathetic hand on Tavis' arm.

Aye, Tavis returned. *A few hours ago, actually. He knew about Rhys, of course, but I gather that news of Alister and Jebediah has only just reached court.*

Well, perhaps it's best he goes ahead and works out his grief. The poor lad must have gone through hell, having to hear that news in open court and not react the way he really felt. He seems quite unsettled.

With an ironic little smile, despite his sympathy for Javan, Tavis moved himself and Queron farther into the hallway and turned to look squarely at the older Healer, though he left the door ajar.

I'll tell you what's probably got him at least as unsettled as his grief, he sent. *Let me show you what he did to the poor, unwitting guard who happened to be lurking inconveniently where Javan was supposed to wait for me . . .*

When the older Healer had assimilated the report of Javan's work on the hapless Norris, he cocked his head and raised a half-disbelieving eyebrow.

But, that's a Deryni ability. Where in God's name did he learn to do that?

I'm not sure what role God had to play in it, Tavis replied, *but shall we ask Javan?*

I think we certainly should, came Queron's reply.

They gave Javan a few more minutes, waiting until they saw him sit back on his heels and begin wiping at his eyes with his sleeve. When the snuffling sounds subsided, Tavis cleared his throat discreetly and pushed the door wider again, Queron at his side as he went back into the chapel. The boy looked up at their approach, awkwardly getting to his feet as he saw that Tavis was not alone.

"It's—Dom Queron, isn't it?" the prince murmured, eying the newcomer's white robes uncertainly. "I believe we met—last year sometime, wasn't it?" he finished lamely, apparently not wanting to call attention to the fact that it had been after Tavis' injury, when both he and Tavis had been afraid of the elder Healer's visit.

Queron gave him a kindly smile, tactfully avoiding the issue as well.

"Yes, I believe we did, your Highness. And I believe that many things have changed since that time—at least some of them for the better."

Javan glanced at the floor, obviously grateful for the change of tack, but his mood was still somber as he looked up again.

"This was not for the better," he murmured, gesturing vaguely toward the three tomb slabs. "I only just found out, tonight. You must pardon me if I seem a little distracted."

"Distraction in such a cause is certainly forgivable, your Highness," Queron murmured. "And I understand that it was very little distraction earlier this evening, when you had to deal with what could have been a—an unfortunate encounter."

Stunned, Javan looked at Tavis in question, obviously feeling betrayed. "You told him, didn't you?" he said accusingly.

"I felt I had to, Javan," Tavis replied. "He's—part of the team, now that Rhys and the others are gone. I want you to trust him. *I* do."

And do *you?* Queron sent, with a hint of gentle laughter, though his expression did not change.

"But—"

"You need to learn to work with others, my prince," Tavis said, laying an arm around the boy's shoulders in comfort as he continued his mental conversation with Queron. *And I haven't any choice, after the trust* you *displayed, earlier tonight—though now that I have Rhys' rather dubious talent, I don't suppose you could hurt me, even if you wanted to. Does it bother you that that's the basis of our trust?*

Queron shook his head gently, for the benefit of both his audiences. "Let's leave the dead in peace, shall we?" he said, gesturing toward the door. "There may be others who wish to pay their respects, and we can work as well elsewhere—perhaps in your quarters, Tavis, since I have none assigned as yet. Javan, I've trained many a young Deryni. Perhaps I can be of help to you as well."

And Tavis, he continued, for the other Healer's benefit alone, *it has just occurred to me to wonder whether Rhys' rather dubious talent would work on Javan's powers. Don't answer now, but think about it as we go.*

Think about what? Tavis retorted, as they left the chapel. *I've been working my heart out, trying to help him* develop *his powers, and you want me to take them away?*

Just think about it, Queron repeated. *I only want you to consider the implications.*

Tavis hardly could have avoided considering Queron's implications as they made their way to the former Michaeline cell that was now his room. He was only amazed he had not thought of it before, and wondered whether any of the others had. He wished he knew more about what Joram and the others had done to Javan and his brothers, the night King Cinhil died. Whatever it was, it seemed to be the source of what was manifesting now in Cinhil's second son.

But why in Javan and not in Alroy or Rhys Michael? Especially, why not in Alroy, who was now the king? He wondered whether there was any way he might get to Alroy and find out. And meanwhile, what if Javan's burgeoning powers *could* be blocked?

"I think the first thing we ought to do is to let Queron read you, Javan," Tavis said, gesturing for the boy to sit on the bed as he closed

the door and conjured fire for the rushlight set in the little niche at
the bed's head.

Javan sat gingerly, sinking into the saggy mattress, uneasy at
Queron's presence, so still and ghostlike as he stood near the foot
of the bed. He clearly was uncertain whether to regard Tavis' behavior as a betrayal.

"I—don't know if I'm ready for this yet," he whispered. "Dom
Queron, I mean you no insult or disrespect, but I—Tavis, *must* I?"

"I think it could be very useful, if you did," Tavis said, leaning
against the closed door. "Obviously, he isn't going to force a reading,
but I think you ought to allow it. In some respects, he's far better
qualified than I to teach you some of the things I think you'll need
to know."

He regretted having to appear to turn on Javan, but Queron's
question had sobered him, for it underlined the need for others to
know of Javan's abilities—such as they were, or were becoming—
so that the boy could be guided more productively.

"But, I—I've never let my shields down for anyone but you,"
Javan whispered.

"No, but you've let them down for me and then let Alister and
Joram and Jebediah read a little *through* me," Tavis replied. "Queron
has worked with all three of them, and he's a Healer and a Gabrilite,
to boot. Do you think he'd harm you and violate his vows? And do
you think I'd *let* him?"

"I—suppose not."

"Lie back, then, and let's get on with it," Tavis said a little impatiently. "Really, Javan, you're not usually this unreasonable."

"No, I don't think he's being unreasonable," Queron interjected,
crouching down at the foot of the bed so he did not tower so over
Javan. "There's a difference between unreasonable and apprehen-
sive. And despite his undoubted maturity for his age, he's still just
a boy of twelve, and very new to what's been happening to him in
the past few months. May I make a suggestion?"

"Certainly."

"Why don't you work with him a little first, just as you usually
do, and then I'll join in? We'll take it slowly. There's no reason to
frighten him any more than he is already—is there, Javan? And
knowing the way you feel, I wouldn't press for this tonight if I didn't
fear it might be some time before we get another chance. It isn't
going to get any easier for you to make these nocturnal visits—and
if you can make the most of the time you have, when you do come,
it will be safer for all concerned."

"That—sounds reasonable," Javan murmured hesitantly.

"There, you see?" Queron glanced at Tavis for confirmation, immediately given. "Why don't you lie back, then, as Tavis suggested, and just do whatever it is you usually do when you and he meet to exchange information? I'll tell you right now that I'm already prepared to be impressed, after what Tavis has told me, so don't worry that you think you might not measure up."

Javan actually managed a faint smile as he swung his feet up on the bed a little self-consciously and lay back, shifting a belt pouch and dagger to more comfortable positions as Tavis moved in to kneel by his head. Tavis knew exactly how Javan must feel, having been put on the spot himself to perform in front of Queron, a Deryni mage of almost legendary reputation. He knew that Rhys must have experienced similar misgivings, the first time he demonstrated his new-found talent in front of Queron and Emrys.

"Well, I think you know the drill by now," Tavis murmured, chancing a quick grin as he brushed the sable hair from Javan's forehead before settling to the usual contact points of hand at Javan's left temple and stump set under the right ear. "Take a couple of deep breaths to relax. Close your eyes. That's it. I'm right with you. Relax and center. Start lowering your shields now. That's right . . . good . . . excellent!"

He drew the rapport close, soothing the last vestiges of Javan's nervousness before quickly taking the report Javan had always intended to give him of the past five days' events at court—and imparting the briefing he would have passed on to Javan in turn, whether or not Queron had been present. They had done that before, so Javan weathered it very well—so well that he hardly even noticed when Tavis deftly brought Queron into the link and then pulled back to observe just from the edge of Javan's consciousness, leaving Queron in passive but flexible control. Javan started a little when he realized what had happened, but Tavis was still there and had not abandoned him; and when Queron did not try to insist that the link be held open, Javan quickly managed to settle enough for the elder Healer to get a fairly good reading.

Queron let Tavis bring Javan back, though, merely sitting back from the edge of the bed a little and watching quietly until the prince finally opened his eyes.

"Impressive," Queron murmured, smiling as Javan blinked. "I see that I shall have to consult with Joram and Evaine to find out how all of this began—that is, if they'll tell me. I see that they haven't decided to tell you, yet."

"It—all has something to do with the succession," Javan said hesitantly. "But I don't need to explain to you now, do I? You already know everything I know about it."

Solemnly Queron nodded. "A distinct advantage, don't you agree? It saves so much time over merely telling. I shall look forward to the opportunity to work with you again."

"Truly?"

"Truly. But for now, I think you must let Tavis take you back to Valoret, before you are missed." He touched his hands palm to palm and held them out to Javan. "My hands in your service, my prince."

Shyly, almost reverently, Javan took the clasped hands briefly between his own in the age-old gesture of fealty accepted, then released them and tried to sit up in the sagging mattress, laughing a little self-consciously as both Tavis and Queron had to assist him.

"You're right. I'd better get back. Ah—have I been gone very long? I always lose track of time, when Tavis and I work together."

Chuckling even as he admired the boy's resilience, Tavis shook his head.

"Not very long, my prince. And your good guard Norris will be keeping the way clear for your return. But next time we meet, I'll try to show you how to do it right, in case you must deal with Norris or one of his brethren again. Queron, we'll speak more on this."

"Oh, we shall, indeed," Queron agreed, as the two left him sitting in the rushlight. "We shall, indeed."

CHAPTER FIVE

For thou bringest strange things to our ears: we
would know therefore what these things mean.
—Acts 17:20

Queron did not appear in the Council chambers the next morning,
for Joram had advised him to spend the day sequestered, in preparation for his own induction into the Council that night. Still, when
the newly augmented Camberian Council met to hear Tavis' report
of his meeting with Prince Javan, Queron instantly became a subject
of interested if passing speculation—for Queron was the first of
them besides Tavis to be permitted direct access to Javan's mind.

But it was neither Queron nor Javan whose discussion caused
their planned morning meeting to extend well into the afternoon.
The contents of Javan's report were themselves sufficiently disturbing to warrant additional consideration, never mind the implications of the prince's gradually increasing abilities. The regents'
treatment of the captive Declan Carmody underlined the increasingly untenable position of *any* Deryni so interned, and the return
of Ansel's mother and her family to court made the question even
more immediate.

"Well, collaborators are no new thing," Joram said, when Tavis
had reiterated his assessment of the Carmody situation. "We've
known for months that the regents were doing some forcible re-
cruiting. Rhun had several Deryni with him at Saint Neot's. Didn't
Dom Juris tell us he thought one of them was Carmody?"

"Carmody *was* one of them," Tavis replied. "Also a man called
Sitric, though he isn't nearly as well trained. They both came back
with Rhun's troops, after the Saint Neot's massacre, but I never

actually got to talk to either of them. Javan says that Carmody's put up more resistance than most—which is why he's still in chains. He hasn't knuckled under easily, the way Oriel did. And the regents are pushing him really hard. I don't want even to think about what might happen if he breaks."

Jesse, a look of consternation on his tanned, beardless face, cocked his head in question.

"But, a simple Truth-Reading of a cooperative human subject isn't that much of a strain, Tavis," he said. "It isn't as if they made him force another Deryni, or—or read past a death block or something."

"Humph!" Gregory gave a derisive snort, fidgeting between Joram and Evaine. "It's only a matter of degree, son. Only a matter of degree."

"Precisely," Tavis agreed. "From a purely objective vantage point—which I doubt very much that any of us can manage—I suppose it does seem innocuous enough, as such things go. Javan certainly didn't see it that way, though—maybe, in part, because of what the working had to confirm. That was the first he'd heard about Father Alister and Jebediah, after all."

That reminder silenced them all for several seconds, but then Ansel sat forward uneasily.

"Certainly, that could have been a factor," he murmured. "But he's seen Oriel work, for God's sake—and kill with his powers, even though that wasn't intended. For that matter, Tavis, *you* were in Oriel's and Carmody's position, not so very long ago."

"I had good reasons!" Tavis began hotly.

"Ultimately, of course you did," Joram returned, a little impatiently. "I think, however, that even you will admit that your original motives were not entirely altruistic—something about wreaking vengeance on the men who cost you your hand, as I recall."

Tavis closed his hand over his stump and bowed his head. "I am not proud of those days," he said quietly.

"No one said you were, son," Gregory said with a sigh, shooting Joram a glance of forbearance. "Nor, I'm sure, are Oriel and Carmody and the other fellow proud of what they are doing. But just as your ultimate reason for staying was to help Javan, so are these other men doing what they must do to protect the ones they love."

Tavis nodded miserably, not looking up. "I cannot fault them for that. But Javan said that Carmody seemed so—so cowed. God, to have to live under such conditions!"

"No one is unsympathetic to Carmody's plight," Evaine said quietly. "But unless you propose to slip into the castle and block him and every other Deryni there—which would only alert the regents that such a thing can be done—I think we must keep our energies directed more constructively."

"Very well, then," Ansel said. "Let's talk constructively about my family."

"What *about* your family, Ansel?" Joram said.

"Well—they can't have come back of their own free will!"

"No?"

"No!" Ansel snapped. "When Jamie took them all off to Kierney last fall, after Davin was killed, he told me they intended to stay there, away from all of this. And if Manfred's son has taken a special interest in the girls—"

Gregory, whose special interest in geneaological matters was almost encyclopaedic, nodded sagely.

"Ah, yes. The MacLean sisters. Cinhil gave their wardship to Elinor and Jamie Drummond several years back, didn't he, after their father died?"

"He did," Joram agreed. "They're Iain MacLean's nieces—and they'd be his co-heiresses, now that the direct line is extinct."

"The direct line is not extinct!" Evaine said sharply, the bright fire of anger and still unresolved grief flashing suddenly in her blue eyes. "No, hear me out!" she went on, as Joram grimaced and would have made placating noises. "This is very important to me. I know what you meant, but this is never to be forgotten. *Never!* Adrian's son still lives, his life bought at the expense of *my* son's life. *Camlin* is Adrian's heir. And when Camlin's grandfather dies, *Camlin* will be Earl of Kierney."

In the shocked silence that followed her words, Ansel slowly shook his head, his voice coming barely in a whisper.

"Aunt Evaine, I'm sorry. No one has forgotten what Camlin's life cost. Do you think *I* could ever forget? I saw what they did to your Aidan, thinking he was Camlin." He drew a deep breath and went on, still sympathetic, but now also stark and brutal in his truth.

"But as for Camlin being earl after his grandfather, it isn't going to happen. You know it isn't. Camlin will no more be Earl of Kierney than I am Earl of Culdi. You ought to be rejoicing that the regents think Camlin is dead; because if they ever found out otherwise, they'd never rest until they hunted him down and rectified their earlier mistake—just as they're out for *my* blood. No, when Camlin's grandfather dies—or meets some conveniently arranged accident at the hands of the regents!—Giesele and Richeldis MacLean will inherit all of Kierney. Given that prospect, it's no wonder at all that Manfred's pimply-faced son was sniffing around them at the wedding feast."

"But, they're still babies," Evaine whispered, tears welling in her eyes. "They're only—what?—twelve or thirteen?"

Tavis snorted. "And how old is Udaut's daughter, who was wed to the Murdoch whelp yesterday?"

Shaking his head, Joram sighed. "So MacInnis' son is sniffing around. I suppose the next question is, can we do anything to stop it? And do we really want to stop it?"

"Do we want to stop it?" Evaine gasped. "Joram—"

"No, just listen. Perhaps we've all been missing a really important consideration here. We've been discussing the purely political ramifications of this situation: Who will end up with Kierney? However, as distasteful as it may be to think about a Kierney in MacInnis hands, it would still be by marriage to a MacLean—and in the long run, it's surely better for Kierney to remain in a family that has at least some MacLean blood than to have the line totally extinguished, the Kierney lands escheated to the Crown, and the lands and titles handed over to someone who has absolutely no ties with the land, such as happened with Culdi."

Young Jesse glanced at his elders and frowned. "I think Joram's certainly raised a point worth considering," he said. "However, that only leads to an even more immediate question. Would Manfred MacInnis, whose brother is a regent and the Archbishop of Valoret, actually consider joining his house to one that has such close Deryni ties? For that matter, just how Deryni are the MacLeans?"

"Not very," Joram said. "The only Deryni blood in the line comes from my father's sister Aislinn, who died at Trurill. Richeldis and Giesele are her granddaughters, and Camlin is her great-grandson. Actual Deryni ability is pretty dilute, at that remove. Given the financial gain involved, the MacInnises mightn't mind. And after another generation—" He shrugged.

"I'm not sure that's good enough," Tavis said, shifting uncomfortably on his stool. "I think what worries Ansel is how the blood manifests in the girls' generation. Do they have shields? Truth-Reading ability? Can they conjure handfire? Work simple spells? What? Ansel, do you know?"

Ansel shook his head. "I haven't seen them for years, Tavis. I simply don't know what they might be able to do. I'm worried enough about my mother. And I've got a half-sister and brother who are even younger than the MacLean girls."

"All right, then. Tell me about them," Tavis persisted. "Your mother has undeniable Deryni ties: widow of a son of Saint Camber, mother of a renegade earl who was killed trying to assassinate the king's brothers—"

"Davin wasn't trying to kill anyone!" Ansel retorted, slamming a fist against the table. "He was trying to protect Javan and Rhys Michael!"

"Yes, I was there, as you'll recall," Tavis went on, unperturbed. "And *I* know that, and *you* know that, but the regents have chosen to interpret events otherwise—which is why *you* were outlawed. Just how Deryni *is* your mother, Ansel?"

Ansel forced himself to take a deep breath and let it out slowly, pushing down his momentary anger. "Not enough to make much difference in any positive sense," he conceded, shifting in his chair. "She's a Howell by birth, and the Howells are not a particularly strong Deryni strain. She has shields. I suppose she can Truth-Read. That's about all."

"So there isn't much she could do directly against the regents," Gregory said cautiously, glancing at Tavis. "Hopefully they realize that. What about your stepfather?"

Ansel sighed. "Please don't take what I'm about to say as a criticism of Jamie, because I'm very grateful that he's been able to give my mother another chance at happiness, after Father—well, I needn't go into that, I hope. But Jamie's Deryni gifts don't run much beyond shields, either. I'll grant you that Drummond blood was fairly strong three generations back, when the first Drummond–MacRorie link was forged—but there's been nothing but pure human lineage in Jamie's direct line since then. My half-sister and brother can hardly claim any Deryni blood at all—even less than Richeldis and Giesele."

"Then, none of them probably has enough Deryni blood to worry about," Jesse said. "It sounds as if it isn't enough to protect them—but it isn't enough to damn them, either."

"That depends on how the regents are feeling about Deryni on any given day, doesn't it?" Evaine said. "What if they should order Oriel or Carmody to start sniffing about, and something shows up that we haven't anticipated? We all know how unreliable Deryni inheritance can be, at that remove, sometimes skipping generations—"

Tavis sighed. "I can see where this is leading," he said softly. "Ansel, if you want me to block them, why don't you just come out and say so?"

Tavis' words brought utter silence to the chamber, for here at last was the first practical challenge to the measure they had been proposing, in theory, almost since discovering Rhys' ability to block

Deryni powers—that ability now resident solely in Tavis O'Neill. The silence deepened as all eyes gradually turned to Ansel.

"Ansel," Evaine said quietly, "*is* that what you're asking?"

Ansel nodded, unable to speak.

"And have you considered that your mother might not agree?" Evaine went on. "How long has it been since she's spoken to you, Ansel?"

The boy hung his head. "Not since last fall, when Davin was killed," he murmured. "She refused to see me. Jamie said she holds us to blame—all of us—that we *used* Davin and spent his life on a futile cause."

"And do *you* think Davin died in vain?" Evaine asked.

Blinking back tears, Ansel shook his head, though he would not look up at any of them.

"No."

"I see." Quietly Evaine glanced at the others—Joram, Gregory, Jesse, Ansel himself—and Tavis. The young Healer gave her an almost imperceptible nod as their eyes met, and she slowly returned her gaze to Ansel.

"You haven't answered my question, Ansel," she said quietly. "If the Council authorizes what you ask—keeping in mind that we risk Tavis, who presently is the only living person we know can block Deryni powers—if we authorize what you ask, are you prepared to put your own life on the line as well, to help him do what is necessary? Before you answer, also remember that Jamie and Elinor, at least, may not agree with what you propose. Are you prepared to use force against your own mother and stepfather?"

Ansel sighed. "As things stand, she and Jamie and the children are in mortal danger that increases with every day that passes," he said quietly. "Yet she cannot help us directly, even if she were willing. If she and the rest are blocked, they will be safe from that threat, at least; and none of them will be able to hinder our cause."

"Answer the question, Ansel," she persisted. "Would you use force against your own mother, and do whatever else Tavis might deem necessary?"

Looking very, very weary, Ansel nodded. "Aye. And God help us all."

"Aye, God help us." Evaine glanced at her hands, then at Tavis. "I take it that you are willing to undertake this task, Tavis?"

"If the Council will permit it, yes. I realize that my talent is unique just now, but this would be an opportunity to test our theory under—ah—less stressful conditions, before trying to work with Revan and the Willimites. Besides that, I already come and go in

Valoret Castle on a regular basis. I think the danger is minimal to me—and it increases daily for Ansel's family."

"Reasonable arguments, all. Joram, do you agree?"

Her brother nodded.

"And Gregory, Jesse?"

Father and son also nodded.

"Very well, then. Ansel, I shall leave it to you to work out the details with Tavis."

"Very well," Tavis said. "Ah, I realize it's getting late in the afternoon, but there *is* one other thing I ought to mention, and then I'll leave you to—whatever else you need to do. I gather, from the rapidly fraying tempers around this table, that perhaps not everyone has yet recovered from last night's work; and the prospect of having to repeat so demanding an operation so soon has surely placed undue strain on all concerned. I apologize if I've contributed to the strain."

"Your apology is noted and accepted," Joram said quietly, as Tavis rose. "What other point did you wish to make?"

"Well, it's something that came up with Queron last night. Nothing to do with Javan's report directly, but it does concern Javan."

"And you'd really rather not discuss it," Evaine said, smiling slightly, "but you feel you ought to."

Tavis quirked an uneasy smile at the room at large. "I'm afraid the question was bound to come up eventually, but—well, Queron wondered whether my blocking talent would work on *Javan's* powers, even though he isn't Deryni."

At the looks of astonishment and near horror on the others' faces, he went on with alacrity.

"Now, don't look at me as if I were some kind of a monster! You know what I can do; I've practiced enough on all of you! And *having* that ability and its attendant responsibility, I certainly would never use it lightly. God knows, I wouldn't want even to think about taking Javan's powers *away*, when he's only just getting them and they may be the only thing to save him in the weeks and months to come. But—what if it *could* be done?" He looked searchingly between Joram and Evaine. "I mean, consider all the implications."

Evaine chewed on her lower lip at that, glancing at Joram in surprise and a little apprehension. Not only Javan but Alroy and also Rhys Michael were affected by what Tavis had just proposed. One of these days, she and Joram really *were* going to have to find out exactly how much Tavis actually knew of what had been done to the three Haldane princes—but not here and now, and certainly not until and unless they decided to make him the seventh member of the Council, with all the binding oaths that implied, to keep the secret safe.

"As you say, Tavis, the implications of what you have just suggested are—staggering," she said quietly. "Just now, however, you're entirely correct in pointing out that the rest of us have another difficult night ahead of us, and that, accordingly, this is not the time to explore this issue fully. Tomorrow, perhaps, when we've all had some sleep."

Tavis looked disappointed, but he could hardly object, since he alone was not involved in the night's work—though he longed to be.

"As you wish," he said, making a gracious little bow. "Have I your permission to go to Dhassa for the night, then? Bishop Niallan has extended a standing invitation to drop in for additional training, whenever I can spare the time."

"Of course," Evaine replied. "Please convey him our regards."

When he had gone, Gregory let out an explosive sigh.

"That was damned awkward. Why don't we just take in him— *and* Niallan—and be done with it? You *had* eight members in the beginning."

Evaine sighed, and Joram shook his head.

"Maybe it will come to that, Gregory," Joram said. "God knows, it's an almost impossible choice, if we have to take only one—Niallan's maturity and level-headedness against Tavis' enthusiasm and unique talents."

"However," Evaine said, pausing to indulge in a giant yawn, "it isn't anything we can even consider until after Queron is part of our company—which will never happen, if we don't finish up our final preparations. So if you gentlemen will all proceed down to the *keeill*, we should be finished in time for everyone to have a few more hours' rest."

As they filed out, Ansel lingered to press her hand in wordless thanks for the decisions made regarding his family.

CHAPTER SIX

*He hath set fire and water before thee: stretch
forth thy hand unto whether thou wirt.*
—Ecclesiasticus 15:16

Later that night, when they were sure that the rest of the residents
of Saint Michael's slept and Tavis had, indeed, gone to Dhassa, it
was Ansel who was sent to fetch Queron. Ansel found the Healer-
priest in the chapel, kneeling before the three blank slabs closing
the tombs of the men that Jesse, Queron, and one other would replace. Though the green-badged white mantle of a Gabrilite Healer
was draped around Queron's shoulders, he wore the simple grey
habit of the Servants of Saint Camber beneath it, and his feet were
bare.

"Dom Queron, it's time," Ansel said softly.

Sighing, Queron rose, a sad little smile on his face as he turned
to greet the saint's grandson.

"I am ready," he murmured. "I only hope I may be half as valuable to the Council as these were. May Saint Camber be my guide
in these next hours, as he was theirs."

Ansel said nothing, though he obviously noticed the Saint Camber medal that Queron wore on a silver chain around his neck, along
with a Healer's seal on a green cord. Not meeting Queron's eyes,
he only turned and gestured toward the open chapel door. Silence
accompanied them all the way to the Portal chamber, Ansel finally
speaking with his mind only, when he laid his hand on Queron's
arm as they stepped onto the Portal.

Our destination is no secret, but I'm to take you through Blind,
Ansel sent. *You're to do nothing to help or to hinder. Do you agree?*

Of course.

As further assent, Queron immediately closed his eyes to eliminate mere visual sight and began a slow, deep breath, stilling and pulling back his shields to give over control of his *other* Sight. He was pleased to realize that Ansel did not seem intimidated by him—though he was certain some of the others still were, even though they should not be.

Softly, very tentatively at first, he felt the younger man's controls surround and bind him. The shift, when it came, was so smooth that Queron hardly noticed it—just a slight catch to his breath as he reoriented vaguely, *knowing* that they had passed to the Portal outside the Council chamber. His opening eyes confirmed that it was so.

Leave me a control link, came Ansel's further instruction, as they stepped into the dimly lit landing before the great bronze doors of the Council chamber, and Ansel conjured handfire with his free hand. *Follow my handfire. We'll take a turnpike stair. Go slowly, because it's steep. I'll be right behind you.*

A section of the wall slid back before them as the handfire touched it, opening into a downward-spiraling wooden stairwell whose location Queron had not even suspected, though he had known such a stair must exist. Joram had told him the day before of the *keeill*—the ancient word meant sanctuary or chapel—the *keeill*, which lay directly beneath the Council chamber.

Ansel's grip shifted to his shoulder and urged him forward, controls still lightly but firmly in place. The boy was *very* good. Queron braced his left hand against the newel post as they started down, his other hand just brushing the stone on his right, and kept his mind stilled, receptive. At the bottom of the stair, a few steps beyond, Ansel's handfire came up against another bronze door—this one single, not nearly as tall as the ones above, and carved with several of the intricate, spiraling motifs anciently called staring patterns.

"I'll release your controls now," Ansel murmured, shifting his grasp to Queron's left elbow, "but don't raise your shields." His free hand seemed to press the handfire into the carvings of the top spiral so that it glowed like molten silver. "Work the first staring pattern. It's a spell for centering. I'll follow it with you."

Nodding, Queron drew a deep breath and complied. He knew the pattern well—probably far better than the younger, less experienced Ansel, but that might not be a safe assumption, based on the last quarter hour. So he made himself trace it slowly—no short cuts—savoring the gradual stilling and centering as his eyes tracked every curve of the mystical maze. At the centerpoint, the spell in place, he closed his eyes for just a moment and took another deep breath, letting it out slowly as he opened his eyes again to await further instruction. The glow of the staring pattern was fading as Ansel pushed the door open with the flat of his hand and ushered Queron in.

The *keeill* was round, rather than octagonal like the chamber above it. Stone floored the perimeter, wide enough to walk around, but a circular dais of seven steps dominated the room—grey-black slate whose planes of shadow and darker shadow seemed to swallow up the light of the torches at the four quarter-stations. In the center of the dais, the others were waiting around a cubic, waist-high altar that looked like giant ward cubes piled in two layers, the black and white cubes alternating. Pillars the thickness of a man's upper arm—two each of black and white—supported a mensa of some stark-white stone atop the cubes, and the whole rested on a base slab of obsidian black.

He could not see much of what lay on the altar, for Gregory and Jesse stood shoulder to shoulder on its north side, dark-clad backs blocking most of his view, but the purplish glow of a lamp of handfire at the altar's center spilled beyond them, revealing Joram's expected presence in the south. Evaine waited in the west, head bowed, her golden hair unbound and spilling down her back, ethereal and almost fragile-looking in white.

"This way, please," came Ansel's low voice, his hand guiding Queron to the left rather than up the dais steps.

They had entered between two massive, rough-cut ashlar pillars flanking the door. Queron could see more of them set hard against the outer perimeter of the chamber, with dark, shadowed spaces between, barely wide enough to hold a man. Making a quick mental count as Ansel backed him partway into the nearest of those spaces, Queron realized there were twelve in all—which meant twelve niches as well, if one counted the one containing the northern door—apt symbolism for a magical working place.

But, there would be time enough, later, to ponder more subtle meanings. For now, Ansel's mind remained close at the edge of his shields, one hand now clasped lightly around Queron's left wrist as he reached into his dark tunic to produce a length of fine white woolen yarn.

"Give me both your hands, please," Ansel murmured, deftly looping the yarn around the captive wrist and then the other one as Queron complied. "This binding of your wrists is symbolic of the loyalties and obligations which have bound you up until tonight," he explained. "A little later, you will be asked to sever these bonds yourself, to free you for the commitment you are about to make. Stand against the wall behind you now."

Yielding to the pressure of Ansel's hand against his chest, Queron eased back a step. The floor was cold and gritty beneath his bare feet, the space between the two pillars claustrophobic, like standing in a tomb, the pillars confining his elbows close against his sides, the stone icy cold along his back, even through his mantle.

Nor was he reassured when Ansel backed off a step to raise both hands to shoulder level, palms turned toward the pillars. The air began to tingle between them—irritating to Queron, with his shields still lowered—and he guessed that Ansel was about to invoke a stasis spell of some sort, perhaps similar to the Trap effect sometimes layered over a Portal to keep unauthorized users in place until they could be dealt with.

But Ansel totally surprised him. Instead of standard stasis, which would have immobilized Queron inside his tomblike niche, Ansel somehow called up a stasis veil. It skimmed the edge of Queron's niche like a fragile purple soap bubble, apparently of the most ethereal and insubstantial nature—but neither fragile nor insubstantial, as Queron quickly discovered. Not only would it keep Queron in, but absolutely *nothing* besides light and sound could penetrate that veil until it was dispelled from outside—not even air! It was a far more serious binding than the cords looped around Queron's wrists—which he could have broken in an instant, had he wished—*very* substantial magic! That knowledge was infinitely sobering, for though he truly believed he trusted this company implicitly, he had not thought they would place him so completely at their mercy and so soon!

He fancied he could feel his air growing stale already—and he *knew* his heart was pounding beneath the bound wrists clenched hard against his chest—but he made himself begin relaxing. He had submitted to this testing voluntarily; he would face far more serious threats than mere physical helplessness before the night was over. If he could keep his breathing light and shallow, he should be all right until they went on to the next test.

But it took him several more slow, controlled breaths before he could raise his eyes to Ansel's, watching coolly from beyond the glow of the stasis veil. The boy studied him intently for several seconds, apparently assuring himself that Queron was in no great distress, then gave him a respectful inclination of his head and turned on his heel to mount the seven shallow steps, careful to approach exactly opposite the door in the north. Queron, in an attempt to put his own situation out of mind as much as possible, set himself to note and remember everything that happened. The stasis veil obscured even light and sound a little, but he was able to follow without too much difficulty.

He watched with understanding and growing respect as Ansel paused and turned at the top of the steps, to crouch and pick up the ends of a dark cord or rope lying almost invisible in the angle between the dais and the step just beneath it. As Ansel knotted the ends loosely, right over left and left over right, closing the dais in a circle marked out by the cord, Queron reflected that the tradition was one not often observed these days, except in very special circumstances—yet it seemed entirely appropriate for the working intended tonight. The cord tied, Ansel glanced at him again before going to take a place at the east of the altar.

The general form of what followed was very familiar to Queron, though some of the nuances were subtly different. The first task of any magical working was to establish the boundaries of the working place, to purify it, and to invoke the presence and protection of appropriate Guardians. Thus, it was no surprise when Evaine took up an aspergillum and, beginning in the East, walked the perimeter of the circle sunwise while sprinkling it with holy water, accompanied by Joram's recitation of the beautiful Psalm of the Shepherd and pausing at South, West, North, and East again to make especial salute. He supposed that the torches already burning at the Quarters must signify for the stations of the four great Archangels who would later be summoned, for no additional lights were placed at the edge of the dais before Evaine began her circuit.

Joram censed the circle next, bringing a thurible to the eastern edge of the dais and raising it to the symbolic source of Light. Queron was pleased to note that the Michaeline had donned the customary blue of his Order for tonight's working and knew that the familiar and much-loved habit must give Joram comfort.

Bowing, Joram passed then to his right to trace the circle a second time, taking up his Psalm again, the thurible's chains jingling musical counterpoint to his voice. Incense smoke hung on the air in a blue-white trail that rose higher at each new quarter where he paused to salute again, though its scent did not reach Queron through the stasis veil.

But when Joram had finished in the East again and returned to his place, setting the thurible back on the altar, it was Gregory who took up the sword to seal the circle, carrying it under the quillons with a no-nonsense expression as he moved briskly to the East.

There he paused to bend one knee for a moment, head bowed to the weapon's cross hilt, before rising to execute quite a proper military salute. At the end, all in one graceful movement, he grounded the tip of the blade against the dais edge and turned sunward, steel slithering against slate as he began tracing the final circuit of the circle's casting. Light sprang up where the sword passed, a silvery ribbon a handspan high, laid on edge, enclosing the circle at the first step off the dais, just outside the knotted cord.

Gregory's performance took Queron a little aback, for he had not guessed that Gregory was particularly trained as a ritualist. But Gregory cut the circle with classic precision, never looking beyond its boundaries, not stopping until he had closed the two ends of the circle, back in the East. And there he did something that almost took Queron's breath away.

For just an instant Gregory paused there, the tip of his blade still impaling the silvery ribbon. Then he turned slightly toward the south, the blade now slanted obliquely across his body, and swept the blade slowly upward in a wide arc from east to west, following the path of the sun.

The fabric of the ribbon of light rose in answer, as if Gregory somehow had snagged the light and stretched it upward to canopy over their heads. The apex of a growing silvery triangle followed the path his blade traced, ever widening and broadening at its base until, as the tip was earthed between him and the altar, a softly glowing dome of energy enclosed the circle. Queron could hardly believe what he had seen.

But the imperturbable Gregory did not seem at all amazed by what he had just done. He held for several heartbeats, the sword grounded at his side, then drew the blade in a straight line in front of him, west to east—*completing the circle's dome as a sphere below their feet*, Queron suddenly realized! Bringing the hilt to his lips again, he turned eastward one more time to bring the blade down smartly to the side in final salute. After that, almost nonchalantly, he shifted his grip below the quillons and brought the weapon back to the altar, circling behind Joram and Evaine to lay it before himself and Jesse on the white surface.

Queron hardly dared to let himself breathe until the sword was out of Gregory's hands. He had never even *heard* of an effect such as Gregory had just produced. And the theoretical knowledge implied by Gregory's physical act of completing the sphere was almost too staggering to contemplate! He wondered what other surprises tonight might hold in store for him, if the mere casting of the circle could contain such revelations.

He was almost relieved as Ansel, Joram, Evaine, and Jesse turned in unison and moved to the edges of the dais, each facing one of the Quarters—even though that meant that his own part in the ritual surely could not be far away. They would call the Quarters now—though whether it would be in any form familiar to Queron, he would not even hazard a guess. In the past little while, he had only just begun truly to realize the scope of the knowledge the Council must have been retrieving from the ancient records; and his very soul both rejoiced and trembled that he was about to gain access to it.

"By rites ancient and powerful have we prepared this place," Gregory said quietly, laying the fingertips of both hands on the sword again—though he did not pick it up. "Now, therefore, by ancient calling do we summon, stir, and call up the great, archangelic hosts."

In the East, on cue, Ansel threw back his head and raised both arms in supplication, his young voice ringing with confidence.

"In the name of Light arising do we summon Raphael, the Healer, Guardian of Air and Wind and Tempest," he said, "to guard this company and witness the oaths that shall be sworn. Come, mighty Raphael, and grace us with thy presence."

He conjured handfire as he spoke—a sphere of golden light that grew above his head and then, at his direction, arrowed across the darkness of the *keeill*'s vaulting to merge with the fire of the eastern torch in a white-gold flash.

Queron was stunned, for he had never seen such an effect before. Nor, shielded behind the veil of his stasis spell, could he sense the Archangel's Coming immediately—though he saw, from the look on Ansel's face, that *he* was aware of it.

Gradually, however, Queron had the impression of a great wind filling the *keeill*, groaning through senses that had nothing to do with hearing. It raised the hackles at the back of his neck, sending a shudder down his spine, ice-cold against the stone wall behind him, and he pressed himself harder into his protective niche, hoping he was invisible, as Ansel's arms were lowered and Joram's raised.

"In the name of Light increasing, we summon Michael, the Defender, Lord of Fire and Prince of the Legions of Heaven," Joram said, his voice echoing in the *keeill* as he threw back his head. "May he guard this company and give due witness to the oaths that shall be sworn. Come, mighty Michael, and grace us with thy presence."

Joram's handfire whooshed toward the southern torch with all the sudden alacrity of a lightning strike, heavenly fire returning to its true source, blinding-bright. When Queron could look at it again, blood-scarlet burned in the heart of the flame; and Michael's sudden and undeniable Presence was all but visual, as *he* loomed all at once in the shadows beyond Joram—fire bright, yet not thus to physical sight—which was all Queron had, veiled behind the stasis spell. But the Healer-priest would not allow himself to dwell on what was not possible, for Evaine was about to summon Gabriel, who was his own especial patron.

"In the name of Light descending," said Evaine, offering her own supplication, "we likewise summon Gabriel, Lord of Water, Heavenly Herald, who didst bring glad tidings to our Blessed Lady. May this company be guarded and our oaths witnessed. Come, mighty Gabriel, and grace us with thy presence."

The gentle, sea-blue fire that Evaine conjured was soothing balm to Queron's now shaky perceptions, and he gave quiet and humble thanks that he did not need to see with his eyes to know that Gabriel approached. Breathing silent prayer and welcome to that One, Queron closed his eyes briefly, feeling himself settle at last into something approaching peace, now that Gabriel was nearby to sustain him.

It was Jesse who summoned the final Witness to their rite—Jesse, youngest of them all and little-tried, but confident as he raised his hands in entreaty, somehow setting just the proper seal on what was being done.

"In the name of Light returning, we also summon Uriel, Dark Lord of Earth, who bringest all at last unto the Nether Shore," came Jesse's Call, quiet but assured. "Companion of all who offer up their lives in the defense of others, guard this company and witness our oaths. Come, mighty Uriel, and grace us with thy presence."

All at once, as Jesse's sphere of emerald green merged with the torch just outside Queron's niche, dark-feathered wings buffeted the other side of the stasis veil. Gasping, Queron ducked his head in acknowledgment of *that* One—to whom, he suddenly realized, he might well have to answer before the night was over. By now, he had been made most uncomfortably aware that the Camberian Council had access to knowledge and powers far beyond even the vast lore of Queron's Order—and Gabrilite training was usually accounted among the best available. Not only in symbol did his life hang in the balance tonight.

For a dozen heartbeats, he trembled in that realization, all too aware of the awesome Powers gathered in the space between the pillars and the circle's dome, watching the *keeill*'s mortal occupants gather around the altar again, as the immortal Ones loomed outside the circle.

And he must pass among *them*, in order even to beg admittance to the circle's sanctuary! Small wonder that he had been left behind the safety of the stasis veil—and what was he going to do when it was lifted?

"We stand outside time, in a place not of earth," came Evaine's low-voiced words, intimately familiar to Queron from very ancient tradition. "As our ancestors before us bade, we join together and are one."

Joram's priestly hands were raised to reinforce his sister's declaration as he gave the answering invocation that Queron expected.

"By Thy Blessed Evangelists, the holy Matthew, Mark, Luke, and John; by all Thy Holy Angels; by all Powers of Light and Shadow, we call Thee to guard and defend us from all perils, O Most High. Thus it is and has ever been, thus it will be for all times to come. *Per omnia saecula saeculorum.*"

As the others answered, "Amen," making the sign of the cross, Queron followed suit as best he could, with his hands bound. All bowed their heads for several minutes after that, before Evaine spoke again—this time, in words unfamiliar to Queron.

"Now we are met. Now we are one with the Light. Regard the Ancient Ways. We shall not walk this path again. So be it."

"So be it," the others repeated in unison.

Then Gregory was taking up the sword again, leading the others in procession to the northern quarter. There they ringed behind him in a semicircle, observing in silence while he knelt and laid the blade close along the dais edge.

Reaching across it and down then, carefully avoiding the shimmering dome of the circle itself, Gregory untied the knotted cord and folded the ends back past the sword's pommel and tip, wide enough for a gate. This he then traced with the sword, rising with the blade in his hand once more to touch its tip to the left-hand side of the incipient opening, sweeping the blade up, arching across to his right and back down. The passage of the blade inscribed a line of brighter silver, outlining a door, and the door became a magical gateway through the circle's dome as the blade rang against the edge of the step on the right, the outline completed.

They would come for him now—or Gregory would, Queron amended, as Gregory stepped through the opening alone, the sword held horizontally before him by hilt and tip. As Gregory descended, heading directly toward Queron, the sword projected a swath of silvery light before him that *stayed*, rippling down the steps like a quicksilver carpet, a moon-bright path of safety for Gregory's feet to tread.

It and he stopped at the bottom step, an armspan short of Queron's niche, but the blade turned in Gregory's hand even as his arm extended. The magical blade pierced the stasis veil and shattered it on contact, before Queron could even think about raising his bound hands in futile attempt to defend himself.

Impossible! He had *never* heard of a stasis veil doing *that*!

Dumbfounded, Queron caught his breath and froze, for the tip of the sword now was poised directly over his heart, pressed hard against his flesh like burning ice—inescapable, for the unyielding stone of the chamber wall was at his back.

Yet the threat of the sword, even a magical one, was as nothing compared to what lay beyond—for *they* were out there. With the stasis veil dispelled, he could almost see *them*, the circle's Guardians, towering vaguely shadowy but altogether potent, still filling the space between the circle's dome and the pillars. Only the path of light on which Gregory now stood offered refuge—and a vast distance separated Queron from it, for all that, physically, he could have encompassed the space between his two arms.

"Queron Kinevan, why have you come to this place?" Gregory asked, his voice snapping Queron back to the more immediate threat of the magical blade. The blue eyes were cool and implacable, the long fingers steady on the hilt of the sword, and Queron knew that if his answer was not wholly satisfactory, Gregory was quite capable of slaying him where he stood, either with the blade itself or with the awesome power obviously directed through the blade by Gregory's will.

"I come—to offer a bond of blood and spirit and sacrifice to this company," Queron said quietly, "in the service of the Light."

"Do you come of your own free will," Gregory asked, "prepared to set aside all previous ties and loyalties, ready to give your life, if need be, in the service of the Light?"

Queron nodded gravely. "I do."

To his relief the blade was lowered, though Queron knew that this did not necessarily diminish the danger.

"Know, then," Gregory continued, "that you stand before the Great Abyss, that dark night of the soul which each of us must cross, and cross alone, at least once in every lifetime. The true adept may face it many times, in many different forms. Nor is any crossing necessarily easier, for having faced the ones before.

"You have faced the sword's first challenge." Gregory knelt to lay the sword across the gap between them, the hilt resting on the first step and the point at Queron's feet. "But the greater challenge is yet to come. The Sword of Justice has rightly been called the Bridge over the Abyss. The Abyss, in this place, is a living symbol of the ties you are being asked to cast aside tonight, many of which have been binding, indeed. One may walk upon this Bridge, if one has courage. But you must know that the Way is even more perilous than you think."

Pointedly shifting his own gaze to the blade, Gregory turned it so that its edge was uppermost, presenting only a thin, sharp line of silver between Queron and the safety of the silvery path where Gregory knelt.

"Only by casting yourself free of these previous commitments, by binding yourself to a purpose higher than yourself, may you essay the crossing in safety," Gregory went on, looking up at him again. "Are you prepared, then, to offer yourself in unreserved dedication to the service of the Light?"

"I am," Queron breathed.

"Then, set your right foot upon the Sword Bridge," Gregory said, "as a sign of your willingness to proceed, and cross the Chasm confidently, borne above all earthly dangers and temptations by your resolve."

CHAPTER SEVEN

Yea, a sword shall pierce through thine own
soul also, and the thoughts of many hearts
shall be revealed.

—Nicodemus 12:5

The Sword-edge Bridge stretched before Queron in all the stark physical symbolism of the inner Ordeal that the very concept suggested. The Bridge over the Abyss was a classic means of progression on the path toward adeptship, but that path was in no wise an easy one. The fact that Queron had crossed lesser chasms gave him little comfort as he faced this latest incarnation of the Ordeal, for each passage was different, presenting its own perils.

He knew he was not expected literally to walk across the edge of the sword—but what seemed to yawn beneath it was infinitely more menacing than any mere steel. He had never thought himself particularly wary of heights, but the vast chasm he could sense gaping before him encompassed far more than just physical space. All of his worst personal fears and petty failings leered up at him from the churning maelstrom that howled below, ready to snap him up and rend his soul at the slightest hesitation or misstep. Failure might not bring about his literal death, but the psychic battering of a spiritual tumble certainly would render him unfit for any immediate usefulness to the company he sought to join; and recovery might take a lifetime—or more.

But he must not dwell on that danger. His inner strength and his dedication to the rightness of their cause must lend him the courage to proceed. He must offer up his weaknesses upon the altar of his heart and let them be consumed by the fire of the Ordeal. He could sense the uncompromising scrutiny of immortal as well as mortal watchers as he set his right foot lightly on the line of shining steel, and he made his pledge of faith a prayer for support.

As he had known it must be, the sword was withdrawn before he could put his weight full upon it, but the narrow hairline of silver that remained, so slenderly bridging the Abyss, was surely no less terrifying as he slowly shifted his weight full upon it and then stepped out with his other foot, balancing a little awkwardly with his bound hands. Gregory had risen and backed a few steps farther onto the path of light as Queron stepped, and stood now with the sword resting across his right shoulder, his left hand held ready to reach out to Queron—but only after the Healer-priest had safely reached the other side by his own devices.

Each step was a trial. The line of light seemed to burn into the soles of his feet like molten silver. Though a part of his mind told him it was only stone he walked upon, perfectly firm beneath his feet, another part shrieked of the Abyss gaping beneath him. Given what he had witnessed so far, without even entering the circle, who could say which perception was correct?

But he persevered, despite the cold terror clutching at his soul, and finally, he was across. As Gregory took his elbow to steady him, turning to lead him up to the safety of the circle—now an honor escort—Queron's relief knew hardly any bounds. Gratefully he stepped into the circle at Gregory's side, only closing his eyes for a few seconds to breathe deeply as Gregory closed the gate behind them with the sword.

Then Gregory was returning to stand at his left. Joram and Evaine were before him, flanked by Ansel and Jesse. All of them looked very, very solemn, causing Queron to wonder whether he had, indeed, passed the test of the sword.

"Queron Kinevan," Joram said quietly, "we welcome you to this circle and acknowledge with respect the courage you have shown, to venture into this place. But you came before us with obligations and commitments which bound you to other loyalties. The faith we require must be without reservation—saving that for priests, such as you and myself, the seal of the confessional must be unbreached, whatever else may befall. For as the Scriptures remind us, 'Thou art a priest forever.'

"Saving only that reservation, then, and even including the vows you made as a Healer and as a member of the Order of Saint Gabriel, are you now prepared to surrender all other ties and loyalties, relegating them to a lesser place, that our work in the service of the Light may come before all other considerations?"

Queron had prayed long and hard over this requirement and had known it would be demanded. He had pondered it before disposing of his *g'dula* the night before—for that, too, was a loosing of ties. So was the putting aside of his Gabrilite robes, later on. He had not been ready, then, also to cast aside his Healer's mantle, but now its weight on his shoulders reminded him that this, too, was a binding—though he would never cease being a Healer, any more than he could cease being a priest.

But he found that, having crossed the Abyss this time, he could now let go of everything that lay outside that core that was the heart of his priestly and healing vocations. He could give it up gladly, in the service of the Light. Almost of their own volition, his bound hands rose to loose the cloak-clasp at his throat. As the Healer's mantle slipped from his shoulders, whispering into a heap of dull, wrinkled white behind him, he felt infinitely lighter. He considered taking off his Saint Camber medal and his Healer's seal as well, but those no longer held the weight they once had, and did not bind him at all.

"I am prepared," he said quietly, looking into Joram's eyes unflinchingly.

"Then, sever the bonds which bind you physically, even as you have dissociated yourself from the ties that bind in heart and soul and mind," Evaine commanded, as Gregory held the sword closer to him, bracing the hilt with both hands.

The woolen yarn parted easily as Queron drew his bonds along the blade—far more easily than he had parted himself from the ties the yarn represented. He felt at peace, however, as he watched Joram catch up the severed pieces, and he followed without hesitation as Evaine led him sunwise around the altar to a place in the west, to end up standing on her right. The others also returned to their places; and as Joram laid the cords in the thurible, still smoldering in the south, and the sharp stench of burning wool briefly drifted upward, Queron at last had an opportunity to examine the items on the altar, if only superficially.

Nothing appeared to be immediately out of the ordinary. The thurible and aspergillum he had already seen, as well as the sword Gregory laid back in place. Nor could he take exception to the other items: an incense boat, a footed clay cup of water, a small bowl of what appeared to be salt, and a small silver dagger that he thought he had seen Evaine wear before. All of this lay on a white altar cloth, totally unadorned.

But in the exact center of the altar was something that was—not precisely out of the ordinary—simply unexpected on an altar. Though its top was covered with a square of fine linen, Queron could see that the object beneath it was a square wooden box, perhaps twice the span of a man's hand and half as tall as it was wide. A lamp burned in a cup of fine-blown purple glass on top of the box, fueled by a small vigil candle. As Jesse moved the lamp aside and Joram removed and folded the square of linen, Evaine laid her left hand on top of the box and turned slightly to face him.

"You have already faced the most difficult part of this night's working, Queron," she said softly. "What remains, however, is by far the most solemn. Beneath my hand are tokens of all the previous members of the Camberian Council. It is upon these relics, made sacred by the dedication of those who have gone before you, that you will be asked to swear your oath. Since the days of the original five founders—myself, Joram, Rhys, Alister, and Jebediah—all members have sworn a like oath and bound their pledge into harmony with the rest."

As she opened the box, hinging the lid back toward Ansel, Queron had an impression of purple, cord-like threads and something that flashed silver. The latter proved to be a signet ring with a plaited hank of threads loosely knotted through it.

"This was my father's ring," Evaine said, taking it out and displaying it on her open palm, nested in the coils of the plait. "Whether or not one holds him saint—and opinions vary, even in this circle," she added with a faint smile, "by including this token, in his memory, we honor his vision and his dream, that one day Deryni and humans should live and work together in harmony, in all and for the sake of all. The braided cords you see wrapped through the ring were prepared last night, after Jesse swore his oath, with each of us contributing a strand. Tonight, we will prepare a new set, all of us renewing our own vows as you make yours."

She put the skeined ring back into the box, then pulled a long strand of purple silken thread from underneath the edge of the altar cloth before him, laying it ceremoniously across the hands he tremblingly raised to receive it.

"To that end, we ask that you first bind this cord across your brow, as symbol of the new obligations you assume tonight, binding upon mind and soul as well as body—a tie connecting you with all our ancient tradition, linking you with the Light we all strive to serve.

"Remember that the purple thread has long been the symbol of excellence," she went on, helping him knot it at the back of his head, as the others donned similar threads, already tied. "In this company, and in matters pertaining to the integrity of its members, it also carries all the weight of the priest's purple stole, and the absolute confidentiality implied by the seal of the confessional, even unto death."

She paused to slip her own cord around her forehead, then gestured toward the open box.

"Now lay your hands upon these relics and swear us your oath, ever mindful that a part of all those who have gone before us remains with us in this company. And may you never be called upon to make a more solemn pledge."

Queron's mouth was dry as he obeyed, and it was only by pressing his hands hard against the edge of the box that he was able to keep them from trembling. He closed his eyes as the others also reached out to touch the box lightly with their fingertips, aware of their scrutiny—though they did not touch him physically or psychically. He could feel Camber's ring cool and potent beneath his right hand—surely a saint's relic!—and as he forced himself to draw a deep breath and center in, reaching for some hint of contact with the men who had gone before him, he felt himself relax, knowing that, indeed, he *could* make this commitment without reservation.

"I swear by all I hold most holy—by my love of God, by my vocation as a Healer and a priest, by my honor as a man—that I will bear faith and truth to this company, named in honor of the blessed Saint Camber; that if need be, I will lay down my life, my honor, and even my immortal soul to preserve our people in the Light, so long as that be not to the harm of the innocent. All this I pledge, God aiding me, as a humble servant of the Light, in the name of the Father, and of the Son, and of the Holy Spirit. Amen. So be it."

The others drew back as he opened his eyes, except for Evaine, who pressed her hand over his, preventing his withdrawal.

"Well and truly have you sworn, Queron Kinevan," she said. "Now that you have spoken these vows, will you open your mind and heart and soul to us, your brethren, as a final seal of your good faith, saving only those things pertaining to your office as a priest?"

"*Volo*," Queron whispered, already lowering his shields as he bowed his head in submission. *I will.*

He shuddered a little as he felt Evaine's hands upon his head, Joram's joining them, but he had half expected this. They were the children of Saint Camber, and he had sworn to them, and he could not refuse anything they asked. He sensed their minds enveloping his, surging in relentlessly as he let his shields buckle and fall before them, wholly giving up control. He had not bared his mind and soul this way since his Healer's examinations, many years before, and the occasional deep readings shared with very trusted and much-loved confessors, in the years since—and he could not bring himself to even care.

Deeper and deeper they took him. Briefly, he drifted beyond all awareness of just how deep, unable to prevent or even sense their entry into any of his most intimate depths, if they wished. But in fact, though they did read deeply, they did not read extensively or for long—and told him so, as they eased him back to a level permitting more equal rapport—content, perhaps, that the opportunity had been freely offered, that Queron had been *willing* to permit this most intimate of all contacts as a sign of his trust.

They let *him* choose the direction of their rapport for a while after that, acquiescing readily when he indicated a desire to explore the psychic ripples surrounding the tokens beneath his hands—for this was the heart of the group soul that was the Camberian Council. Camber's ring drew him like a moth to flame, plummeting him abruptly into a cool, lavender stillness that sucked Joram and Evaine in with him.

And then, stark as any physical presence he had ever noted under the brightest noonday sun, Queron saw Saint Camber's face floating before his psychic Sight, pale silver-grey eyes boring into his.

A part of Queron shouted that this was impossible, that he had hardly even met Camber MacRorie in life—some few passing conversations during a retreat, many, many years ago—but another part of him knew that it was Camber, indeed, regardless of any mere facts.

And yet, what more appropriate than that the Deryni saint should vouchsafe an appearance to one who had just made an unreserved commitment to the company that bore his name? In his mind's eye Queron saw Camber lift his hands in blessing—or beckoning?—and sensed the shock and confusion of Joram and Evaine, still locked with him in unshatterable rapport.

Yet Queron was not afraid, and he sensed they were not afraid either. Camber was their father, after all, for all that he was a saint. Still, Queron seemed to sense their pulling back, a garbled exchange of communication flashing between them that he could not catch.

Then the saintly image was gone, and Evaine was cautioning him to say nothing of this to the others.

These visitations sometimes happen, she told him. *Joram and I have become somewhat accustomed to them, but the others are newer and less tried. To reveal this now might disrupt the pace of the rest of the night's working. This vision was for you. We will speak later on what it might mean.*

At his confused but elated assent, they slowly began bringing him up then, returning him but gradually to normal consciousness and sensation. And as they withdrew, and he jerkily removed his hands from the box, flexing his fingers cautiously, he fixed his eyes for just an instant on Camber's ring, even as he quickly ran through the mental assessment that all trained Deryni were taught to make after such a contact.

"Welcome, Dom Queron," Jesse said quietly, jarring Queron back to physical reality. As Queron looked up, still a little dazed, he saw the little silver knife in Jesse's hand. The boy obviously was unaware of any of what had just transpired.

"Well and truly have you given the bond of your spirit and your mind," Jesse went on. "Will you now give us the bond of your blood as a final seal and symbol of the sacrifice you may be called upon to make in the service of this covenant?"

Breathing a weary and relieved sigh, for this part was easy, compared to what he had already experienced, Queron held out the hand closest to Jesse—his left.

"Take it gladly, as token of my trust and truth."

He did not flinch as Jesse grasped his left ring finger and nicked it smartly with the dagger. Evaine removed the cord from around his brow, not meeting his eyes, and he watched dispassionately as she smeared the knot with his blood and then Jesse held the dripping finger over the cup and let a drop fall. It dissipated immediately, quickly invisible to mere sight, but Queron sensed other blood in the cup and guessed that it would have some later part in the proceedings.

But not immediately. First they collected the other cords, the knot of each one already sealed with the owner's blood. These cords Joram and Evaine wove together in a pattern Queron recognized of the ancient cording lore—though he could not have said which particular one it was, especially in his still befuddled state. He sucked absently at his wounded finger as he watched, but he did not Heal it as he might have, choosing instead to let its natural healing remind him of all that had happened tonight. When Joram and Evaine had finished with the cording pattern, Evaine took the previous night's braid off of Camber's ring and replaced it with the new one, depositing both in the box before closing it and replacing the linen cloth and lamp.

"Behold now this salt, a symbol of earth, which purifies and perserves, banishing all evil," she said then, indicating the dish that held it. "Into this cup of our covenant, which bears the blood of all this company, we add this salt, in token of the tears we may be called upon to shed in the service of our vows." Taking a pinch of the salt between thumb and forefinger, she sprinkled it into the water.

"Even as this salt dissolves in water, so may the Light diffuse through us as we drink of this cup, refining and multiplying the element of Light within us so that we may become Its perfect servants. So be it. Amen."

"So be it. Amen," the others repeated, as Evaine raised it to her lips.

They all drank from it then, Evaine passing it to Gregory and on, sunwise, as Joram admonished them to remember those who had gone before and to cherish those now bound in their company. Jesse, when he had drunk, went to the north, where the gate had been, and retied the circle cord, signifying that this most recent incarnation of the Camberian Council was once again duly sworn and complete. Ansel drank in special memory of his brother, who had been one of those to give their lives in the cause, even though he had not been a member of the Council *per se*. Joram spoke of the memory of Alister Cullen, Jebediah of Alcara, and Jaffray of Carbury—Michaelines all.

To Queron the cup came last, and he invoked the memory of the martyrs of Saint Neot's and Saint Camber's at Dolban, and of Saint Camber himself, before draining the cup to its dregs. The water did not taste of blood, but the presence of that bond was no less real for being overshadowed by salt. Tears were welling in his eyes as he upturned the empty cup and set it carefully before the box.

After a short period of final meditation, they quietly set about the necessary rites to close down the circle. Queron was allowed to observe, for he needed no additional demands placed upon him after the evening's work. Even when it was over, no one spoke unnecessarily. Ansel took Queron out, to return him to his quarters, and when Jesse and Gregory had also gone, Evaine glanced at her brother.

"He's the one, Joram," she said quietly.

"He's the one what?"

"Queron is the one to help us bring him back. I think that's why Father showed up during our working tonight."

Joram sighed wearily and sank down on the topmost step of the dais, picking up the fat ball of the circle cord that Ansel had rewound as they dismantled the circle. He did not look at Evaine as she sat down beside him.

"You're really determined to do this, aren't you?" he said.

"Yes."

"And what makes you think he'll agree to help? Evaine, he still thinks Father was really a saint! You saw the medal he was wearing tonight. And he didn't take it off, even when he shed his Healer's mantle at the circle's gate."

"I suspect he meant it as a mark of respect for his favorite saint, in whose memory the Council is named," Evaine said.

"In whose honor he founded a religious order that we *know* to be based on a lie!"

"*Do* we know that, Joram?" Evaine retorted. "You yourself expressed at least a contrary possibility not two weeks ago, as I recall. Just because the official canonization was supported by illusion, by a *misinterpretation* of the truth, that doesn't make *him* any less what he is or isn't—including a saint, if that's what God had in mind for him!"

Joram gave her a sour and slightly scandalized smile.

"I see. So now you're claiming to know the mind of God."

"Certainly not! Besides, whether or not he's a saint is hardly the point. For that matter, it isn't even important that Queron founded a religious order in Father's honor. That order has just been brutally suppressed, and Father's sainthood has been rescinded. Despite that, Queron still was willing to make an unreserved dedication to the Council named in Father's honor. I can't imagine that he wouldn't be willing to help us, under the circumstances."

Joram sighed and ducked his head, fingering the cord-ball uneasily.

"Do we have to tell him *all* the ghastly details?"

"Let me answer your question with another question," she replied. "Given the fact that a Healer is essential to our attempt to bring Father back, would you want to work with one who didn't have all the background of the situation? Remember, this isn't just a matter of healing physical wounds."

Joram snorted. "I know that. And the fact that Father manifested here tonight, right while we were in Queron's mind, seems to be a clear indication of *his* preference. I'm not arguing that."

"Then, what *are* you arguing?"

"*I don't know!*" Joram blurted. "Queron scares me! Even after going into his mind the way we did tonight, the very *thought* of having to face him one-on-one—"

"You know, you really *are* going to have to work past this irrational wariness you have of him!" Evaine said sharply. "You've let what used to be a survival habit become an obsession. After all, if we *do* draft him, we'll have to *tell* him everything you've always been afraid he'd find out."

After a stunned silence, Joram slowly began to chuckle. "You're right. If we tell him, I don't have to be on guard any more, do I? After twelve years of protecting the illusion, it's easy to forget."

"Yes, it is."

"Mind you, I *still* don't have to like it," Joram went on. "The notion will take some getting used to. But as you say, a Healer is essential—and there aren't any other Healers I'd trust with the information, or who have the training to handle the working."

"No, there aren't," Evaine agreed. "The only other one who even comes close is Tavis—and we certainly can't spare *him* for such a working, even if his training were up to it. It's bad enough that we have to send him into Valoret with Ansel."

Joram sagged back against the step and rubbed a weary hand over his eyes. "Aye, that bothers me, too. Blocking Elinor and her family is one of the last things I would have chosen to do—but for now, not being Deryni is the only thing likely to keep them all alive and safe."

"Very true," Evaine said, rising and holding out her hand to help him up. "And if all goes well, at least it will be a good trial run for Tavis' work with Revan. We won't even *think* about what happens if things don't go well."

"You'll get no argument from *me*," Joram said, slipping an arm around her shoulders as they headed down the dais steps. "For that operation, we'll let Ansel and Tavis do the thinking."

CHAPTER EIGHT

*I am become a stranger unto my brethren, and
an alien unto my mother's children.*

—Psalms 69:8

More than a week passed before Tavis was able to agree on a plan
with Ansel and coordinate its implementation with Javan. The
prince readily agreed to assist them, confirming their fears that the
regents were showing uncommon interest in the young MacLean
sisters, but he warned of some other machination afoot as well—
something of which he had been able to glean only vague hints that
an important event was brewing.

"I couldn't begin to guess what it's all about," a worried Javan
told the Healer, at their last meeting before the planned operation.
"Not even Rhys Michael knows—and he usually has some idea
when the regents are up to something."

Tavis sighed. "Well, we're just going to have to do the best we
can. What about the other Deryni in the castle? Have they paid any
particular attention to the girls?"

Javan cocked his head quizzically. "Now that you mention it,
no. In fact, I haven't seen most of them, lately. I know that Rhun
took Carmody and Sitric out on winter maneuvers with him, right
after you last came, but I have no idea why, or how long they're
supposed to be gone."

"Well, that's two less to worry about, anyway," Tavis murmured.
"What about Oriel?"

"He's scheduled to go with Hubert to Ramos, midweek—though
I understand he's been down with a bad cold and fever for several
days."

"What's happening in Ramos?"

"Some religious convocation, I suppose. Murdoch and Tammaron are planning to go along, too. I suppose they'll use Oriel to keep everyone else in line. Oh, and Manfred's got a pet Deryni now, too, name of Ursin O'Carroll, but I don't know anything about him."

"I do," Tavis muttered. "A failed Healer, but a very powerful practitioner, otherwise. He and I started Varnarite training together."

"You know him, then."

"Aye. Not well enough to predict what he'll do, but too well not to be recognized, if he saw me."

But he agreed to the delay that Javan suggested, until Hubert and the others had gone to Ramos. The night of the twenty-first, just before midnight, found Tavis peering cautiously out of the garderobe Portal below the King's Tower, Ansel at his back. Javan was waiting for them in the shadows, just past the first set of torches. No guards were anywhere to be seen or sensed.

"We're really in luck," Javan whispered, as the two bent close to hear. "None of the regents are in Valoret tonight. Hubert and his cronies left yesterday, as planned, and even Manfred and his pimply-faced son have gone off to Caerrorie. They left this morning, and they took that Ursin O'Carroll fellow with them. Word came back a few hours ago that they're spending the night and won't be back until midday tomorrow."

Ansel nodded grimly. "Good. What about my mother?"

"She and Lord James retired early. Their quarters are at the end of the west wing, above the old queen's gallery. Your little sister and brother are in an adjoining room to the right, with the MacLean girls in a separate suite beyond that." Touching both men's hands simultaneously, Javan flashed them a picture of the precise location. "It's one of the better places the regents could have put them, actually. That part of the castle is never heavily guarded. You shouldn't have any trouble getting in and out without anyone the wiser. In that part of the castle, at this hour, I doubt you'll see more than one or two guards."

They saw *no* guards, once they reached the west wing—which almost made Tavis more nervous than if there *had* been guards. After sending Javan back to his quarters with instructions to go to bed, he and Ansel spent nearly a quarter of an hour working their way through the west wing—slipping stealthily from shadow to shadow on soft, indoor boots that made no sound, all but invisible in stone-colored tunics and hoods. They were never challenged. Outside his mother's door, Ansel kept watch while Tavis set his magic to the working of the lock. The faint, metallic snick of the tumblers falling into place sounded like the crack of doom to heightened Deryni senses, but the two were in and across the room, drawing back the curtains on the great, canopied bed, before a groggy Jamie Drummond even began to rouse from sleep, starting to sit up in alarm.

"What—"

But he never got out more than that one word. Even as he lunged for the sword hanging over the head of the bed, Tavis was on him, stripping James Drummond of what little Deryni power he had and then plunging the older man into sudden, unresisting sleep. Simultaneously, Ansel clapped a hand over his mother's mouth, pinning her struggles beneath the blankets and the weight of his body as his mind sought the psychic link they once had shared.

"*Mother!*" he whispered, trying to seize her attention and stop her struggling. "Mother, stop it! It's Ansel. I don't want anyone to get hurt."

She went limp at that, though her mind instantly shuttered behind surprisingly imposing shields. As Tavis slowly straightened on the other side of the bed and glanced at her, breathing hard, his hand still spanning the upturned throat of the unconscious James Drummond, her eyes flicked to him in horror and she started struggling again.

"It's *all right!*" Ansel whispered, giving her a shake and trying again to quiet her as Tavis conjured handfire so she could see their faces. "Jamie isn't hurt. Tavis has just put him to sleep. Now, will you promise not to scream, if I take my hand from over your mouth?"

Her eyes flashed outrage and anger, but she nodded. Ansel was still wary, though, as he eased his hand from her mouth.

"I'm sorry, Mother. I had to see you, though."

She snorted, but her reply was the required whisper. "Do you think it necessarily follows that *I* wish to see *you?* What have you done to Jamie?"

"I told you, Tavis put him to sleep. We couldn't risk him raising the alarm."

"Which he surely would have done, since my son the outlaw chose to creep into my bedchamber by night, like some common ruffian! I have nothing to say to you, Ansel."

"I regret that, Mother," Ansel murmured. "But I have something of great importance to say to you. Why have you come back to court?"

She grimaced and turned her face away from him and from Tavis, tarnished blond hair tangled on the pillow like a young girl's. "Did we have a choice?"

"What has been said about the children?" Ansel replied. "I know Manfred MacInnis' son has been paying court to the MacLean sisters."

She closed her eyes briefly. "It's none of your affair, Ansel," she breathed. "Just leave us alone."

Ansel shook his head. "I can't do that. What of my little sister? What about Michaela?"

"I told you, it isn't any of your concern. I don't want to discuss it."

"Have any of the Deryni here at the castle paid particular attention to any of them?" Ansel insisted. "Mother, it's important that I know."

"And what possible difference could it make? Isn't it enough that your brother died a traitor's death and you are rapidly following in his footsteps? Must you destroy what is left of this family?"

Her voice had started to rise on that last question, and Ansel clapped his hand over her mouth again, to her utter fury.

"Not destroy it, Mother. I'm going to have to do the only thing I know possibly to save it." He glanced at Tavis and gave him a reluctant nod. "I'm sorry."

She bucked under him, trying at least to throw off his hand to scream, but once Tavis' hand made contact, it was over in an instant. Ansel's mind surged in behind the shields that were no longer there, to read an even more frightening prospect than he had dreamed—for the regents planned to foster Ansel's half-sister, the ten-year-old Michaela Drummond, to the household of Manfred MacInnis and his wife; and Michaela's brother Cathan, now eight, would become a page in the household of Prince Rhys Michael. As for the MacLean girls—

Ansel withdrew briefly, horrified, suddenly aware that Tavis had gone into the other room to deal with his half-siblings—which was absolutely essential now, after what Ansel had just learned. Quickly he returned to Elinor's mind, erasing all memory of his visit and what they had done, substituting harmless memories of what little Deryni ability Elinor had had. In that, at least, they had been in time, for neither Elinor and Jamie nor their children had warranted any special attention from captive Deryni since their return to court.

But was Ansel in time to save the MacLean girls? As he completed the necessary adjustments in his mother's mind and withdrew for good, Tavis was gliding back into the room, a satisfied smile lighting his face for just an instant as he nodded to Ansel.

They'll remember nothing, he sent. *They didn't even stir. Shall we move on next door?*

Ansel conveyed his worries about the MacLean sisters to Tavis as the two of them moved through the anteroom and toward the door to the corridor, but they had to wait there as heavy footsteps tramped past—one of the inevitable guard patrols they had not encountered earlier. Ears pressed against the door, Deryni senses tensed to their limits, they heard a door open and close, farther down the corridor, and then more feet continuing on out of hearing. When nothing else occurred to jar their caution for several minutes, Ansel cautiously eased the door open a crack. The corridor was deserted.

Let's go, he ordered.

The door relocked behind them as easily as the next door yielded to their magic. They slipped inside without mishap, Ansel remaining to keep watch while Tavis glided deeper inside to locate their quarry. Near the window, a rushlight burned feebly on a coffer between two narrow beds mounded with sleeping furs. Tavis bent briefly over the bed on the left, doing what needed to be done, then moved on to the one on the right—and went rigid with shock.

Ansel, come here!

The summons did not brook delay or even question. Instantly Ansel was dashing across the room, to look on in horror as Tavis drew back the edge of sleeping fur that covered the silent, unmoving form of a young girl just entering puberty, the soft curves of her child's face barely beginning to streamline to the stronger planes of young womanhood.

Except that little Giesele MacLean would never become a woman now, for she was quite dead.

"My God, what happened?" Ansel breathed, dropping to his knees, not daring to touch her.

"I didn't do a thing," Tavis replied, pressing his fingers hard along her throat in vain search for some thread of pulse. "I haven't a clue what caused it. She's just dead—and only quite recently, too."

"Recently enough to revive her?" Ansel dared to ask, knowing that Healers sometimes could bring a patient back from the brink of death, if damage was not too severe.

Tavis slipped his hand along the side of her head, resting his thumb against her temple, and pressed his stump against the right side of her neck. After a few seconds, he shook his head.

"Can't bring her back. But this soon, I *should* be able to read something of how it happened. Niallan has taught me several interesting techniques in the past few months."

"To hell with Niallan!" Ansel muttered under his breath, though he did not interfere as Tavis closed his eyes and set to work.

The Healer bowed his head over the dead girl as he drew a long, slow breath to trigger the very deep trance he must achieve to work a Death-Reading. He could feel the faint flutter in the pit of his stomach that confirmed his readiness to proceed, and he breathed a silent prayer that little Giesele's suffering had not been too great. His teachers had taught him well, for very quickly he was in the memories of her last few seconds of life—and suddenly reliving them!

She had been dreaming about her father at first—happy, carefree memories from her earlier childhood, before death carried off Lord Geoffrey MacLean in a hunting accident. Giesele had been just six.

But then the dream had shifted to nightmare—a vividly imagined scenario of her cousin Adrian's death by torture, spun from the graphic and triumphant reports that swept through the court when the perpetrators returned, and embellished in terrifying detail by a frightened twelve-year-old.

The horror of it had jarred her from sleep, but only to plunge her into far more immediate terror. Already trembling and gasping for breath, she opened her eyes to a hazy, sleep-blurred glimpse of someone towering over her narrow bed. But she never had time to scream—only to catch a final impression of a hard, bearded face and a vast, leather-covered chest, just before gauntleted arms pressed something soft and suffocating hard against her face.

She had tried to escape, flailing wildly underneath her sleeping furs at first; but the man set a knee across her chest to hold her, relentlessly crushing out the breath she had managed to catch before the pillow began pressing her closer and closer to the darkness. Consciousness seeped away fitfully, even as the slender body twitched and gradually was still, the terror eventually giving way to a resigned peacefulness, until even that was gone.

Tavis was never sure exactly when she slipped away; only that, at last, Giesele MacLean was no longer there. As he drew another deep breath and opened his eyes, blinking back tears, he thought her body underneath his hand was already cooler than it had been when he began. As he bent to press his lips to her forehead in final farewell, he brushed at his tears with his stump.

"What happened?" Ansel whispered.

Tavis sighed, drained. "They had her killed. Smothered. To look as if she died in her bed. Children do sometimes, you know."

"But—"

Shaking his head, Tavis reached out and took up one of Ansel's hands, sending his reading across the bond of flesh before Ansel had time to do more than draw a startled breath.

"Dear *Jesu*," Ansel started to breathe, as the full horror hit him. But Tavis could not allow him time to think about it here.

"This has all been carefully orchestrated, don't you see?" he whispered. "It has to be the reason that *all* the regents are conveniently away tonight—and *especially* all the MacInnises. If foul play is even suspected, they all have an alibi."

"But, *why*?" Ansel asked. "What did a twelve-year-old girl ever do to deserve—"

"She was *alive*, Ansel! Think about it. Now that she's dead, her older sister is sole heiress of Kierney—a very valuable marriage prize for young Master Iver MacInnis! I'd wondered how they planned to work that out, with co-heiresses, but it never occurred to me that they'd murder a child."

Impulsively Ansel glanced at the still-sleeping Richeldis.

"Let's steal Richeldis, then," he said. "At least we can foil *that* part of their plan."

"Don't be stupid," Tavis snapped. "If we did that, she'd be attainted, the same way you were, and all the Kierney lands would escheat to the Crown on Iain MacLean's death—which you can be *sure* would come quickly, or *his* attainder—and Iver MacInnis would *still* get Kierney. We've lost this one, Ansel. Let's get out of here, before we lose us, too."

"But—"

In less than a heartbeat, Tavis surged his mind across the bond of flesh again and touched the triggerpoint in Ansel's mind, at once blocking all his Deryni abilities and setting irresistible compulsions to obey.

Sorry, Ansel, but we're leaving, he ordered. *I haven't time to argue with you. Now, move!*

Disobedience was not possible, even though Tavis removed the block to Ansel's powers as soon as his compulsions were in place. Ansel moved, his body guiding him to the door with smooth, silent precision, even as his mind raged at Tavis for what he had done—for the Healer had left him with all memory of the event. In unshakable physical harmony, the two eased open the door and slipped back down the corridor, making their way stealthily toward the King's Tower and its haven of the Portal. So they might have continued without incident, had they not rounded the last bend but one and nearly ran into the arms of two surprised guards.

All four men froze for just an instant. Tavis managed to avert his face before either of their adversaries could get a good look at him, thrusting his handless wrist behind him and dashing in to grasp the nearer of the guards by the neck. The man crumpled before his sword could even clear its scabbard.

But Ansel was not so fortunate. Armed with only a dagger, his offense quickly became a frantic parry as the other guard made a wild slash in his direction with one of the biggest swords Tavis had ever seen. Ansel managed to deflect the first blow, the steel ringing against stone in a tocsin that surely must have roused the entire Valoret garrison, but the second connected with the sickeningly solid thud of a butcher's cleaver in flesh, opening a broad gash in Ansel's left thigh that cut clear to the bone.

Ansel could not even cry out. The very force of the blow left him breathless, though the first, numbing shock changed immediately to fire as the leg buckled under his weight and blood fountained from his thigh. As he clutched at a wound almost too wide to span with both his hands, blood-slick dagger falling forgotten as the hot blood spurted between his fingers, it hardly mattered that in that instant Tavis had managed to dart in and put Ansel's opponent out of commission with more Deryni magic.

"*Jesu*, we've got to get out of here!" Tavis gasped, taking a quick, disbelieving look at Ansel's leg as he seized his arm and urged him to his feet. "Come *on!*" He brushed the wounded man's forehead with his stump, blocking both Ansel's powers and his pain. "Put the pain aside!" he ordered. "You have to walk, no matter what it costs. I'll help you. Let's *go!*"

And the pain was gone, though crucial muscles were cut, and Ansel could not manage more than an awkward shuffle. How they made it down the turnpike stair of the King's Tower, Ansel never knew; only that suddenly he was sitting in a growing puddle of his own blood at Tavis' feet, on the stinking floor of the garderobe Portal, and Tavis was clasping his head between bloody hand and stump and willing him to surrender, to give over control—and Ansel gladly obeyed, no longer caring that his life's blood was pooling around him, and his consciousness receding, even if Tavis' controls had not been taking him . . . elsewhere.

CHAPTER NINE

*They will lay lands on the sick, who will
recover.*

—Mark 16:18

"Somebody, fetch a Healer!" Tavis shouted, conjuring handfire even as he found his footing in the haven's Portal chamber, staggering under Ansel's dead weight. "Queron! Dom Rickart! Hey, help! Somebody, get another Healer in here, right now! I need more hands!"

He heard the faraway buzz of alarmed voices and running feet approaching, but he pushed them to the back of awareness as he collapsed to his knees beside the fainting Ansel. He had kept his hand clamped to Ansel's wound as best he could, while they made their escape, but an anguished glance beneath it confirmed that the wound was even more serious than he had feared. Tavis had to stop the bleeding, and soon—or at least slow it until help could arrive— or Ansel was a dead man. They already had left a terrible, bloody trail behind them in Valoret, and Ansel continued to pump out his life's blood here on the Portal floor.

Heartsick, Tavis jammed his stump hard against the femoral pressure point at Ansel's groin and, at the same time, eased his fingers into the wound as far as he could. The bloody opening in Ansel's legging hampered him physically, too small by half to let him really feel or see what he was doing; but with only one hand, there was little he could do about that until help arrived. Skipping the usual preliminaries, he plunged himself into Healer's trance with dizzying speed and cast out with his powers, trying to begin assessing the worst of the damage.

The wound was deep as well as wide. It had cut right to the bone, also damaged, but Tavis bypassed that for the moment, hunting for the major sources of bleeding. The vital femoral artery seemed to be intact—else Ansel would be dead by now—but some of its major branches surely must be badly damaged, judging by the amount of blood that continued to well up around Tavis' hand, even with the pressure point.

"Where's another Healer?" he screamed again, really becoming alarmed as he was forced to divert some of his attention to Ansel's suddenly erratic heartbeat.

"Oh, no you don't! Stay with me, Ansel!"

All at once, others were crowding to assist him, several other pairs of hands reaching in to help shift Ansel into the antechamber outside the Portal itself and give Tavis room to work. He scuttled along with them, maintaining contact. To his intense relief, Evaine took over monitoring functions at Ansel's head, even as they moved him.

"He's going into shock. Jesse, go get Queron!" Evaine ordered, cradling Ansel's head in her lap as they straightened him out on the floor. "Gregory, tear that legging open wider, so Tavis can see what he's doing, and then take the pressure point."

The blood-soaked fabric parted between Gregory's already bloody hands with a soggy, ripping sound, and blood spurted again as he relieved Tavis, the heels of both hands applying pressure in the angle of Ansel's groin. From Tavis' left, another pair of hands smoothly eased into the wound to either side of Tavis' one, the directing mind linking in with trained precision and urging them both to deeper levels, so that healing might be effected.

"Easy," the other murmured. "You've got your extra hands now. Sylvan's my name."

The name was vaguely familiar to Tavis, but he did not know that mind. Without doubt, however, Sylvan was a Healer well accustomed to dealing with wounds of this kind. A battle surgeon?

That's right, came the other's brisk reply. *Let's see if we can get him stabilized now. You work on the bone damage, and I'll try to stop the bleeding.*

It was a logical division of labor, with Sylvan's two skilled hands to Tavis' one, and Tavis bent to his task without question, though he had to rely solely on touch until someone sluiced warm water over the wound to clear their working field—Fiona MacLean, Tavis' quick glance confirmed.

Even then, and with Sylvan at last making headway with the bleeding, repairing the damaged bone was trickier than Tavis had expected. Though Ansel's femur was not broken, the blow that had caused his wound had also pried up a chip of bone as the sword twisted in its wielder's hand. Tavis managed to mend it without getting in Sylvan's way too much, but he sensed his own fatigue and after-reactions to the night's events beginning to set in as he finished, potentially affecting both skill and judgment. He pulled back gladly as another unfamiliar Healer joined in across from him— not Queron or Rickart, to his surprise, though the newcomer was Gabrilite, and known to Sylvan.

Leaving further physical manipulation to them, he shifted his own dwindling energies to bolster Evaine—for Ansel's vital signs had steadied, but they were still dangerously weak. For a while, he tried to maintain a secondary link, prepared to drive further power into their working if it should be needed, but he made no false protest of bravado when the other two finally eased him from the link entirely, as aware as he that he was nearly spent.

When hands suddenly dropped onto his shoulders from behind, it was Queron's mind that wrapped around his in compassion and offer of healing for the Healer, even as the hands drew him back, head tipping against Queron's knees. Tavis caught a glimpse of the Healer looking down at him as his eyes rolled back under his lids, already responding to Queron's command to let go, but he did not even think of resisting. Surrendering all thought of what he had just done and witnessed, he let Queron's reviving spell work its miracle for those few seconds. He could feel new energy coursing through him as he opened his eyes, Queron's support remaining with him in a light Healer's link still open between them. And since Sylvan and the other Healer still were working and seemed not to need their help, Tavis allowed himself a quick scan of the rest of the room.

He was not surprised to see Joram and Jesse, of course, watching quietly from the shadow of the Portal, where they would not be in the way; and Gregory still knelt at his right, Evaine cradling Ansel's head beyond him.

He remembered that he had noticed Fiona in the room, too. Just now, she was setting a steaming basin of water on the floor by Ansel's feet, damp little tendrils of dark hair standing out around a face flushed from exertion.

What he had not expected was the children—though, on second thought, perhaps that should come as no surprise. They lived here, after all, and hardly could have slept through his frantic cries for help. Beyond Fiona, a wide-eyed and trembling Rhysel Thuryn hugged an enormous stack of towels to her breast, her face almost as white as the folded linens. And a little to her right, pressed hard against the wall, the twelve-year-old Camlin MacLean crouched beside an agitated-looking Tieg Thuryn, both comforting and restraining the younger boy with arms around his shoulders from behind.

Of course Tieg would have been drawn to the call for a Healer, even if the others had not. Tieg was a Healer's son and already known to be a future Healer himself, though the Healing gifts generally did not begin to manifest until near puberty. At three-and-a-half, formal Deryni training of any kind must be negligible, but Tieg's Healing potential was prodigious enough to have shown already, as Camlin certainly had cause to know full well. Though Evaine had been the one to *direct* that Healing, its source had been Tieg.

"It's all right, Tieg," Tavis reassured the boy. "We're nearly done. He's going to be fine."

Indeed, the unknown Gabrilite Healer already had withdrawn physically, though he kept one hand resting lightly on the back of one of Sylvan's to augment, as the battle surgeon finished up. Tavis could not see much of the Gabrilite's face, for his head was bowed over the patient, but the hair pulled back in the sleek braid of his order was bright blond, untouched by grey. Quite possibly, he was not much older than Tavis. Somehow, he had managed not to get blood on his white habit, either—which amazed Tavis, because the rest of them looked as if they'd been working in a slaughterhouse.

The Healer Sylvan certainly had not escaped tonight's blood bath. He was nearly as bloody as Tavis. His fine, green woolen tunic, neatly embroidered with tiny Healer's badges all around the neck and sleeve edges, would never be the same; and even his smooth, clean-shaven face was spattered with blood. In profile, he appeared to be in his early thirties, but age was difficult to judge without looking at his eyes, which were all but closed. Mostly, all Tavis could see was a shock of light brown hair, cropped short all around his head—as if someone had used a pudding bowl for a cutting guide.

He certainly seemed competent, however. Even as Tavis watched, the last of Ansel's wound sealed under the other's hand, leaving only a long, moist-looking line that Tavis knew would soon fade. Sylvan breathed a heavy sigh of relief as he opened his eyes and, before Tavis could even think about trying to prevent it, shifted the less bloodied back of one hand across Tavis to touch the side of Ansel's neck. Tavis was not surprised when the Healer tensed almost immediately, startlingly hazel eyes darting to Evaine's blue ones in surprise and alarm.

"Are you shielding him somehow?" he demanded. Quickly he reached his other hand beside the first, to bracket Ansel's jaw and read even deeper—that there was nothing Deryni there to read.

"Good God, you aren't doing it at all, are you?" he whispered. "But—I thought you said this was Ansel MacRorie. *This* man isn't even Deryni! Aurelian, *read* him!"

As the young Gabrilite moved in to confirm, both Healers' shields snapping up in reflex defense against this unknown, little Tieg suddenly darted between Camlin and his mother to lay both chubby hands on Ansel's cheek before anyone could stop him.

"You leave my Uncle Ansel alone!" he piped up, turning wide, indignant eyes on his mother as she closed him in the circle of her arms and tried to shush him.

"No! *Not* pull Tieg away! Why that man says this not Uncle Ansel, Mummy? And why is Uncle Ansel clear? If I close my eyes, I don't see him."

For just a stunned instant, Tavis could not think clearly—he could only guess that Tieg must be reading Ansel's lack of shields—perhaps even his lack of power! And right here, in front of the two stranger Healers!

He could sense the others' alarm as well, especially Queron's, even though reason told him that these surely must be more of the Healers Gregory and Jesse had been bringing to be screened for the blocking ability. A frantic glance and question at Joram confirmed it—and also that the two had received no preparation whatever. There had been no time.

Nor were the present conditions precisely optimum for a reasoned introduction to the notion of blocking Deryni powers—especially their long-range plans for Revan. The young Gabrilite might hesitate to take any serious action against what surely would be perceived as a threat, for his Order was sworn to nonviolence, but Sylvan, at least, was battle-tuned and already far too jumpy. Drastic action was necessary on Tavis' part—though he must set things up so that the two would not realize it was drastic, until too late.

"Relax, gentlemen," Tavis said quietly, only shifting his hand to one of Ansel's slack wrists as he glanced at the two Healers, trusting Evaine to deal with any unexpected reaction little Tieg might make, and watching Joram move a casual few steps closer to the young Gabrilite. "He *is* Ansel MacRorie, and he *is* Deryni. Evaine, if I put him back, will that interfere with your monitoring?"

Evaine shook her head. "Not at all. I've already set commands to sleep and to follow doctors' orders until he gets his strength back." She managed a faint smile as she encircled Tieg more closely. "Despite my nephew's usual penchant for doing what *he* thinks is best, I suspect we'll find him a model patient."

"Right, then."

Tavis already had the physical point of contact he needed with Ansel, his hand to Ansel's wrist. Reaching across the link with his mind, he reset the triggerpoint with only casual effort, then drew back. The Gabrilite gasped and leaned closer to the patient, Sylvan also edging closer on his knees to stare without comprehension—and in that incomprehension lay their downfall.

"What in the—"

"That simply is not possible!" the Gabrilite murmured.

But Tavis ignored their predictable astonishment. Snaking his left arm behind Sylvan without warning, he clamped the man's neck between stump and hand long enough to trigger a block and control before Sylvan even knew to struggle, forcing him deeply and instantly into sleep. At the same time, Joram moved in and pinned the young Gabrilite's upper arms from behind, while Queron reached across to catch the man's wrists—all before Sylvan even began to crumple. As Tavis rose, giving Sylvan into Gregory's keeping as he prepared to step across Ansel and repeat the process with the Gabrilite, he sent silent suggestion to Queron, who agreed.

"Dom Aurelian, isn't it?" Queron said briskly, diverting the younger Healer's attention so Tavis could make his move. "Ah, but don't be frightened, little brother. No one is going to harm you. Nor is your friend Sylvan harmed, I assure you. However, this *will* be easier on everyone if you don't fight us."

By then, it was too late for Aurelian to fight. Tavis' trigger and control brought horrified astonishment and oblivion within the space of a single heartbeat, and the Healer-priest slumped unresisting between Joram and Queron, only twitching a little as Tavis set commands to permit a deep probe, even once the block was removed.

"I'm sorry we had to do things this way," Queron murmured, observing Tavis' operation with interest and not a little envy. "I remember this young man from Saint Neot's—a promising Healer, Dom Aurelian. He was ordained shortly before I left the Order."

Preoccupied, Tavis nodded and reset the triggerpoint in Aurelian's mind, then delved deep, looking for the ability to block. He did not expect to find it, so he was not overly disappointed as he withdrew and gave control over to Queron.

"Just like all the others, I'm afraid," he said. "Oh, he's fulfilled the Healer's promise you remember, Queron, and he certainly justified his existence by helping Heal Ansel—but unfortunately, he hasn't got what we're looking for. I'll let you make the appropriate memory alterations while I check the other one."

As Queron sighed and nodded, setting resignedly to his task, Tavis rose and stepped back across Ansel to turn his attention on the other man, now sprawled unconscious in Gregory's arms, eyes closed.

"This is Sylvan O'Sullivan, my household Healer and battle surgeon," Gregory said in a low voice, as Tavis knelt and set hand and stump to the other's temples, confirming that identity. "I still wish I knew how you do that."

"So do I," Tavis said, smiling mirthlessly. "Hmmm, Varnarite trained, like myself. Too bad that the resemblance probably ends there. But—let's set his powers back in place and see what he's got."

No further resemblance became immediately apparent, as Tavis reset the triggerpoint and skirted the edges of Sylvan's mind. Where Tavis had been trained primarily for civilian Healing, Sylvan O'-Sullivan's emphasis was as a battle surgeon—which was why Gregory had employed him. Where Camber had found Tavis' Varnarite training philosophically deficient, compared to Gabrilite or Michaeline training, Sylvan's was even less sophisticated. He certainly did not have the esoteric background possessed by so many other hopefuls that Tavis had read in the last few weeks, searching for another like himself. Nor would Sylvan have presented any challenge to the brilliant Rhys Thuryn, in sheer Deryni power—though he had worked with Rhys, on occasion.

But as Tavis restored Sylvan's powers—though not his waking consciousness—and pushed deeper past Sylvan's now unresisting shields, he suddenly realized that the ability to trigger a power block was there! Tavis was as sure of that as he was that he himself could strip *any* Deryni of his or her powers.

"Dear God, he's got it!" Tavis murmured, looking up at Gregory and Evaine, then at Queron and Joram, with awe in his eyes and in his voice. "He was right here, practically in our reach, all this time." He swallowed uneasily. "Sweet *Jesu*, I can hardly believe it. Shall we tell him now, or wait?"

Cautiously Joram rose from where he had been crouching beside Queron and the sleeping Aurelian.

"First, let's get the good Dom Aurelian bedded down for the night, shall we? He doesn't need to know anything else about this. No sense having to tamper with his memories any more than we've already done."

"I agree," Queron said. "I've already taken care of tonight's little incident. So long as nothing else happens to change his conditioning, he'll be fine, come morning."

"I'll take him to a room, then," Jesse said. "Unless you'd rather."

"Do that, Jesse," Joram replied, before Queron could reply. "Queron, if you don't mind, I'd rather you took charge of Ansel now. I know you'd like to observe Sylvan when he's brought around, but I think a Healer should stay with Ansel until we're sure he's out of danger—and Tavis is going to be a little busy. I'll send you a couple of men to help you get him to his room."

Queron, after surrendering Aurelian's control to Jesse, stood back and gave a resigned nod as Joram helped Jesse get the groggy Healer to his feet.

"I'll see to Ansel, then, if that's where I'm needed most," he said, watching Jesse walk Aurelian out. "The most important thing will be to keep him quiet and make sure he takes plenty of fluids for the next few days, to compensate for the blood loss. Fortunately, we have some medications that should speed that aspect of recovery. I'm sure Tavis is familiar with them."

Tavis nodded his concurrence, though he had yet to take his eyes or his hand from Sylvan, who still lolled bonelessly in Gregory's arms.

"I promise to give you a full report, Queron," he murmured. "I know how badly you wanted to be the one."

Queron shrugged. "We are not always given all the gifts we desire." He glanced up at the waiting Fiona. "May I ask your assistance, my lady? If we clean him up here, perhaps we can avoid tracking any more blood through the compound. I'm afraid young Jesse's already left bloody footprints in the Portal and landing of the Council chambers, when he came to get me, and Joram did not improve matters by standing in it."

Joram glanced at the soles of his boots and grimaced, and Evaine gave the anteroom and its occupants a wistful appraisal.

"Let's *all* get cleaned up," she said, rising, "and give Tavis a chance to gather his wits about him before we pursue this further. And *I* have *children* to put to bed!" she added, taking little Tieg's hand and glancing meaningfully at Rhysel, whose eager young face mirrored instant rebellion over her stack of towels. "None of you should have been here, you know—not even Camlin, who thinks I don't see him, hiding behind Joram—though I suppose, if he's willing to help scrub floors, he may stay."

Camlin raised his chin with all the haughty indignation of any precocious twelve-year-old mistakenly presumed to be a child still by his elders.

"Do you think I'm too proud for that?" he asked. "It *is* Cousin Ansel's blood, after all—and he certainly cleaned up enough of mine, at Trurill. Besides, Saint Camber's blood flows in his veins—and was spilled for us tonight. Of course I'll scrub floors."

"I want to help, too," Rhysel chimed in. "May I, Mummy, please? I promise I'll go right to bed, when we're done."

"Me, too, Mummy!" Tieg piped. "I help, too."

"You're far too young—both of you."

"But, Mummy, I'm nearly eight!" Rhysel protested.

"Rhysel, you were just seven in November."

"So? That's big enough. Nobody *ever* lets me—"

"Rhysel—"

Fiona, smiling despite her efforts to keep a straight face, set her hands on Rhysel's shoulders.

"Why not let her help, Evaine?" she said. "She's seen worse—and she's old enough to fetch more water and towels. I'll see that she gets to bed when we're through. We can use the extra hands. And it's certainly easier than arguing."

Evaine sighed. "Oh, very well. But Tieg *is* too young, and he's going to bed *now*." She scooped up the indignant Tieg and braced him on her hip. "Gregory, why don't you take charge of Sylvan, while Tavis gets changed, and we'll all meet in the chapel in half an hour."

As she carried the squirming and protesting Tieg out of the room, Gregory glanced up at Tavis, over Sylvan's head lolling against his chest.

"Do you want to block him again, before I take over? It might be easier, all around."

Tavis almost flinched physically at having to let Sylvan go, now that he had found him, but he triggered the block and turned over control to Gregory without comment, forcing himself not to think about Healers at all as he watched Gregory rouse Sylvan and take him out.

He thought about blood instead as he shed his bloody mantle and outer tunic and tugged off his bloodied boots, leaving all in Camlin's charge. He doubted the felted soles would ever come really clean—but at least he left no more bloody footprints as he took his leave and padded toward his own quarters in stockinged feet, to wash and change into clean clothes.

He had left bloody footprints aplenty in Valoret, though. So had Ansel. And by now, the regents' soldiers would have followed that bloody spoor directly to the only Portal in the castle that Tavis still dared to use—and that would confirm that Deryni had been in the castle.

Please God, that bloody trail would not lead also to Prince Javan. Tavis knew there was no physical evidence to link Javan with the Deryni intruders, but he was willing to bet that some way would be contrived to lay young Giesele MacLean's death at the feet of same. And if, on their return, the regents should set their Deryni sniffers to questioning Javan, along with everyone else left at Valoret Castle tonight . . .

And that raised another question. What an interesting coincidence—if coincidence it had been—that all the regents and their assorted Deryni sniffers had been conveniently away from Valoret tonight. A most convenient coincidence, indeed, given the fate of Giesele MacLean. With Giesele dead, her sister Richeldis was now sole heiress to lands that the regents wanted very much for their own.

But these were questions for which Tavis had no answers—at least not yet. All the speculation in the world would not bring answers when he was not yet even sure of the questions. The important thing for now was that another Healer had been found who could block Deryni powers—and that raised its own set of questions, rather apart from all the ones concerning the regents.

As Tavis went into his cell and began stripping off his bloody tunic to wash, he found himself thinking about Sylvan O'Sullivan, and wondering how Sylvan was going to take to the whole idea.

Evaine also was wondering about Sylvan as she carried Tieg toward his room—or she was trying to wonder. For though Tieg had stopped wiggling once they left the bloody Portal chamber, he had begun crying instead, and that was almost worse.

"Tieg, this isn't making things any easier for Mummy," she said.

"Don't care!" Tieg sobbed. "Put Tieg *down*! Don't *want* to go to bed. Why you don't let Tieg help?"

Evaine shook her head as she pushed open the door to the cell that Tieg and Rhysel shared for sleeping quarters, conjuring handfire so she could see to light the little oil lamp set on a small table between the children's two pallets. Tieg continued to wiggle and whine until she plopped him onto his bed

"Now, that's about enough of that, young man," she said, as she pulled his sleeping furs from under him and pushed him back against the pillow. "You're too young to stay up any later, and that's the end of the discussion."

Lower lip protruding in a teary pout, the hazel eyes still stormy, Tieg flounced onto his side and turned his freckled little face to the wall, curling into a ball and scrunching a wad of fur coverlet under his chin.

"*Not* too young!" he muttered. "Don't *want* to go to bed yet!"

"I know you don't, darling, but we can't always have exactly what we want." She sat down beside him on the pallet and began stroking the rigid little head and back. His hair was silky and blond like hers, but reddish where hers was sun-golden—the legacy of his Healer father.

"Listen to me, my love," she went on. "I know you're upset. I know it must have been very frightening to see Cousin Ansel so badly hurt, but you were very brave. That makes Mummy very proud and happy."

Tieg snuffled, unstiffening not a whit. "Tieg wanted to help."

"But you *have* helped," Evaine replied, patiently continuing to rub his back. "You were a very big help, just by being there with me while we helped Tavis and the other Healers make Ansel well."

Tieg snuffled again, though this time he turned his face slightly toward his mother.

"Tieg helped?"

"Yes, of course, darling."

She could sense him mulling that as he rolled onto his back to look her in the eyes. After studying her gravely for several seconds, he finally allowed himself a wry little smile.

"Funny."

"What's funny, darling?"

"Uncle Ansel was clear." His little brow furrowed. "Why he clear, Mummy?"

Evaine breathed out with a sigh. She had been hoping Tieg would not remember that. How could she explain to a three-year-old about blocking Deryni powers, when he scarcely knew what powers were?

"Does that worry you, that you couldn't see him except with your eyes?" she asked, trying to fathom what he might really be asking.

Tieg scrunched up his face even more, trying to understand.

"Did it hurted Ansel to be clear?" he asked.

"Noooo," Evaine replied honestly. "Tavis made him clear so that he and the other Healers could work on him more easily. Ansel's leg was hurt, but what Tavis did didn't hurt him."

"Hmmm, good." Tieg nodded sagely, then broke out in an impish smile that turned into giggles.

"What's so funny?"

"Oh, nothing. But Tieg can do that, too," he announced.

Evaine's heart leaped into her throat.

"Can do what?" she whispered.

"Make people clear." He pursed his lips at her little gasp. "Mummy not believe Tieg?"

"Darling, it isn't that I don't believe you, but I don't know if you understand what you're saying," she murmured. "Making people clear is very hard."

Tieg shook his head confidently. "Not hard. Tieg can do."

"But—"

"Tieg can do!" he insisted. "Show Mummy?"

"You mean, make Mummy clear?" she breathed.

"Uh-huh," he nodded.

"Tieg, it isn't a game, you know."

"No game. But Tieg can do." And before she could make further protest, he touched a chubby hand to her cheek, cocked his head and blinked—and she was Blind.

CHAPTER TEN

*Therefore night shall be unto you, that ye shall
not have a vision; and it shall be dark unto
you, that ye shall not divine.*

—Micah 3:6

Evaine gasped in the first shock of it, reeling from the sudden psychic jolt of being all at once stripped of power while still retaining her awareness of precisely what had happened.

Dear God, Tieg had said he could make her "clear," and he had! Little Tieg, who would not be four until August, had done what only a very few highly trained adult Healers could do—as casually as an ordinary child his age might recite his prayers or show his mother how he could turn a somersault or hop ten times on one foot and not lose his balance. Could he have any inkling what it meant?

Still hardly able to comprehend it herself, much less believe it, Evaine could only stare at him aghast, unsure whether to be horrified or elated. She knew she ought to reassure him that she was all right—but she was *not* all right! She was psychically Blind! Who would have thought that *Tieg*—

"Mummy clear now," Tieg said, very matter-of-fact, too pleased with himself to be anxious quite yet. "Clear like Cousin Ansel, see?"

"Yes, darling, I do," she answered automatically.

Something in his tone made her suddenly think of Rhys. She had let him block her many times in those early days after he first discovered the ability, while they worked to understand its potential uses and limitations. Being blocked was still one of the most disconcerting sensations she had ever experienced, in a lifetime of awareness augmented as only Deryni could do. Perhaps she should have expected that the ability might manifest in Rhys' Healer son—

103

though the notion of a three-year-old child being able to use it instinctively, without any notion of the ultimate consequences, was appalling.

But was it any more appalling than Tieg's early manifestation of his Healer's powers, so strongly realized that Evaine, not a Healer herself, had been able to channel those powers through her own experience and direction and use them to Heal the crucified Camlin, in the ruins of Trurill? No, of course not! Lack of *control* over such power was appalling—not the power itself.

No, the discovery of Tieg's ability simply meant that they now had *three* Healers who could block Deryni powers—though it must be many years before Tieg had the training, experience, and judgment to put his ability to practical use. In fact, perhaps she ought not even to tell the others just yet, lest desperation one day suggest to one of them that Tieg should become involved prematurely in the work with Revan and the baptizers. Yes, best simply to have him restore her, and then broaden the already existing controls that she and Rhys had planted long ago, to include prohibitions against using this new talent unless specifically directed to do so.

Nodding at her decision, Evaine let her eyes refocus on her son. Though she knew her internal debate had not taken long, some trace of her anxiety must have shown in her expression, because Tieg all at once sat up, fearful concern written large in the hazel eyes.

"Mummy all right?" he whispered. "Tieg not hurt Mummy?"

He was too young and untrained actually to scan her, to read her thought processes—even precocious Deryni had to learn to do that, and rarely before the age of eight or nine—but he obviously was sensing that she no longer had the ability to shield him from her emotions, even if he did not know why. Trying anyway to shield her inner turmoil, or at least calm it, she drew a slow, deep breath and shook her head, giving him what she hoped was a reassuring smile.

"No, you haven't hurt Mummy," she said softly. She had to pause to swallow carefully. "And I'm very proud to know that you've learned how to make people clear. But I don't want to be clear right now."

"Not clear?" Tieg replied, cocking his head at her.

"No, dear, not just now. Do you think you can put things back the way they were? Mummy has important things to do. I—want to check on your Cousin Ansel. And it *is* time you went to sleep."

Tieg pursed his lips. "Tieg not want to go to sleep. Want to *help*."

"Well, you can help most by making me not be clear anymore," Evaine replied, hoping that this was not going to turn into a bargaining match in which she would have to use force on her own son. "So why don't you do that, and then Mummy will help you go to sleep? When you wake up, it will be morning and you can go visit Cousin Ansel. *He's* asleep right now, you know."

Considering that, Tieg at length gave her a nod.

"Okay, I do it."

"Fine. Anytime you're ready."

Very gravely, he reached up to lay his little hands on either side of her head, not at all self-conscious as he gazed dreamily into her eyes. *She* was self-conscious, however, and closed her eyes lightly, waiting.

And waited, and waited—until finally he choked back a whimper and his hands fell away. The look on his face, as she opened her eyes, was positively stricken.

"Tieg, what's the matter?" she asked softly, taking him by the shoulders. "Baby, what's wrong?"

"T-Tieg forgot," he managed to stammer. "C-can't *do* it!"

"Of course you can," she reassured him, though a sick dread rose in her throat at the thought that maybe he could not. "Remember how Tavis did it? That's how you learned, isn't it? Just do what you saw Tavis do. *Try*, sweetheart."

But he would not even try again, shaking his head and dissolving into tears as she gathered him to her breast.

"I s-s-sorry, Mummy," he sobbed. "I sorry. Don't be mad at Tieg."

"Oh, Tieg, I'm not mad," she murmured, stunned, rocking him and making soothing noises while she tried to think what to do. "There, darling, don't cry. I'll go see Tavis, and he'll put everything right."

And meanwhile, she must make sure that Tieg did not make anyone else "clear"—because it suddenly had occurred to her that she did not know for certain whether Tavis *could* restore her. What if a block could only be removed by the person who placed it? No one knew. Up until an hour ago, they had never had more than one person at a time who could block powers. What if Tieg could only block and not restore?

"Come on, darling," she murmured, standing to pick him up, setting his arms around her neck while she braced his weight on her hip. "I'm going to let you sleep in my bed tonight. Would you like that?"

She did not give him the chance to protest or approve. Still crooning little endearments to comfort him, she caught herself just before foolishly trying to conjure handfire and picked up the little lamp instead. Her monologue shifted to lighthearted cajolery as she carried him next door, eliciting smiles and even laughter by the time she set him down on her narrow pallet.

She wheedled him into playing bears then—a favorite bedtime game guaranteed to take his mind off what was bothering him. The horseplay gave her ample opportunity, under cover of tickling and pouncing, to try triggering the few purely physical cues that normally would have plummeted him into sleep without resistance.

But without her powers to nudge him along, he simply did not respond—and she dared not take him to the others until his potential to do harm was safely neutralized. Fortunately, she had the means to do that another way, though it was not her first choice.

He was giggling and squealing with delight by the time she told him breathlessly that it was time to climb under the sleeping furs and settle down, once again the merry, happy child she remembered, his recent anxiety apparently forgotten. She continued to banter with him when he burrowed under the furs to "hide," taking that opportunity to open a low chest set at the foot of the pallet. Rhys' Healer's satchel lay under a folded Healer's mantle inside, and she quickly inspected and discarded several vials and ampoules from it before finally choosing a tiny vial of dark blue glass and a little glazed brown jar sealed with a cork the size of her palm.

Tieg poked his touseled head out from under the furs, still pretending to growl like a bear as she sat down beside him, but he sobered instantly as he saw the jar in her hand—and the vial she laid casually beside the lamp, on the little table at the pallet's head.

"What's that?" Tieg asked, his little brows converging in a disapproving expression exactly like his father's.

"Just something from Papa's satchel to help you sleep," she said truthfully. "You've had a very busy night. I think it might be awfully hard to get to sleep by yourself, and Mummy has to check on Cousin Ansel."

"Medicine. Ugh!" Tieg said, wrinkling up his nose. "Tieg hates medicine."

"Well, I know that, darling, but sometimes we need to take medicine, even if we really don't want to." Casually she loosened the jar's stopper, though she did not remove it. "I promise you, though, it isn't nasty medicine. In fact, it's rather sweet—almost like nectar. Don't you remember how you used to suck the stems of honeysuckle flowers last summer and how nice they tasted? This even smells like honeysuckle."

"Honeysuckle?"

Still a little suspicious, Tieg propped himself up on his elbows, craning his neck to see the jar better as she held it closer.

"Tastes nice?" he said.

"Oh, very nice. See how good it smells?"

As she said it, she lifted the cork to one side and held the jar under his nose. She had counted on him taking a big sniff, and he obliged. The hazel eyes were already dilating as he glanced up at her in muzzy surprise.

"Mmmm, is nice."

"Breathe again, a good, deep breath," she murmured, herself not breathing as she caught him behind his back and neck with the hand that held the cork, to keep his head upright, and tipped the jar much closer under his nose to make sure he got at least another whiff or two of the now hazily visible vapor curling upward like smoke.

Only as he went quite limp against her arm, eyes rolled up in their sockets, did she recork the jar and allow herself to breathe again, taking up the little blue vial as she set the jar aside. A cloying trace of the vapor remained in the room, which might or might not be responsible for the blood pounding in her temples—she could not tell, with her powers gone—but opening the door quickly cleared her head. And before it could clear Tieg's as well, she dosed him from the vial.

Her hands were shaking as she recorked it and carefully set it next to the jar. She was not concerned about the medical consequences of what she had just done. In Rhys' practice as a Healer, she had seen him use this same combination of drugs often enough, especially on children, to avoid the trauma of physically forcing a patient to take more conventional medication. With her powers blocked, she could not blur Tieg's memory of the subterfuge, as Rhys would have done; but she would see to it, once Tavis restored her— or *he* would see to it, if she could not be restored.

That worry had been gnawing in the back of her mind ever since it occurred to her—and even more in its implications for Tieg than for herself. For if Tavis could not restore her—or if Sylvan could not—they would feel compelled to delve deep into Tieg's young mind to find *his* power to do so. And if that risked harming Tieg in the process, she knew they would do it anyway, counting her value far greater than that of an untrained child. Nor could she prevent them, with her powers blocked. Suddenly, even the notion of using Tieg prematurely as some adjunct to Revan's baptizer cult seemed far less threatening than what she must face now.

But perhaps her worry was for nothing. In any case, delaying the question certainly would do no good. She tried not to think about either possibility as she picked up the now deeply slumbering Tieg, wrapped him in a sleeping fur, and carried him toward the chapel, where the others surely must be wondering what kept her. In her absence, she hoped they had brought Sylvan around by now and briefed him, so that he might be of some help.

The new Healer was conscious, at least, by the time she got there—though he looked as wrung-out and shaken as she felt, sitting limply on one of the stone benches built out from the southern wall of the chapel, not far from Rhys' tomb. He had changed his blood-stained Healer's tunic for a black monk's robe and had drawn its hood over his head, which was tipped back against the wall behind him, and Gregory and Tavis flanked him on the bench, each with a hand resting on one of his wrists.

Joram and Jesse had drawn a wooden bench close before the three of them, and turned to look as she entered the chapel. The two rose out of simple deference to her sex at first, Joram a trifle sour-looking at her tardiness, but then he and Jesse were practically tripping over one another to run to her, as they realized what she carried.

"What's happened?" Joram demanded, as he and Jesse tried to relieve her of her burden, only to be rebuffed by her headshake. "Evaine, what is it? Is Tieg ill? Why on earth did you bring him here?"

"Read my shields and it should be abundantly clear," Evaine replied, smiling faintly as he did just that and recoiled in shock, as did Jesse and then the others, at a distance.

"For Tieg's sake as well as my own, I'm hoping that Tavis can set things right," she went on, talking to cover her own nervousness as she continued toward the now-standing Healer, her eyes locked on his—terrified lest he could *not* set things right. "Regardless of how I end up, Tavis, Tieg will need to be blocked and then have deep controls set, to make sure he doesn't do this again—because he doesn't know how to turn it off. I'm praying that it's the operation and not the operator that's crucial in blocking and unblocking—but we don't really know, do we?"

She could tell by their horrified expressions that none of them had considered that possibility before. She stumbled as she came between the benches, finally letting Jesse take Tieg from her as Joram and Tavis supported her.

"Evaine, for God's sake!" Joram began.

But Tavis shook his head and signed for Joram to ease her to a seat on the bench behind her, shifting his hand and stump to bracket the sides of her neck while Jesse laid the slumbering Tieg on the floor and did his best to make the boy comfortable.

"Gregory, go have Dom Aurelian take over with Ansel and bring Queron here," Tavis said, beginning to push calm into Evaine's mind and body like a gently rising tide. "He may not be able to block, but he's studied it more than anybody, myself included. Evaine, I want you to relax and let someone else worry about this for a while. I'm not even going to attempt to unblock you yet, because I want to see first what Tieg did. Close your eyes now."

She was aware of Gregory leaving, but she hardly cared by then, sinking back in Joram's arms with an anxious little whimper as Tavis brushed his hand briefly downward over her closing eyes and sat beside her.

"Now, review for me exactly what happened, of your own conscious recollection." Tavis' fingers slid gently into her hair so they cupped the left side of her head, thumb resting on her temple, and she could feel his stump pressed firmly behind her right ear. "That's right—from the beginning. Saves me sifting through a lot of other memories, looking for the information I need. Don't worry about sedating Tieg. That was precisely the right thing to do, under the circumstances."

Reassured, she did as he commanded, moaning softly as he locked onto the pertinent memories and took her deep, beyond conscious awareness and then into blessed oblivion, where her fear did not intrude and the passage of time had no meaning.

The next thing she knew, she was back in her body, her fatigue greatly diminished—and her powers were hers once more. Never before had she felt such relief as she ran quickly through the standard mental assessments that most Deryni learned early in their training and found everything intact.

"Oh, thank God!" she murmured, sighing heavily as she opened her eyes to stare at Tavis in grateful relief. "Thank *you*, Tavis. I really was afraid that the block might have to be undone by the one who put it there."

Tavis smiled wistfully and glanced at the one in question, sleeping peacefully unaware at their feet in Jesse's arms.

"Fortunately, a false alarm—though you were certainly right in recognizing the other danger. If he'd somehow gotten to me and Sylvan as well—"

Swiftly, before Evaine could even react, he reached down long enough to clamp his hand briefly around the boy's wrist. Jesse hardly even blinked.

"But we don't have to worry about *that* anymore, do we?" Tavis said, raising a reddish eyebrow as he sat back to watch her. "He won't be blocking anybody now—or Healing, or doing anything else Deryni, until Sylvan or I reset the triggerpoint—which neither of us is going to do until his controls have been altered. I assume you'd prefer to do that yourself?"

She would—and did, taking only a few dozen heartbeats to elaborate on the controls already in place to keep a Deryni child from misusing his powers before he learned wisdom. That Tavis would *not* have restored the boy until that was done, she had no doubt. In that, they were in total agreement.

When she was done, she helped Jesse tuck Tieg's sleeping fur around him more closely and sat back on the bench again with a sigh, more relieved than she could say. Gregory had returned with Queron at some point, and the two had settled on either side of Sylvan, who still looked more than a little dazed by what he had seen. Queron gave her a sympathetic and knowing nod, obviously brought up to date in the interim, and she relaxed and allowed herself the utter luxury of a yawn she had been fighting since she regained consciousness.

"Well, at least Tieg's little problem is solved," she said with a smile and a faint chuckle, her usual balance restored. "Tavis, you can unblock my horrid child whenever it suits you—years from now, if you think the lesson would do any good."

"Oh, he didn't mean any harm," Tavis said. As casually as he had blocked Tieg, he reached down and touched him again. "He was showing off for his mum—wanted to make her proud, do what the grownups can do. He seems to be quite good at observing Deryni power in operation and then picking up on what to do. Isn't that how he decided he was going to help you heal Camlin?"

Evaine shrugged and smiled. "I suppose it is. But *you* weren't on the receiving end." She turned suddenly shy eyes on Sylvan. "Which is more than we can say for you, isn't it, Sylvan?—though at least Tavis knew what he was doing. Talk about baptism by fire—I take it they'd briefed you before I came barging in with instant field experience?"

As Joram nodded, the Healer in question managed a weak, tentative chuckle.

"I'm sure I haven't realized all the implications yet," he ventured, "but I'll certainly do everything I can to help. It's a pleasure to see you again, Lady Evaine. I only wish that Rhys—" He flushed and ducked his head, embarrassed. "I'm sorry. I'm afraid I'm not thinking clearly yet. This is all quite—extraordinary."

"Yes, it is." She drew a deep breath and let it out slowly, not letting her gaze stray to the left, and the three new tombs—or think about Tieg.

"But you mustn't be shy about mentioning Rhys," she went on

resolutely. "I miss him more than I can ever tell you, but I'm not going to break down and cry at the sound of his name. He's the reason we knew to look for the talent in you—and I'm sure he would have been pleased to find that *you* share this somewhat dubious honor."

She was *not* sure what he would have thought of Tieg also sharing it, but she was not about to raise that point just now. In the back of her mind—and Tavis, at least, must be abundantly aware of this— the fear persisted that they might eventually want to use Tieg in the baptizer scheme, if it proved impractical to use Tavis—though Sylvan surely would be suitable, wouldn't he?

Gregory snorted, recalling her to the immediate discussion.

"And *I'm* the one Rhys did it to first! I still say that if we'd told Sylvan about it from the start, we could have saved a lot of needless to-ing and fro-ing, looking for someone else who could do it. But everybody was so damned secretive about it."

Joram chuckled, reaching across to clasp a hand briefly to Gregory's shoulder.

"There you go, second-guessing us again, Gregory. You know why we've kept the search close to our chests. If the regents got wind of this, we'd ruin all chance of using it to protect our people."

"And the subject of regents brings us back to Valoret," Queron said archly. "I know we've all been a little busy, thanks to young Tieg, but I wonder whether anyone has thought to enlighten Evaine about what happened there besides Ansel's rather unfortunate altercation with a blade?"

One look at their faces told her she had not heard the worst of it. As she turned to look at Joram, her brother sighed and laid his hand on hers, answering mind to mind rather than with words.

Mission accomplished, in five out of six cases, he sent, *with some unfortunate complications. Don't ask needless questions; just read what happened.*

The foreboding that clutched at her heart was well merited. As she slipped into familiar rapport with Joram and let the information come, she was horrified to learn of the casual and cold-blooded murder of Giesele MacLean. And the hue and cry sure to be raised by the witnesses to Ansel's and Tavis' bloody escape promised dire dangers to all Deryni and their sympathizers.

"I'm pretty sure I wasn't recognized," Tavis said, as Evaine emerged from trance and opened her eyes, "but we have to assume that Ansel was. And we left a trail of blood leading straight to the Portal—which, you can be sure, they now know is not a garderobe."

Gregory shook his head, setting his hands stubbornly on his spread knees, pale eyes burning in red-rimmed lids.

"Deryni in the castle! The regents will have apoplectic fits. You can guess who'll get the blame for the poor girl's murder."

"But, why should Deryni want to kill her?" Evaine protested. "What could we possibly have to gain? And why spare her sister? There's no motive."

"According to the regents, when have Deryni ever needed motives to justify their nefarious deeds?" Joram replied. "The question simply won't come up. Just as it will never be pointed out how convenient it was that all the regents were absent from Valoret tonight, so that none of *them* could be blamed—since they *did* have a motive. God knows how they planned to cover it, if we hadn't blundered into their little plan."

"Probably, they would have tried to claim she simply died in her sleep," Tavis offered. "People do, sometimes, you know. But then we obliged by showing up and giving them a much more useful explanation." He sighed and propped his elbows on his knees, eyes closed, massaging his temples with hand and stump. "God, what rotten luck! If we'd asked in advance what would help them most, we couldn't have done more!"

"Well, you *could* have let yourselves get caught," Jesse said mildly, raising an eyebrow and one corner of his mouth in bitter smile as Tavis' head snapped up to stare at him aghast. "Of *course* I'm being facetious. But you shouldn't be so hard on yourself. There's no way you could have known any of it was going to happen. Certainly no one has said it was your fault. And you did manage to block Richeldis and the rest of them. That certainly counts for something."

Exhaling softly, trying hard to convince himself that he really believed it, Tavis nodded, curving his lips in the bleak semblance of a smile that fooled no one, not even himself.

"I'd argue that things might have gone differently if we'd spent less time with Elinor and Jamie, or gone to the girls' room first, but you're right. It isn't useful to anyone for me to try to second-guess, after the fact." He set his stump into the palm of his hand and rested his forearms on his knees, bowing his head. "I still have to wonder what they'll consider a decent interval, before they marry Richeldis off to that MacInnis sprat."

Evaine suppressed a shudder, knowing it would happen exactly as Tavis suggested—and grieving for the thirteen-year-old Richeldis—though at least the girl would be alive.

"It's a story I fear we'll be hearing more and more in the next months," Evaine whispered, "of Deryni heiresses being married off to the regents' favorites. And the tale also will be told of how Deryni assassins came through a secret Portal and murdered Richeldis' sister—and would have murdered her as well, had they not been startled from their most foul deed by the timely intervention of the regents' loyal guards."

"No one startled *anyone* until we were almost back to the Portal," Tavis said indignantly.

"No, but that isn't the way the regents will tell it," Joram replied. "Even if Ansel *wasn't* recognized, Deryni will look bad. They'll say that the Deryni assassins attempted to flee the way they had come, one of them being grievously wounded in the process—but their trail of blood led the loyal guards to that most fiendish of Deryni devices—a hitherto unsuspected Portal, most treacherously disguised as a garderobe."

"Which eliminates our only way of getting into the castle now, doesn't it?" Jesse said.

Tavis nodded. "Trying to use that Portal right now would be suicide. You can bet they'll have at least a dozen men guarding it. And if they don't destroy it outright, as soon as they find a Deryni who can do it, they'll at least block it up. Either way, it can't be used again—and that finishes any further contact with Javan."

"What *about* Javan?" Queron asked. "You don't think they can connect him with anything that happened tonight, do you?"

Tavis shook his head. "I shouldn't think so. A lot depends on what use they make of their Deryni, for questioning people. But I made him promise he'd go right to bed after he left us, and stay there. So if he followed my instructions, they shouldn't really have any cause to suspect him."

"Please God you're right," Joram murmured. "I don't envy him the next day or two."

"Aye, poor lad," Evaine said. "Now he really *is* alone."

CHAPTER ELEVEN

For thou indeed mayest be tyrant over
unrighteous men, but thou shalt not lord it
over my resolution in the matter of
righteousness either by thy words or through
thy deeds.

—IV Maccabees 2:58

Being alone in a general sense was one of Prince Javan's least concerns just then, as his Deryni allies discussed his fate at Saint Michael's, for he did not yet know the isolation that the night's events eventually would bring him. Like most princes, he was accustomed to being alone—or to being surrounded by courtiers and servants and household, which was practically the same thing.

Left motherless from a very tender age, he and his brothers had been reared by a succession of competent but stodgy servants and tutors, most of them of advanced years. The little princes had one another, but theirs was not a happy childhood. King Cinhil was not demonstrative by nature and, after his wife's death, found it increasingly difficult to take much part in the upbringing of children whose very existence was an embarrassment to his former priestly status—especially when Javan's lameness daily proclaimed God's displeasure over Cinhil's abandoned vocation. Far easier to let others take over the running of the royal nursery, preparing the eldest ultimately to succeed his father—which at least was a justification for *his* existence—and keeping the others in reserve, quietly out of the public eye, where Cinhil would not be reminded of his failure.

The king's attitude mellowed as the years passed, but the young princes' exposure to outsiders still was restricted and closely monitored, ostensibly for safety's sake. Until shortly before Cinhil's death, when the sons of the future regents began to attend occasional sessions in the royal classroom, even commerce with other children was rare; and the friendship that grew between Javan and his Healer, Tavis O'Neill, was truly unique. Cinhil thought he was doing what was best for his sons, shielding them from the harshness of the world he once had renounced and then been forced to re-enter, and never realized that, in fact, their benificent isolation left them most pitifully lonely.

Nor had the princes' seclusion eased much after Cinhil died, though all three boys were long past the age when such rigid supervision was strictly necessary for their personal safety. Two of the more somber personal realities of royalty—the lack of privacy and the lack of true companionship—had been most emphatically underlined when the regents decreed that Javan and his brothers henceforth should have separate households. "To encourage them to mature on their own," Archbishop Hubert had informed the accession council, in the smooth, pseudo-pious tone that Javan had come to loathe.

The real reason, Javan had long suspected—and his Deryni friends concurred—was to keep the royal brothers shut away from outside ideas and divided among themselves, so they would never develop any independent thinking or even compare notes on how they thought princes ought to be treated. Events of the months immediately following Alroy's coronation certainly tended to support that theory. With the twins' twelfth birthday and completion of their formal classroom schooling, all their favorite tutors and even occasional classmates gradually disappeared from court, along with most of the Deryni, replaced by professional courtiers and retainers from the regents' families and favorites, who seemed to be everywhere. And Tavis' forced flight, just after Christmas, had left Javan most isolated of all, for only with Tavis had the prince dared to carefully explore the powers he was developing—for which the regents would kill him, if they only knew.

Not that Javan's isolation gave him any more privacy than he had known before. He was almost never alone. Such official engagements as he was permitted were almost always in the company of one or the other of his brothers or one of the regents, always with a plethora of attendants. Most evening meals turned into semistate occasions, taken in the great hall and surrounded by functionaries of the regents' growing court.

Outings to ride or hunt in the surrounding countryside were hardly less formal, altogether too rare, and almost always accompanied by at least one regent and a host of hangers-on. The officers of Javan's tiny personal household were hand picked by the regents.

Regent Hubert even appointed Javan's official confessor, who was himself confessed by the archbishop.

And whether Javan was engaged in the "state" duties designed to make him think he was participating in the process of governing, or trying to fill his "free" time in ways which would not arouse either the disapproval or suspicion of the regents, his constant companion was a clever, tow-headed young squire named Charlan, who was attentive to the point of often being underfoot. Charlan served him at meals, dressed him and attended to his personal toilette, sparred with him in the exercise yard, partnered him at Cardounet or other indoor games, and slept on a pallet at the foot of his bed. Charlan even prayed with him when Javan retreated to the chapel as the one refuge where he could have a few minutes almost alone, though the squire never intruded beyond his mere presence.

Not that praying displeased the regents—or its gradual increase, as Javan realized it was permitted. On the contrary, Javan found that the regents interpreted this pastime as a growing inclination toward a religious vocation, following in the footsteps of his late father. Such a vocation for this middle son surely was to be encouraged— for if Javan could be persuaded to enter the religious life, that would remove him from the succession, clearing the way for the biddable Rhys Michael to succeed Alroy, if Alroy died before producing an heir.

Javan did not disabuse them of their notion. He did gain much from daily attendance at Mass and the frequent observation of other religious devotions, when his schedule permitted, but what he gained was not always what the regents thought. And sometimes, Charlan gained more than he realized, too, for the centered stillness produced by prayer in squire and prince alike often afforded Javan an unsurpassed opportunity to tamper with his watchdog's mind.

Oh, Javan liked Charlan well enough, if he had to have a constant shadow, chosen by the regents, for the young man was only a few years older than himself, and had a wry, easy sense of humor that helped to pass the time. He was also well educated and conversant with most of the court gossip that went on in the castle—information he readily shared with his young master.

But Charlan had also told Javan quite openly that one of Earl Murdoch's agents held weekly interrogations of all three of the principal royal squires, always with a Deryni sniffer present to Truth-Read the sessions. Which meant that anything Javan said or did in front of Charlan was as good as said or done in front of the regents themselves, whether or not Charlan meant to betray his prince's confidences—unless Javan blurred the squire's memory, of course, which was precisely how he had covered his several secret meetings with Tavis. Javan was becoming fairly confident in his ability to carry out reasonably sophisticated tampering—though Tavis had warned him that using his fledgling powers without real need was senselessly risky and that princes must not flaunt their powers, whether political or esoteric. Javan believed him.

Neither sort of power was to give Javan much success in finding out what happened to Tavis and Ansel that night, however. He realized rather quickly that something must have gone wrong, for he heard the faint echoes of swordplay in the King's Tower shortly after midnight—an altercation that surely must involve his friends, though he dared not let on that he knew. For an hour thereafter, the corridors of Valoret Castle had resounded to the sounds of running feet and shouted orders. His one cautious attempt to ease his door ajar and ask a passing guard about it had produced only a polite but inflexible request, bordering on a command, to go back to bed, all was under control.

Nor was Charlan any more successful in gaining information, when Javan sent him out an hour later to fetch them a snack—and Charlan was as curious as he. Charlan returned under guard, with bread, cheese, ale, and a tale of nearly having his ears boxed for venturing out after being told to stay put. The continued presence of two guards outside suggested that the story was true, and Truth-Reading confirmed it. Javan's own, more authoritative attempt to question those guards only produced a grim, taciturn sergeant who assured him in even stronger terms that all was under control—and if Javan persisted in asking questions and did not go back to bed, he might consider himself temporarily under house arrest, prince or no prince.

Javan did not have to feign his indignation, though he backed down, nonetheless. He learned later that he had not been singled out in this, for both his brothers had received identical treatment, but he still resented it. It also meant that the situation *was* serious, and the frightened castle garrison were taking a holding action while they awaited further direction, the regents presumably having been informed and summoned back to deal with the crisis. Knowing the probable cause of the crisis, Javan did not fear for his own safety or that of his brothers, but he spent an uneasy remainder of the night worrying about Tavis and Ansel, only dozing fitfully when Charlan finally insisted he at least lie down.

Even hints of what actually had happened did not come until late the next morning, when Javan at last was summoned to the regents' private withdrawing room beyond the great hall, no reason given. Javan left his rooms with some foreboding, for Squire Charlan pointedly had *not* been invited.

"Can't you tell me *anything*?" Javan demanded of the guard assigned to escort him, as they headed down the stairs to cross the castle yard. He had dressed carefully in a conservative tunic and cloak of nondescript greys, and he pulled the fur collar of his cloak closer against the wind as they stepped outside.

"Connor, slow up, will you? You're walking too fast, and the cobbles are slippery. Be a sport, and tell me what's going on."

The guard Connor, a freckled, stoutly built fellow barely out of his teens, glanced uncomfortably at his royal charge, though he did shorten his pace to accommodate Javan's slight limp. This particular man was inclined to humor all three princes, but he clearly had his orders.

"You know I'm not supposed to say, your Highness," he murmured. "You'll find out, soon enough."

"Then, what difference will a few minutes make? Connor, I'm dying of suspense. Please?"

Connor snorted good-naturedly. Javan could tell he was wavering. They were nearly across the snow-covered courtyard, preparing to mount the ice-slick steps to the great hall entrance, so as the man set his hand under the prince's elbow to steady him, Javan reached out just slightly with his mind and nudged.

"Come on, Connor, tell me!" Javan whispered fiercely. "Just a hint. Am I under arrest, or is this about last night?"

Connor snorted and glanced around uneasily as they climbed, wiping at his nose with a casual brush of his sleeve. The gesture also covered the slight movement of his lips.

"Nah, it isn't you, lad. It's the trouble last night," he admitted in a low voice. "There's Deryni involved, and someone was killed. That's all *I* know. But you never heard it from me!"

Javan faked a stumble to cover his reaction, mixed of relief for his personal safety and horror for his friends, but he was able to manage a wry grin as he caught himself on Connor's arm.

"Heard what?" he whispered.

He feared for Tavis and Ansel, though, as he followed Connor through the great hall, for he was remembering another day, not four months past, when the dead body of Ansel's brother had been brought to this very place. Please God, it was not Ansel today—or Tavis!

Fortunately, no dead bodies occupied the hall or the regents' withdrawing room this time—though Jamie Drummond gave him a scare at first, sprawled unmoving in an armchair against the right-hand wall. A closer look reassured him that Jamie was breathing, though unconscious, and since the Healer Oriel was in attendance and did not look concerned, Javan relaxed a little.

But he was not at all sure he liked the looks of the priest standing beside Oriel, also watching Jamie. The man appeared to be in his early forties, with bright black eyes that missed nothing. The badge embroidered over his left breast was quite unfamiliar to Javan, as was the unusual cincture of braided red and gold knotted over the black cassock. Javan could not imagine what Order wore such a habit. He supposed the man could not be some strange new sort of Deryni sniffer, given the regents' ban on Deryni priests, but that supposition did not make him any less uneasy.

He became more uneasy when he saw that Ansel's mother, the Lady Elinor, also had been included in the morning's gathering. She was dressed all in black, her fair hair partially covered by a veil of black lace, and she had been weeping. Her chair was set in the center of the room with its back to where Jamie slumped, a guard standing directly behind her so she could not see her husband if she turned. The Deryni sniffer Declan Carmody, no longer in chains, crouched beside her with a cup in his hand, nervously dividing his attention between her and Archbishop Hubert, who stood in front of her—which made Javan wonder whether Tavis had succeeded in blocking her Deryni powers before disaster intervened, for Hubert looked suspicious. But then, Hubert almost always looked suspicious.

Murdoch and Tammaron stood beyond, with Manfred MacInnis and Manfred's seedy son Iver, all of them congregated around a chair of state obviously meant for Alroy, though the king was not yet present. Manfred had been making some emphatic point to Tammaron, but he abandoned it immediately as Javan came into the room, all four of them sketching him offhand bows. Beside them, a few paces to the right of the state chair, Javan could just see Rhys Michael silhouetted against the fireplace behind, gaily clad in royal blue and white, looking almost excited at whatever was taking place.

"Ah, your Highness," Murdoch said, motioning Javan to a stool beside Rhys Michael's as Hubert also turned his attention on the prince, pink rosebud lips pursed thoughtfully. "No doubt you are wondering why you have been summoned here. I apologize for the mystery. It seems a Deryni plot was interrupted last night. We are just wrapping up the loose ends, as you see. A pity your Tavis O'Neill is not here to assist these others of his race who have consented to use their accursed talents for the good of the realm."

God, could they *know*? Had they captured Tavis or Ansel last night and now were testing Javan? And if Tavis *had* been captured, would he want Javan to defend him to the point of compromising his own situation?

"O'Neill?" Javan managed to put a full measure of scorn and bitterness into his voice as he limped toward his seat, pointedly favoring the lame foot and taking care to feign far more discomfort than he usually felt, even on bad days, hating what he knew he must say. "I trusted him and he abandoned me! Good riddance to *that* one."

Fortunately, Alroy's arrival spared Javan having to answer any challenge someone might wish to make of that denial, though he knew it was what the regents had long hoped to hear. The lack of challenge probably also meant that Tavis had *not* been caught or killed. All rose at the king's entrance saving Jamie, who appeared to be either ill or drugged—he definitely was not dead. Elinor had to be helped to her feet by Carmody's hand under her elbow, so dazed was she.

Alroy noticed that and gave Hubert a sour glance as he flopped down in the chair of state. He actually looked annoyed, which was rare for Alroy. Haldane crimson cloaked him, and the Haldane sword clattered against the chair as he settled, but he had not bothered with any kind of circlet or crown. His black hair was rumpled from pushing back the fur-lined hood attached to a capelet around his shoulders, and dark circles stained the fair skin under his eyes. Nor did he look as if he had slept much.

"Would someone please tell me what is going on?" he said. "I can't seem to get a straight answer out of anybody." His face showed even more disapproval as Elinor wobbled back into her chair and leaned her head on her hands. "I heard an unholy commotion last night, but no one would tell me what had happened. What's wrong with the Lady Elinor, and what have you done to Jamie Drummond? Surely you don't expect me to believe that the two of them somehow were to blame."

Shaking his head, Hubert came over to Alroy and bowed over his hand, smiling with prim forbearance.

"Do not trouble yourself, my Liege. Deryni intruders entered the castle through a hitherto unknown Portal last night. Whatever else they may have come to do, they murdered a young girl."

"What?"

"Since one of the assassins is believed to have been the outlaw Ansel MacRorie, Lady Elinor's son," Hubert went on blithely, "we thought to question her and her good lord about the matter—and to ascertain, at the same time, just how much of a Deryni threat they themselves might pose. It should have been done when they first returned to court," Hubert added, at Alroy's expression of stunned outrage. "They have always claimed to be of very little Deryni blood, but one never knows."

Javan managed not to show his own dismay—at least no more than Alroy was doing—but inside, he was near panic.

God, it had been *Ansel* who was recognized!—though apparently not caught, for Hubert had said they only *believed* that to have been the identity of one of the intruders. And Tavis must have gotten away as well, thank God!

But what girl had been killed? Surely not by Ansel or Tavis. And what had been done to Elinor and Jamie? With Oriel and Declan Carmody present, Javan's imagination suggested a variety of unpleasant possibilities that might be applied to his own person with equal ease, if anyone had cause to suspect he had any knowledge of last night's events. He must try to be invisible to the two Deryni and pray that suspicion did not turn his way.

And *who had been killed?* Maybe Rhys Michael knew, since he had gotten here first. Surely no one would take it amiss if Javan evidenced a curiosity about that.

Leaning a little closer to his younger brother, Javan poked him in the ribs, hardly moving his lips as he whispered, "Who got killed?"

"The Lady Giesele MacLean," Rhys Michael whispered back. "They think somebody smothered her with a pillow—probably Ansel."

"He *smothered* her?" Javan gasped, though at Tammaron's sharp glance he immediately stifled further reaction.

Fortunately, his near-outburst was completely overshadowed by Alroy's reaction to what Hubert had said. The king had come to his feet during Javan's exchange with Rhys Michael, and he looked as if he might faint.

"What have you done to Lady Elinor and her husband?" the king demanded. "You—you haven't harmed them, have you?" he ventured, voicing an even more immediate concern to Javan than Giesele's death—for his own fate might be the same as theirs. "The lady has always been so kind to me, and I have never had reason to doubt Lord Jamie's loyalty."

Manfred snorted derisively. "Sire, *really!* Your dear Lady Elinor was previously married to one of the sons of the heretic Camber himself. Her son Davin died a traitor, not a year ago, and her son Ansel apparently means to follow in his brother's footsteps. He certainly left his own footprints in blood, when he fled our men last night. Oh, do sit *down*, Sire! You're making far too much of this."

Ansel had been wounded, then. Javan prayed it was not serious.

And as Alroy sank back into his chair, cowed by the insolent Manfred—on whom Javan wished only the cruelest of fates!—Javan silently applauded his brother for this rare display of backbone in attempting to defend Elinor and Jamie.

"I—cannot speak for Lord Ansel, of course," Alroy said, only a little more meekly than before. "I believe I have not seen him since my coronation. But is the lady to be held accountable for the actions of her grown sons? I was given to understand that there had been little contact with them, even at the time of Lord Davin's death— that she had severed almost all contact with the MacRorie family when she married Lord James."

Murdoch smiled mirthlessly and leaned both arms along the back of Alroy's chair, forcing the king to twist around if he wished to look up at him—which he did.

"Fortunately for both the lady and her second lord, Master Declan has confirmed that there was no recent contact," Murdoch said. He looked almost disappointed. "And since your Highness seems to value them so highly, I am pleased to be able to tell you that neither the lady nor her lord shows any sign of the accursed Deryni blood we feared might sway them to treason. Father Lior and his Order are becoming quite adept at ferreting out secret Deryni."

He gestured toward the stranger priest, who made the king a respectful bow, right hand to breast, but Alroy only stared, the grey Haldane eyes dark and frightened.

"I ask you again, what have you done to them?" he whispered. "And who is this Father Lior, that he can discover who is Deryni and who is not? I do not recognize the habit."

"Nor should you, my Liege," Hubert replied, "though all shall be revealed in due time. Father Lior, bring in the Lady Richeldis and proceed. We must set the king's mind at ease."

As the priest left to do Hubert's bidding, Javan tensed inside. He now liked the mysterious Father Lior even less than he had before, and wondered who else might fall under scrutiny before Lior was done—and whether Tavis had gotten to everyone that he intended. Drugs of some kind were being used in conjunction with the Truth-Reading Oriel and Declan obviously were supplying, for he could see Oriel stirring something in a horn cup, over beside the unconscious Jamie. Certain drugs were Deryni-specific, Javan knew—like the one called *merasha*, which would affect a Deryni but only put a human recipient to sleep—but he had no idea what Oriel was using.

Whatever it was, it had not betrayed Elinor or Jamie. He could only hope that Richeldis would react the same—and young Michaela and Cathan Drummond, if it came to that—and that *he* would not be required to undergo a similar testing.

He tried not to look disapproving or even particularly interested as Iver MacInnis and a guard picked up the chair bearing the now sleeping Elinor and deposited her beside the equally somnolent Jamie. He even yawned as Father Lior came back in with another priest of his unknown Order, leading a frightened-looking Richeldis MacLean between them.

Or, *was* it Richeldis? Javan had to look twice to be sure. He had never paid that much attention, but this girl seemed a good deal more grown up than the slightly plump adolescent he had seen at the wedding feast, not a week before. The black gown was partially responsible—and also made her look slimmer—and her dark hair had been pulled back off her face and braided, the plaits pinned across the top of her head to show off a long, graceful neck—though a sheer black veil kept him from getting too close a look. Why, she was almost pretty—though not with her eyes all puffy and red-rimmed from weeping, of course.

Nor was Javan the only one to notice the difference, as Lior and his companion brought Richeldis before the king. Murdoch and even Tammaron accorded her far more than fatherly interest as she dipped in a wobbly curtsey, on the verge of tears again, and Manfred's son Iver looked so pleased and even proprietary that Javan abruptly wondered if *he* could have had a part in the death of Richeldis' sister.

Or if not Iver himself, then someone else on his behalf. After all, Giesele's death made Richeldis sole heiress of the Kierney lands and titles, once Earl Iain died—and Iver had been paying court to both girls at the wedding feast.

"My condolences on your loss, my lady," Alroy said without prompting, sitting ba k restlessly in his chair—oddly disquieted for Alroy, who usually did not resist the regents' direction. "If it is within my power, you may be certain your sister's murderers will be brought to justice."

The frightened girl said nothing as she rose from her curtsey, only going a little paler as she stole a glance at her guardians slumped senseless in their chairs. At a snap of Hubert's fingers, a guard brought another chair into the center of the room and set it behind her. She sat because she knew she had no choice, hands clenched white-knuckled in her lap, but she held her head a little higher as Father Lior folded the veil back from her face—a true daughter of the nobility, though her chin quivered with her terror. Oriel came over with his cup, and the other priest withdrew to stand by Declan and the Drummonds.

"My Lady Richeldis, I am required to ask you certain questions," Father Lior said quietly. "Father Burton has already taken your oath to answer truthfully." He gestured toward his fellow priest with a square, workmanlike hand. "I shall remind you that you imperil your immortal soul if you lie—and that retribution shall strike you in this world, before you can even plead before a heavenly Judge, if Master Oriel discerns any shred of deliberate misdirection or omission. Do you understand?"

Tears swam in the dark, swollen eyes, but she bobbed her head in assent.

"Excellent. Now, please tell us what you remember of last night. What time did you go to bed?"

She swallowed, glancing fearfully at the impassive Oriel.

"It—it was not long past Vespers, Father," she whispered. "My—my sister and I said our prayers, as we always do, and—and we went to sleep."

"And when did you awaken?" Lior asked.

"I—I don't know exactly."

"What woke you then?"

"I—heard shouting in the corridor outside. I was frightened. I ran to the door, but there were soldiers running back and forth, and no one would tell me what was happening. And then my sister—"

"Go on. What of your sister?"

Richeldis swallowed noisily. "She—didn't wake up. And when I went to her, and tried to rouse her, she—"

"Yes?"

"She wasn't breathing."

Richeldis' voice broke off in a tiny sob as she buried her face in her hands, but Lior was not content with that. Signalling Oriel with a brusque jerk of his chin, he took the cup the Healer handed him and watched Oriel take the girl's wrists, pulling her hands from her face. She continued to weep as the Healer stared at her—Javan guessed he must be probing fairly deeply—but then he shook his head and released her, sinking to one knee to slide an arm around her shoulders in compassion.

"She conceals nothing, Father," Oriel murmured, looking up at the priest with sick despair in his eyes. "She knows nothing of her sister's murder—I swear it! Richeldis woke. Her sister did not. Nor is she Deryni, by any test I know to apply."

"You have not yet applied this test," Lior replied, holding out the cup.

"Is that really necessary?" Alroy suddenly blurted, his tone sharper than Javan had heard it in a long time. "If Oriel says she isn't Deryni, then she isn't Deryni."

"I would prefer to have independent confirmation of that pronouncement, your Highness," Hubert snapped. "She is, after all, the granddaughter of Camber MacRorie's full sister. We do not know how potent that blood might be. Oriel, the cup, if you please."

Sighing, Oriel took it and returned his attention to the girl, who was trembling as she stared at what was in his hand.

"Drink it, child," Oriel murmured, shaking his head as she set her hands against his to keep it at a distance. "Please, little one. I desire this no more than you, but you *will* drink, if his Grace says you must. I promise, you have nothing to fear. The draught will act as a sedative. It will be good to sleep, after all that's happened. That's right," he encouraged, as she ceased resisting and let him set the cup to her lips. "Small sips, but you must drink it all. There's my brave girl."

He handed off the cup to Lior when she had finished, letting her bury her face against his shoulder and sob while he held her in simple human comfort. After a few minutes, when he raised his eyes to Lior's and shook his head, Declan came, at Lior's summons, and set his hands lightly on her shoulders. By then, her sobbing had ceased and she was still.

"All is as Master Oriel has said," Declan said after a moment, his face devoid of expression. "She has been acquainted with many Deryni, because of her family, but she herself shows no sign of the blood. She certainly is no threat to your plans."

"Careful, Carmody," Hubert warned. "We'll have no show of your disapproval."

"Disapproval, your Grace?" Declan said mildly, ignoring Oriel's startled gesture to subside. "Why should I disapprove of being forced to use my powers in ways not intended, to further the goals of avaricious men who probably envy the very things in me they say they fear?"

"Hold your tongue, sir, if you care for your family!" Murdoch ordered. "You are on the dangerous edge of insolence."

"Were it *not* for my family, you would see far more than insolence," Declan retorted, his voice harsh with his hatred as he stepped out from behind Richeldis' chair. "How long do you think a man can live this way, Murdoch? Do you think we have no honor, simply because the bishops say our souls are damned because of what we are?"

"Carmody!" Tammaron said. "Don't be a fool! Standing orders are that if any harm comes to one of us while you are present, your family will be executed in the most excruciating manner possible. Are you willing to risk that for the sake of a moment's satisfaction?"

For an instant, Javan was afraid Declan was willing to risk precisely that—and secretly almost hoped he would—but then the captive Deryni drew a deep breath and let it out in a sigh, head bowing in surrender as he dropped his hands to his sides. Oriel, still on his knees with the sleeping Richeldis, ducked his own head as well, obviously appalled at what his fellow Deryni nearly had been driven to do and praying that the regents' retribution would not fall upon him as well.

And retribution there would be, too. That was obvious as Murdoch stepped from behind Alroy's throne, arms folded across his chest. Alroy looked a little scared, and Rhys Michael as well. Javan did not like what he saw in Murdoch's eyes as the regent studied Declan with calculating intent.

"I will have your apology, Deryni," Murdoch said quietly.

Declan did not lift his eyes, whether as further act of defiance or because he did not yet trust himself to maintain control.

"You have it, my lord," Declan said, the words toneless and without expression.

"No, you will give it on bended knee," Murdoch said, pointing to the floor before him. "You will crawl to me and beg my forgiveness, and you will place my foot on your neck in token of your submission. Any other action—" His voice rose sharply on the last three words, as Declan's head snapped up to glare outrage.

"*Any* other action," Murdoch repeated coldly, "will result in dire consequences for your family. For your wife, perhaps, and maybe even your pretty little sons. Yes, I think my soldiers might enjoy such playthings, don't you, Carmody?"

CHAPTER TWELVE

*Who will rise up against the evildoers? or who
will stand up for me against the workers of
iniquity?*

—Psalms 94:16

Declan blanched and then colored, swaying a little on his feet as he
sucked in an agonized breath between clenched teeth. His hands
had balled into fists, though he managed to keep them at his sides,
and Javan hoped never again to see the look in Declan's eyes. Almost,
he could fancy he saw faint sparks beginning to crackle in the Deryni's hair like tiny, captive lightnings.

"Murdoch, you push him too far!" Tammaron gasped.

"No, it's *he* who pushes too far," Murdoch said coolly. "He for-
gets his very precarious place."

The colossal arrogance of the man only reaffirmed all Javan's
loathing. Both appalled and furious that Murdoch could be so stupid,
he watched the regent slide one proprietary hand along the back of
Alroy's chair, the thumb of the other hand hooking casually in the
gilded belt, very near his dagger—as if either would help, against a
Deryni! Alroy himself reminded Javan of a trapped mouse, caught
between the menace of a cat's claws and the striking range of a
deadly serpent. As a guard scuttled outside to summon help, Hubert
and the other regents began backing warily away from the throne,
Father Lior retreating beside his fellow priest. Only Murdoch seemed
to be without fear.

"Go ahead, Carmody," Murdoch said contemptuously. "Raise a
hand against me, and you won't leave this room alive." As if to
underline his threat, half a dozen archers crowded into the doorway
with bows at full draw. "Not only that, your family will *still* die."

He jabbed a warning forefinger at Oriel as well. "Yours too, Oriel, if you *let* him! Now, on your knees, Carmody, and crawl! *Now!*"

Declan was shaking like a man with palsy, clenched fists risen to waist level now, self-restraint clearly near the breaking point.

"Declan, it isn't worth it," Oriel whispered, in a room that all at once had become far too quiet, and far, *far* too small. "Don't do it, Declan. Don't throw everything away. Do as he says."

Declan did not seem to hear him. The thickening silence swallowed up the sound. From their place of hoped-for safety, flattened against the wall with the two priests, Tammaron and then Manfred began making cautious, urgent gestures for the king and princes to come away—for they were far too close to Murdoch, if Declan lost control. Iver had ducked behind the chair where Jamie Drummond slumbered on, oblivious to the danger.

At least Rhys Michael finally saw the danger, slowly easing far enough above his stool to step backward over it and then inch almost imperceptibly toward the other regents. But Alroy still seemed frozen in his chair. Javan, as much concerned for the fate of the two Deryni as he was for his own safety, stayed put on his own stool, within an arm's stretch of Murdoch, trying to decide whether he really could see a faint aura beginning to surround Oriel's head as well as Declan's.

"Do as he says, Declan," Oriel repeated softly. "It isn't worth the price you'd have to pay. And you'd make me pay it, too. Please, Declan. Don't make *me* turn against my own kind, any more than I already have."

For another endless instant, Javan was not even sure anyone in the room was breathing—and could not believe that Murdoch did not realize how closely he was courting death. The arrogant fool stood glaring across at his intended victim as if the weight of his office would actually afford him some protection if Declan went over the edge. Javan had never seen a Deryni unleash the full force of his power against an enemy, but he did not want to start now—even to be rid of the despicable Murdoch!

He did not have to. All at once, Declan's face contorted in a silent sob and he sank slowly to his knees, eyes closed, biting back a low, animal moan of grief as he pitched forward onto his hands. For a moment he stayed that way, panting as his head wove back and forth in useless denial. Then he began crawling jerkily toward Murdoch.

Other than the harsh rasp of Declan's breathing, only the hollow thud of his hands against the wooden floor and the soft, irregular drag of his knees intruded on the silence as he drew nearer Murdoch's polished boots. Very cautiously, Javan began to breathe again, aware of others doing the same. Behind Declan, still crouched beside Richeldis' chair, the watching Oriel had assumed almost an attitude of prayer. By the door, at Hubert's tiny, cautious hand signal, the archers relaxed to only half-draw, watching in wary amazement as Declan stopped at Murdoch's feet.

Fascinated almost against his will, Javan noted the spurs glittering on Murdoch's heels, golden rowels and silver chains flashing in the light of torches and fire behind as the regent shifted weight. Not a man but held his breath as Declan slowly stretched a trembling hand toward Murdoch's right ankle.

"Say the words first, Carmody," Murdoch commanded, before Declan could touch him.

Declan froze, his fist clenching empty air as his head drooped lower between his shoulders. At his stifled little sob, Murdoch nudged the fist with the toe of his boot.

"Say them!"

"I—b-beg—forgiveness!" Declan managed to choke out.

"You are forgiven," Murdoch replied. "Now complete your penance."

Blindly Declan groped for Murdoch's boot again, now intent only on ending the humiliation as quickly as possible; but Murdoch clearly had other plans. The regent lifted his foot as Declan touched it, but not far enough to reach the bowed neck—not with Declan still on hands and knees.

Declan understood what more Murdoch intended, though—and all at once, Javan did, too. With an impotent whimper, Declan collapsed onto first one and then the other elbow, drawing his knees up close beneath his chest. Then he bent his forehead to the floor, finally setting Murdoch's booted foot on the back of his neck. Murdoch held it there for a full count of ten, its spur glinting in Declan's brown hair, before lifting it disdainfully to back off a step. Declan did not stir.

"Now get up," the regent said in a low voice. "And if you *ever* defy me again, I swear I'll make you sorry you ever lived."

But Declan did not get up or even move, other than to collapse weakly onto his side, one arm protectively cradling his head as his body slowly curled into a rigid, trembling ball. Indeed, he seemed not even to hear as Murdoch's repeated order to get up gave way to shouts and then to increasingly emphatic proddings with Murdoch's boot.

"No! Don't! You're hurting him!" Oriel pleaded, scrambling to Declan's side. "Declan? Declan!"

But even Oriel could not rouse his fellow Deryni from the bleak twilight world of futility and despair into which he had withdrawn. Murdoch had, indeed, pushed Declan too far, if in a different manner than the one Tammaron had feared.

"What's wrong with him?" Murdoch demanded, as the other regents cautiously gathered round to stare down at the stricken man. "Why doesn't he respond?"

Tight-lipped, Oriel shook his head, motioning for one of the priests to bring him his Healer's satchel. "He can't, my lord."

"What do you mean, he can't?" Hubert chimed in. "And what do you intend to do, without even asking anyone's leave?"

"First, I'm going to give him a strong sedative," Oriel replied, as he snatched the bag from Lior and began rummaging in it. "He's retreated deep into his own mind to escape what you made him do. If I can force him to sleep deeply enough, before that escape becomes too entrenched, he should be able to endure waking up properly when the sedative wears off."

"Why, Master Oriel," Murdoch said softly, "do I detect a certain note of—ah—disapproval of my methods?"

Oriel produced a blue glass vial from the bag and worked the stopper loose. "What you think you detect may be quite different from what I might *mean*, my lord," he said, grimacing as he had to force the selected drug between Declan's clenched teeth. "But for now, you must excuse me. For this treatment to work, I must try to go into his mind for a time and sort things out. I will not be able to converse while I do so."

"Now, see here!" Manfred began.

But Oriel did not wait for permission to proceed, only setting his hands to either side of Declan's head and closing his eyes, his own head bowing lower and lower over Declan's as he pushed himself deep into Healing trance. Nor did anyone dare to challenge him.

Javan watched in awe, the regents more in apprehension and even irritation. Manfred finally summoned guards to take Richeldis and the sleeping Drummonds out of the room, when it became clear that Oriel's task would not be quickly done. A little later, when more guards brought in the two Drummond children, Oriel was still bowed motionless over Declan's supine form. The children looked frightened, clinging to one another for comfort as the guards gave them over to the charge of Fathers Lior and Burton. Earl Tammaron drew Hubert a little aside as he saw them, though Javan still could hear what he said.

"Must we go on with this?" Tammaron murmured, stealing a

look at the quaking Michaela. "Surely you don't believe these little ones know anything."

Hubert, returning his attention to Oriel for a few seconds, scowled as he glanced back at Tammaron. "Are you suggesting that the children should not be questioned?"

"To what purpose?" Tammaron replied. "They can't have seen or heard anything."

"Probably not," Hubert conceded, "but I would prefer to be sure. And besides that, there is still the question of their blood."

"Their blood?" Tammaron snorted. "You mean you still think they might be Deryni? That's preposterous. You saw their parents tested."

"We saw their mother and her husband tested," Hubert amended. "You assume that James Drummond is, indeed, their father."

Rolling his eyes heavenward, Tammaron gave an enormous sigh. "I suppose you have reason to believe he is *not*?"

"Not at all. In fact, I think it most improbable. But it is not impossible, Tammaron; and the Deryni taint is insidious. I'll not chance having their spawn brought up among us, unbeknownst."

"Then, have Lior test them with *merasha*, and be done with it," Manfred said, joining the conversation. "If they're truly innocent, it will only make them sleep."

"Hmmm, true. And it need not be Oriel who questions them, I suppose." With a thoughtful expression on his face, Hubert glanced at the children, trembling between Fathers Lior and Burton, then crooked his finger for the two to approach. The ten-year-old Michaela raised her chin bravely and took her younger brother's hand as, together, they came before the archbishop. The girl bobbed in a tiny, nervous curtsey and the boy ducked his head in a bow.

"Please, your Grace, can you tell us what has happened to our parents?" Michaela asked. "No one will tell us anything, and there were so many guards rushing to and fro last night."

"You needn't concern yourself, child," Hubert murmured, setting his hand briefly on her head and then brushing her brother's cheek. "Your parents are quite safe. You shall see them a little later, after you've answered a few questions."

"What—questions, your Grace?" Michaela asked.

"Simple questions, my child," Hubert said softly, "requiring simple answers. So long as you tell the truth, you have nothing to fear." Fingering the jewelled pectoral cross lying on his ample chest, he glanced at Cathan. "Tell me, young Cathan, how old are you?"

"Eight, your Grace," Cathan replied.

"Excellent. And have you made your First Communion yet?"

As the boy gave him a tremulous nod, Hubert echoed it, his rosebud lips pursing in a priggish smile.

"Good. And since I know that your sister is old enough to have done so, that means that I can be certain you both know right from wrong, and what God will do to you if you lie." He shifted his placid blue gaze to Michaela. "You do know what happens to children who lie, do you not, Michaela?"

Michaela swallowed noisily, her lower lip trembling as her blue eyes swam with tears. "They—they are damned for all eternity, your Grace," she whispered.

"Alas, that is correct," Hubert said sadly. "But if you are truthful with me, you have nothing to fear, do you?"

"N-no, your Grace."

"Good. Now, with your hands on this cross, I require that you answer my questions as fully as you can." As he spoke, he took their right hands and set them on his pectoral cross, holding them flat there beneath his own. "Remember that you swear on holy relics, and if you lie, the angels will weep. Do you understand?"

Tremulously both children nodded.

"Excellent. My first question is this, then. Do you know what happened to your cousin Giesele last night?"

The two glanced at one another and then back at Hubert.

"She—died," Michaela said.

"Do you know how it happened?" Hubert persisted.

Cathan's eyes widened, and he nodded sagely. "She was *smothered with a pillow!*" he said, with all the conspiratorial fervor of a child who does not truly understand what death means.

"Smothered with a pillow, eh?" Hubert replied. "How do you know that?"

Michaela whimpered a little and snuffled. "We—we heard the guards talking. They say that—that our brother did it. But Ansel wouldn't do a thing like that! That was wicked! *Wicked!*"

"It was, indeed," Hubert agreed. "I don't suppose either of you saw or heard anything?"

But neither child had. Javan was as certain of that as if he had Truth-Read them—though he did not dare to do that, with Oriel still in the room and deep in working trance. Fortunately, Hubert's further questions only served to confirm their innocence.

"Very well, then, children. Your answers please me greatly," he said, smiling unctuously as he released their hands and sketched the sign of blessing over their nervously bowed heads. "Father Lior, I believe our young friends have had quite enough fright for one day, and precious little sleep last night. Perhaps you might give them some soothing draught to help them get a little rest, eh?"

As Lior bowed, bringing out cups that had been ready for some time and extending one toward each child, Michaela stiffened, her arms slipping protectively around her brother's shoulders, and Cathan glanced up at his sister for reassurance. Michaela's lower lip trembled a little as she glanced from the cups to Father Lior and back to the archbishop.

"And, it please your Grace, I should rather not sleep until we have seen our parents," she whispered. "The knowledge that they are safe will be far more soothing than any draught drunk from a cup."

"And *I* should rather that you drank the draught that Father Lior has so kindly prepared," Hubert replied, the smile evaporating from his face. "I trust that I shall not need to make threats to gain your cooperation."

"But you said we might see our parents," Michaela said plaintively, on the verge of tears. "You promised we could."

"I said you might see them later," Hubert said coldly, taking the cups from Father Lior and thrusting them in front of the two. "*I* shall determine when that might be. Now, do as you're told."

Javan dared not move, praying that Michaela would not make a scene. But while he prayed, his younger brother took more direct persuasive action.

"Don't be silly, Mika," Rhys Michael said, coming to take the cups from Hubert and offer them himself. "It's for your own good. You, too, Cathan. It will only make you sleep for a while. I saw your parents. They're perfectly safe. And *I* promise you, you shall see them after you've slept—certainly no later than tomorrow morning. Isn't that right, your Grace?" he added, giving Hubert a sharp glance.

To Javan's surprise, Hubert only bowed, making Javan wonder whether the archbishop actually had backed down or had only recognized the expediency of allowing Rhys Michael appear to have influence over a regent's wishes. Javan preferred not to think about what it would mean if Rhys Michael really was now in the regents' camp and ready to do their bidding.

But whatever Rhys Michael's motivations, the two young Drummonds responded in the manner Hubert had always intended, taking the cups from Rhys Michael and quickly draining them, though Cathan made a face and Michaela averted her eyes. When, after a minute or two of further reassurance on Rhys Michael's part, both children began nodding off, with no other sign of the drug's effect, Hubert had guards take them out to return them to their beds. By then, Oriel had finished with Declan, emerging pale and exhausted from his trance. Javan watched him go paler still as he saw the guards disappear with the children.

"I've just saved you the further tedium of questioning the Drummond children," Hubert said, frowning at Oriel's reaction as he, Rhys Michael, and the other regents returned to stare down at the Healer and his now peacefully slumbering patient. "How is Carmody? Will he be all right?"

Breathing out with a soft shudder, Oriel sat back on his hunkers and made a visible show of folding his hands so they would not tremble. "I think so, your Grace, though I'd like to keep him heavily sedated for several days. And I beg you to excuse him from any further work like today's for at least a week or so. We cannot do this kind of work indefinitely and not have it take its toll."

Manfred snorted. "Are you pleading for yourself as well, Oriel? Good God, man, you look like death!"

"I—beg pardon if my appearance causes offense, my lord," the Healer whispered, staring glassy eyed at Murdoch's boots. "I m-must rest. Dealing with what I—have just done—takes a great deal out of me."

"What, squeamish, Oriel?" Murdoch snapped.

Oriel swallowed noisily. "M-my lord, I beg you to permit me some faint vestige of professional pride. You have never seen me shrink from any medical challenge appropriate to my function as a Healer. But to—"

He shook his head, clasped hands clenched hard under his chin as he tried again to steady his nerves. "Surely you can appreciate the position in which you placed me, my lord, knowing that if I could not persuade Carmody to back down, I must use whatever means I had at my disposal to stop him. You made it quite clear what would be the consequences if I did not stop him, did you not? And I was prepared to do it!"

"Which is your function," Murdoch replied coldly, "just as it is your function to exercise your abilities in whatever other ways the regency may see fit, in exchange for preferential treatment not meted out to others of your race. You are in our service by choice, after all."

"Yes, my lord," Oriel whispered, "because it is the only way I may hold any reasonable hope for the safety of my family. In addition, I am a realist. With the—incentives you offer, I know that there will always be someone of my race ready to do as you require— and possibly not do it as well as I. I can do nothing about the use you make of the information I help you gain, my lord, but at least

I can make sure that the gaining of that information is done with as little distress to your subjects as is within my power."

"Why, Oriel," Murdoch purred, eyes glinting dangerously, "if you are not satisfied with the terms of your employment—"

"Oh, let him be!" Tammaron muttered, crossing his arms on his chest with an explosive sigh. "Surely Oriel's demonstrated his loyalty enough for one day, and in very unpleasant personal circumstances. Can't you see he's exhausted? You already pushed Carmody too bloody far!"

"Carmody brought it on himself," Murdoch retorted, "and Master Oriel's impertinence is beginning to wear a little thin."

"*Will* you let it pass, Murdoch?" Hubert said. "Regardless of your unfortunate confrontation with Carmody, Master Oriel surely has shown himself loyal, for whatever reason. It would be petty to push him beyond his endurance, just to make a point that, in his case, does not need to be made. Oriel, you are excused from further duties for the rest of the day, and I shall place you on limited duty for the next week. During that time, I expect you to bring Master Carmody back to full function. I shall require twice-daily reports on his progress, with resumption of full duty for both of you at the end of a week."

"I—thank you for the respite, your Grace," Oriel murmured, bowing his head deeply. "I shall do my best. I—am not certain I can guarantee Carmody's full recovery in that time, however."

"I would do my utmost to make certain he *is* fully recovered within that time," Murdoch said sharply. "A Deryni who cannot fulfill the terms of his employment is of little use to us—or to his family either."

"My lord—" Oriel began, appalled.

"We will entertain no further discussion," Murdoch said. "Archbishop Hubert has been more than generous. Guards, assist Master Oriel to take Carmody to his quarters."

And that was the end of it. When the guards had taken Oriel and Declan out of the room, Javan was left huddled next to Alroy's state chair, nervously eying Rhys Michael as he chatted with the two priests, while the regents clustered in the center of the room. Alroy himself looked grey and exhausted from the strain of the morning, near to fainting. Javan had the feeling his own continued presence in the withdrawing room was almost as much from oversight as design, and tried to make himself a part of his stool, as invisible as possible, as he watched Archbishop Hubert pace the floor.

"I trust you're all aware that we have a far more serious potential problem than just the question of how the MacLean girl died," Hubert said after a moment. Something in his manner convinced Javan that the archbishop knew *exactly* how it had happened. "What concerns me most is that Deryni were able to enter this castle without hindrance. God alone knows how many others may have come and gone without our knowledge."

"Well, they won't come through *that* Portal again," Murdoch said, seating himself on the arm of the king's chair with a casual familiarity that infuriated Javan, though Alroy did not seem to mind. "I have a team of stonemasons blocking up the one we found. In fact, they're filling it with stone. Any Deryni who tries to use it from now on is in for a severe shock—hopefully a fatal one."

As Javan shivered a little, wondering what *would* happen if Tavis or one of the others tried to use the Portal, Tammaron nodded thoughtfully.

"Hmmm, yes, that's all very well, but can we be sure there aren't any more? We know that the Deryni themselves destroyed one in the cathedral sacristy. But what if there are others?"

Hubert nodded. "My thought, precisely—which is why I suggest that, as soon as the weather breaks, we move the court back to Rhemuth. This is a very old castle, my Liege," he added, at Alroy's pained grimace of distaste. "Five Deryni kings had their courts here during the Interregnum, with unknown numbers of other sorcerers to support them. We have no way of knowing what other, even more sinister magic they may have left behind, perhaps even worse than a Portal. Besides, Rhemuth is far more comfortable, now that restoration is so far along."

More comfortable for the regents, Javan thought, as agreement murmured among the adults in the room. The move would bring *him* no comfort, though. For though there might be Portals at Rhemuth as well as Valoret, Javan had no idea where the former might be.

Not that the other one he knew of in Valoret would do him any good either—or anyone else, for that matter, since it lay in Archbishop Hubert's apartments. Tavis had told him of using it that awful Christmas Day when Rhys was killed, but Javan did not even know its exact location, much less whether he could work a Portal on his own. Besides, the very notion of sneaking into the archbishop's palace to look for it was so unthinkable as to be near suicidal. Discovery in Hubert's quarters could cost him his freedom or even his place in the succession, not to mention his life. For he was the expendable prince, the already inconvenient spare—and if he made himself too inconvenient, the regents might decide to be very conveniently rid of him.

"How soon would we go?" Alroy asked. "The snow is still awfully heavy."

"Oh, four to six weeks," Hubert replied. "Certainly before the start of Lent. That's ample time to make all the necessary preparations for a move of that magnitude."

"That suits *me* fine," Murdoch said with a tight little smile. "The hunting is much better, farther south."

Javan had the impression Murdoch was not referring only to animal game.

"Quite true," Tammaron agreed. "I confess, I've grown rather tired of Valoret, knowing the greater comforts awaiting us at Rhemuth. And I know my wife will prefer it."

Manfred cleared his throat, controlling a tiny smile. "Ah, yes, connubial harmony. Which reminds me that it might be well to—ah—'regularize' certain other considerations in the next few months," he said. "May we discuss the Lady Richeldis?"

"What did you have in mind?" Hubert said, as Iver became instantly more attentive, drifting closer from his vantage point nearer the wall.

"Well, ordinarily, I would not have pursued the matter for another year or two, since the girl is barely twelve, but I think last night's events clearly demonstrate that the remaining MacLean heiress may not be totally safe under the mere protection of her present guardians, innocent though they may be of any—ah—subversive leanings."

Tammaron raised an eyebrow. "You propose to bestow her wardship elsewhere?"

"Not only her wardship but her hand," Manfred replied. "Surely you're aware that my son has developed a fondness for the girl." Iver at least had the good grace to blush as his father laid an arm around his shoulders. "I propose that the marriage be celebrated immediately, as soon as the banns can be read, so that the MacLean lands may be secured with a family strong enough to protect them."

"But her uncle still lives," Alroy blurted, consternation clouding his brow. "And surely such haste is less than seemly, with her sister not yet dead a day."

"Why, do you fancy her yourself, Sire?" Murdoch retorted, chuckling unpleasantly as his eyes raked Alroy's thin form and the boy went bright red. "I had no idea you were so eager."

Iver stifled a snigger, and Hubert coughed self-importantly.

"There'll be time enough for that," the archbishop muttered. "In the meantime, I agree that the marriage should go forward as soon as a decent interval has elapsed. The Lady Richeldis must have a more potent protector. Perhaps we might make the happy event the first major court function upon the return of the king to his new capital. Sire, you surely do not object to that?"

After the derision he had already suffered, Alroy certainly had no objections that he was willing to voice. Nor did Javan, though he now was virtually certain that either Iver or, more likely, his father, had had a hand in Giesele's murder—*someone* among the regents, in any case. Some lackey had done the actual deed, of course, while his superiors secured their alibis by being prominently elsewhere, but Manfred's family certainly had stood to gain a great deal.

Far more than the unfortunate Richeldis, who must be sacrificed on the marriage bed to the loutish Iver MacInnis. But Javan dared not voice his suspicions, lest he add himself to the list of sacrifices.

So he kept his own counsel and tried to be at least polite in congratulating Iver MacInnis on his coming marriage and wondered what the archbishop had to say to Father Lior, when the two stayed to confer while the others began dispersing for a midday repast. He found out on Candlemas, little more than a week later, when the regents pulled their biggest coup since ousting Alister Cullen from the archbishop's seat—the formal institution of a new religious order to replace the Michaelines.

CHAPTER THIRTEEN

*Woe be unto them that decree unrighteous
decrees, and that write grievousness which they
have prescribed.*

—Proverbs 10:1

"Archbishop Hubert says it's going to be a splendid order!" Rhys
Michael told Javan excitedly, just before they entered the cathedral
on that chill February morning. "The Michaelines will look shabby
by comparison. Just wait until you hear all the details!"

Javan wondered how his younger brother had become privy to
such details when he was not, but he dared not inquire further as
he and Rhys Michael followed Alroy down the center aisle. The
regents and their families preceded and trailed them in casual
procession, all too readily placed to overhear anything said among
the royal brothers and report it back to Hubert. Behind the regents
came half a dozen royal squires, at least some of whom Javan knew
were also more loyal to the regents than to their royal masters.

Javan supposed he should have guessed that something of this
sort was in the wind. No one had explained the mysterious scarlet
and gold cinctures, even Tammaron brushing him off with an eva-
sive answer the one time he dared to ask, but they had been showing
up with disturbing frequency and regularity, their wearers obviously
in the archbishop's confidence and favor.

"Where *ever* are they going to put everyone?" Alroy wondered
in a low stage whisper to Javan, as they passed into the choir and
entered the stall set aside for the royal brothers.

Javan, all too aware of the throngs packing the nave and the
audience this would give the archbishop's newest triumph, could
only shake his head and murmur, "Good question." He refrained

from adding his own hope that perhaps the new order would be very small.

"Well, at least we have some of the best seats," Rhys Michael observed, slipping to his knees on the other side of Alroy and craning his neck toward the altar area. "The ceremony's supposed to be really impressive. I suppose it is going to be crowded, though."

Indeed, if only for reasons of logistics, Candlemas—which was also the Feast of the Purification of the Blessed Virgin—seemed particularly ill-suited for the institution of any new religious order, of whatever size. Not only was the day's usual liturgy considerably lengthened because of the feast itself, but the very process of blessing all the candles for the coming year was a formidable physical undertaking in its own right, requiring a fair amount of space and time. Javan doubted they would be out of here by noon. Hundreds of candles had been piled before the altar, boxes and baskets of them, from the tall, elegant brands used on the altar down to humble votive lights and the tapers for lighting all of them. Their honey-sweet fragrance filled the sanctuary and choir and drifted into the nave— a soothing scent, were it not for the fact that Javan knew his every reaction to be under scrutiny by watchers of a most critical disposition.

Murdoch, Tammaron, and their wives and children faced the princes across the choir, up behind the two rows of choir monks who would sing the day's responses. In the fourth and last row, returned from his wedding trip at last, Rhun of Horthness sat flanked by his bride of a few weeks and a dark-eyed girl someone had said was a daughter of a first marriage. The recently made Earl of Sheele seemed far more interested in fondling his new countess' shoulder than in watching what was about to occur, but Javan knew that the outward air of dissipation concealed a sharp intellect and awareness that missed very little. No, things would not be easier, now that Rhun was back.

Nor was the disposition of attendees on the king's side of the choir any more reassuring. The royal squires formed a buffer row immediately behind the princes, young Cathan Drummond now among them, but behind them knelt Manfred and his family, with little Michaela Drummond now among the attendants of Manfred's wife, the Lady Estellan. The parents of Cathan and Michaela were nowhere to be seen. A thinner and very sad-looking Richeldis MacLean, still wearing black for her dead sister, sat sandwiched between her future mother-in-law and her affianced husband, their marriage banns having been read for the first time the previous Sunday.

Javan saw little to hint at the day's double intention as the ritual began, though he sensed a large number of men standing quietly in the ambulatory aisle that ran behind the high altar. Dawn was still a faint glow behind the stained glass beyond as a splendidly vested Archbishop Hubert entered, attended by his auxiliary bishop, Ailin MacGregor, and several priests Javan did not recognize. Hubert's cope was a rich, stiff brocade of violet and gold, heavily embellished with gold bullion on orphreys and hood. MacGregor's was hardly less sumptuous. Even Hubert bowed more deeply under the weight of his vestments as he stood before the altar with its piles of candles and began to sing the day's opening prayers.

"Dominus vobiscum."

"Et cum spiritu tuo," the choir answered.

"Oremus. Domine sancte, Pater omnipotens, aeterne Deus, qui omnia ex nihilo creasti. . . ." Holy Lord, almighty Father, eternal God, who didst create all things out of nothing, and by thy command didst cause this liquid to become perfect wax through the work of bees. . . . we humbly beseech thee . . . graciously to bless and hallow these candles for the service of men. . . . Be pleased to grant that as these lights, kindled with visible fire, dispel the darkness of night, so may our hearts, enlightened by that invisible fire, the radiance of the Holy Spirit, be free from all blindness of sin. . . .

The prayers for blessing the candles were lengthy and threefold, and seemed interminable to Javan, dreading what would follow. When Hubert had finished singing, he sprinkled the candles three times with holy water while the choir sang the antiphon, *Asperges me*. Next, he censed the candles thrice. The pungent bite of the incense smoke mingled with and overpowered the honey scent as he finished, making Javan sneeze.

Silence for a few seconds, as Hubert handed off the thurible and temporarily changed places with MacGregor, who had taken up one of the large, blessed candles. The choir shifted to a new set of canticles and antiphons as MacGregor presented it to Hubert, who lit it from flint and tinder struck by a waiting deacon and then held the lit candle aloft in salute to the altar.

Then, when Hubert had given it to MacGregor, both received the other clergy in the order of their rank, to distribute candles to all. Each man knelt before Hubert to kiss the candle humbly and then the hand that gave it, before moving on to MacGregor, to light the candle from Hubert's original.

But they did not form up for the procession that should have come next. Instead, Hubert's clergy gathered to either side of his episcopal throne, bowing as he passed between them and took his place. His costly vestments bent stiffly around him as he sat, and the precious miter a chaplain placed on his head glittered like an earthly crown in the candlelight.

As a master of ceremonies came forward in a lesser cope, bearing a large scroll that dangled half a dozen seals pendant from as many different colored ribbons, two lines of priests in the most austere of black cassocks began to file into the choir from either end of the ambulatory aisle. They were led by a tall, lanky, barefooted man of about fifty, also all in black, who prostrated himself at Hubert's feet as his brethren knelt all around him, heads humbly bowed. Javan could not quite place the man, though he looked vaguely familiar, but there was no mistaking Fathers Lior and Burton among the kneeling others, even without the odd cinctures they had worn the last time Javan saw them.

The men remained kneeling, their incipient leader still stretched prostrate among them, as the master of ceremonies read out the charter.

"*In nomine Patris, et Filii, et Spiritus Sancti, Amen. Salutem in Domine, omnes gentes. . . .*"

The document began innocuously enough, with the conventional Latin words one always expected of such formal documents. But after the introductory phrases, the text shifted to a vernacular translation, as if to ensure that there could be no mistaking the charter's intent.

"So, therefore, do we, Hubert John William Valerian MacInnis, Archbishop of Valoret and Primate of All Gwynedd, in accordance with the recommendation and consent of our Council sitting in Ramos, authorize, institute, and found a new religious order, under our direct and especial patronage. And the name of this Order shall be the *Custodes Fidei*—the Guardians of the Faith—and its purpose shall be three-fold.

"First, so that the teachings of Holy Mother Church may be transmitted in accordance with holy writ and canon law, free from the taint of heresy, especially the heresy of the Deryni contagion, the Order shall have charge of all education whatsoever in this land—from infants' schools through universities and seminaries—under the direct supervision and execution of the Order's Chancellor General.

"Second, so that the purity of God's holy priesthood may be preserved, uncorrupted by the taint of Deryni magic, as set forth in the Statutes of Ramos, all examinations for entry into Holy Orders of whatsoever kind shall be conducted by members of the Order, who shall have all means at their discretion to ensure the good faith of candidates, even unto capital trial. To this end, all seminaries presently instituted for the training of priests or religious of any kind are hereby made over to the *Custodes Fidei*, and all ordinations to any clerical degree whatsoever are temporarily suspended, for a period not to exceed six months. During that time, the Order shall take such steps as are necessary to bring all such seminaries into accord with the new guidelines promulgated by the Council of Ramos, so that by Lammastide next, in the second year of the reign of our Lord King Alroy, an officially sanctioned series of approved seminaries may be duly reconstituted and the training of priests resumed, to the greater glory of God.

"Third, so that Holy Mother Church may once again have an honorable company of Christian Knights to defend her and do homage before Our Lord, to be His arm upon this land, we do institute a sub-order of Knights of the Most Holy Guardianship, *Equites Custodum Fidei*, who shall live under monastic rule and owe direct obedience to the Primate through their Grand Master and Vicar General.

"And as an especial sign of the favor of this Order in the eyes of the Crown, it has been the pleasure of the King's Grace to grant unto said *Custodes Fidei* a double cincture of Haldane crimson and gold, intertwined, in token of the Order's mandate to unify holy and secular law. And though all members of the Order shall wear black as a sign of humility and their death to secular concerns, their mantles shall be faced with Haldane crimson, lest anyone forget that the Order bears the special patronage of the Crown of Gwynedd.

"And the badge confirmed unto this Order shall be *gules*, a winged golden lion *sejant guardant*, its head ennobled with a halo, holding in its dexter paw an upraised sword, emblematic of the Order's duty to maintain constant vigilance in defense of the Faith. . . ."

There was more of the proclamation, mostly pertaining to specific lands and houses being granted to the Order at its institution, but Javan hardly heard. Now he understood how the regents planned to enforce at least some of the restrictions the Council of Ramos had placed on Deryni, especially the ban on Deryni priests.

He watched numbly as the first members of the Order came forward to make their vows to the archbishop, Hubert raising up their leader first—Paulin of Ramos, who stepped down as Bishop of Stavenham to become the *Custodes'* first Vicar General, and who undoubtedly would continue to spearhead the council that shared his name. No wonder he had looked so familiar.

And now Paulin was giving up a bishop's miter to head the *Cus-*

todes. Him the archbishop invested with a wide scarlet sash, tying over it the cincture plaited of Haldane scarlet and gold cords. The black mantle laid around his shoulders was wholly lined with scarlet, clasped with a pair of haloed lion heads at the throat, and bore a larger version of the haloed-lion badge appliqued over the left shoulder. His staff of office likewise bore the lion badge in three dimensions, and the thought crossed Javan's mind that the hand-high sword in the lion's paw was a lethal weapon, as was Paulin himself. Certainly, that Paulin had chosen to give away a bishop's miter for it bespoke much of the power the new Vicar General expected his order to wield in the future.

Following Paulin, his immediate subordinates made their vows and were installed. One Marcus Concannon became Chancellor General, in charge of the seminaries—a man well known as a Deryni hater as well as a scholastic. A tall, gaunt monk identified only as Brother Serafin became Inquisitor General. Javan shivered to hear Father Lior named as his assistant.

And as the Order's first Grand Master, to command the new ecclesiastical knights, Paulin named his brother, the former Earl of Tarleton, a widower-warrior of some prominence who had resigned his earldom to his teenaged son but a few days before, and now took the name Albertus in religion.

Then came the rank and file of the new Order. In addition to nearly four-score clergy, over a hundred fighting men took the vows of the *Custodes* that morning, promising poverty, chastity, and obedience in exchange for the accolade of an *Eques Custodum Fidei*, conferred by Grand Master Albertus. The professed brethren's plaited cincture of scarlet and gold became a cordon when worn about the left shoulders of the new ecclesiastical knights, and black surcoats bore a red moline cross charged with the haloed lion's head of the Order's device. The pristine white sash formerly used to denote knighthood among the Michaelines acquired scarlet fringes when bound about the waists of the new ecclesiastical knights. To Javan, the fringe evoked the imagery of blood dripping from the ends of the sashes, desecrating the very concept of chivalry. Nor did the swooping black mantles with their scarlet facings make the *Equites* look like anything other than birds of prey.

And the Order's lethal intent seemed only underlined by Hubert's next act, for he called all the newly vowed *Custodes* to kneel before him and there bestowed upon them the notorious Benediction of the Sword, which granted the recipient automatic forgiveness for malicide. In general terms, malicide had always been understood to mean any justifiable killing of the wicked. In practice, its use in the past had almost always been confined to times of war, when malicide was not only expected but encouraged. Giving the *Custodes* such a sanction in peacetime amounted to a license to murder Deryni, so far as Javan was concerned—for who better than the Deryni, in the regents' estimation, currently embodied the most prominent example of wickedness?

Unfortunately, Javan could do nothing to prevent it. And when he attempted to query Alroy about it, while the newly vowed and exonerated *Custodes* filed forward finally to receive their candles from the archbishop's hands, Alroy could not seem to understand why Javan should object. Nor could Rhys Michael, when Javan shifted his questioning to *him*—and the exchange brought a *shush* and a very stern look from Manfred, back behind the row of royal squires. The reprimand silenced Javan immediately, but it did not still the turmoil in his brain.

Hubert's triumph was not yet complete, either. For as the *Custodes* took up their candles, they went not to the ambulatory aisle whence they had come, but filed into the nave to line the center aisle. The ostensible reason was to provide a guard of honor, for when the morning's original ceremony resumed where it had been broken off to institute the new order, all laymen present, beginning with the king and his brothers, were expected to come forward as the clergy had done and receive *their* candles from the archbishop.

Javan had known he would have to do that, and had innured himself to the necessity of kissing Hubert's pudgy, pink hand, but he had not reckoned how difficult he would find it to pass among the *Custodes* without flinching. He seemed to feel their eyes boring into the back of his neck as he followed Alroy forward, though he knew they could not know his true feelings about them, and he was chilled to find Brother Serafin, the Order's new Inquisitor General, gazing directly at him as he limped closer, to kneel at Hubert's feet.

Hubert's hand was moist and soft, and the archbishop insisted on resting it on the heads of each of the princes in blessing after they had kissed it and taken their candles. Javan managed not to show his revulsion as he went through with the required charade, even finding some measure of charity in his heart as he bowed before Bishop MacGregor to light his candle, but on his way back to his place, he feigned a sneeze so that he could wipe his sleeve across his nose and mouth, in at least a symbolic gesture of wiping Hubert's taint from his lips.

As he knelt in his place once more, staring into his candle flame as the seemingly endless parade of the faithful came and went in orderly lines, he begged God's pardon for any disrespect his gesture might have carried for the gift—but not the giver!—and tried to let the rise and fall of the choir's sung antiphon lull him into more seemly observation of the day's intent.

"*Exsurge, Domine, adjuva nos: et libera nos propter nomen tuum. . . .*" Arise, Lord, and free us for the honour of Thy name. . . .

The words had most of their desired effect, after being sung enough times, so that, when all the congregation had returned to their places, Javan was able to observe the archbishop's procession to the doors and back with only scant animosity. During the procession, the choir sang of the presentation of the Child Jesus in the temple, when Simeon had taken the child in his arms and said, blessing God, "*Nunc dimittis servum tuum, Domine, in pace.*" Lord, now dost thou let thy servant depart in peace.

But even during the Mass that followed, Javan was able to derive no real peace, all too aware of Paulin and his *Custodes* assisting Hubert in the Eucharistic celebration—and the Knights now kneeling along the center aisle. The Sacrament itself seemed oddly hollow to Javan, and made him wish he had dared to stay in his place instead of going forward for Communion, for receiving it in his present state of mind was perilously near blasphemy, so much anger did he bear Hubert and his cohorts.

Afterwards was hardly better, for then he must be gracious and pretend he approved of the entire thing, both in the informal chatter that surrounded the royal party as they left the cathedral and then at the feast that followed in the archbishop's great hall. No women were allowed to attend, and the regents and the three princes were the only laymen present.

The afternoon stretched on interminably. Javan's knees ached from kneeling all morning, and they sat him between Tammaron and the new chancellor general, neither of whom said much to him. Soon, as a result of allowing too much wine to be forced upon him, his head ached, too.

The one positive result of the misspent afternoon was that he got a look at parts of the archbishop's palace he had not seen before—knowledge that would be vital if he ever got up the nerve to look for the Portal in Hubert's apartments—the Portal the archbishop did not know he had. Today's events made it even more imperative that Javan communicate with his Deryni allies—at least before the regents packed him off to Rhemuth.

But not tonight—though a ghost of a plan had begun to form in his mind of how he might gain more ready access to the palace and, more important, to Hubert's apartments. He would have to think further on it and consider whether he dared the other risks that went along with it.

CHAPTER FOURTEEN

For thy power is the beginning of righteousness.
                    —Wisdom of Solomon 12:16

Javan's Deryni allies, of course, had no inkling of the risks their prince was contemplating. Losing the use of the Valoret Portal—and hence, their means of communicating with Javan—was but one of the setbacks of the night of Giesele MacLean's murder, and one that allowed of being pushed temporarily to the background while they dealt with more immediate considerations arising from the incident. Once Ansel was out of danger and they had resolved their initial panic regarding young Tieg, their chief priority in the following fortnight became the further evaluation and integration of Sylvan O'Sullivan—for upon his cooperation and ability might rest the entire success of what they had planned for Revan.

Fortunately, Sylvan proved to be both an apt and an enthusiastic pupil, once he recovered from the shock of his unexpected initiation into higher arcana. Not only Tavis and Queron but also Joram, Niallan, and even Ansel all instructed him in the days and weeks that followed his arrival, so that both his knowledge of Healing techniques and his general adeptship increased almost twofold—no mean feat for a man whose Healer's training hitherto had been oriented almost exclusively toward battle applications.

"So Revan is simply going to be a decoy for what's really happening?" Sylvan inquired of Queron, early on in his training, as he and the senior Healer relaxed with a jug of mulled wine Queron had brought, after a particularly tiring afternoon's work.

Queron handed Sylvan a steaming cup. "That's right—though

you mustn't underestimate the sheer charisma a gifted human like Revan can project. Still, it behooves you and Tavis to make Revan look good—because he can stand up to official scrutiny, where the two of you can't."

"Against *merasha*, you mean?"

"That seems to be the preferred form of coercion just now—yes. I predict that the *Custodes Fidei* will have much to answer for, when they finally are called before God's judgment. In any case, we can't give you any defense against *merasha*, other than to block you."

"Which makes us no use to Revan," Sylvan reasoned.

"Precisely. Which is why our first preference is that none of you come to the particular notice of the authorities at all—even Revan. Besides the obvious danger of *merasha* and perhaps other substances, my guess is that the *Custodes* are not above more physical means of persuasion—even outright torture, if it suits their purposes."

Sylvan grimaced. "Well, I can cope with that, if I must. I suppose it's the John the Baptist parallel that still makes me uneasy. It seems to me that we're skirting perilously close to blasphemy—and I don't even want to think about heresy. Mind you, I can't argue from the same philosophical premises as you or Joram." He flashed the senior Healer an amiable grin. "In the last few days, the two of you have made me woefully aware of the inadequacies of my Varnarite training for anything but battle surgery. But isn't it awfully risky, doctrinally speaking, using the framework of baptism to cover blocking Deryni?"

Smiling, Queron blew lightly on his hot wine to cool it. "If we meant it as a substitute for Christian baptism, most assuredly. However, the mere concept of baptism is not exclusively Christian. We know that at the time of Christ, baptism was common to many different sects. Nor did it always have the sacramental nature we now attach to it in a Christian context."

"No?"

Queron shrugged in easy camaraderie. "Well, I could quote you chapter and verse from a multitude of sources—a few of which might even be familiar to someone of Varnarite training—but take my word for it. As just one example, the Prophet Elisha prescribed baptism for purification. That's in the Second Book of Kings. And all four Gospels speak of John's form of baptism in almost exactly the same words, as a sign of inward repentance for the remission of sins."

" 'Repent, for the kingdom of heaven is at hand,' " Sylvan quoted promptly.

"Correct," Queron agreed. "A plus for Varnarite training! And

John said, 'I indeed baptize you with water; but one mightier than I cometh, the latchet of whose shoes I am not worthy to unloose; and he shall baptize you with the Holy Spirit and with fire.' "

"So we simply avoid baptizing with the Holy Spirit or fire?" Sylvan retorted with a wry smile.

Chuckling, Queron raised his cup in salute. "Something like that—though I'll grant you, it's a delicate balance. Somehow, we must go back to some of those earlier traditions and devise a form for our current situation that will be acceptable to the most conservative of the present Church hierarchy, yet still induce people to believe it might have some efficacious effect. Now perhaps you understand why the Lady Evaine spends so much time poring over her scrolls."

The conversation seemed to clear away whatever remaining doubts Sylvan might have had. Furthermore, once he understood the scope and magnitude of what they planned, he had new ideas to contribute, and readily offered to assume the primary Healer's role of working directly with Revan—for Tavis, with his missing hand, would be all too conspicuous among Revan's growing band of "disciples," if he tried to take too prominent a part.

"You do understand the risk you're taking, though?" Tavis asked him, when their new recruit had reiterated the offer for the third or fourth time. "Right now, you could still be free to go back to Trevalga with Gregory and Jesse. If you join up with Revan and me, and the regents' agents expose the baptizer cult for what it really is, you're likely to get killed with all the rest of us."

Sylvan only laughed. "Why should *you* have a monopoly on taking risks? Besides, I think I'll be in good company. There *are* causes worth dying for, Tavis."

The sentiment was one that Evaine shared, though in an additional context to the one occupying Tavis, Sylvan, and most of the rest of the sanctuary household. Once she was reassured that Sylvan's timely arrival had at least temporarily suspended any need to consider drafting little Tieg for their purposes—and that Tieg himself was not going to become a problem, by using his blocking talent for childish whims—Camber's daughter pursued her own purposes increasingly, though only Joram knew her true intent. Her first priority was to begin assembling the texts that might contain clues on how to bring their father back.

The documents stashed at Sheele seemed a logical place to start. She and Ansel had secreted a number of scrolls and other valuables under the flags of the Sheele Portal before fleeing to Saint Mary's at Christmas. These must be retrieved before Sheele's new lord took

formal possession, probably in the spring. Just now, Rhun of Horthness was occupied with the festivities of winter court at Valoret and
besotted with his new bride; Sheele was occupied by a small garrison
of knights hand picked by Rhun. Evaine felt it likely that such men
would not presume to usurp the apartments usually reserved for the
manor's lord—including Rhys' former study, where Sheele's Portal
lay.

She and Ansel went a week after his wounding, when he was
fully recovered, in those dark, quiet hours after midnight when men
sleep most soundly and the watch was likely to be least attentive.
As anticipated, the study was deserted. They had a tense moment
or two, when footsteps passing in the corridor outside paused and
someone tested the doorlatch; but no one entered. While Ansel pried
up the heavy flags forming the floor of the Portal, Evaine kept guard
by the door, scanning for danger and noting the changes already
wrought in the name of Sheele's new owner, missing the familiar
things that had made the study a refuge when she and Rhys had
called Sheele home.

Gone were most of the volumes of medical lore he had collected
over the years, especially the ones having to do with a Healer's
special abilities. Gone also was the entire section of Deryni litera-
ture—the scrolls of poetry, the histories, the collected poems of
Pargan Howiccan, the treasured scroll of the Lays of the Lord Llew-
ellyn. In fact, anything to do with Deryni at all had disappeared.
The ashes Evaine prodded in the cold fireplace grate bore mute evidence of the fate of at least one of the scrolls; and charred remnants
of a fine old leather binding brought tears to her eyes—for to burn
a book, any book, seemed to her one of the most heinous of sins.

But there was no time to linger or to nurse her grief and indignation. All too quickly, Ansel's soft hiss called her back to the Portal,
the flags now set back in place, his leather satchel bulging with the
booty he had recovered. The information she sifted from the salvaged
volumes kept her busy for the best part of several weeks, while the
others continued their indoctrination of Sylvan.

Other discoveries there were as well. Just after Candlemas,
Bishop Niallan reluctantly quit besieged Dhassa for good, bringing
with him several large boxes of scrolls and bound volumes of Deryni
lore that, if left behind, were sure to be consigned to the flames
when the regents' army took the city—which they were sure to do,
once the spring thaws came, if not before. Most of the manuscripts
were classic texts, already well known to Evaine, but one long, narrow chest contained a cache of documents dealing with the early
days of the Varnarite College at Grecotha. The bulk of them had to

do with the day to day running of the college, and were of only passing interest, but several purported to extract direct quotes by some of Grecotha's most famous lecturers, among them the great Orin himself. One lot, almost overlooked under a dusty sheet of parchment lining the bottom of the chest, bore a seal of dull green wax ringed with faded script.

"Look at this, Joram," Evaine said, holding the packet gingerly by the edges as she blew off a puff of dust. "I don't think it's been touched for years—maybe centuries."

Joram, who had been helping her catalog the new acquisitions, pushed aside his list and moved a rushlight closer as she laid the packet flat on the table.

"What's the seal? Can you tell?"

"I'm not sure. The lettering is odd looking—no, it's reversed. Maybe a coin impression."

Joram ran a finger over the seal and peered at it more closely.

"Hmmm, I think you're right. It looks like another of those old dower coins—like the one that led us to Cinhil so many years ago. If I still had access to the records at Saint Liam's, I could look it up."

"There's writing around the edge," Evaine replied, groping toward a pottery jar of dry brushes as she squinted at the tight, crabbed Latin. "Maybe that will give us a clue. Hand me one of those brushes, would you?"

While Joram watched, she carefully cleaned away another layer of dust, gradually bringing up two concentric rings of faded, spidery brown script.

Hoc est sig Jod Carneddi fil luc soc Orini mag. In hoc sig minist altissimi sacrat sum. Dmna ang ora pro me.

"Oh, my," Evaine breathed, when she had finished scanning the abbreviated Latin for the first time. " 'This is the sign or seal of'— it has to be 'Jodotha of Carnedd,' Joram! Yes, 'daughter of Light, colleague or associate of the Great, or the Master, or the Adept Orin'—that last depends on whether we read *mag* as *magni* or *magi*. Dear God, do you suppose *she* wrote this?"

Joram smiled. "So, you've finally gotten your hands on something from one of your childhood idols. I'm pleased for you."

"Not just for me," she replied, grinning as she bent to the rest of the translation. "Jodotha was a Healer, as Jerusha is going to be. What a legacy for my little girl!"

"You do realize, I hope, that it's probably a shopping list for the steward, telling him how many loaves to buy and how many hogshead of ale to brew for supper," Joram quipped, though his smile showed that he appreciated Evaine's excitement. "What does the rest say?"

"Joram MacRorie, it is *not* a shopping list!" she muttered, though she smiled as she said it. "Let's see. 'By this sign or seal, to the ministry, service of the Most High, I was'—*sacratus*—'bound? Wed?' "

"*Sacratus*—more in the sense of consecrated, I should think," Joram replied. "And what was that last bit? 'Lady of the Angels, pray for me.' Hmmm, was she a religious?"

Evaine rubbed at her temples in concentration. "Not that I know of—but then, I don't know that much about Orin, either. Not about his clerical status, at any rate."

"Well, let's see if what's inside sheds any light on the question," Joram said.

They tried to pry off the seal, hoping to preserve it intact, but the edge fractured very early on, so that Joram was forced to take the time to draw out the design—which was well, because the seal shattered utterly before they finally could free it enough to open the packet. The contents proved to be transcripts of several of Jodotha's lectures at the Varnarite College, plus an extract of a paper she had written on memory, bearing the sigil of the long-vanished Healer's Schola at Portree.

"But nothing here to suggest any clues for our actual research," Evaine said, crestfallen.

Later, on closer reading of the other texts, they found references to the Varnarite library and hints that some of the most valuable volumes might have been placed in a secret archive before the school moved to its new quarters in Grecotha, but no hint of its actual location ever materialized. Joram retraced the drawing of the seal on the other side of the parchment, so that they had a positive image of the coin used to imprint the original seal—which Queron was able to identify as belonging to the *Templum Archangelorum*, a long-destroyed abbey with ancient esoteric antecedents. But they still were not ready to confide in him the reason for their interest, so dared not question him too closely.

Meanwhile, Queron and Tavis continued to work with Sylvan, perfecting their blocking techniques until at last, toward the end of the second week in February, they finally felt ready to bring Revan in to give him final instruction on the specific form his incipient baptizer cult must take. Since Queron had been with Revan the previous month and would not be viewed as a complete stranger by Revan's Willimite brethren, he again was selected to make the contact.

"I worry about your going there blocked, though," Joram murmured, as he, Sylvan, Ansel, and Tavis gathered outside the sanctuary's Portal chamber to see Queron off. "Even on foot and in the snow, it shouldn't take you more than two days each way, starting from Caerrorie, but that's still a long time."

Queron smiled wanly, adjusting the worn but serviceable cloak they had given him—heathery grey tones, to cover a tunic and leggings of nondescript brown. His hair had been raggedly barbered just to cover his ears, all signs of tonsure or Gabrilite braid now obliterated, and his beard had come in wiry and dark.

"If they found me out, I'd be dead a long time, too," he reminded them. "But, don't worry. With any luck, I'll be back with our Revan in less than a week. In the meantime—" He eased to one knee expectantly. "—how about a blessing to speed me on my way, Father Joram? You surely don't want your Daniel to have to go among the lions unprotected."

Even Joram had to smile at that as he laid one hand lightly on Queron's head in benediction.

"May almighty God bless and protect you, dear brother, in the name of the Father, and of the Son, and of the Holy Spirit, Amen," he murmured, making the sign of the cross over Queron's head. "And may all the lions be asleep when you go into their den."

"Amen to that," Tavis said, moving in closer to take Queron's elbow as he rose. "And on that note, let's be about our business."

Tavis was dressed like Queron, for he would accompany the older Healer part of the way to Revan's camp before blocking his Deryni powers, but Ansel, already waiting in the Portal behind them, was clothed all in black, with a dagger at his waist. As the two Healers crowded into the Portal to either side of him, it was Ansel who took charge, closing a hand around each man's inside wrist. Almost as one, the Healers opened to him, allowing the control Ansel needed to take them through to a Portal neither of them had used before. A moment to steady the link, and Ansel was reaching out to warp the familiar energies, punching the power through, so that, in the space of a single heartbeat, they were no longer in the Michaeline sanctuary.

None of the three of them moved as Ansel released the link, all of them questing out with their minds in the darkness to test for danger. After a few seconds, Ansel conjured a small, dim sphere of handfire and crouched where he was, carefully scanning the floor of the corridor just outside the Portal. Dust lay undisturbed upon it, and he let out a tiny sigh as, rising, he willed his handfire to brighten.

"So far, so good," he whispered, stepping into the corridor as he continued to scan. "Thank God my ancestors thought to build a secondary Portal for Caerrorie. No one's been here since I left it, after my brother died."

He led them into the corridor at that, heading downhill, pointing out several branching tunnels and identifying their destinations until, at length, they came to a wall of blank stone.

"The wood is on the other side of this," he told them, setting his hand against the counterweight. "A few dozen paces straight ahead you'll pick up a game trail that will lead you directly to the road. Make a mental note, so you'll be able to find it again, Queron, because you'll be coming back without me or Tavis. You should try to bring Revan in this way, but if, for any reason, it doesn't look safe, you can always try coming through the village church. Getting into the sacristy might be tricky, but that tunnel is an even more direct route back to the Portal."

"I'll be there," Queron muttered. "Just make certain *you* are. With my powers still blocked, a Portal won't do me a bit of good if you aren't around."

Ansel smiled. "I shall *marry* that Portal until you turn up safe. Seriously, it should take you at least four days to make the round trip, but I'll wait here for two hours at midnight every day for the first three, just in case anything goes wrong—God forbid. And of course, I'll be here constantly thereafter. Any other questions?"

"I think it's a little late for questions," Tavis replied with a grin. "Take care, Ansel. We'll see you in a few days."

When Ansel had seen them safely on, he waited an hour to be sure they would not come back immediately, spent another hour checking the other tunnels to be sure they had not been breached, then returned via the Portal to the Michaeline sanctuary. Sylvan was waiting just outside the Portal chamber, shivering in too thin a mantle.

"Are they safe?" he asked.

Ansel smiled, far more used to intrigue than the older man.

"As safe as we can hope for, this early in the operation. Go get some sleep, Sylvan. There's nothing you can do for now."

The next days passed uneventfully for those at the haven, though Sylvan fretted increasingly as the passage of time made danger more likely for the two missing Healers. He found it difficult to concentrate on his training; and his agitation was passed on to his teachers,

who were no less concerned for Tavis and Queron—simply more
used to coping with this kind of stress.

Javan, too, fretted in Valoret, though for different reasons, becoming more and more anxious as the time approached for the departure of the Court to Rhemuth. The fact that his Deryni allies
had not yet discovered a new way to communicate with him was
unnerving, for he had much to tell them. Besides the obvious news
of the founding of the *Custodes*, and the increasingly restrictive
legislation being generated by the regents' new religious advisors,
Javan himself had new developments to report. Two days before the
scheduled departure from Valoret, during a practice session at the
archery butts, he unexpectedly found himself almost alone with his
elder brother, for the first time in many, many weeks. Rhys Michael
had gone far downrange to retrieve arrows with Cathan and another
junior squire, and the weapons master, Sir Radan, had been called
aside by one of the officers of the Royal Haldane Archer Corps, well
out of sight and earshot.

It was not an ideal opportunity, but it was the best one Javan
was likely to have for some time. Trying to read Alroy here in the
open would be tricky—and God help him, if Alroy's command of
his powers was greater than anyone supposed—but Javan thought
he could do it. He had even hit on the perfect opening gambit, as
he watched Rhys Michael and the squires running toward the straw-
stuffed targets.

"You're shooting well this morning," he said to Alroy, propping
his bow against a rest. "Isn't that vambrace bothering you, though?
It looks a little loose at the wrist."

Even as Alroy made vague noises of disagreement, turning the
leather-bound wrist to demonstrate that it was fine, Javan caught
the hand and slipped his fingers between leather and flesh, ostensibly
checking the adjustment but also making the direct physical contact
he needed to try a probe.

"Here, let me see if I can improve things."

In that same instant, he projected a mental command for Alroy
to sleep—and was astonished when the king's eyelids fluttered and
then closed, the royal breath exhaling in a soft sigh.

Remain standing! Javan sent, tightening his hold as Alroy
swayed a little on his feet. *Open your eyes, but remain deep asleep.
Just watch my fingers. Do not resist. There is no danger.*

Immediately Alroy steadied and opened his eyes, at once bending
his head to watch Javan fiddle with a vambrace buckle.

No time for lengthy preparations. Javan must be in and out in a
few seconds, before Rhys Michael and the squires finished picking

up the arrows—and before Sir Radan returned from his consultation, which could happen even sooner.

Punching past a lethargy that had far more to do with the regents' constant sedation than with any compulsion Javan had set, Javan dipped deep into his brother's mind, shocked to find that Alroy had only the most rudimentary of shields. Nor could he detect any hint of the power potential he sensed increasingly in himself and which should have been far more potent in an anointed king—nor any awareness or will to resist what was being done to him by the regents.

You will only remember me adjusting your vambrace, he ordered, withdrawing all at once as he suddenly realized Sir Radan was fast approaching. "There! I think that's got it," he said aloud.

Alroy turned the vambrace to and fro, flexing his wrist experimentally as Radan drew up to look at them curiously.

"Yes, that does seem better," the king agreed. "Thank you." The smile he flashed his brother was open and unaccusing, but pinched with the old fatigue and tension. "Ah, Radan, do you think I'll ever be the archer Javan is?"

"Of course you will, Sire." Muttering, Radan picked up Alroy's bow and put it in his hand. "You just need more practice. You lads, hurry up with those arrows!"

I had an anxious moment or two, but I'm certain no one detected a thing, Javan wrote that afternoon, when his squire thought he was napping, adding to the report he had been compiling for nearly a week now. *He hasn't much in the way of shields, though. Nor does he seem at all aware of the power potential you say all three of us should carry. Maybe it's because the regents keep him full of sedatives all the time. That can't be good for him.*

He went on for several more paragraphs, expressing his concern for his brother's general health and bringing the final length of the report to three closely crabbed pages. He would have continued except that he felt he dared not make the packet any thicker than it was already going to be. After rereading what he had written, he sanded the final lines to finish drying them, then twice folded the three sheets together into thirds, sealing the packet shut with his signet pressed to a wafer of crimson wax. He debated whether he should leave it unaddressed, but then went ahead and inscribed Tavis' name on the outside—for that would be no more damning than what was inside, if he was caught before he could deliver it.

After that, he slipped it inside the breast of his outer tunic, next to his heart, and went out into the receiving room that adjoined his sleeping chamber, yawning. Charlan and Tomais, Rhys Michael's senior squire, were playing at Cardounet over near the fire, but both rose as the prince entered.

"Ah, who's winning?" Javan asked, coming over to survey the board. "Charlan, I think he's trouncing you."

Sheepishly, Charlan put down the piece he had been about to move. The men were carved of ebony and ivory, the board inlaid with light and dark woods. The set once had been the property of Javan's father.

"Well, then, your Highness, I'd thought to *let* him win this time, he usually does so badly!"

Javan smiled. "Is that true, Tomais?"

The dark-haired squire grinned. "He wasn't saying that just a while ago, your Highness, when I captured his war duke."

"I see." Javan surveyed the board again, then reached for a warm, fur-lined cloak he had left draped over a stool beside the table. "Well, I hate to spoil your fun, Tomais, but I'm afraid you'll have to find another opponent. Charlan, I thought we'd go to Vespers in the cathedral this afternoon. We may not get another chance for a while, since we're leaving for Rhemuth the day after tomorrow."

It was clear from Charlan's expression that Vespers at the cathedral was not high on his list of priorities, for snow was coming down steadily outside, but he nodded amiably enough, tipping over his priest-king in surrender before helping Javan with his cloak. Javan had already drawn on heavier boots than his usual wont, as well as donning an extra tunic, and waited patiently while Charlan also changed into more suitable attire for venturing outside.

They arrived at the cathedral early for Vespers, though the light was fast failing because of the snow. Servers were already lighting the candles as Javan and Charlan slipped into their places in the royal stall, close up beside the altar on the Gospel side. What praying Javan did, while they waited for the service to begin, was directed more toward the success of his plans than spiritual enlightenment, but he was heartened to see that at least a part of his prayer had been answered when the elderly and kind Father Stephen entered with the choir to conduct the service. Javan paid little attention to the actual scriptures sung that evening, but he excused himself as soon as the service was over to follow the old priest into the sacristy.

"I'd like Father Stephen to hear my confession," he told Charlan. "Wait here. I shan't be long."

The old priest was putting his surplice away in a vestment press when Javan eased open the door of the sacristy, and looked up in surprise as the prince entered.

"Your Highness. You really shouldn't be here, you know."

Javan ducked his head contritely, trying what he hoped was one of his more disarming expressions. "We shall be leaving Valoret in a few days, Father, and I—wanted a chance to say good-bye."

The priest's face immediately softened. "Oh. That's right. I had nearly forgotten. Why, that's very kind of you, my boy. I'm very touched that you should think of a humble priest like myself."

"Well, you have given me some very moving spiritual direction," Javan murmured, trying to edge a little closer to the part of the Kheldish carpet that Tavis had told him once marked the room's Portal. "In fact, I was hoping you might hear my confession one last time, before I go."

"Oh." The priest seemed quite taken aback. "Well, of course, my son, if you wish it," he murmured. "But—would your Highness not prefer to go out to one of the confessionals?"

"Oh, no," Javan replied, gesturing toward the little vesting altar, with its tabernacle and Presence lamp. "In here, He is closer by, to give me strength while I unburden my soul. I pray you, let me kneel here at your feet, to receive your shriving this last time."

"Ah. Very well, then."

As the priest turned to rummage in the press for a stole, Javan cast out with his mind, searching for the Portal, but he had found nothing by the time Father Stephen turned back to him, setting a stole of purple silk around his shoulders.

"Come here, then, my son," Father Stephen beckoned, as he settled himself on a stool beside the press.

Dutifully folding his hands, Javan came to him, knowing that he must try a desperate measure if he hoped to find what he was looking for. He had controlled the guard Norris; he had read his own brother without his knowledge. Now he must try to put this old priest to sleep, so he could pursue his own investigations.

He made himself stumble as he went to kneel before Stephen, so that it was a completely natural thing to catch himself on the hands the priest automatically raised to steady him. At the same time, as the contact was made, he sent his command racing across the link, to *sleep!*

Stephen's eyelids fluttered and closed even as his breath, drawn to caution Javan not to fall, exhaled in a slow, relaxed sigh and the priest subsided on the stool, head bowing onto his chest.

Good man, Javan breathed. *Sleep deep now, even as I release your hands, and do not stir until I command it.*

The old man did not move as Javan rose, and remained sunk deep in slumber as Javan dared to step back from him a few paces.

Success! He had done it! He had put Stephen to sleep, at least.

Whether he would be able to revive him without any memory of the incident was another story, but Javan was sure he could do that, too. Drawing a deep breath, he darted back to the sacristy door and locked it, already framing a plausible explanation, should anyone try to enter, then returned to the squared design on the carpet. Kneeling, he turned back the edge to expose the stone flooring underneath, not at all surprised to see that the square of the carpet no longer coincided with the squared design he could make out in the stones themselves. The carpet must have gotten turned, when it was put back down, after Bishop Kai allegedly destroyed the Portal.

Unfortunately, "allegedly" no longer seemed to be the operative descriptor, for when Javan laid one hand on the square and the other on the stones outside its boundaries, he could feel a difference between the two; but what he felt from the square was not the distinctive tingle of an active Portal, but a dull, buzzing sensation that jangled his nerves after only a few seconds.

Blast! Then, Kai Descantor *had* destroyed the Portal. Which meant that, if Javan hoped to deliver his report, he must gain access to the one in Hubert's quarters. He had tried not even to think about that possibility, but he did have at least a ghost of a plan, loath though he was to try it.

But he could do nothing here. And certainly, he could do nothing if he did not get Father Stephen back to normal and none the wiser for his experience.

Sighing softly, Javan folded the carpet back into place, crept quietly to the door to listen carefully for a moment before unlocking it, then tip-toed back to the dozing priest to kneel again at his feet, setting his hands on Stephen's as he had when he pretended to catch himself. He extended his controls again then, blurring the priest's memory just a little—for only a hundred heartbeats or less had passed while he made his inspection—and pressed hard on Stephen's hands as he released him from sleep, at the same time wobbling a little on his knees.

"Ah, your pardon, Father! Sometimes my foot gives way, especially when it's cold."

"Oh, does it pain you, my son?" Stephen said, leaning out to look at the foot in question. "I'm sorry to hear that. It must be very vexing."

Javan dared to smile, fairly certain now that the priest had noticed nothing. "I try not to complain, Father. It is a cross I must bear, so I try to endure it as cheerfully as I may. In due time, perhaps God will make its purpose known to me."

"In due time, I am certain He shall," Stephen agreed. "But, you wished to confess, my son. Shall we proceed?"

"Certainly, Father." Javan bowed his head and signed himself as he began the ritual exchange of phrases with the priest. "Bless me, for I have sinned. It has been a week since my last confession. These are my sins."

In truth, it had been only a few days since his last confession, and he dared not confess certain things that he now did regularly—like what he had just done to Father Stephen himself—but he was able to produce enough petty failings and general contrition to satisfy the priest. When they had finished, Javan took his leave and went out into the choir again to kneel before the High Altar, lifting his eyes to the *Christus* there while he recited the few prayers that Father Stephen had assigned him as penance.

After that, he bowed his head to rest on his folded hands, elbows propped on the altar rail, and considered how he was going to get into Hubert's apartments tonight—for tonight it must be, since tomorrow would be a flurry of activity in preparation for the next day's departure. He heard Charlan shift, back in the choir stall where he had left him, but the squire knew better than to interrupt his young master at prayer. Besides, what possible harm could there be in kneeling before the High Altar?

Nearly an hour later, with the snow coming down even harder outside and the high windows black beyond their stained glass, Javan still had not moved, though he had begun to think of a plan. He ignored Charlan's increasing coughs and shifts of position as well as the excruciating pain in his knees from kneeling on the unpadded marble of the altar step, waiting for footsteps. Very shortly, his patience was rewarded when one of the cathedral canons entered through a side door near the south transept, intending to close up for the evening. The canon might not have recognized Javan immediately, muffled all in greys and furs, black hair all but invisible in the light of votives only, but Charlan's crimson Haldane livery was distinctive, even muffled under his black cloak. The other figure kneeling closer to the altar could only be one of the royal princes, and the canon could guess which one.

"Your Highness, it's getting very late," he murmured, resting a hand on the altar rail as he leaned close to Javan's right ear. "In fact, I'm not even sure you can get back to the castle, it's snowing so hard."

Which was exactly what Javan had hoped to hear. Lifting his head, he turned a tear-streaked face toward the priest. He had worked hard to produce the tears while he knelt there, thinking back to all the saddest things he could, and the effort was rewarded by the look of dismay on the priest's face. Now, to get the man on his side.

"Your Highness, is anything wrong?" the priest whispered.

Swallowing visibly, Javan made a point of turning his face back to the altar. "I—hoped I might stay here all night, Father," he whispered. "I—have the feeling that God is trying to tell me something, only I—I don't know what it is. It's important, though. I know it is! And just now, I felt as if I were on the verge of a major revelation."

The announcement clearly took the priest by surprise, orders warring with concern for a young man obviously greatly moved.

"Well, I—really don't think you can stay here, your Highness," he murmured. "The cathedral is normally closed at this hour to all except the Night Offices of the cathedral chapter. Besides that, I—don't think the regents would approve of your staying out all night."

Snuffling, Javan looked back over his shoulder at the rose window in the west wall. He could hear the wind whining in the doors and the snow hitting the glass; inwardly he rejoiced that the weather was worsening by the minute.

"I've kept all night vigils before, Father, in the Chapel Royal," he murmured, glancing back searchingly at the uneasy priest and knowing he was going to have to help things along just a little. "I—you mustn't tell anyone, but I've been thinking about a religious vocation." He seized the priest's hand with both of his and bowed his head over it, at the same time sending subtle encouragement for the man to help him.

"I don't know what to do, Father. Right now, I'm torn between my duty to my House and what I think God is trying to tell me. How did you know, Father? How does anyone know what God intends for him?"

He had kept sending his suggestion as he spoke and he knew he was succeeding when the priest, tears in his eyes, gently rested his free hand on Javan's head, tremblingly stroking the raven hair.

"My dear, dear boy," the priest murmured. "I had no idea. Does the archbishop know about this?"

Snuffling again, and feeling vaguely hypocritical—for he did not feel any inclination whatever toward the religious life—Javan nodded. "He knows a little," he whispered. "And I'm sure he wouldn't disapprove. Maybe—maybe I could go and pray in his Grace's chapel tonight, if you're worried about me staying here. I can't imagine that he would mind, and I'd certainly be safe enough."

He felt relief flood through the priest, at being offered so easy a solution to an otherwise awkward problem, and soon he was following the man through the maze of covered passageways that led out along the cathedral yard and into the complex of the archbishop's palace, Charlan walking resignedly behind—for Javan had, indeed, kept all night vigils before, especially in the last few weeks, already laying the groundwork for just such a mad scheme as he now sought to employ.

CHAPTER FIFTEEN

He discovereth deep things out of darkness.
—Job 12:22

Simply gaining access to Archbishop Hubert's Portal was not Javan's real problem, of course. He was certain he could contrive some way to do that, if simple escape were his only aim.

Getting to the Portal *secretly*, however, using it to deliver his report, and then getting back out again, with no one the wiser, was another story entirely. Javan had no clear idea just how he was going to accomplish all that, but being admitted to the archbishop's chapel, which he understood to be on the floor below the one where Hubert's quarters lay, at least seemed like a good start.

It was a very grand chapel, too, for all that it was much smaller than Javan had expected. Javan's jaw dropped as his escorting priest, whose name was Father Aloysius, threw open the gilded double doors and stood aside for him and Charlan to enter.

Javan had never seen such a room, all floored and walled and vaulted with some white stone that glittered slightly in the light of dozens of vigil candles set before a life-sized statue of the Virgin, just to the left of the altar. Behind the altar, a carved frieze of the same stone, some of it gilded, seemed to explode with angels bearing trumpets and thuribles and palm branches, all hovering above the splendid jewelled tabernacle that stood beneath an equally ornate Presence lamp. And the ceiling—

"I'll tell the chamberlain you're here, your Highness," Father Aloysius told him nervously. "He'll have a messenger sent up to the castle, so no one will worry. And did you wish to see the arch-

163

bishop, or would you rather just be left alone? I believe His Grace may be entertaining the Vicar General of the *Custodes Fidei* to dinner this evening."

"Oh, you needn't disturb His Grace," Javan replied, lowering his eyes in some alarm. And he *certainly* had no wish to face the *Custodes'* Vicar General tonight. "I don't mean to put anyone out. Besides, I don't think this is really anything that anyone else can help me with. I need to work it out alone. I—feel that if I can just have this quiet time, maybe—I don't know. It's all so very confusing, Father."

"I know, my son," the priest whispered. He started to touch the prince's bowed head for comfort, as he might have done for any lesser boy, but then thought better of it and merely made the sign of the cross above him. "God bless you in your quest, Prince Javan."

"Thank you, Father."

When the man had gone, Javan glanced sheepishly at Charlan, who was standing by the closed doors with a look of patient forbearance on his handsome face.

"Poor Charlan," Javan said with a slightly embarrassed smile. "All this excessive kneeling doesn't mean a great deal to you, does it, yet you endure it for my sake, when you'd far rather be back in your bed, especially on a night like this."

Charlan shrugged deprecatingly and returned the smile. "It's my honor to serve you, your Highness. If it pleases you to spend the night in prayer, then I am proud to watch with you."

"Truly?"

"Truly, my lord."

Javan smiled and shook his head, briefly resting a hand on one of Charlan's wrists in a gesture both comradely and compelling. "Well, I can't fault your loyalty. But do keep your watch here by the door, where you can at least sit for part of the time. And feel free to doze, if you like. I have some heaven-storming to do, but there's no reason you should miss an entire night's sleep."

He turned to move farther into the chapel at that, but not before he saw Charlan covering an enormous yawn with one hand as he sat down on a bench set into a niche to the right of the doors.

Good. The yawn confirmed that the squire was now primed to do Javan's bidding without question, and could be used with impunity to further Javan's plan—once he figured out what that plan was.

But for now, before he could even think about actually doing anything else, Javan had to make sure his physical scenario was plausible, if anyone should come in. He bowed his head as he made his reverence before the altar, kneeling on the hard sleekness of the bottom altar step rather than at the single *prie-dieu*, for that surely must be Hubert's. There was no altar rail to lean on, so he sank back on his heels and folded his hands in his lap, closing his eyes to the glitter of the chapel while he tried to think.

Timing was his main consideration from now on. If Hubert was entertaining the new Vicar General of the *Custodes*, that should mean that he would be late returning to his quarters—though how late was anyone's guess. So Javan dared not wait *too* long.

But nor dared he begin his venture too early, either, for the archbishop's household would still be about until at least after Compline, even if their master was otherwise occupied. That Office must be nearly upon him by now, for it normally fell some three hours after Vespers, at least half of which time Javan had spent in the cathedral with Father Stephen and after. He wondered, as he strained his ears for some faint echo of a Compline bell, whether they would sing it here or in some other chapel—for he gathered that there were several within the precincts of the archbishop's palace. This one did not seem large enough for the entire episcopal household. Nor was it really set up for other than private meditations and celebrations of Mass. He hoped it would not be here, for he did not want to endure more questioning about the vocation he knew he did not have. But he would submit with good grace, if he had to.

Meanwhile, Charlan already had begun to snore softly behind him, chin resting on his chest above folded arms, and the chapel seemed secure. Later, Javan would try to check outside and figure out which way he had to go to find Hubert's apartments. For now, he would try to get his thoughts in order, and plan what he would do if Hubert did or did not come in to question him.

Nor did he have long to wait for a resolution to that set of options. Though no one came to the chapel in response to the Compline bells that soon sounded, the doors did open about half an hour later, at about the time the office would have been over. Javan started at the sound, turning to look as he also heard Charlan shuffling to his feet with a murmured apology. To his consternation, but no real surprise, not only Archbishop Hubert but also Paulin of Ramos were entering the chapel. Paulin showed his usual sour expression, but the archbishop's pink face was wreathed with smiles.

"Why, Prince Javan, how pleasant to see you. And why are you kneeling on the cold, hard floor, dear boy? You're quite welcome to use my *prie-dieu*."

Javan rose as the archbishop approached, suddenly certain of the suggestion he would try to plant in Hubert's mind as he kissed the archbishop's ring. Again he used the ruse of pretending to stagger a little on his lame foot, catching himself on Hubert's hand, to prolong the contact.

"Your Grace," he murmured. "I'm very sorry to have interrupted your evening. I only wanted to keep a vigil, and Father Aloysius didn't think the cathedral was appropriate."

"Hmmm, yes," Hubert replied. "And he did right not to send you back to the castle in this storm. You're certainly most welcome to keep your vigil here." He smiled wider. "Am I to understand that a vocation is making itself known?"

Javan lowered his eyes. "Well, I—I'm not certain, your Grace. That's what I have to find out."

"Would it help to talk about it?" Hubert offered. "I'm sure you must know that I've given spiritual direction to many young priests."

"I—think that might be premature, your Grace," Javan replied carefully. "I wouldn't want to waste your time, especially when you have a guest."

"Oh, it would hardly be a waste of time, your Highness. I'm sure that Father General would be as delighted as I if you were to discover that you have a vocation like your dear father—God rest his soul. But I won't press the issue. It's an important decision, and these things take time to discover. I'll leave instructions that you're not to be disturbed for the night. And if you *should* feel a need for counsel, my quarters are just down the corridor. You have only to ask."

Javan could hardly believe his good fortune, for not only had Hubert responded to the suggestion to leave Javan alone for the night, but this chapel was not the one Javan had thought. His quick probe, as he kissed the archbishop's hand again in farewell, caught a clear picture of the archbishop's apartments, but three doors down—and his ability to make the probe undetected reassured him that he could probably deal with Hubert if he were discovered, later in the night.

His heart was pounding with excitement as he made the expected responses to the archbishop's parting blessing, but he forced himself to pretend that nothing was amiss, sinking down piously on the *prie-dieu* before Hubert and Paulin had even gotten through the doors, to be certain that picture was etched in Hubert's memory—for he planned to leave Charlan kneeling here in his master's cloak, when he eventually went out to visit Hubert's quarters, just in case anyone should glance inside and expect to see him.

He agonized for the next half hour, wondering how long Hubert would stay out with Paulin. Should he try to go soon, hoping to be in and out before Hubert returned, or wait until he had a fair expectation that Hubert slept, and try to sneak in and out under the archbishop's nose? Either option had risks that Javan would as soon avoid, but he was going to have to do *something*, if he had any hope of delivering his report.

And what if, overcoming the risks, he succeeded in finding the Portal in Hubert's quarters and then discovered that he could not operate it after all? He had been making all his plans under the assumption that he *could*, but the fact of the matter was that he never had done it all on his own. Tavis had expressed faith that Javan was about ready to try it, and Javan *thought* he understood how it was done, from watching Tavis—but what if the theory and the practice were miles apart?

He sighed and rubbed his hands across his face, glancing up at the splendor of the altar without really seeing it. He must not allow himself to get bogged down in doubts or he would end up doing nothing—which might be best in the long run, a more cautious part of him counseled. It was what Tavis himself would probably advise, reckoning no report worth the risk Javan was preparing to take.

But Javan was convinced that his information was vital. Furthermore, with the collapse of his communication network with his Deryni allies, he was foundering in uncertainty. He *had* to know how they were faring—or at least let them know how he was faring. Caution had no chance in the face of youthful zeal.

And so, very shortly, Javan went quietly to the back of the chapel, reaching the dozing Charlan just as the squire was startling out of sleep at the approach of his master.

"Go back to sleep, Charlan," Javan commanded, reinforcing the order with a hand across the squire's eyes as Charlan wavered, half in and half out of his seat, and then subsided. "I want you to put on my cloak and go up to the *prie-dieu*. Don't stir for anyone." While he guided Charlan to stand, he worked the clasp of his cloak with his free hand. "You'll remember none of this. Just go up and kneel by the altar. Put the hood up."

He helped Charlan pull it forward as the squire adjusted the cloak over his own, walking with him then to see him safely ensconced at the *prie-dieu*. When he had finished, he stepped back to look at Charlan. From behind, hunched over the *prie-dieu* and swathed in Javan's grey-fur cloak, Javan was sure no one could tell the difference. He doubted anyone would look in, after Hubert had given orders, but if they did, the sight of anyone bowed in such intense meditation should deter any further intrusion. He drew a deep breath as he set his hands on the door latches, listening to the silence outside for a dozen heartbeats before he dared to turn the handles and slowly ease one door ajar.

Nothing moved in the corridor outside. Torches in cressets spaced along the long, wood-panelled walls splashed dull pools of firelight along the stone flags, but no one seemed to be lurking in the shadows. By the sounds drifting up a stairwell at the end of the corridor, which must lead down to the part of the palace Javan had thought he was in, initially, he judged that Hubert's dinner for Paulin was still in progress—which should keep both Hubert and most of the rest of the staff occupied for at least a little while yet. And Javan had already decided that he was looking for a garderobe, if anyone should come upon him—an excuse that should save him, up until the very moment he set his hand on Hubert's door.

And if there was a servant *inside*, and Hubert not yet there, Javan could always say that the archbishop had invited him—which even Hubert would verify. But it would all be so much simpler, if no one was there at all!

He forced himself to walk casually as he headed in the direction of Hubert's door. He had not seen it when Father Aloysius brought him in, because it lay just around a corner, beyond the chapel. But as Javan turned that corner, pretending to inspect the other doors to either side, there was no mistaking which one was Hubert's. The wide architrave surrounding it was carved and gilded, with cherubim set at the corners and the symbols of the four evangelists ranged across the lintel. The doorjambs bore full-sized croziers carved in deep relief. The door itself displayed the full heraldic achievement of Hubert MacInnis, second son of the Baron of Marlor, his family arms impaled with those of the See of Valoret and the whole surmounted by the miter and mantling of an archbishop.

Javan walked on past it the first time, straining his ears and his powers for any hint of someone within, continuing on to the next corridor intersection to get his bearings before heading back. He did not *think* there was anyone inside, but now that he was about to run out of plausible excuses, if he was caught, he thought briefly of giving it all up.

But only briefly. For when he slipped his hand inside his tunic to feel the sealed packet of his report, still nestled next to his heart, the touch brought back all the urgency of what so many others had risked, many of them for *him*, and he knew he must put his own fears aside and proceed.

To his relief, no one responded when he tapped lightly on the door. He tapped again harder, and when still no one responded, he gently tried the latch—and found, to his utter relief, that the door was not locked. And why should it be, for who would dare to enter the archbishop's apartments without permission?

Hardly daring to breathe, Javan slipped inside and glanced around quickly, flattening himself against the wall beside the door. The anteroom into which he had entered was dimly lit by a vigil lamp burning beneath a painted icon of Saint Sebastian, its reddish gleam picking out the gilt on the arrows piercing the martyr's body—all too vivid a reminder of his own fate, if he was caught, figuratively, if not literally. Beyond, another door standing slightly ajar led into a larger room furnished with several comfortable-looking chairs piled with cushions and furs, grouped around a large, stone-manteled fireplace, the floor before it covered with a dark-patterned carpet and more furs. Javan inspected the room as he entered, looking for another door or curtained opening that might conceal the oratory, but he remembered that Tavis had said it opened off the sleeping chamber—and a closed door, just to the right of the fireplace, must lead to that.

Now he was really getting daring, left with no possible explanation, once he went into Hubert's bedroom. Cautiously he tried that door, holding his breath as the latch moved beneath his hand and the door swung silently inward. At least it did not creak. He caught the gleam of another votive light off to the right, which must certainly be the oratory; but just before he was able to close the door behind him, he heard someone come into the anteroom from the corridor outside, closing the door with no attempt to be quiet.

Good God, it was either Hubert or a servant, and either way, someone was almost certain to come where Javan was!

In an instant that seemed like eternity, he scanned the room. Hiding in the oratory was his first thought, but that was out of the question because the curtains across its entrance were open. If Hubert decided to pray before retiring—

And there was not enough light to see what other hiding places the room might afford—and which would continue to offer hiding, once the candles were lit. The only thing Javan could make out for certain was the location of the great state bed, directly across from the still partially opened door, its vast canopy and hangings looming dark and forbidding in the gloom.

That was all too obvious a possibility, and truly audacious, but as Javan heard footsteps passing from the anteroom into the one with the fireplace, panic triumphed over reason, and he darted to the bed's far side, there to drop to his belly and slither underneath as quickly as he dared, even as he realized he *could* have gone into the oratory, and simply said he was waiting there for Hubert, at the archbishop's invitation. He prayed that whoever had just come in would not notice that the bedroom door was not closed all the way.

His heart was hammering as he inched his way as close toward the head of the bed as he could get, curling up in a tight, miserable ball. The bed was high enough that he could lie on his side, his back hard against the wall, but it was also high enough that someone just might think to look under it, before the archbishop mounted the steps on the bed's other side to get into it.

Javan would not be anything but dead if that happened, for he could offer no excuse for being found here. And the packet he carried next to his breast would surely seal his fate.

He tried to make himself consider options as he lay there in the dark, certain that anyone who came in now would instantly hear his heart pounding and yank him from his hiding place. Numb with terror, he forced himself to take deep, careful breaths and slow his racing pulse. Gradually the booming in his ears receded until he could pick out the faint, desultory sounds of someone moving around in the next room.

Brighter light began to spill through the crack of the partially open door. Soon the scent of woodsmoke and the crackle of a good fire underscored Javan's realization that a servant must be responsible, making things ready for the master's return. Briefly the prince considered trying to make a dash for the oratory, so near and yet so far away, in hopes that he might yet use his excuse of waiting there for Hubert. But he gave up that idea immediately as stronger light approached the partly open doorway and then a hand pushed it open, sandalled feet below a black monastic robe carrying the light around the room to light several candles in wall sconces and on the chest to the right of the great bed.

Javan tried to breathe very, very softly as he watched the feet move back and forth, their owner laying out night robes and water for washing up and even slippers, just beside the bed steps, so close that Javan could have reached out and touched them. He wondered briefly whether contact with the man's foot would be sufficient to let him extend control and concluded that it probably would. He decided not to try it, though, not knowing when Hubert might show up to interrupt.

The decision was a prudent one, for Hubert returned very shortly in the company of someone who lingered long enough in the outer chamber to have a cup of wine before taking his leave. The monk working in the sleeping chamber went out to serve them, but he left the connecting door open and continued to move back and forth between the two rooms, finishing up his chores. Javan never did learn who the visitor was, but he heard his own name mentioned several times. Nor did he catch the gist of what else they were discussing, though at least their tone was positive.

All of which was very fine, but then the visitor left. Javan spent the next half hour or so in sheer, quaking terror, while Hubert padded around the sleeping chamber, getting ready for bed. After the monk had assisted him from canonicals to nightrobes and left with his blessing, Javan had to watch the fat feet pacing back and forth in their embroidered slippers, their owner pausing from time to time to gaze out at the snowfall while he had another cup of wine. Javan approved of the wine, for it increased the chances that Hubert would sleep deeply when he eventually did go to sleep, but *when was he going to do it?*

Apparently, not for a while, Javan soon realized. Hubert had another cup of wine—or perhaps it was water; Javan could not tell from under the bed. Then he had to use the garderobe. Then he came out to kneel in the oratory for a little while.

Finally he rose and came back into the room, drawing the curtains before the oratory and extinguishing the candles in the wall sconces, and Javan thought he might be going to bed at last. Hubert did get into bed, dangerously straining the lattice of ropes that supported the mattress so close over Javan's head. But then he took up a scroll from the chest beside the bed, where a candle still burned, and began to read.

The situation was fast growing intolerable. Javan now believed he was reasonably safe from discovery here under the bed—and eventually, Hubert *would* fall asleep—but he was beginning to worry about Charlan, left waiting in the chapel. The squire would stay indefinitely the way Javan had left him, but what if someone tried to speak to him? Javan had never planned to be gone this long.

So he must move things along. With the curtains now closed across the oratory, Javan felt reasonably certain it was safe to try using the Portal—once Hubert was asleep. But could he somehow help Hubert along? He dared not touch the archbishop directly, so long as there were signs that he was still awake—as occasional rustlings of the scroll periodically attested—but perhaps he could encourage Hubert to sleep without actually having to touch him. Javan knew that trained Deryni could communicate at a distance with individuals whose minds they already knew; and they could certainly Truth-Read without touching someone, as he himself could do. And earlier, Hubert had responded to his suggestion that no one should disturb him. If he could combine all those principles . . .

Slowly, carefully, he shifted until he could lay his right hand flat against the underside of the mattress just above his head, visualizing Hubert's bulk only a double handspan above it. Closing his eyes, he gathered all his concentration, the way Tavis had taught him, and began sending the soft, gentle command to *sleep*. He synchronized his breathing with Hubert's, having to speed his own up considerably in the beginning; but when he began to slow his, Hubert's followed.

So sleepy, so drowsy, Javan continued to send, as he slowed the breathing yet again, certain now that he was having an effect.

After another minute or so, his labors were rewarded. As he drew a deeper breath, letting it out with a soft sigh, Hubert's sigh was deeper still, the scroll slowly slipping from his hands and sliding, first to the bed-steps, then softly onto the carpet beneath, to roll back on itself. Javan did not falter in his concentration, lest the sound should have jarred Hubert from his dozing—for if Hubert bent down to retrieve it, he might see the huddled form lurking under his bed—but the archbishop did not move.

After another deep sigh and the alarming vibration of the bed moving above him, Javan realized that Hubert was simply settling in, slipping ever deeper into sleep. Liquid-sounding snores soon confirmed it. A few seconds later, Javan was easing out from under the other side of the bed to peer gingerly up over the edge, hardly able to believe his good fortune.

Hubert was definitely asleep. His ponderous bulk was propped up on half a dozen fat pillows, his head tipped back so that his jaw fell slack, and Javan almost had to laugh at the ridiculous, fur-lined nightcap covering the archbishop's head and ears. Ridiculous, but it also would help to muffle any inadvertent sound Javan might make in the course of his escape.

And there was more that might be done to ensure that escape, first to the Portal and then from the room. Now confident that Hubert would respond, Javan slowly reached across to touch his fingertips to the archbishop's forehead, at the same time commanding even deeper sleep and an opening to Javan's will. Hubert moaned softly, but he did not stir, and Javan knew he had him. Reinforcing the command, he made the suggestion that the archbishop should settle into a more comfortable position for sleeping, maintaining contact while the man obeyed. Hubert groaned and shifted farther under the sleeping furs, burrowing into his pile of pillows, then was still, his mind blank and receptive.

Now remain sleeping until I tell you otherwise, Javan sent. And as he cautiously drew back his hand, Hubert did not stir.

Excellent! This was even better than Javan had dreamed and well worth the anxiety he had endured to reach this point. Touching one hand to the breast of his tunic to confirm that his report was still in place, he headed across the room and slipped between the heavy curtains hiding the little oratory. After all the difficulties he had already overcome, he was all prepared to have to search for the Portal, but its intact presence blazed up in his heightened senses like a warming flame, directly in front of the little altar with its Presence Lamp.

Thank God! Now, if he could only work the Portal. He would have only one chance. Either he could do it or he couldn't. Drawing a deep breath, he visualized the Portal in the Michaeline sanctuary, reaching out for the energies. He could feel them, like a tangle of fiery skeins, but he paid no attention to the heat, wrapping his mind around them and then, with a faintly breathed prayer that this would work, wrenched the energies.

CHAPTER SIXTEEN

In a dream, in a vision of the night, when deep
sleep falleth upon men, in slumbering upon the
bed; then he openeth the ears of men, and
sealeth their instruction.

—Job 33:15–16

Javan staggered as the floor lurched under his feet, flinging his arms to either side for balance. Simultaneously, he opened his eyes to torchlight rather than a Presence Lamp, the light coming from beside him rather than in front. One hand smacked into stone, but the one toward the light flailed into empty space, nearly hitting a man who had not been there an instant before.

The man caught his wrist and yanked him from the Portal before he could even cry out, deftly spinning him around so that suddenly Javan's wrist was twisted up behind his back, pressure arching him backward with pain and the promise of real damage to the wrist if he made the slightest attempt to escape. At the same time, the man's other hand slid around his neck from behind and clamped hard across the carotid pressure points, even as crisp, efficient Deryni shields wrapped around his mind, testing. Javan pawed at the choking hand with his free one, vaguely trying to dislodge it, but his vision was already tunnelling in toward blackness.

"Don't even *think* about fighting me, son," a strange, brisk voice commanded, just beside his left ear. "I don't want to have to hurt you."

"You're already hurting me!" Javan managed to gasp, though he made an immediate effort to stop struggling. "Who *are* you?"

The tension on his trapped wrist backed off just a fraction, and most of the pressure eased from his throat, but escape still was out of the question.

"Odd, I was about to ask you the same question," the stranger murmured. "So since *you're* the intruder here, suppose you tell me first."

Javan's alarm gave way to vague indignation at the presumption of this glib stranger to take such liberties with the person of a Haldane prince, but now was hardly the time to quibble over niceties of protocol. The man's very presence in the Michaeline sanctuary declared him no enemy, for all the menace of the hands still holding Javan quite immobilized and the mind surrounding his, Truth-Reading him.

"Fair enough. I'm Javan Haldane, and I need to see Tavis right away."

"Ah, and so you are. He didn't tell me to expect you."

The hands released him immediately, their owner stepping back to make him an apologetic bow of the head. The man appeared to be in his mid-thirties, with kind-looking hazel eyes twinkling beneath a shock of shortish brown hair—somewhat surprising, in light of the force he had just displayed to keep his prisoner under control. He wore a Healer's badge and some other on the shoulder of his plain brown mantle, and his sparse beard and mustache looked only recently grown.

"Sorry, your Highness," the man said. "I'm afraid Tavis isn't available. Will someone else do?"

"He isn't available?" Javan repeated. "But, he has to be. What about Queron, then? Or one of the MacRories?"

"Not Queron. But I can fetch Joram or Evaine within a few minutes."

"No, I daren't stay that long. I'm on borrowed time as it is." Javan took the packet out of his tunic breast and hefted it in his hand, looking the Healer up and down, Truth-Reading in turn. "The fact that you're here ought to mean that I can trust you. Tell Father Joram that the regents are moving the entire Court to Rhemuth the day after tomorrow, so I don't know when a direct contact will be possible again. And give him this." He handed the packet to the Healer. "It's a report of what's been happening in Valoret for the last three weeks, since Tavis and Ansel were there." He cocked his head at the man. "Ansel *is* all right, isn't he? The last time I blithely assumed that someone had recovered from an injury incurred on my behalf, it was Rhys—and he hadn't."

The Healer's smile was bittersweet as he fingered the sealed packet.

"In that regard, I *can* assure you, your Highness. Ansel is fine. I was personally involved in Healing him, when he came back. In fact, so far recovered is he that he's out on a mission now. Dom Queron has gone to fetch Revan back from the Willimites, and Ansel is waiting for them with Tavis at the Portal outside Caerrorie. They could return at any time—which is why I was waiting here. Oh, and my name's Sylvan O'Sullivan. I was one of Earl Gregory's battle surgeons before Tavis—ah—recruited me."

"Tavis recruited—then, you can *block*? They've finally found another?" Javan breathed.

"Oh, yes. For that matter, Lady Evaine's little son can, too—though, hopefully, we'll never have to use him."

"You mean Tieg?"

"Yes, that's his name."

Javan sighed, closing his eyes briefly. "Babies. It isn't enough that *I* don't even get a chance to grow up."

"Beg pardon, sir?"

Javan shook his head. "Don't mind me. It's been a very difficult night. I—ah—used Archbishop Hubert's Portal to get here—left him sleeping just on the other side of some curtains. I *think* I've covered all the details, but I've got to get back before somebody tries to wake him or I'm missed from where I'm supposed to be."

"Wait a minute." Sylvan set his hand on Javan's shoulder to hold him from going back into the Portal. "Am I to infer that *you* put Hubert to sleep?"

Javan gave him a sheepish grin. "Yeah. I had to hide under his bed, and I didn't dare touch him at first, but I managed. Don't worry. He won't remember anything."

"You'd better pray he doesn't," Sylvan muttered, looking troubled as he glanced again at the sealed packet. "And this report doesn't have a word about any of that, does it?"

"Well, no. Of course not. When I wrote it, I didn't know I could do it."

"But you know now. And what's more important, the others should know." Sylvan tucked the report under his belt. "There *is* a way to remedy that, of course. You could let me read you before you go back."

Javan's heart went into his throat at the very thought of letting this stranger enter his mind. He had been Truth-Reading the man for some time and accepted that Sylvan O'Sullivan was exactly who and what he said he was, but consciously permitting what Sylvan asked was a very frightening notion.

"I—don't think I dare take the time," he whispered, offering a milder excuse than his own fear.

Smiling, Sylvan made him a slight bow, one hand to his heart. "I don't blame you for your apprehension, your Highness. Tavis is your mentor, and you hardly know me. But with all due respect, what I'm asking would only take a few seconds. Queron has been teaching me rapid reading techniques, so I can gather information from subjects while they're being 'baptized.' I can strip out the information *very* quickly, without the subject even being aware." He grinned. "Of course, that normally would occur after I'd blocked them—and Tavis has made it quite clear you're not to be blocked, after he's worked so hard to help you awaken your powers—but with your cooperation, the process should differ very little."

"But I really should be getting back," Javan whispered, trying to edge a little closer to the Portal entrance.

Nodding, the Healer dropped one arm between Javan and the door frame, blocking the entrance.

"Do you think I don't know what I'm asking?" Sylvan said quietly. "And I'll make my request even more unfair by pointing out that I don't know how long it will take for regular contact to be reestablished with you. That makes a detailed report all the more valuable at this time. But I won't insist, if you feel really uncomfortable about it."

Biting at his lip, Javan sighed. Sylvan was correct, of course, and had offered the undeniable argument. Tavis and the others *should* know about these most recent developments. That realization did not make Javan any happier about the proposition, but he knew he must concede the point.

"Very well," he said quietly. "Make certain you don't do anything that would prevent me going back, though, or interfere with handling Hubert. I really don't dare stay much longer."

"We'll be done before you realize," Sylvan murmured, setting one hand across the back of Javan's neck and the other on his forehead. "Draw back your shields and close your eyes. No need to be nervous. Visualize a door opening, and hold that image. I'll do all the rest."

Javan obeyed, surprised to find the requested action much easier than it had been in previous attempts. Because he was looking for it, he felt the faint, gentle tickle of Sylvan's mind wrapping around his own, then a gentle, swooping sensation that momentarily set him a little off balance, so that he swayed between Sylvan's hands. Then the hands had shifted to his shoulders and he was looking up into Sylvan's smiling face.

"You're a young man of many surprises," Sylvan allowed. "Audacious—but perhaps that's what's necessary in these troubled times. I'm proud to be in your service. But you mustn't let me delay you any longer. As soon as you've settled in at Rhemuth, you must try to establish as public a daily routine as you can. We'll find some way to contact you." The Healer's hands propelled Javan gently toward the Portal. "Godspeed, your Highness—and be careful!"

Javan's mind was whirling with the praise and the heady excitement of having exceeded Sylvan's expectations, but he schooled his thoughts to the necessary discipline as he stepped into the Portal, raising a hand to the Healer in farewell before closing his eyes to orient himself. This time, he braced his feet a little farther apart so that he would not overbalance on contact. Just before he warped the energies, he wondered what he would do if someone had come into the oratory while he was gone—unlikely but possible—but only silence met him as torchlight gave way to the little oratory's Presence Lamp. He waited, listening, for several dozen heartbeats, then cautiously parted the curtains enough to peep outside.

The door was still closed the way Javan had left it, all quiet save for Hubert's gentle snores. Nor were there any sounds of movement from outside the room. Greatly reassured, Javan crept softly over to the bed and parted the hangings, considering what else must be done before he fled.

The archbishop had not stirred in Javan's absence, other than to burrow his tonsured head more comfortably into the hollow of the pillow. One plump hand rested on the coverlet beneath his multiple chins, the jewel of his archbishop's ring glowing darkly in the light of the single candle still burning at the head of the bed. With his blond head cradled on the silk of the pillowslip and the rosebud lips relaxed in sleep, Hubert hardly looked capable of the monstrous acts of which Javan knew him to be guilty. He did look incredibly vulnerable—and was.

For several long seconds, the temptation simply to kill Hubert and be done with it was very strong. Certainly the archbishop deserved to die for what he had done—and for what he *would* do, if only through the terrible instrument he had created in the *Custodes Fidei*. How many more must suffer before Hubert earned some tangible wrath of a just God? It was all very well to say that Hubert would reap his reward at the Final Judgment, but could not justice find him a little sooner?

Savoring the temptation, Javan considered the various means at hand. Most direct was the quick satisfaction of a dagger drawn deftly across the fat throat. More fitting, perhaps, was a pillow—of which the shade of Giesele MacLean certainly would approve. Held fast in the thrall of Javan's emergent powers, Hubert would not even be able to struggle against the smothering press of feather-stuffed silk— a fair exchange, since Giesele had not been able to fight the physical restraint of her murderer. Whoever eventually found the body might even attribute the death to natural causes—far more believable in the case of the corpulent Hubert than in Giesele's case. Ah, tempting thought!

Briefly tempting, too, was the realization that Javan could probably make Hubert take his own life! It would require more active control than Javan thought he could manage just yet, but a more telling reason for rejecting that notion utterly was the Church's teaching regarding suicide. If Javan were to *make* Hubert kill himself, he was more guilty than Hubert. No retribution, however just and sweet, was worth that.

Nor was any retribution possible just now, Javan realized. It was not even the killing itself that bothered him. He had killed once before, defending Tavis against assassins on the day Davin MacRorie died.

But killing a man in battle was one thing. Even ordering an execution after proper trial was justifiable, if only to ensure that the guilty would commit no further crimes—though no death could cancel out crimes already committed or bring back the innocent dead.

But killing a man while he slept, regardless of his guilt, was quite another matter and made the killer little better than his victim. Not only that, if Hubert died, who might be his successor, both as archbishop and as regent? It could even be two individuals. Hubert's brother Manfred was a likely regent, already functioning almost as a sixth regent for some time. And for archbishop, Javan guessed it might be Paulin of Ramos, now that his *Custodes* were established and he had their might behind him. Somehow, Javan didn't think Paulin would refuse an archbishop's miter. However bad Hubert was in that respect, Paulin would be worse. At least Javan knew what to expect from Hubert, for the most part.

Or did he? And might there be something Javan could do to improve Hubert's predictability? For that matter, might Javan improve his own standing with the archbishop?

This temptation, unlike murder, was too enticing to resist. Javan knew he dared not try anything too drastic or someone else might suspect tampering, even if Hubert did not. Whether Oriel or one of the other Deryni sniffers could detect specifics, if they tried to investigate, Javan had no idea—but he didn't want to find out. Which meant that any suggestion planted in Hubert's mind must be subtle—nothing that would actually *change* Hubert's basic attitude, but perhaps just soften it a little.

Quite suddenly, Javan thought he knew how to do that. In fact, he had already laid some of the groundwork. Even the plan's success held its dangers, however.

He had been leading Hubert to believe he was considering a religious vocation. As a means to an end, the premise had suited Javan admirably, since it allayed whatever suspicions Hubert and his staff might have had about Javan being in the episcopal palace tonight—a vital necessity if Javan was to use Hubert's Portal.

Support of Javan's potential religious vocation had suited Hubert very well, too, since Javan's eventual acceptance of Holy Orders would almost certainly promise his removal both from Court and from the royal succession, thus clearing the way for the more biddable Rhys Michael to succeed Alroy. The danger was that if Javan played his part too well, and Hubert got impatient, Javan could end up locked away in a monastery for the rest of his life, regardless of whether or not he had a true vocation. Javan was sure that Paulin of Ramos would know of several small, secure, out-of-the-way monasteries suitable for immuring inconvenient princes—if Hubert did not simply arrange a convenient accident.

The challenge, then, was to strike just the right balance: saying neither yea nor nay to the religious life, shutting no doors; to exploit his youth in seemingly earnest indecision and avoid taking any steps that might raise real impediments to his eventual succession—all without getting himself locked away or killed. For now, telling Hubert at least a little of what he wanted to hear seemed the wisest course. Also, a Hubert trying to encourage a vocation was more likely to be a Hubert inclined to indulge Javan a little.

And even if the only result of that indulgence was a degree more freedom, a bit less stringent monitoring of his every word or action, that was all to the good—and it was the only way he had any hope of eventually reestablishing contact with his Deryni allies. Moving to Rhemuth was bad enough, but at least they now would know not to seek him in Valoret any more. And meanwhile, he would work through Hubert as best he could.

That was as far as Javan thought he dared go—at least for this time. He would plant the seeds of indulgence in Hubert and see how they grew—and also set triggers to enable him to continue the venture at a later date, if the first phase proved successful. In the end, if things came to an ultimate showdown, Hubert still was his, to do with as he must, even unto death.

Briefly Javan put his hand on Hubert's forehead again, setting his suggestions, eradicating any memory of the night's tampering. Then he was withdrawing, creeping back across the room to the door to the audience room, and through it to the anteroom, where he scanned the corridor outside for several seconds before slipping outside to head back for the chapel. He met no one enroute. By the time he was taking his cloak from Charlan's shoulders and sending the squire back to his post by the door, he was reassured in the knowledge that no one had even looked in during his absence.

He seemed to put on exhaustion with the cloak as he took Charlan's place at the *prie-dieu*—and small wonder, considering what he had been through—but he bowed his head in formal thanks as he fastened the clasp at his throat, at the same time schooling his mind to obscure the details of the night's adventure from any casually attempted probe by castle Deryni. After that, he shifted off the *prie-dieu* to prostrate himself before the altar steps, knowing that would please anyone looking in from now on.

And if they chose to report it to Hubert as evidence of heightened piety, so much the better. Meanwhile, it was a far more comfortable way to spend the rest of the night, until he could return to the castle and his bed. He thought about the very interesting Sylvan O'Sullivan as he settled his head on the pillow of his folded arms and wondered what Tavis and the others would say when they found out what Javan had done.

Joram and Evaine knew of it within the hour. Tavis and Queron would have to wait several days, by which time Javan would be already on his way to Rhemuth. Sylvan found the two MacRories poring over some of Evaine's manuscripts in the Camberian Council chamber. Young Jesse MacGregor was with them, apparently asleep in his chair, though Sylvan knew the younger man actually was monitoring a passive link set with Queron, operational only when the blocked Healer slept. Queron seemed not to have slept the night before—or at least not in sufficient depth for anyone to activate the link; and the depth of Jesse's trance, wide-open for the least hint of Queron's readiness, indicated that the Healer was working late tonight, too.

"Sorry to intrude," Sylvan said, tossing Javan's report between Joram and Evaine as they looked up in question. "I've just met Prince Javan. No one told me he was able to use a Portal."

Joram's jaw dropped in astonishment, but Evaine looked pleased.

"He's learned to use a Portal?" Her smile faded as she realized what else that must mean. "But which Portal? Sweet *Jesu*, he didn't come through *Hubert's*?"

"The very one," Sylvan replied. "Not only that, he controlled our beloved archbishop—put him to sleep. Is there anything you'd like to tell me about this young Haldane? I've suddenly been made very aware that he's no ordinary thirteen-year-old—and it has nothing to with the fact that he's royal."

Joram, who had cracked the seals on the packet and started to unfold it, glanced at Evaine and then back at the Healer, setting the parchment on the table before him. Jesse had not stirred.

"We told you he was something special, Sylvan," Joram said quietly. "What else did he tell you, to make you this surprised?"

Snorting, Sylvan pulled a stool closer and sat between Joram and Evaine, extending a hand to each of them.

"He didn't have time actually to *tell* me much at all, but he did permit a quick reading before he went back. You *are* aware that, other than the arcane knowledge, he has almost the identical abilities of a fairly well-trained Deryni?"

Evaine, laying her hand on Sylvan's, simply smiled and nodded. "Don't feel that you're being singled out, Sylvan. He keeps surprising us, too. Let's have your reading," she added, as Joram joined in the link.

The information was transferred with the usual economy they both had come to expect of Sylvan. Joram sighed and sat back in his chair as the link was dismantled, already calculating the possible ramifications of Javan's night's work, and Evaine nodded distractedly as she, too, digested the new information.

"I think you're probably right that he got away safely, since he didn't come back through the Portal in the next few minutes," Evaine said to no one in particular. "He's playing a dangerous game, though. I hope he realizes how dangerous."

"At least we have a better chance of sending him help, once the court is installed at Rhemuth," Joram said. "We can infiltrate the staff there; I doubt the regents will take their entire domestic household from Valoret. Provided he isn't watched too closely, and no one's suspicions have been aroused unduly by tonight's little escapade, we should be able to make contact with him somehow."

"A bogus clergy contact, perhaps," Evaine said, "since that's the cover he seems to have chosen. It's clever, but I hope he doesn't wake up one morning to find himself a monk in some godforsaken monastery."

Joram nodded. "All too possible. It would be a convenient way for the regents to rid themselves of a troublesome prince without resorting to murder—and who would question it, if Javan has been seen to display an open interest in the religious life?"

"Who, indeed?" Evaine replied. "His father was a priest, after all."

"In the meantime, however," Joram went on, "I think we can at least confirm that he hasn't suffered as a result of what he's done tonight. The departure of the court from Valoret will be something of a state occasion, if I know the regents. I'll arrange for someone to observe. It might even be possible to get him a message."

"Be careful on *that*," Evaine said, glancing at the still motionless Jesse. "It's a shame Ansel isn't back yet. He could handle this to a fare-thee-well."

Joram smiled and rose. "He could—and might still, if he gets back in time. In the meantime, I have several Michaelines who can do the job. Care to help me set this up, Sylvan? Jesse doesn't need our distraction, and you'll want to take up your post at the other Portal anyway."

When the two had gone, Evaine sat back in her chair and gazed across at Jesse, well aware that it would take more than mere conversation to distract the young Deryni when he was so deeply entranced. Watching Jesse made her think of those for whom he waited, and she wondered how long the wait would continue and whether all was well with Queron and Revan.

CHAPTER SEVENTEEN

*A prophet shall the Lord your God raise up
unto you of your brethren.*

—Acts 7:37

Queron Kinevan pulled his shabby cloak more closely around him and tried not to think about the cold, pretending to be asleep. Across the cave, by the light of a tiny fire, Revan was conversing quietly with three of his favorite disciples.

So far, everything was going well enough. Other than taking nearly four days to make a journey that should have taken two, partly from dodging the expected patrols of Earl Manfred's men and partly because of weather, Queron had made the journey from Caerrorie without real incident, arriving two days before. The disguised Tavis had accompanied him, his missing hand filled out with a lump of bandage and shrouded by a grubby sling that hid much.

But Tavis did not enter the Willimite camp. Nor would he allow Queron to do so until he had blocked the elder Healer's powers, for discovery as Deryni could be as good as a death sentence.

Which was not to say that there were no Deryni among the Willimites. Indeed, one of the disciples sitting with Revan was Deryni—a quiet, balding older man called Geordie—and there were more in the ranks of the less favored disciples, camped at the foot of the mountain. The Willimites, while despising Deryni for their unholy magic and for what one of that race had done to their patron, Saint Willim, granted refuge of a sort to those Deryni who publicly abjured their evil magic and promised henceforth to lead lives of humility and public penance. Public penance in the Willimite sense included denouncing any other Deryni who might try to infiltrate the Willimite ranks without also giving up their powers. Geordie had been one of the first to swear the public oath the Willimites now required as a matter of course, and now used his powers only to unmask the deceptions of other Deryni and induce a parting from their evil ways. The Willimites deemed it not only permissible but praiseworthy to do so—a fitting act of expiation, for having been born Deryni in the first place.

The skewed logic of such reasoning eluded Queron, who thought such individuals some of the saddest he had ever seen, to so deny their birthrights, but too much sympathy with their self-imposed plight could be deadly. Under the rigid, fundamentalist code of the Willimites, undeclared Deryni were liable to meet a speedy and awful end. Hanging seemed to be the preferred method of execution, but he had heard of stoning, impalement, and even crucifixion—though the latter was not often used, since it offered the victim too close an identification with the crucified Christ, Who surely despised Deryni sorcery fully as much as His Willimite devotees.

Had Queron been willing to make the public abjuration the Willimites required, he might have passed among them with his power intact if unused, but any hint of clandestine and illicit activity might have cost him his life. There were enough Deryni about, just watching for the chance to inform on recusants—and thus enhance their own spiritual standing—that such a risk simply was not worth it.

Hence, Tavis' block, at least until they determined whether Revan had been successful in purging his most immediate circle of abjuring Deryni. Except for Geordie, he had—and Geordie had been retained for a reason. In fact, though Revan had begun to preach the imminent coming of a new age, hinting that even Deryni might hope to be worthy of a new heavenly grace, his words had served to make many of the other Willimite Deryni withdraw for a time of fasting and meditation, abject in their hope that Heaven might yet hold out some chance for their forgiveness. Revan encouraged such withdrawal, knowing that Deryni themselves, not Heaven, might soon hold out that hope.

The few Deryni who remained, even among the Willimites at large, became targets for Tavis, who ghosted silently around the outskirts of the camp after dark to pick his prey, carefully and selectively blocking those whose presence might interfere with the plans he and Queron had for Revan. By ones and twos, such activity was risky but possible—incapacitating a subject long enough to alter his or her memories, planting reassuring false memories of earlier visual acquaintance with the wiry little grey-haired man who now accompanied the prophet Revan increasingly, squelching any further curiosity about the bleary-eyed beggar with the bandaged arm, and then resetting the triggerpoint with the subjects none the wiser for their experience.

The process was not without its dangers, but the results had been well worth it, thus far. Tavis was never detected, and Queron had been accepted without question. During the first few days, when Queron remained blocked, he found maintaining his charade a tiring proposition, unable to influence any of Revan's followers other than by ordinary persuasion, but Revan himself was good enough at that and had chosen his chief disciples well. Brother Joachim had been the first of the Willimites to heed Revan's preaching and remained his staunchest and most loyal supporter. Flann, a firebrand of a youth with wild black eyes and an even wilder mane of curly black hair, represented the more radical elements of the Willimite brotherhood. The Deryni Geordie had become more valuable to the mission than he knew. Even now, Revan was telling this unlikely trio that he felt called to go into the wilderness to fast and pray for a fortnight, and wished these three, of all his company, to come with him.

Queron could have helped him this time, for Tavis had contrived to pass close enough to touch him earlier in the evening, restoring his powers for their imminent departure—but best not to meddle unless there was real need. Right now, the three were listening with rapt devotion as Revan outlined his hopes for the retreat. Later, when they all prayed—as was always Revan's custom before embarking upon a new venture—Queron would establish the necessary controls to ensure that no one should prove anything but the most amiable of travelling companions.

But for now, a bit of neglected business remained on Queron's part. He had hoped to report back to the Council the night before, through the passive link that Joram and Evaine had set in him to work, even with his powers blocked, but his work with Revan the previous night had not even allowed him much sleep, never mind the privacy necessary to allow the linking safely. Now, with his powers restored and Tavis lurking in the darkness outside to waylay any too-curious Deryni who might try to interfere, Queron could hope to initiate the necessary contact himself.

Drawing a deep breath and exhaling slowly, Queron shifted his mind into a meditative state, not only opening himself for the contact but actively seeking it. The Willimite medallion hanging on a leather thong around his neck became a physical focus for his concentration, and he clasped it in his hand, feeling its edges bite into his palm as he pressed his closed fist to his chest.

All at once, he was linked with Jesse MacGregor, basking in the restoring energy of a connection augmented by the latent power of the entire Camberian Council, of which power Jesse was custodian at the moment. Wordless greeting and relief flooded through Queron as Jesse widened the link and locked in on him, and also surprise that Queron was functioning with full powers.

Are you sure that's safe? came Jesse's cautious query. *Nothing's happened to Tavis, has it?*

Sending assurance and an admonition not to worry, Queron compressed his report into a brief, intense burst of information. Jesse took it as fast as Queron could send, which was fast indeed. Within seconds, Jesse was privy to all that had occurred since Queron's last report, just before arriving at the Willimite camp.

Tavis shouldn't be taking such risks! came Jesse's first, worried response. *Not that there's much you can do, if that's what he feels is necessary, I suppose. How soon do you think you'll be back? Two or three days?*

No more than that, Queron replied. *I'll try for another contact tomorrow night, but tell everyone not to worry if I don't manage it. It may just mean that we're busy dodging Manfred's men again. Oh, and we'll be bringing three guests.*

Guests?

Three of Revan's disciples. Can't help it, Jesse. If we tried to slip away without any of them, the Willimites might not let him go. He's got quite a following. These three are excellent subjects, though. Altering their memories shouldn't be difficult. Just be ready.

Very well, but Joram isn't going to like it.

I don't like it either, but I'm afraid we have no choice. Anything we should know?

Hard to say, came Jesse's reply. *Sylvan just brought in a report from Prince Javan, who apparently managed to use Archbishop Hubert's Portal to deliver it—*

Javan used a Portal? Queron interjected.

Yes, and quite handily, from what I gather, Jesse replied, *though I'm not sure I'd let Tavis know about it yet. I suppose you can tell him that we've learned the court is moving back to Rhemuth in the next few days. Evaine is still digesting the report, but she doesn't seem to be terribly concerned—not about Javan, at any rate. Nothing that can't wait until you get here, so far as I can tell.*

The hint to terminate the contact was clear. Nodding to himself, Queron sent his acquiescence.

Very well. We'll get the full details when we return. Our greetings to all.

And God keep all of you, Jesse responded, just before he withdrew.

Both heartened and troubled, Queron opened his eyes to the same dim firelight and drone of voices that had been with him before he sought out the link, and he carefully cast out for danger. Outside the cave, he sensed Tavis waiting nearby—and the fainter presence of others, farther down the mountain, settling into camp for the night, but nothing about Deryni at all. Good.

Revan was going on about his visions, enthralling his listeners with the lure of similar experiences if they followed his guidance. The three men looked absolutely spellbound, caught in a magic that had nothing to do with Deryni but only the magnetism of Revan's own personality. Quite suddenly, Queron realized that it was no longer entirely a charade for Revan—that the younger man had already set the foundations for a quite viable cult in its own right, owing nothing whatever to the Willimites or the manipulations of the Camberian Council. Queron recognized all the earmarks from his own experience with the Servants of Saint Camber and wondered whether Revan realized how powerful a charisma he possessed. Queron also became aware that the younger man was stalling for time, waiting for him to wake up.

Yawning, Queron sat up and pretended to blink sleep from his eyes, once again putting on his persona as the intense, hot-eyed disciple.

"Forgive me, Master, I didn't mean to sleep so long," he murmured contritely, easing his feet under him to duck-walk over to the four, in the low-ceilinged cavern. "God give you blessings, brethren. I didn't hear you come in."

"Brother Aaron got little sleep last night," Revan said easily, referring to Queron by the name they had agreed upon as biblical and close to Queron's own. "He watched with me while I prayed for a sick child—young Erena's babe. I'm happy to report that the child seems to be much improved, so the lost sleep was surely worthwhile."

He did not mention, nor did Queron, that a Healer's knowledge of herbs and such, to break the child's fever, had not hurt matters any. Had Queron had access to his Healing power, the cure might have been effected even sooner, but the child had recovered, nonetheless.

Joachim gave the master a knowing nod, Geordie muttering that he had noticed the restored child that morning, while Flann attributed all to Revan's prayers.

"Nay, little brother, you must not attribute such power to *me*," Revan protested, holding up both hands in denial. "If praise is due, it should be lifted up unto the Lord, Who is the Doer of all good things. I am only His humble servant. But, come, my brethren," he went on, spreading his hands to either side and inviting them all to draw closer. "'Tis time to ask God's blessing before embarking upon our sacred mission."

None of the men seemed to notice how Revan directed their movement, so that when they all joined hands, Queron had a link with Flann on one side and Geordie on the other—who had a link with Joachim. With the physical contact, and as Revan led them in prayer and lulled their senses with the drone of his words, Queron was able to ease the three under his control without anyone realizing what had happened, extending through Geordie to secure even the veteran Joachim.

"We can go now," he said softly, looking up at Revan as he released the men's hands. "Our brethren shall surely be the most agreeable of companions."

Revan eyed the three carefully before releasing their hands himself. "Douse the fire, would you please, Brother Flann, and we shall be away."

Minutes later, they had safely negotiated the rocky path leading down the mountainside and joined Tavis, who led them softly away from the Willimite camp. By dawn, as the sun thrust its first rays above the hills before them, they had reached the main road and were joining their voices with those of the birds in a paean of praise to greet the new day, their three Willimite companions quite convinced that they and "Brother Aaron" were all on a pilgrimage to the wilderness with their master. The morning was brilliant with the promise of coming spring. If the weather held, and they ran into no hostile patrols, Queron thought they might reach the Caerrorie Portal late the next day.

Neither the carolling of birds nor the rays of the rising sun penetrated to the chapel where Prince Javan greeted the new day, but Archbishop Hubert's early arrival made it clear that the long night was over. Hubert's fat face was wreathed with smiles as he first poked his head into the room, then entered boldly, startling Charlan to his feet and admitting a wash of brighter light and a cold draft from the corridor beyond. Javan, just beginning to rouse from fitful drowsing on the cold, hard floor, knuckled sleep from his eyes and struggled to a sitting position, half tangled in his cloak, fearful that his previous night's work was about to receive its ultimate test.

"Forgive me, your Grace, I fear I must have dozed off," he whispered.

Hubert made a deprecating gesture, bishop's ring winking in the dim light, and came to lower himself heavily to one knee beside Javan.

"So did Christ's disciples, when they tried to keep watch with Him in the Garden," Hubert said. "You need not beg *my* forgiveness, my son. Sometimes God grants His greatest revelations during that twilight time when the soul hangs suspended between sleep and wakefulness. To offer up one's night before the Blessed Sacrament, prostrate before the Altar of Heaven, can only benefit the supplicant."

"I pray you may be right, your Grace" Javan murmured, bowing his head. When he did not go on, Hubert set a pudgy hand on his shoulder.

"Have no doubt of it, my son," Hubert said. "God will not desert His own. Tell me, have you any recollection of what He might have revealed to you while you meditated?"

Javan swallowed and shook his head. "I—am very young and foolish, your Grace," he replied. "I—am not certain I should understand His words if I heard them. Perhaps I have not yet learned to listen properly. If—if your Grace were to instruct me—"

As he turned the grey Haldane eyes on Hubert, projecting as much as he could of innocence and honest bewilderment, the archbishop smiled happily and took Javan's hand in both of his.

"My dear, dear boy, of course I will instruct you. Come. The chapter will be singing morning prayers in my household chapel. Afterwards, I must celebrate Mass in the cathedral. Perhaps you would care to be my server. God will make His will known, all in good time."

The plan presented no compulsion to do anything Javan had not done dozens of times before. Javan and both his brothers had often served at Mass. Such service was a part of the general religious training of all well-born boys, though the function generally diminished as boys grew into men, unless they were intended for the religious life. Nor was Javan a stranger to regular attendance at other devotions. It was expected of reasonably pious individuals, and princes must set an even better example.

Most important of all, Hubert had not once referred directly to the formal religious vocation he hoped Javan would embrace, and seemed content this morning to let the prince continue his own slow, noncommital exploration of the possibility. That represented a notable backing off from the previous night's more aggressive encouragement, hopefully as a result of Javan's cautious tampering.

Using the physical link of Hubert's hands surrounding his, Javan cautiously tested his continuing ability to influence the archbishop. Sending the gentle suggestion of an itchy nose brought a casual, off-hand brush at the proboscis even as Hubert lumbered to his feet, steadying himself on Javan's shoulder. At Javan's further subtle urging, Hubert also crossed himself from right to left instead of left to right, as they both reverenced the altar a last time before departing.

"Come, young Charlan, you may accompany us," Hubert said, including the squire in his gesture as they swept out of the chapel. "I know you have no inclination whatever toward the religious life, but attendance at yet another Mass will not hurt you."

Javan felt as if every eye was upon him as he and Charlan entered the archbishop's household chapel behind Hubert, and he thought the morning prayers would never end. Serving Mass afterwards was better, since people had grown accustomed to seeing the princes occasionally perform this function, but Javan had to keep reminding himself that it was the priestly office he assisted and not the man. He loathed the individual who offered up the Sacrifice and suspected that Hubert would just as soon sacrifice him, to gain his own ends.

In response to that fear, just after the Consecration, when Hubert offered the Sacred Victim as an homage to God's Infinite Majesty and for the welfare of all the faithful—"*hostiam puram, hostiam sanctam, hostiam immaculatam*"—Javan even flashed on a *most* disturbing vision of himself laid bound and naked upon the altar, like Isaac before Abraham, his bare throat stretched back to accommodate the descending knife. Only, the hand wielding the blade was his own father's, not Hubert's.

Shuddering, Javan shook off the vision—and, in fact, paid it little more heed for the duration of the ritual. For ironically, he also felt the faint tugging of a fancy on his own part to be in Hubert's place, were his own place not so urgently dictated by his position in the succession—not as archbishop, to be sure, but as priest. All at once he understood a little of what his father must have suffered, having to set aside such a calling in the interest of royal duty. He also understood why Cinhil Haldane had always found it so difficult to express affection for his sons, a part of him always resenting those individuals who were the tangible signs that he had abandoned his priesthood for a crown. Javan himself must have been a particular trial, his lame foot seeming to Cinhil to give physical confirmation of all Heaven's disapproval of that abandonment, vital though it had been for the well-being of the kingdom.

Javan did a lot of growing up in that hour, and hardly minded that Hubert took his thoughtfulness afterwards as a sign of softening. A further irony was that Javan found himself in the cathedral sacristy, both before and after—easy access now to the place visited only by dint of great effort the night before, though the Portal was no more functional than it had been. In all, however, Javan counted the last twelve hours well spent.

And as eventful as those hours had been, the rest of the morning and, indeed, the day passed absolutely without any occurrence to mark this day different from any other, except that the servants were busy with their final packing for the move to Rhemuth on the morrow. Javan returned to the castle with Charlan just before noon to find his quarters nearly stripped of all personal effects, only temporary bedding and a change of clothing remaining unpacked for their last night in Valoret.

They poked around the trunks and parcels and baskets until a senior steward chased them out, then raided the kitchen for something to eat—which incurred the wrath of Cook, trying to organize that night's supper, but also gained them a handful of scones hot from the oven, a slab of rich, buttery cheese, and a couple of tankards of hot mulled ale. They took their spoils to a window embrasure in the great hall, where Javan and Tavis had been wont to sit and eavesdrop on the regents as they supervised Alroy's hearings of the assize courts. After they had eaten, Javan pretended to nap. In fact, he observed the comings and goings of the increasingly informal court and reminisced on the old days, wondering where Tavis was now.

He continued to think about Tavis and the others later that evening, as he sat through supper, and was glad that the next day's planned early departure gave him excuse to retire early—for his previous night's lack of proper sleep was catching up with him. He did not even dream that night, and managed not to embarrass himself by crying when he had to ride out of Valoret on the morrow, in the midst of the royal household, with no idea how and when or where he might next be able to reestablish contact with his Deryni allies. The loneliness was setting in with a vengeance. They would be on the road for at least a week.

It was on Javan's second day out of Valoret, just after dusk, that Tavis and Queron drew Revan and his spellbound disciples into the welcome shelter of the tunnel entrance that led beneath Caerrorie

Castle. Most blessedly, the weather had held—no certain thing in Gwynedd in March—and Earl Murdoch's patrols seemed elsewhere occupied.

Tavis set his hand on the back of old Geordie's neck, drawing him under deeper control as Queron did the same with Flann and Joachim and Revan secured the opening. Closing the door blocked out all light, but Tavis conjured handfire where the Willimites could not see its source, until Revan could strike a light to the candle left in a niche by the door. Revan allowed himself a faint sigh of relief as the wick flared up.

"How far now?" he whispered.

Queron gestured deeper into the tunnel. "Not very. Go ahead and lead."

They moved off in single file, treading as quietly as possible. Gradually the tunnel changed from dirt and rock to brick and then to cut stone. Ansel and Sylvan were waiting for them a little beyond that, just before the Portal chamber, looking very relieved indeed.

"You made good time," Ansel said. "I'm glad something has gone right for a change."

"Why? What's wrong?" Tavis demanded.

"Oh, everyone is fine. We've even heard from Javan. But let's not talk about it here."

They talked about it in the Michaeline sanctuary later that night, after everyone had eaten a hot meal and the Willimites were locked away to sleep in one of the cells. Joram let both Queron and Revan read Prince Javan's report and filled in other details from Sylvan's direct reading verbally for the benefit of the human Revan.

"So long as he hasn't aroused any particular suspicion as a result of his activities three nights ago, he should be all right," Joram concluded. "We've had reports that he did ride out of Valoret with the rest of the royal household and that everything seemed normal. Once he's settled in at Rhemuth, we can make additional arrangements. Meanwhile, I think his biggest immediate worry will be to keep Hubert from shuffling him off to some monastery."

"How likely is that?" Revan asked.

Evaine steepled her fingertips and tapped forefingers against her lips. "That depends on Javan, doesn't it?"

At Revan's troubled look, Joram smiled and pushed several sheets of closely penned parchment across the table toward him.

"Let us worry about Javan, why don't you? You're going to have your hands full enough, as it is."

Revan picked up the sheaf and scanned the first few lines of the top page. "What's this?"

"Your preliminary briefing," Evaine replied. "After you've digested that, we'll move on to your actual preparation. It won't be easy, but I think it just might work."

In the days that followed, all of them began to think it might work. Revan proved an apt pupil. The manuscript Joram had given him was a lengthy scenario of how the institution and extension of Revan's new movement should go. Revan not only made it his own but embellished upon it, quickly mastering the patter and the mechanics of the "baptism" itself and then adding his own interpretations.

In addition, Revan soon developed a surprising affinity with Sylvan—which freed Tavis to continue working in the background, on the fringes of the crowds, where he could keep a lower profile and set up subjects for Revan's more public ministrations. Revan and Sylvan had never met, but they quickly forged a brilliant partnership for the outward functioning of the operation. Sometimes, Revan even displayed an almost Deryni intuition where Sylvan was concerned.

Which led to another, unplanned advantage that the Deryni were able to give their would-be messiah, verging much more closely on their own powers yet undetectable, so far as they knew, by any means available to the regents. They had learned from Tavis' early association with Javan that close contact between Deryni and humans sometimes catalyzed near-Deryni tendencies in the human so exposed. Revan had nothing like the Haldane potential to explain a like tendency in himself, but he had worked closely with MacRories and Thuryns for more than half his life. To their delight, they found that Revan also possessed vestiges of extra ability, all but indistinguishable from his own personal charisma. Already, when Revan preached, evangelical persuasion verged on near compulsion in some listeners.

And they found that the tendency could be amplified through the focus of Revan's Willimite medallion, magically "charged" by one of the Deryni. Drawing on that power source, and reinforced by the laying on of hands and the expectations of his subjects, in conjunction with baptism, Revan could actually induce an effect ranging from disorientation and dizziness to near fainting.

"What about this, though?" Revan asked, fingering the medal thoughtfully, after trying his enhanced talent on several of Evaine's compliant men at arms. "If I'm put to the question, as you *know* will have to happen eventually, won't a Deryni sniffer be able to detect something?"

Bishop Niallan shook his head. First he and then Tavis had been sworn into the Camberian Council on Queron's return, finally bringing that body back to its original complement of eight, and he was now an active and enthusiastic member of the team.

"Remember that religious medals are always blessed, Revan," the bishop said. "And whether the blessing is done by a human or a Deryni, it's long been known, at least among Deryni, that the act of blessing places a special imprint on the object blessed. It's a kind of magical 'charge' that has nothing whatever to do with being Deryni, and the effect can be so subtle that not even a Deryni cleric can always isolate it. A Deryni layman certainly won't be able to tell the difference—if he detects a change at all. If anything, your own status as a holy man will be enhanced."

They also determined that the working of Revan's new skill was not affected by *merasha*, except as the usual sedative effect of the drug in humans would slow Revan down and eventually put him to sleep. Revan made the acquaintance of that bane of Deryni more than once, as they refined their techniques, and learned not to fear it.

"Being neutral to *merasha* should be the clincher, when they eventually do question what you're doing," Queron informed him. "The drug has been the great leveller for centuries, ever since its effect was first noted. Everyone who knows anything at all about Deryni knows that we're universally vulnerable to it. When you don't react, that will be the final confirmation that, whatever else you are, you aren't some new, insidious kind of Deryni."

They had allotted a fortnight for melding the different members of the team into a cohesive unit, but well before the second week had passed, all of them were letter-perfect in their parts.

"Given our time constraints, I think you've probably taught me all that's feasible," Revan told the assembled company on the night he declared himself satisfied with his preparation. "I don't see that further delay will accomplish much. We still have to do our forty days' retreat in the wilderness. If we start by mid-April, we can time our return to coincide with Pentecost. One could hardly wish for a more auspicious beginning."

Two things remained to be done before they left. The next morning, Revan was introduced to Torcuill de la Marche, who was to become Revan's first public Deryni "convert." Torcuill's family were already safely lodged with Gregory at Trevalga, but the Deryni lord would have quite a different story to tell about them when he came to Revan in a few weeks' time.

"You won't have much of a chance to chat, when you meet in the river," Evaine told the two, when she had brought them together in the library of the Michaeline sanctuary. "Actually, Torcuill, I think you might have met Revan at Sheele, years ago, when he was my children's tutor."

Torcuill managed a nervous smile. "I seem to have some vague recollection to that effect. Young man, I admire what you're doing for us."

Revan met Torcuill's eyes squarely, with a dignity and self-assurance that had not come entirely of his mentors' indoctrination of the past week or so.

"I only wish that I might do more besides play a part," Revan replied modestly. "Without Sylvan or Tavis, I am nothing."

Which was not precisely true, as Evaine had cause to know full well. The burgeoning charisma first noted by Queron had become a powerful force in itself. Revan spent some time with his three disciples each day, Sylvan making a fourth. Even without Deryni tampering, the three Willimites were convinced that Revan was a genuine prophet and were ready to believe that eventually he would work miracles.

He certainly looked the proper prophet now, with his sheepskin mantle and robe of unbleached wool and sandal-shod feet. A pouch of hairy goatskin hung from his leather girdle, and a staff of twisted olivewood rested in the crook of his arm.

Only his efforts to cultivate a properly biblical beard had come to naught. Even after more than a year, his hirsute adornment was still sparse and fair, only faintly shadowing his upper lip and jaw. What beard he did have, however, was perfect foil for his eyes—a warm light brown verging on gold that somehow seemed almost luminous in dim light. His straight brown hair brushed the shoulders of his robe. The fine hands were more calloused than they had been in the days when he was scribe and tutor to the Thuryn family, but the nails were clean and neatly tended, as was everything else about him.

Slowly Torcuill looked him up and down, shaking his head a little as their eyes met again.

"I thought that holy men were supposed to be filthy and vermin-ridden, and lead a simple life," he said with a nervous chuckle.

"Why, are holiness and simplicity to be equated with dirt?" came Revan's amused rejoinder. "Water will play an important part in my ministry. Should I not, then, have more than a nodding acquaintance with it?"

"Some would deem cleanliness a vanity of the body," Torcuill retorted.

"Say, rather, that it betokens a respect for the body, as temple of the soul. If our purpose in life is to seek reconciliation and reunion with our Heavenly Father, why should His Indwelling Spirit wish to occupy a filthy temple?"

Revan's sly smile was infectious, and Torcuill burst into hearty laughter.

"You won't trip him up that easily, Torcuill," Evaine said, when the Deryni lord had wiped his streaming eyes. "We may have pushed him into the role of holy man and prophet, but he was a scholar before that. Rhys and I trained him, after all."

"Oh, I can see that."

"But, I think I'll let you wait to see how *well* we trained him, when you show up to hear him preach in a few months' time. I wouldn't want to dampen the spontaneity of your response, so we probably oughtn't to discuss much more of what's actually going to happen."

Evaine had Jesse take Torcuill back to Trevalga then, to spend what might be his last few weeks with his family. Jesse returned, though, for he and the Healer Sylvan had been close for most of Jesse's life. Later that night, Jesse was among those who gathered in the sanctuary chapel to witness a brief but very special ceremony, as Sylvan, Revan, and Tavis presented themselves before God's altar to offer up their mission.

The little chapel had not been so crowded since that night, more than thirteen years ago, when Cinhil Haldane prepared to go and claim his crown. Fifty Michaeline Knights had packed the chapel then, reconsecrating their swords to the Haldane cause.

Michaelines were not so many tonight, only Joram and a handful of his exiled brethren wearing the distinctive Michaeline blue. Nor were the presiding clergy preparing to consecrate swords, but men—though such weapons could be far more potent than mere metal.

Two renegade bishops received them. After initial prayers, the three laid themselves prostrate before the altar, Revan between the two Healers, while the assembled company sang a litany hallowed by more centuries of use than the age of the faith in which they now worshipped. The sense of the ancient words hung on the air even after the litany was finished, underlining the silence as Joram, Evaine, and Jesse helped the three to their knees.

After that, the Deryni Bishop Niallan and the human Bishop Dermot gave the three a commission just short of priestly ordination, imparting the authority to preach, to heal, to bless, and to absolve. Laying their consecrated hands upon the head of each man in turn, the bishops thrice called down Heavenly Grace to bless the work and protect the workers.

The three had been to confession before Mass that morning, but now they received Communion from the Reserved Sacrament one more time, for priests were few among the Willimites, and it might be long before they could partake again. This final Sacrament took on even more solemn dimensions when Dermot used the wording usually reserved for the dying or mortally ill.

"*Accipe, frater, Viaticum Corporis Domini Jesu Christi.* . . ." Receive, my brother, this food for your journey, the Body of our Lord Jesus Christ, that He may guard you from the malicious enemy and lead you into everlasting life. . . .

And finally, as a seal on the night's work and to underline the deadly dangerous situation into which the three were about to place themselves, Niallan gave each man an amended version of the Last Anointing—for no Last Rites might be possible later on, if they were discovered in what they went to do.

"*Per istam sanctam Unctionem et suam piissimam misericordiam indulgeat tibi Dominus quidquid per animum deliquisti,*" Niallan said, signing each man on the forehead only. By this holy anointing and His most loving mercy, may the Lord forgive you whatever wrong you have done by the use of your mind. Amen.

After a final blessing, all but the three themselves filed quietly out of the chapel, those who had conceived the plan making their way to the corridor outside the Portal chamber. Thus were Joram, Evaine, Queron, Jesse, and Ansel waiting when the three eventually made their way to the sanctuary's Portal, Ansel shepherding three deeply entranced Willimite disciples. No word was exchanged as the travellers took their leave and quitted the sanctuary, and those who were left did not speak of what had happened.

CHAPTER EIGHTEEN

*So shall the knowledge of wisdom be unto thy
soul: when thou hast found it, then there shall
be a reward, and thy expectation shall not be
cut off.*

—Psalms 24:14

The forty days that Revan planned to spend in the wilderness with
his disciples provided a breathing space that Evaine, in particular,
found most welcome, since it gave her both time and opportunity
to pursue the research that was becoming increasingly uppermost
in her personal priorities. Immediately after Revan's departure,
Evaine and the others of the Council resumed round-the-clock monitoring, receiving daily and sometimes twice-daily progress reports
until Sylvan could finally confirm that he and their little band were
safely ensconced in their high desert "retreat." Once that was accomplished, and for the duration of the forty days, surveillance
dropped to an hour at midnight each night, in case some urgent
report needed to be made. Otherwise, those at Sanctuary could do
nothing to advance Revan's cause besides wait. It freed up everyone
for other pursuits, such as these were within the confines of
Sanctuary.

Nor could such pursuits yet include any attempt to reestablish
contact with Javan—and for Javan to take the initiative again was
out of the question. For one thing, though there were several Portals
reasonably accessible in Rhemuth, and at least one in the castle
itself, Javan did not know about them. For another, he had not yet
arrived in Rhemuth. Joram's agents were following the southward
progress of the royal party and reported that the prince appeared to
be in good health and under no duress, but the regents had halted

their progress at Tarleville, one of Earl Tammaron's estates on the Eirian. There they might remain for as much as a week before continuing on to the restored capital. And time must be allowed after that, while the royal household settled into some semblance of a predictable routine, before anyone ventured an infiltration.

Accordingly, the dwellers in Sanctuary had time on their hands. Joram and Evaine spent the first few days of their enforced hiatus reviewing the fruits of her research to date.

"I started with the four volumes of Orin's Protocols that we retrieved from Sheele," Evaine told him, fanning out the neatly penned pages of her notes on the table before them. "As you know, they're bound with different colored cords, which give them their names— Black, Vermillion, Green, and Gold. We were working from the last when we helped Father assimilate the Alister memories."

"But we've known for years that the suspension spell isn't in any of those," Joram objected.

"No, but I've done a closer reading of all four Protocols, as well as contemporary commentaries and annotations on Orin's work. Neither Orin nor his redactors come right out and say it, but I gather that the spell we're looking for might be an extension of what we did thirteen years ago—a vast extension, I might add. I've also come upon several references to a rumored Fifth Protocol, bound in blue, that's sometimes referred to as 'The Scroll of Daring.' Apparently it was a later work, perhaps still in revision when Orin died."

"So we're looking for a Fifth Protocol?"

"Not necessarily." Evaine pulled another sheet forward. "The Mearan poet MacDara, who flourished about two hundred years ago, alluded to a spell for defying death in a work called, 'The Ghosting of Ardal l'Etrange.' I don't think it was just poetic license. More recently, here's a reference to an obscure text called *Haut Arcanum*, by a Gabrilite philosopher called Dom Edouard. I need to ask Queron about that one. And I think there might be more in something called *Liber Ricae*, or *The Book of the Veil*. It's very rare—I've never seen a copy—but the old Varnarite library is supposed to have had one."

Joram shook his head, drawing the last notation closer and tipping it slightly toward the single rushlight. He and Evaine had taken over one of the small, vaulted cells on the same level where Camber's body lay locked away in its magical slumber, both chambers heavily warded against all intrusion. Half a dozen document chests were stacked against the end wall, and the table in the center left room for only two backless stools.

"The Varnarite library, you say? Now, *there's* a challenge, trying to get in there. Edward MacInnis probably has Grecotha swarming with episcopal troops by now. We wouldn't dare do it by conventional means."

"Implying that there might be unconventional means we could try?"

"Mmmm, maybe." When he did not seem inclined to continue, Evaine sighed and pulled out a stool, settling on it like a broody hen, with her fur-lined mantle puffing out all around her.

"Come on. Give."

Joram shrugged and also took a seat. "Well, you'll recall my telling you how Father took me down into the ruins under Grecotha, that first autumn after we restored Cinhil. Later on, he let me see the old plans for the bishop's residence. Did he ever show you those?"

"No."

"Well, the place was honeycombed with secret passages and chambers. It had been a secular manor house, built on an old Varnarite site."

"I remember hearing about it. I never saw the plans, though. He kept meaning to show them to me, but we never got around to it. I don't suppose you know where they are?"

Joram replaced his note on top of all the others and folded his arms. "Unfortunately, no. I never got back to them, either. With all that happened in the years after that, I suspect the plans got pushed back into the archives where he'd found them. I don't know whether he got to do much exploring on his own, but casting back in my memory of the documents themselves, I seem to remember some branching passages that at one time led in the direction of the present Varnarite library. Not that I know whether I could find them or not, or whether they're passable after all these years. Even the parts he showed me were in very poor condition, and very dangerous in places."

"But he and Jebediah did go through part of those ruins to make their escape toward Saint Mary's."

Joram nodded. "Very true. And I'm willing to try to find the branching passages that lead toward the library. I just want you to know that it may not be possible. And if I find them, they may not be passable."

"That's understood." Evaine stared off thoughtfully at the wall behind the rushlight for several seconds, then glanced at Joram. "It sounds as if our first task, then, is for you to duplicate the plans. Are you up to it?"

Joram gave her a wan smile. "Well, I'm no draughtsman, and I'll need some help remembering, after so long, but yes, I'm up to it. I didn't have any other plans for tonight. Did you?"

"Not immediately, no," she replied, rising to fetch pen and ink and a sheet of fresh parchment as he belatedly gathered up the sheaf of notes and pushed them to one side. He could feel the bond of their rapport already strengthening as she came around to stand behind him, and he drew a deep breath and let it out slowly as her hands lightly clasped his shoulders, dropping his shields to allow the even deeper rapport she now began to request.

"Close your eyes now and let me direct you," she whispered, drawing him back to lean against her, cool fingertips slipping up to rest against his temples. "Go deeper now, and deeper still. Suspend all conscious thought and let yourself drift back to that day at Grecotha, when Father showed you the plans he'd discovered. See him spread the plans before you now. Remember your fascination as his finger traces what he's discovered. Study what he shows you. Recall every detail with such clarity that you can read each word and line."

Drifting at her command, Joram let the image form—smiled lazily as the requested details came bobbing up from memory to focus in his mind's eye.

"Good," came her encouragement, just at the edge of his awareness. "Now fix the image in your consciousness and, when you're ready, open your eyes and see the lines superimposed on the blank parchment in front of you. When you open your eyes, you'll remain in trance and the image will persist, as real as actual lines, so that all you have to do is trace over the lines on the parchment. Begin when you're ready."

Slowly he opened his eyes to the now familiar plans, dreamily reaching across to pick up the quill and dip its point precisely in the inkwell Evaine steadied. His hand seemed to take on a life of its own as he bent to his task. The pen glided along the ghostly lines with uncanny sureness, delineating corridors, rooms, and stairwells, inscribing abbreviated legends in a tight, archaic style that was nothing at all like his own handwriting. He could feel Evaine's control, light and reassuring, as his pen raced on, only interrupted by occasional forays back to the inkwell. A detached part of his consciousness laughed with her at the sheer joy of being able to tap such resources of the mind.

He drew and wrote for nearly two hours and over several pages, never faltering, his hand never cramping from the exertion. When he had laid the pen aside, he sat back with eyes closed and let Evaine bring him up slowly, pausing briefly to share his memory of the one time he had actually been where the plans showed. When he opened his eyes again, she was sitting on her stool once more, studying what he had drawn.

"I wish this extended farther to the east," she said, tapping a fingernail against the right-hand edge of one of the pages. "These two corridors look as if they *might* lead where we need to go, but it's impossible to tell from this."

Joram shrugged and stood to stretch, indulging in a yawn. "Sorry, but that's all the farther the originals went. I do know that the original exercise was all about clogged drains. That's what made him consult the plans in the first place. A work crew had broken through into the upper levels of the old complex. Father had them block that all off, and I suspect he adjusted folks' memories a little, to make certain no one remembered where the blocked passages were. But what's been blocked can be unblocked. One of those might take us where we need to go."

"Hmmm, very likely. It's certainly worth a try." She sighed and sat back from the parchment, considering for a moment, then cocked her head at him. "You aren't going to like this, but I think it's time we took Queron into our confidence."

Joram's face went very still as he sat down again. "You're right. I don't like it."

"That doesn't alter the fact that doing what we're considering is probably more than two people can handle, just from the physical aspect—not just for shifting rubble and unblocking masonry, but for actually infiltrating the library, if that becomes possible. The possibility of injury in either activity makes a Healer an excellent choice."

"We could have Gregory send us a Healer from Trevalga," Joram ventured. "No one would have to know why we need the Varnarite texts. For that matter, Queron need not know."

Evaine snorted. "You think Queron wouldn't ask questions? Besides, we need his expertise. Remember that Father's research suggested that the Gabrilites were a precursor or offshoot of the Varnarite School. Queron is our only available Gabrilite, and he has a scholar's background—which means that he might know things he doesn't even know he knows, regarding some of the esoteric sources we're trying to track down."

"I won't argue any of those points," Joram agreed. "But just how much did you propose to tell him?"

"Everything."

"Everything? *Now*?"

Evaine shrugged. "He has to know sometime, Joram. Besides, he's a very observant man. Now that Revan's operation is well and truly launched, I can hardly continue to pretend that all this research is on baptizer cults, now can I?"

"I suppose not."

"Shall we tell him tonight, then?"

Joram sighed and bowed his head in his hands, elbows supported by the tabletop. For several seconds he stared unseeing at the table, at the plans and the sheaf of notes fanned across the scarred wood, then sighed again and sat back on his stool to look up at her, hands spread flat on the table.

"I suppose you have the approach all worked out."

Smiling, she laid her nearer hand over one of his, inviting their old rapport.

"Try this scenario," she whispered, as she began to show him.

Half an hour later, a knock at Queron's door roused him from his meditations. He had been sitting cross-legged on his pallet, with the readings for the next morning's Mass spread around him, but he closed the volume in his hands and swung one foot to the floor as he called, "Come in."

"Good evening," Evaine said, smiling as she opened the door and entered. "I hope I'm not disturbing you."

Queron raised a disparaging hand and returned her smile. "A welcome disturbance, I assure you. I've been trying to gather my thoughts for some kind of coherent homily tomorrow, but I'm afraid all I've gathered so far is wool. I think I'll sleep on it, and put the onus on the Holy Spirit to inspire me at the appropriate time. I've found that's usually better than trying to force the issue. What can I do for you?"

"Well, I'd like to confide something to you," she said lightly, leaning against the doorjamb with her hands behind her. "You see, Revan's baptizer cult isn't the only reason I've been doing research for the last few months. It doesn't have any direct bearing on that, or even on Javan's problem with the regents, but it's very important to me personally. I'm going to need a Healer's help. Since Rhys isn't available any more, you're elected."

Concern furrowed Queron's brow, and he slowly got to his feet. "You aren't ill, are you?"

"No, nothing like that," she said, smiling. "Believe me, it's nothing you would guess in a million years. And I can't reveal anything else unless you agree beforehand to lower your shields and give me absolute control to *keep* them down afterwards, so Joram and I can feed you full details of what it all means."

One wiry eyebrow arched in surprise, but no trace of fear crossed Queron's face. "So Joram's involved in all of this too, eh? You make it sound very ominous."

"Queron, it will shake you to the very depths of your faith," she replied honestly.

"I see." He drew a deep breath, obviously considering, then slowly nodded. "Very well. You've piqued my curiosity sufficiently that you know I can't refuse—so what happens now? I assume you won't make this revelation without Joram present, so I gather we have to go somewhere else. Where is it to be? Or, is he waiting outside?"

Evaine gave him a tiny smile. "Oh, he's waiting, but not outside. Come with me."

She conjured handfire before leading him down a stair he had not seen before, descending several levels deeper than Queron had known existed. Torchlight greeted them as they emerged from the stairwell, but Joram was nowhere to be seen.

"In those last days before King Cinhil's restoration, when we had several hundred Michaelines hiding out here, this used to be a stores level," Evaine said, extinguishing her handfire as she took the torch from its wall-mounted cresset. "We aren't so many now, and couldn't reprovision such a large undertaking if we wanted to, but these lower levels do still have their uses."

Queron said nothing, only following with increasing curiosity and a little apprehension as she led him farther along the corridor. He had been expecting Joram, but the Michaeline priest still startled him by stepping suddenly from the shadows of a doorway near the end of the passage. Queron guessed that what they meant to show him was behind that door. Joram nodded greeting as he took the torch from his sister, but he did not speak. He looked very somber, as did Evaine. Unaccountably, Queron could feel his heart beginning to beat faster.

"I'll need that control now," Evaine murmured, turning to face him in the torchlight, her blue eyes locking with his dark brown ones. "I promise you won't be harmed, but we can't proceed without your cooperation."

Pushing down a vague sense of foreboding, Queron smiled faintly and rested both his hands on the upturned palms she held out to him. "I did this for your dear husband once, when he first showed me his blocking talent," he said. "He scared me silly. You've scared me, too, on occasion—both of you—but you've never betrayed my trust. So go ahead and do what you think you must. I won't resist."

His shields subsided even as he spoke, like contained flame

slowly dying in a covered jar. Carefully and deliberately, he made himself vulnerable, letting her will engulf him like a pool of purifying light, blood-warm, feeling her mind insinuate controls into every source of his strength, to depths he had not dreamed she would require.

She was good at what she did—very good. His powers were intact, of course, but he could not have used them against her to save his very soul. He found himself praying that his trust had not been misplaced, for he knew she could destroy him with a glance—could even make him destroy himself, so absolute was her hold upon him.

But she demanded nothing yet, only smiling faintly as she released his left hand and gently turned him to face away from the doorway where Joram still stood vigilant watch with the torch. He heard the door open then, and let himself be guided through it backwards, watching Joram close and bar it before setting his torch in a cresset to its left. More light streamed from behind him, deeper in the room, reflecting from the still, watchful whiteness of their faces.

"There is a glamour on what you are about to see," Evaine warned, releasing his hand so he could turn. "What you will *think* you see is not necessarily what is."

Queron did not even notice when Evaine brought Joram into her control link. Indeed, he forgot all about controls as he gaped at the blue-clad body laid out on the bier. Candles burned in tall, freestanding candlesticks at the bier's four corners, shedding their uncompromising light on the face of a man Queron himself had helped to bury, but a few months before.

"But, this is Alister Cullen," he breathed, forgetting all about Evaine's warning. "I don't understand. Why have you brought him here?"

"I told you, what you *think* you see is not necessarily what is," Evaine repeated, setting her hand lightly on his left wrist. "Look again."

Before Queron's very eyes, the face of the body before him began to waver and then to change. Queron gasped and leaned closer, catching himself on the edge of the bier with both hands, lightheaded with shock as the new face steadied. All he could think, as he melted to his knees, was that Joram had told the truth about hiding away his father's body all those years ago. It had not been assumed into heaven, but it had remained incorruptible!

"It's Saint Camber!" Queron managed to whisper. "Praise be to God!"

He started to cross himself, but Joram caught his right wrist.

"I can't say whether he's a saint or not," Joram said sharply, "but think again about what you first saw!"

"But—"

"Queron, *my father didn't die in 905*," Joram went on relentlessly. "*Alister Cullen died.* Father and I found his body after the battle, and I helped Father take on Alister's shape, and put Father's shape on *him*, because Cinhil needed Alister Cullen more than he needed Camber MacRorie. All the rest sprang from that substitution. *All* the rest."

"But, the visions," Queron protested weakly. "The miracles—"

"Were all based on misinterpretation of what we were actually doing—at least at first," Evaine murmured. "Show him, Joram. You were the one most immediately caught up in everything that happened. We didn't set out to make him a saint, Queron. We really didn't."

Queron collapsed back onto his haunches as Joram loomed above him, whimpering a little as the Michaeline's free hand dropped heavily to his brow. He could feel Evaine holding down his shields so Joram could enter his mind, and he could not evade the power that he himself had given her over him. Joram's hand was cold on his forehead, pressing his head back against Evaine's supportive shoulder, and the force of Joram's overwhelming sendings made him reel, his eyes rolling upward and closing as the unwanted images began to flow.

Joram helping his father make the shift of shapes that turned Camber into Alister, Alister into Camber . . . Assisting Camber to read the shreds of Alister's memory still accessible in the dead man's mind . . . Making his way back to King Cinhil's camp with the Alister-faced Camber, bearing the dead body of his "father." Only he, Rhys, and Evaine had known the truth, in the beginning.

"Camber" was not even properly buried before the first incident occurred that later contributed to the evidence for canonization, when a compassionate act meant to ease the grief of Camber's almost suicidal former squire, young Guaire of Arliss, had been taken for a supernatural event. Camber had presented the visitation as a dream, but Guaire's elation soon had changed it to something of a miracle.

And close on its heels, though Camber himself had not been consciously aware of it at the time, had come a second incident that truly cemented Camber's saintly status, when later added to the weight of other occurrences that, otherwise, might have been dismissed as pious fantasizing. During an interrupted working meant by Evaine, Rhys, and Joram to help Camber assimilate the memories he had taken from the dead Alister—memories that, if not made his own, would drive him mad—not one but two outsiders had glimpsed Camber's true face. Not knowing what they truly saw, both believed the event to be an instance of saintly intervention. One of the witnesses had been one Lord Dualta Jarriot, a fervent young Michaeline Knight; the other, King Cinhil himself. Both had later testified to their experience during the proceedings to canonize Camber, the king much against his will.

Before all of that, however, had come the single act of conscience that legitimated much of what Camber did in his dual role as Alister Cullen—and also led to his eventual presence at his own canonization. The catalyst was Camber's discovery that Alister Cullen, the Vicar General of the Michaelines, priest as well as knight, had already agreed to accept consecration as a bishop before he rode off to his last battle.

To refuse the office at such a time would have required explanation Camber dared not give. Nor did he feel he dared profane the priesthood that Alister had possessed or the episcopal office he now was expected to assume, by accepting the outward ceremonials without the substance of proper ordination. Had two elder brothers not died while Camber was in his youth, leaving him their father's only male heir, Camber might have become a priest in fact; but he had set aside an honest vocation in the interests of filial duty. Now Joram suggested a way that his father might resolve his present ethical dilemma by taking up his old vocation.

So Camber had approached his old friend Anscom of Trevas, the Deryni Archbishop of Valoret, the night before he was to receive episcopal consecration, confiding what he had done and why, and asking ordination at Anscom's hands so that he might fulfill his new role as conscientiously as possible, given the circumstances. Anscom had agreed, and for many years remained the only one besides the immediate family to know that Alister Cullen was really Camber MacRorie.

So the impersonation might have progressed indefinitely, without further complication, had not young Guaire of Arliss confided his most intimate experience of Camber to a zealous Gabrilite Healer-priest named Queron Kinevan. Queron already had begun investigating a local cult of the "Blessed Camber," arising around Camber's tomb at Caerrorie. Even then, Joram had found the attentions of that cult both disturbing and unwanted, and already had sought a safer resting place for the body of his "father." Secretly moving it from the family vaults had seemed a prudent thing to do, lest someone break into the tomb and discover who it really was— or rather, who it was *not*.

The action had backfired little more than a year later, when Queron brought his evidence before the Synod of Bishops and demanded Camber's canonization, citing the empty tomb at Caerrorie as evidence that "Saint Camber" had been bodily assumed into heaven, in addition to working miracles on behalf of his devotees. Joram's presence at the synod, as secretary to Bishop "Alister," and his inability to explain away the empty tomb with other than the now lame-sounding excuse that he had moved the body—whose location he was magically bound not to reveal—only added fuel to Queron's argument, for neither Joram nor Camber dared defuse the allegations of sainthood with the truth without also giving away the impersonation.

Neither Camber nor Joram had ever told an outright lie under oath, but neither had they been able to deter Queron. Formal canonization ceremonies had been carried out less than a month later, and soon the Servants of Saint Camber, under Queron's direction, were spreading the cult of their patron saint throughout Gwynedd. Camber himself had lived on as Alister Cullen until a few weeks ago, fooling everyone including Queron, until assassins' blades had taken him and Jebediah of Alcara in a snowy clearing near Saint Mary's in the Hills.

Queron reeled under the onslaught of Joram's forced briefing, trying to shake his head in negation as all the implications of the truth of Saint Camber resettled in his consciousness, readjusting "facts." He knew he was weeping for his lost faith, and could not help himself. And Camber's children were not yet finished with him.

Now the relentless drive of harsh, uncompromising, and unwanted knowledge shifted from Joram to Evaine, as Camber's daughter revealed her unshakable belief that Camber even now was not dead, but lay suspended in the binding of a spell not reckoned possible by most Deryni, if they had ever even heard of it. Evaine's research in the matter had been frighteningly thorough, as Queron would have expected of Camber's daughter, and she gave him the weight of *that* information to add to all he had already taken in— along with a plea for his help. She and Joram intended to try to reverse the spell that held Camber suspended in some twilight realm between life and death, and to have Queron attempt to Heal him before true death claimed him at last. The very notion made Queron's mind reel even more dizzily than it had hitherto, and this most rational and disciplined of Deryni would have crossed himself in ritualistic plea for deliverance, had control of physical function remained in his volition.

But the audacity of their intention was tempered finally by a softer flow of yet another strand in their indoctrination—the speculation, jointly shared by sister and brother, that *something* about their father lay beyond the reason even of those who knew the truth about him, and had always known it. A wistful wondering whether something about Camber might not be supernatural after all. The spiritual presence of Camber had been felt more than once in the weeks since his working of the forbidden spell—and by Queron as well as Joram and Evaine, under circumstances that had nothing to do with the cult of Saint Camber now being so rigorously suppressed in the outside world.

What if Camber *was* a saint? Even Joram was forced to consider the possibility. What really constituted sainthood? And how was one to know *anything* for certain?

Evaine backed off then, as Joram had already done. For a moment, she used the skills she had learned by working with Rhys to assess Queron's physical condition—to regularize rapid breathing and heartbeat, soothe bruised psychic pathways, and make shy apologies for what she had felt compelled to do to him.

"It was never our deliberate intention to deceive you, Queron," she murmured, shifting to audible speech as one hand gently stroked his head, now resting in her lap. "Nor was it our intention to hurt anyone, though harm inevitably has been done, in the process of protecting first Cinhil and now his sons. Everything my father did—everything *we* did—was for that purpose. We sought no personal gain.

"Now we need a Healer to help us try to bring him back to continue what he started. But it has to be of your own free will."

He had no free will yet, though. Her controls were still in place, preventing any extreme reaction—which was probably a good idea, because the anger, grief, and pain warring inside him amid all the new information to be assimilated would take a while to resolve. Groggily he opened his eyes to look up at her, aware of Joram crouching beside her right shoulder, tight-lipped and anxious. Even the slight effort of trying to focus on them made him so nauseated he feared he might throw up, so badly did his head ache, right behind his eyes, but she sensed his distress immediately and helped him damp the physical symptoms, also urging him to run through the standard assessment exercise that trained Deryni always used after an involved working.

He found himself resenting her ministrations, even as the respite from pain enabled him to confirm that his faculties were his again, save for his shields. Simultaneously, the thought occurred to him that he still had the ability to lash out psychically—for all the good it would do, since they simply would know what he was going to do and counter it accordingly. And the sane, rational part of him admitted that they had not intended to deceive him, even as another part relished imagining what it would be like to give back hurt for hurt.

"I wouldn't do that, though," he said aloud, a little surprised to find his throat scratchy and hoarse. "You're going to have to give me time to sort this all out, but a lot makes sense that didn't before. What you've done, you've done for all the right reasons. It simply didn't work out the way you planned."

Evaine sighed. "We like to think so. Sometimes, it seems that we were simply swept along on a tide of destiny, unable to alter forces we'd unwittingly set in motion without realizing all the possible consequences. One thing led to another."

"And now you've been led to confide it all to me." He smiled shakily. "Shall I keep this all under the seal of the confessional?"

Joram looked uneasy. "That wasn't part of the original bargain. In all that I've done, I never compromised my priesthood. So far as I know, neither did my father. I certainly wouldn't ask you to do so."

"I don't recall offering to compromise," Queron murmured, lifting shaking hands to rub across his face. "This headache I've got—is it akin to what Camber felt, before he'd assimilated all of Alister's memories?"

"Probably akin, yes, but not the same," Evaine said, smiling tentatively. "A simple good night's sleep will sort you out. If you wish, I'll set a compulsion to that effect, then let you go back to your quarters under your own power. I doubt you'd sleep well here on the floor, especially with *him* up there." She gestured toward the bier with a wry jut of her chin. "And I don't think Joram and I particularly relish the idea of carrying you back up all those stairs."

Queron chuckled aloud at that, patting his free hand wearily against Evaine's, where it still curved against his neck.

"Dear lady, after what we've all just been through, I wouldn't dream of asking. I confess, I'm too numb to think very clearly, so you just do what you think is best. You know what I need, both in body and mind. You've worked with one of the best Healers I ever knew. You just set your orders, and we'll all be off for some well-deserved rest.

"And Joram," he went on, turning his attention to the younger man, "I don't think you ever need to be wary about your ability to operate in my league." He shook his head at Joram's beginning protest. "No, don't deny it. You were intimidated by my reputation, which I've cultivated carefully for many, many years; and I deliberately let you think I was as good as you thought I was. I'm good," he agreed, holding up a finger for emphasis, "but so are you. You were trained by Camber MacRorie, after all—whether or not he really is a saint."

CHAPTER NINETEEN

For thou seest that our sanctuary is laid waste,
our altar broken down, our temple destroyed.
—II Esdras 10:21

Joram took Queron's Mass the next morning. Queron slept until ccmidafternoon and lay on his pallet thereafter, thinking, until Evaine came with a tray of supper, an uncomfortable-looking Joram accompanying her.

"Ah, you're awake," Evaine said brightly. "I've brought you something to eat. How do you feel?"

Queron smiled and swung his legs off the bed, taking the tray on his lap. "Hungry. How *should* I feel, after you've let me sleep all day?" He chose to ignore the look the two exchanged as he bit into a slab of bread spread thick with butter and honey. "I do hope someone showed up to celebrate Mass this morning," he went on, around the bite of sweetness. "It's one of my few contributions to this little flock, in addition to rather niggling Healer's duty when one of the children has a scuffed knee or a stomachache. You should let me do more."

"You've already done a lot," Joram said quietly. His eyes had a faintly haunted look. "We haven't the right to ask more of you."

"But you *have* asked," Queron replied. "And I've thought it over and I accept."

Evaine glanced at her hands, suddenly shy to look him in the eyes. "Searching out the records we need is only the beginning, Queron. If we find what we're looking for, the magical working required almost certainly will be unlike anything any of us has ever done before. Nor will it be without its dangers, perhaps to our very

213

souls as well as our lives. You should know what you're getting into."

Queron started to speak, then paused to pass both hands in a ritual gesture somewhat hampered by the piece of bread in his hand. The impediment did not affect the Wards that rose up around the room in a shimmer of silvery light.

"I wonder, do either of *you* know what you're getting into, where that's concerned?" Queron said, after another bite of honeyed bread. "Oh, you know you must try to reverse a spell that you *think* Camber worked successfully—and I'd like another look at him, now that I've somewhat recovered from my initial shock—but neither of you knows any more than I do about what may actually be involved. You're not even sure how the spell was *set*, never mind how it needs to be reversed."

"I've seen the result of a *failed* setting at rather close range," Joram said quietly, "back when this whole thing began. Ariella tried it, after the real Alister pinned her to a tree with a spell and his sword. Either she died before she could complete it or she did it wrong. Father did neither."

"I believe you may be right," Queron answered softly.

"I was also with him when Rhys was dying," Joram went on, almost daring Queron to deny it. "He was confident enough that he could work the spell that he thought about using it to try to save Rhys until a Healer could get there to do a proper job. He decided that the decision was one he couldn't make for another soul—which means, one must conclude, that he felt there *was* danger that went beyond the mere finitude of existence in a physical body. From that and from the research Evaine and I have done, I think we realize the kind of power we're dealing with. Gabrilite training isn't everything, you know."

"No one ever said it was, son."

For a few minutes, Queron only continued eating, finally pouring himself a cup of ale from the pottery pitcher on the tray and gulping it down.

"I think you'll agree that Gabrilite training *does* offer some unique features, however," he went on, as if the break had not occurred. "In general terms, you're surely aware of some of the things it implies. I'll bend my vows by telling you that it also implies connection with an ancient mystery school whose very existence I'm not supposed to reveal. It's entirely possible that knowledge coming from that source might apply to what we need to do—in which case, I'd have to consider very carefully what I dare share with you. I am still bound by *some* oaths no less strong than those I gave you in the *keeill* a few weeks ago."

Evaine breathed out softly, still not looking up at him. "We're aware of the existence of other traditions alongside the Gabrilite," she said. "You studied with Dom Emrys, didn't you? He once told Father that he'd had his original training in a tradition that was neither Gabrilite nor Michaeline. It was even pre-Varnarite, wasn't it? We'll be looking at some Varnarite texts, with any luck."

As she looked up at him at last, her blue eyes were glowing like sapphires. Joram's face was closed and shuttered, the grey eyes like granite, but no threat could be read from either of them.

"I think," Queron said, setting aside his tray, "that we never quite finished some business in the *keeill*, back when I gave you my oath. I don't think we need go back there for this, do you?" he went on, holding out a hand to each of them. "If I'm to help you, I need to know everything you kept back because it was tied in with your secret about Camber. I can handle it here, if you can, but we need to get this resolved, I think."

Wordlessly, Evaine and then Joram sat down on either side of him, joining hands with him and then with each other across his knees. In a harmony jagged at first, with Queron unused to their three-way linkage, they settled into deep rapport.

This time, there was no holding back save in the areas of Queron's esoteric oaths of secrecy and his and Joram's priestly offices. This Evaine and Joram simply *knew*, with a certainty that echoed the closest bonds any of them had ever had with other Deryni. All knowledge pertinent to the situation was shared, including a full briefing to Queron of all the material they had assembled thus far and what Evaine felt they needed next. Whatever misgivings any of them might have had about one another previously were dispelled by the time they dismantled the rapport.

"I shouldn't think we ought to waste any time, though," Queron said, plucking a piece of cheese from the discarded tray and taking a bite. "The Varnarite library is sure to be an early target for the *Custodes Fidei*, if Bishop Edward's minions haven't already gotten to it."

"You don't think they'll burn the library, do you?" Evaine asked, horrified.

"Oh, very likely. Parts of it, at least." Queron poured himself another cup of ale to wash down his cheese. "That would be a particular pity, since Grecotha had a copy of the *Liber Ricae*, the last time I looked. We should go tonight."

"*Tonight?*" Joram had said it, but both he and Evaine looked surprised.

"But don't you need to rest?" Evaine asked. "We put you through a lot last night."

"Very true," Queron replied, draining off his ale. "Gabrilites have wonderful resilience, though. When this is all resolved, and we have more time, I'll teach you both some of our techniques. Go get changed now, both of you, while I finish eating. Michaeline blue is not conducive to sneaking into establishments run by paranoid bishops these days, Joram. And Evaine—you can't go climbing around ruins comfortably in skirts. Borrow someone's boots and breeches."

An hour later, all of them suitably garbed and fed and armed with implements for shifting earth, their excuses made to Niallan, who must take charge in their absence, the three of them stood outside the door to the sanctuary's Transfer Portal. Though they had not consulted among themselves, all had chosen clothing in shades of grey and black, stone- and shadow-colored. Joram wore a close-fitting leather cap with his ears exposed and handed one to each of his companions.

"Besides providing camouflage for the two of us with yellow beacons for hair, the caps give some protection where headroom is close," he said, as Evaine coiled the braided tail of her hair inside hers and pulled it on. "At least Evaine won't concuss herself, with all that padding," he added with a grin, as she felt the soft cushion on top of her head.

Queron smiled and put on his cap as well. "One would think you'd done this kind of clandestine foraging before," he said. "One of the advantages of Michaeline training, no doubt."

"No doubt," Evaine said, before Joram could reply. "Who's going through first?"

Joram ended up going through first with Queron, since he had been there before, then returned to bring Evaine. Queron's silvery handfire met Evaine and Joram as they stepped from the plastered Portal chamber into a timbered corridor strewn with rubble. Both Evaine and Queron had seen the place through Joram's memory, but it was different, seeing it in person. Different individuals noted different things. Evaine was struck by the dank, stagnant air, overlaid with a faint, sweetish odor she had smelled before.

"Dry rot?" she whispered, brushing fingertips across a crumbling wall panel.

"And wet rot, rising damp, woodworm, deathwatch beetles— you name it," Joram replied, pulling on gloves. "God, it's worse than I remembered!"

"Well, you were here in the autumn before," Queron murmured, his boots making crunching sounds as he ground rubble against the tessellated tiles. "I'd expect winter to be wetter. To the left, I believe?"

Joram nodded, steadying himself with a hand against the wall as he stepped across the debris to join Queron. "As good a direction as any other. You probably ought to see the parts I saw, before we get too far afield. There're some interesting frescoes on these walls ahead. Watch your heads."

The frescoes to which Joram referred had long since ceased to have any artistic merit. If Evaine squinted her eyes just right, she could imagine she saw the scenes of monastic and academic life Joram had noted on his first visit, but that was stretching credibility to its limits. What lay ahead interested her far more, in any case— just around a sharp bend to the right.

The vast doorway once had supported heavy double doors of oak bound with iron. One of the doors had fallen since Joram's last visit, its upper hinge finally rusted through; the lower had been ripped from the wood by whatever catastrophe had brought the place to ruin. Joram did not attempt to push the remaining door ajar, but scrambled up the gentle incline of the fallen one and held out a hand to Evaine when he had jumped down to the littered floor level on the other side of the door sill.

"*Adorabo ad templum sanctum tuum, et confitebor nomini tuo,*" Queron recited behind them, reading from an inscription carved on the lintel beam high above his head. "I will worship toward Thy holy temple, and will give glory to Thy Name." He chuckled softly. "Well, that's apt."

"Yes, but for what?" Joram murmured, as Queron joined him and Evaine. "Father and I were never able to figure it out."

"Oh, it's apt for the folk who built *this* place," Queron replied, gesturing forward. "Shall we?"

The great domed chamber they had just entered was vast, sucking up the feeble light of their handfires even when they each conjured a second sphere. It bore a superficial resemblance to the *keeill* underneath the Camberian Council chamber, but it was much larger. A circular dais of seven steps supported a black and white cube altar very like the one in the *keeill*, but the top level of the dais was inlaid with black and white tiles set in a checkerboard design that echoed the motif of the altar sides. The pavement was badly damaged, as was the top of the altar, perhaps by the impact of something heavy and substantial that had fallen from a length of broken chain dependent from a central boss high above. The chain ended in nothingness well short of the cracked altar top, which once had been a polished expanse of white marble. Above and all around, the ribs and arches of the chamber's domed ceiling disappeared into a gloom that was little dissipated by handfire, even when they sent several additional spheres aloft. Shattered glass and masonry littered the steps around the altar, though the dais itself had been swept mostly clear.

"Father and I did that," Joram whispered, indicating the space.

As Queron glided closer to inspect some of the glass shards, crouching beside the bottom step, Evaine began moving around the room's perimeter.

At least in the evocations depicted on the chamber's walls, the place had been an elemental shrine, Evaine soon realized. As she moved from quarter to quarter, making the complete circuit of the chamber, the cool greens of a shaded forest glade gave way to a dark, brooding sky filled with scudding storm clouds, to the fire of summer lightning, and then the cool, tranquil beauty of a lake shore nestled among craggy mountain peaks. The familiarity was somehow comforting, though the chamber itself was not.

Evaine glanced at Joram, standing near the door and watching their reactions, arms folded across his chest. Queron had ascended the dais steps and was standing at the altar, his hands spread flat on its surface, eyes closed. As she mounted the steps to join him, Queron looked up, still in the trance of his deep reading, a trace of an odd little smile twitching at the corners of his mouth.

"I see what Joram means about the altar still being a power source, after all these years," he murmured, inviting her to feel it for herself.

Without comment, she moved in beside him, setting her hands flat on a part of the altar that had been exposed when the top was smashed, one hand on a black surface and the other on white. Closing her eyes, she felt the upsurge of power almost at once, strong eddies of pure energy that spiralled upward like a gentle tide, washing at the edges of her mind with a force that held just a hint of menace behind the raw potential.

She blinked as she withdrew, unconsciously wiping her palms against the sides of her tunic as she glanced at Queron uneasily.

"Do you have any idea who used this altar?" she murmured. "And more important, for *what*?"

Queron shook his head. "I could hazard a few educated guesses, but I'd prefer to wait until I've had a chance to digest all of this," he said. "Meanwhile, I seem to recall a library that wants finding. We'd best not spend too much time here."

"Come this way, then," Joram said, gesturing back the way they had come. "There's supposed to be a branch off the main corridor, not far from here. We'll start there."

They spent the remainder of the night picking their way through a series of partially collapsed passageways that got worse the farther they went. Toward the end, they had to stop and dig through where a portion of roof had fallen in.

"Father did this," Joram told them in hushed tones, as they shifted the rubble, stone by stone. "A branch of this passageway, farther along, was one of the ones that still led close to the surface. He didn't want anyone wandering down here who shouldn't be. We'll have several places like this, if I've interpreted the plans correctly."

That night's work brought them little closer to their goal, however. The next night was hardly more fruitful. The third night saw them gain hesitant access to an area immediately underneath one end of the bishop's residence, however, skirting a cellar complex that once had held a fine collection of wine amassed by Camber-Alister and his predecessors as Bishops of Grecotha. Only Evaine's curiosity, as she investigated a supposedly blocked up squint in a wall, averted what might have been a fatal mishap. She had to stretch to peer through the narrow spy hole, and nearly gasped aloud at what she saw.

What is it? Queron asked, his question blasting into her mind.

She eased back to let him look, still seeing the scene before her in memory: the dim, close confines of the hall beyond, lit by smoky cressets along the walls, its floor virtually lined with the sleeping forms of dozens of soldiers of the bishop's garrison. And this late at night, the slightest sound made in the hidden corridor that passed so close might be heard and remarked by the men sleeping there.

They beat a quiet but hasty retreat after that, and shifted their operations to the daylight hours in the future, when inadvertant sounds would not carry such potential danger. Since little natural light penetrated to the depths where they moved, the change of time made little difference on that account; they still used handfire, rather than torches, to eliminate the risk of smoke giving away their presence. A difference it did make was the opportunity it gave them to spy upon actual activities instead of sleeping men. On the fifth day, they even gained access to a narrow lancet window that looked out onto the main courtyard of the bishop's manor.

Smoke was curling upward from something smoldering in the center of the yard. At first Evaine thought they were burning leaves or the blacksmith had set up his forge in the center of the yard and was having trouble getting his fire to draw properly.

Then she saw the monks carrying the stacks of parchment rolls and the occasional bound book, lining up to consign the volumes to the flames.

"So, dear Bishop Edward is purging his library," Queron murmured, close beside her ear. "What do you want to bet that our *Liber Ricae* is either in that lot or on its way in there?"

Evaine shuddered and turned away to bury her face in her brother's shoulder. "How can they do that?" she whispered. "How can they burn books?"

"The same way they burn people," Joram muttered. "Books are just as dangerous."

"And they'd gladly consign us to the same fire, if they could," Queron said. "Come, let's be away from here. We can do nothing to stop that, and watching it will only depress our spirits even more."

They lingered for a while longer, even so, and returned to the hidden Portal in silence.

"So, what next?" Evaine asked, when they were safely back in the little study next door to the room where Camber lay. "We needed that text."

"Well, we'll have to make do with something else, unless we're granted a miracle," Queron replied. "In the meantime, we'll go back over the sources that we do have. I've been racking my brain, all the way back. How about Kitron's *Principia Magica*? Have you got a copy of that?"

"Yes, but it doesn't have—"

"Parts of Kitron are coded," Queron said brusquely. "I haven't read it in a long time, but there may be parts that apply. It's also just possible that I still might be able to get hold of a copy of the *Liber Ricae*. We have to do something, though."

Joram nodded. "I was thinking about Jokal of Tyndour, too. I remember Rhys talking about some of the Healing passages, and being surprised by some of the procedures—which means they can't have been straight-forward techniques. Maybe there's a more esoteric connection."

Sighing, Evaine shook her head despondently. "We're grasping at straws, I'm afraid. Maybe we're mad even to think about continuing. Maybe we should just let Father be dead and forget about it."

Neither man answered that remark, all too aware that the temporary setback they had suffered was only that—temporary. And after a while, the three of them went into the next room to pray, and so that Queron could investigate the spell more carefully.

*   *   *

While research continued in the Michaeline sanctuary, Javan had not been idle, either. The royal party finally reached Rhemuth on Quinquagesima, the Sunday before Lent. On Tuesday morning, the new capital was treated to the spectacle of a state wedding, that of Richeldis MacLean, the Heiress of Kierney, to Iver MacInnis, Heir to the new Earl of Culdi. The ceremony was conducted jointly by the bridegroom's uncle, the Archbishop of Valoret, and his younger brother, the Bishop of Grecotha. A bleak-eyed Jamie Drummond gave away his former ward, with the king to witness, and the king's own brothers served at the couple's nuptial Mass, further setting the royal seal of approval firmly on the match. All the regents and their wives attended.

The wedding feast in Rhemuth Castle's great hall would be the talk of Rhemuth society well into the summer. Javan would rather have forgotten it. The thirteen-year-old bride looked thoroughly overwhelmed by the entire affair and burst into tears when the ladies of the court came to convey her to the bridal chamber. The bridegroom, eight years her senior, drank too much, talked too loudly, and strutted like a bandy cock before following after her half an hour later, to hoots of encouragement and ribald suggestion. The next morning, before repairing to the basilica to receive the ashes marking the beginning of Lent, young Iver pronounced himself passing pleased with his new wife, and boasted of having been in Kierney the night before.

Javan hated him doubly for that, for though young Richeldis was not yet Countess of Kierney in fact, he had little doubt that the deficiency would be remedied all too soon. Nor was he surprised when, but a few weeks after the wedding, word came that the bride's uncle had met a fatal accident while hunting.

All Javan's skills as an actor were put to the test when he again was required to lend the legitimacy of his presence as his brother confirmed the new Countess of Kierney in her title and acknowledged her husband as the new earl. The prince had murder in his heart as he stalked off afterwards to pray in the Chapel Royal, the ever-present Charlan at his heels, and spent some hours devising suitable fates for those guilty of Iain MacLean's death, though he knew his chances of carrying out any of them were nonexistent.

At least he felt better, afterwards. Nor did he count any of the regents innocent of the old Earl of Kierney's death. It was as well that they dispersed to other pursuits for the rest of Lent, for Javan found himself hard-pressed to be civil to any of them, even if prudence forced him to spare their lives.

Iver's father, Manfred MacInnis, returned to Grecotha with his younger son, Bishop Edward, to loot and censor the Varnarite School, taking Ursin O'Carroll with him. Duke Ewan headed north to resume his viceregal duties in Kheldour. Periodically, Earl Tammaron betook himself to Caerrorie on Manfred's behalf to oversee the dismantling of the castle there, for Manfred wanted no old Camberian associations remaining when he took up residence in the new manor being built at the opposite edge of the holding. Murdoch and Rhun remained with the king at Rhemuth, but the two made frequent trouble-shooting forays to the north and east, all during those weeks of early spring—which made them relatively easy to avoid, most of the time.

Javan's chief personal nemesis, Archbishop Hubert, returned to Valoret soon after the MacInnis-MacLean wedding, to get on with the concluding business of the Council of Ramos. He took with him Rhemuth's archbishop, Robert Orris, but handed over the care of Javan's soul to Orris' auxiliary, Bishop Alfred of Woodbourne. Javan had respected Father Alfred as a priest, and supposed the man might have turned out to be a reasonably good bishop, had he not succumbed to the temptations Hubert offered in exchange for his integrity, but the prince had no use for Alfred as a spiritual director. Instead, Javan drafted a round, merry priest of middling years called Father Boniface, who was attached to the old basilica in the grounds of the castle. With Boniface, he pursued sufficient scholastic endeavors of an ecclesiastical bent to disarm increasingly any serious worry about him as a rival for Rhys Michael's eventual succession to the throne.

As a consequence, Bishop Alfred and the remaining regents mostly left Javan alone, except when his presence was required for state occasions, of which there were few during Lent. Otherwise, the Lenten season progressed as Lent usually did—for Javan, a welcome respite from the round of endless banquets and other court entertainments that seemed so empty and hypocritical, as he watched his brother's royal prerogatives slowly eroded. Javan worried increasingly, as Lent progressed and none of his Deryni allies managed to contact him even indirectly to reassure him that he was not forgotten, but he continued with what he believed Evaine and Joram would have wanted him to do—spying on the regents and, in particular, trying to find out more about the true feelings of his brothers.

Rhys Michael proved easy enough—still an uncomplicated if increasingly self-centered child, mostly concerned for his toy knights and games of strategy, and whether his governors would allow him sufficient practice time in the weapons yard and in his equestrian pursuits. Midway through Lent, Javan managed an entire afternoon with his younger brother, with Charlan unwittingly distracting Rhys Michael's senior squire over a spirited game of Cardounet while Javan pretended to need help with the translation of a treatise on strategy—which assistance Rhys Michael was only too willing to provide. The youngest prince was never to realize what other assistance he provided by sitting close enough to read over Javan's shoulder and make comments as Javan limped through the translation. Javan left the afternoon's work no better versed in strategy, but convinced that his younger brother had begun no breakthrough whatever into his Haldane heritage—which was how things were *supposed* to be, Javan knew, even though he himself was different.

Seeing his brother the king privately again was yet another story. Several times Javan contrived plausible excuses to be in his elder brother's presence, only to find others with even more plausible excuses. As Eastertide approached, he began to despair of ever managing to attempt a proper reading in reasonable safety. An unexpected opportunity finally presented itself on a cold, rainy Saturday afternoon late in March, when Alroy was confined to bed with a bad sore throat and cold and Javan came to inquire after his health. Alroy's squires had been sent off to weekly confession—and interrogation by one of the regents' agents, Javan had no doubt—and only Oriel was in attendance when the prince arrived. Alroy had been coughing, and his voice was hoarse as he greeted his brother.

"Ah, at least *someone's* come to pay me a visit!" Alroy croaked, seizing Javan's hand as his brother came to sit on the edge of the bed. "Oriel doesn't count, because he *has* to come to see me. Maybe now he'll leave me long enough to run down to the wine cellars and fetch some of that Rhennish brandywine for a new cough posset he's been promising me. I've been fair to hacking my lungs out this afternoon."

"*Has* he, Master Oriel?" Javan asked, glancing at the Healer.

Oriel tried not to look concerned. "I will concede that his Grace's cough has not responded as well as I would like. And if your Highness would agree to stay a while, my mind would be more at ease while I fetch the wine."

"Why, certainly," Javan breathed, hardly able to believe his good fortune. "Go immediately, Oriel. Perhaps my brother would like me to read to him."

Alroy nodded weakly but enthusiastically. "No, just talk to me, Javan. Tell me what you've been doing. I hardly see you anymore."

"I shan't be long," Oriel murmured, bowing out the door.

Alroy nestled down contentedly under his sleeping furs as the door closed behind Oriel, not releasing Javan's hand as he stifled a dry, nagging little cough with his free one.

"So, tell me what you've been up to lately. I hear you've been spending a lot of time on your knees. Earl Rhun makes snide remarks when he thinks I don't hear, but I think it would be a wonderful thing to be a priest the way Father was."

"You sound as if you've got me ordained already," Javan said with a smile, reaching to brush Alroy's damp forehead with his free hand. "Hey, you're running quite a fever. You need to take better care of yourself."

As he laid the hand flat, ostensibly to better judge the fever's intensity, he sent a gentle command to sleep, immediately eliciting a wide Haldane yawn.

"I'm trying, Javan," Alroy whispered, his eyelids drooping. "Really, I am. I'm so tired all the time, though. I've been taking my tonic, but it doesn't seem to do much good."

The king drifted into sleep as he finished the sentence, and Javan encouraged it, easily following up on the reference to Alroy's "tonic." The royal physicians had prescribed it, but Alroy sensed that Oriel did not approve—Alroy had no idea why.

Javan could guess why, though. Tavis had warned him months ago that the regents were keeping Alroy compliant with regular sedation.

But what of Alroy's potential as a Haldane? Further probing of a more general sort elicited stirrings of a beginning ability to Truth-Read—though Alroy counted it as a prerogative of his divine right as king—but no suspicion on Alroy's part of any of the further power that should be his as their father's heir. Appalled, Javan pressed his inquiries longer than was prudent, only suddenly becoming aware that he himself was under scrutiny. He started as he glanced up to see Oriel staring at him from just inside the door, a stone flask almost forgotten in his hand.

"Ah, Master Oriel. I didn't hear you come in," Javan said, quickly drawing back his hand from Alroy's forehead and trying to cover his tracks in Alroy's mind. "Did you get the wine?"

Oriel nodded minutely, his eyes never leaving Javan's. Javan could feel the other's mind probing at his, not hard but determinedly, for several seconds before Oriel broke eye contact and crossed to the table where his Healer's implements were laid out.

"I'll just make that posset now," he said, "though I see that the King's Grace has managed to drift off to sleep."

"I—think it's probably the fever," Javan murmured lamely, "though I'm sure you're aware of that." He did not move—only watching with growing apprehension as the Healer poured a small cup of wine, then dumped in a measured amount of powder from a parchment packet and stirred it briskly with a horn spoon. Oriel said nothing as he came to sit on the other side of the bed from Javan, only nodding his thanks as Javan helped raise the sleeping king to a sitting position to drink the posset. When the cup was empty, Oriel set it aside and motioned for Javan to join him in the window embrasure beyond. The gesture was not an invitation but a command. Javan shivered as he stepped up into the alcove. The yard beyond the diamond-paned glass was grey with rain, and the cold stone sucked away at body heat despite the heavy woolen drapes intended to insulate.

"Are you going to tell me about it, or do I have to make an issue of this?" Oriel said quietly, glancing beyond Javan at the rain as they sat down.

"Tell you about what?"

Slowly Oriel turned his face toward Javan, one hand moving slowly but deliberately to encircle one of Javan's wrists. Immediately, the sensation of the other's mind pressing at his shields intensified, though not to the extent that he felt they might breach.

"If anyone should come in now, I am monitoring your general health," Oriel said quietly. "Unless you tell them otherwise, no one will ever know differently. But what I really want to read is what you are. The king didn't just fall asleep while I was gone, Javan."

"What makes you say that?" Javan persisted. "Of course he fell asleep. He's been ill. He was worn out from coughing. And maybe he was worn out for other reasons, too. He told me about the tonic, Oriel."

"Then I trust he also told you that the tonic was not my idea, and that it's given to him without my approval." Oriel grimaced as he glanced at his hand on Javan's. "It's a sedative, of course—just enough to take the edge off any resistance he might make to what the regents want."

Javan nodded miserably. "I knew they'd been doing that at one time. I didn't think it had continued. Can't you do anything about it?"

"Do anything? Me?" Oriel snorted, glancing out at the rain streaming down the windowpanes. "Oh, I'm free as a bird, with my family held hostage for my good behavior. Have you forgotten that I have a wife and baby daughter I've hardly even seen since the regents took them into custody? Believe me, I'm sympathetic to your brother's plight, but my own family comes first—unless you know even more than I think you do," he added, suddenly looking back at Javan sharply. "Just how *did* you learn to do what you're doing?"

"What am I doing?"

"You're shielding, dammit!"

"I don't know what you're talking about," Javan replied steadily. "Forget about it."

"I *can't* forget about it, and you're lying when you say you don't know what I'm talking about," Oriel whispered, leaning closer to stare into Javan's eyes. "Did Tavis teach you this, or—Good God, was it *you* that those Deryni came through the Valoret Portal to see? Has all this sudden compliance with the regents' wishes just been lip service?"

"I know you can Truth-Read me, so I'm not going to answer those questions," Javan whispered.

"And with those shields, I can't just dig the answers out for myself, either," Oriel murmured. "Lord, I've never seen a human with shields. And I wouldn't even have noticed if you hadn't given me cause to be suspicious. I'm sure the others don't know. I—can it be that you're still in contact with Lord Rhys and the other exiled Deryni, Javan? Do I dare to hope it isn't all over, after all?"

"Some of it is over," Javan said woodenly. "Lord Rhys is dead. I can't speak for anyone else right now. But you tell *me*, knowing that you are being Truth-Read—is your loyalty to the regents based upon anything besides the threat to your family, if you don't play along?"

Oriel closed his eyes briefly, his face contorting in a grimace of barely controlled anguish. Tears glittered in his eyes as he opened them again, and his hand tightened on Javan's wrist.

"I'll answer your question with yet another question, my prince," the Healer breathed. "Can you sense that I'm lowering my shields and giving you access to the controls for those shields as well as access to my innermost thoughts? And know by Truth-Reading me that if you enter my mind, there is *nothing* I can do to resist you until you choose to withdraw. By the lives of my wife and daughter, I can't give you any greater pledge than that."

Every word Oriel spoke was true. Javan knew that with the same certainty by which he was assured of the loyalty of his Deryni allies. And time was growing short. At any moment, the squires or other servants might return, forever rendering this moment impossible.

If you betray me or mine, I'll kill you, Javan sent, as he surged into the other's mind. *I don't care what threat Rhun or any of the others make against your family, because I know you can deceive them if you really want to.*

Oriel harbored no thought of betrayal, however—too overcome to even *contemplate* a deception of this most unexpected and welcome ally.

I'll do anything for you, my prince, if only you'll promise to do what you can to save my family, Oriel sent. *I hate what they've made me do—and myself, for having let them bend me to their will—but if you give me even the hope of a hope, together we might be able to make them pay!*

Together they forged their bond, without need for further words, Javan emerging with the certain conviction that he had made an ally for life. It was well he felt that, for in the first instant that he emerged from trance, that conviction was put to the test.

"Oriel, is he all right?" asked an all too familiar voice, as Javan fought to open his eyes.

Let me handle this, came Oriel's smooth assurance, as his hand came to Javan's forehead and urged relaxation, even as he answered, "He's fine, my lord. I do think he may have a touch of the same fever that has lately plagued the king, however. Cough for me again, your Highness," he urged with voice and powers. "This damp is beastly. You should be in bed."

Javan obeyed, his free hand going to his mouth to help mask his consternation, wondering whether he and Oriel really could pull this off. Thank God it was Tammaron watching the interchange and not Rhun or Murdoch; Tammaron basically was a decent human being, for all that he was one of the regents. Fortunately, Tammaron did not seem in the least bit suspicious.

"The cough really isn't that bad, Master Oriel," Javan said after delivering an appropriately dry, hacky cough, making the expected protests. "I'm fine—really. Must've gotten a breath of dust from these drapes."

"Yes, well, maybe a little rest *would* do you good, your Highness," Tammaron said, to Javan's relief. "I hear you've been spending a lot of time on your knees in cold, draughty chapels of late. I confess, none of us would mind if you found yourself a vocation as a priest, but for now, you *are* the heir. You mustn't endanger your health."

Both Javan and Oriel were Truth-Reading Tammaron as he spoke, and knew that the earl meant what he said, without rancor or deception.

"Perhaps his Highness would allow me to prescribe a posset with a light sedative," Oriel said smoothly. "Did you not say you hadn't been sleeping well the past few nights, my prince?"

Javan picked up the prompt without hesitation. "Aye, but it's just a stuffy head—and my ears feel blocked up. Can you really give me something to help that?"

Smiling, Oriel rose, shifting his hand from Javan's wrist to his shoulder and urging him down out of the window embrasure. "Most assuredly, I can, your Highness. Lord Tammaron, if you'll excuse us? The king will sleep until suppertime now. What I've given him will offer respite from his cough. The squires should be back shortly."

"They're back now," Tammaron replied with a satisfied smile. "And congratulations on convincing Prince Javan that his asceticisms were too much for this cold, damp weather. You take care of yourself now, you hear, son?"

Making vague noises of agreement, Javan let Oriel lead him out of his brother's quarters. As they headed for his own rooms, the two of them refrained from interacting in any way besides verbal small talk, lest they encounter any of the castle's other tame Deryni, but Oriel gave him additional reassurance before bedding him down with the promised posset—a harmless enough drink made of hot brandywine and milk, with honey and an egg beaten into it. The sleep that descended upon the prince when Oriel had gone was a gentle, undemanding one, and Javan felt as heartened as he had been in many a week.

His only worry, as he drifted off, was how, eventually, he was going to rescue Oriel and his family. Maybe he could somehow smuggle them out to Revan . . .

CHAPTER TWENTY

Shall not they teach thee, and tell thee, and
utter words out of their hearts?

—Job 8:10

Lent wore on in the Michaeline sanctuary as well as in Rhemuth—
a bleak succession of dreary days punctuated by increasing reports
from outside of further hostility against Deryni. Before the events
of the previous fall and early winter had brought everything to a
head, Ansel had organized a small but efficient intelligence network
in the Valoret area, partly made up of men who had ridden patrol
with him and Davin in the old days, to try to curb the worst excesses
of young Deryni. A few ex-Michaeline colleagues of Joram's had
joined them since, mostly human.

Now these men became the eyes and ears of the Deryni resistance, such as any resistance could be, so stripped of its leadership
and set off balance by the purely physical reprisals the regents were
setting in motion. A few came directly to the Michaeline sanctuary
to report; others Ansel met nearby in the hills north of Caerrorie,
for the sanctuary, though well hidden underground, could be ac-
cessed from the surface. Despite their best intentions, its location
could not remain a secret indefinitely.

Against that eventuality, Joram, now senior member of the
MacRorie family, made plans to disperse at least the women and
children to places of greater permanent safety, Evaine excepted.
Fiona MacLean had charge of the Thuryn children and waited to
take them to Gregory and Jesse in Trevalga on a moment's notice.
Mairi MacLean, numbed by nightmares of her husband's tortured
death, retreated increasingly into her own world of grief and mind-

less religiosity, spending hours praying for her husband's soul and becoming more and more withdrawn. Even Queron could not reach her and in the end suggested that the kindest thing would be to let her enter some secluded religious house, her scant Deryni powers blocked and her memories altered to protect herself and those at the sanctuary.

"But leave her her grief," Evaine whispered, as Queron prepared to go to Mairi and make the delicate memory adjustments that would forever change her life. "That's the only thing that makes her want to keep living. She prays for him constantly."

"And ignores the fact that her son still lives," Queron said, disapproval sharpening his voice even though he agreed with Evaine's assessment. "She still thinks Camlin died in that castle yard with Adrian."

"The Camlin that she knew *did* die," Evaine murmured, not looking at him, "just as surely as my Rhys and Aidan died. The boy that Ansel takes out raiding with him, with his own memories of that day and the stigmata of crucifixion on his hands and feet, will never again be the boy she knew and loved. Nothing will ever be the same for any of us."

So Queron left Mairi with her memories, softening only those details that might lead a dogged interrogator to those who must be protected at whatever cost. And the night before he took her through the Portal to put her in the charge of the monks and sisters at Saint Mary's in the Hills, little Tieg was called upon to block her, carefully controlled by his mother. Evaine slept with Tieg that night, silently crying herself to sleep after Tieg had drifted off in her arms.

She tried to make more time for the children after that, for she knew that the day would come all too soon when Fiona must take them to a place of greater safety. A Deryni wet nurse already had been found for little Jerusha among the refugees at Trevalga—a shy young widow called Nicaret, hardly more than a girl herself, whose husband and baby had died in a fire set by zealot raiders intent on burning out Deryni—and Evaine sadly began resigning herself to the likelihood that her youngest child eventually would come to call Nicaret or Fiona mother.

The latter days of Lent brought more positive progress in other areas, however. The regular reports from Sylvan, on retreat with Revan in the hills above Valoret, were uniformly reassuring. Nearly a dozen of Revan's original disciples from the Willimite camp now had found and joined him, and he and Sylvan had been working with quiet diligence to set the stage for the desired reception, come Pentecost. Under Sylvan's tutelage and with the help of the Willimite medallion that Sylvan regularly recharged, Revan perfected his laying on of hands to the point that his suggestions of disorientation and dizziness almost always were accepted. The sensation *could* be fought, if the subject were inclined to do so, but those presenting themselves for baptism would be predisposed to experience *something* at the hands of a supposed miracle worker and possible messiah. With this additional resource at his disposal, Revan looked forward to beginning his public ministry with increasing confidence that he could actually pull it off—which greatly reassured those in the sanctuary, who were gambling so much upon him.

Finally, and most immediately important to Joram, Evaine, and Queron, a report came in from Rhemuth, from one of Joram's ex-Michaelines working as a groom in the castle stables, that the royal household at last had settled in and established a regular enough routine that further contact with Prince Javan again might be feasible. Evaine had immersed herself in her researches, spending a portion of each day in meditation by her father's body, in as compulsive a behavior as any Mairi had displayed, but it was she who determined to make the contact, against any remonstration that Joram or Queron could come up with.

"When Sylvan took Javan's last report, he didn't know about Portal accessibility in Rhemuth, so Javan will be expecting our contact to come from outside the castle," she told them, indicating the written report that Ansel had received the day before from his agent. "Nor does he know who that contact might be.

"To that end, he's obviously tried to set himself a reasonably public and predictable schedule of activities. We know, for example, that he takes classics instruction from a monk at the cathedral three afternoons a week—a pursuit appropriate to a prince as well as to a fledgling religious, and which also provides an excellent opportunity for someone to approach him. In addition, he's a daily communicant at the mid-morning Mass at the basilica during the week—another shrewd move, since almost anyone can get into the outer ward if they say they're going to Mass and don't look too suspicious. To broaden his excuse for hanging around the basilica, he's begun treating the rector as his informal spiritual director, and often lingers after Mass to talk. Castle gossip is that he's turning into a regular monk like his father."

"Just as long as he doesn't take any binding vows," Queron muttered. "Oh, he can always be dispensed, later on, I suppose—Cinhil was—but vocations aren't something to take lightly."

"I'm sure he's well aware of the delicate line he treads," Evaine said. "What matters more right now, though, is that he's unwittingly set the scene for an almost ideal contact situation. Of the several Portals still accessible to us in Rhemuth, the one in the basilica was my absolute first choice. We have you to thank for that one, Queron."

The Healer-priest shrugged. "You have the present rector's predecessor several times removed to thank for it," he amended. "Gabrilite adepts set up that Portal when Blaine of Festil, King Imre's father, had a Gabrilite Healer-Confessor, before most of us were even born. It has the distinction of being one of the few Portals I know of that can be used without potentially having to materialize in the open, where anyone around could see."

"Which makes it precisely the kind of Portal we need," Evaine said.

"No one's arguing that," Joram said crossly. "I *am* arguing the advisability of risking you, personally, to make this contact. The risk to Javan himself is bad enough, no matter *who* makes the contact, but if something were to happen to *you*, it could also affect a certain other project that only you can lead."

"I think the risk is minimal," she said, "and I want to see Javan, at least this once. And one of the reasons is precisely because *all* of us run a very real risk when we eventually push that certain other project to its conclusion. Please don't fight me on this, Joram. It's important to me."

Joram sighed, glancing at Queron for support which, surprisingly, was not forthcoming.

"If it's that important, then let her go," the Healer said. "It's no more dangerous than what any of a number of our people are doing daily."

"That isn't the point," Joram muttered. "Besides, this isn't a job for a woman."

"Then, I won't go as a woman!" Evaine retorted. And before their very eyes, her face began to change.

It was not a sudden metamorphosis. The air before her face seemed to sparkle, a shadowed mist gradually building up behind and all around. She was wearing one of the ubiquitous grey habits that many of the inhabitants of the sanctuary wore, and she drew its hood over her hair before lightly covering her face with both hands and bowing her head. Joram, who had seen the transformation once before, only caught his breath a little and stared, suddenly very sure who would shortly look up at him. Queron appeared less concerned as the spell was bound, but he gasped aloud and almost recoiled as the hands fell away from the averted face and then a bearded stranger raised smoky black eyes.

"My *God*!" Queron whispered, crossing himself almost without volition. "Is it—"

"Dom Queron Kinevan, permit me to present 'Brother John,' " Joram said drolly. "Other than myself, Rhys, our late King Cinhil, and one of my Michaeline brethren who has since dropped out of sight, I don't believe anyone else has ever met this good monk, though a lot of people were looking for him in the weeks leading up to Camber's canonization—yourself included, I believe."

"Brother John" made Queron a deferential bow, right hand pressed to his chest. Queron, even knowing what Evaine had done, and drawing on the memories that she and Joram had shared with him of Brother John's only previous incarnation, could hardly believe what he was seeing.

"*This* is how you looked to Cinhil and young Lord Dualta, the night Camber assimilated Alister's memories?" Queron whispered.

"Brother John" lowered his startling black eyes under long black lashes, inclining the hooded head slightly. "If it please your Worship, I am but an ignorant monk, and unlearned in such matters," he replied, in a voice quite unlike Evaine's. "But it did seem to me that some other person was in the room besides the Father General. In fact—" White teeth flashed in the beard as the thin lips parted in a wry smile. "—it did seem to me that there were several people in the room whose presence had not been expected. It was most unfortunate that we had to entertain those extra visitors."

Despite his best intentions, Queron chuckled. "You certainly made *my* work more difficult by disappearing so thoroughly. But then, that was the entire point, wasn't it? Ah, what a tangle we all wove for ourselves."

"It isn't going to get any less tangled, either," Joram said, "if Evaine goes to Rhemuth as Brother John."

The bearded figure shrugged, and in that instant became Evaine again. "I have to use *some* disguise to move about the basilica without suspicion. So would either of you, if you went. Why waste energy inventing a new one? It isn't as if Dualta's likely to show up; and 'Brother John' means nothing to Javan."

Actually setting up the contact took several days. Holy Week was approaching, and preparations for it meant that more people were in and out of the basilica daily, many of them clergy, the majority of them unknown to Father Boniface, as Evaine quickly learned the rector was called. Among so many new faces, a slight, almost frail-looking monk in the deep-grey habit of the long-established *Ordo Verbi Dei* raised not an eyebrow.

The bearded young cleric showed up at Mass several mornings

running, only kneeling piously near the back of the church, not even venturing forward to receive Holy Communion. Nor did he attempt to approach the black-cloaked prince who also came to Mass each day with his squire but knelt in the royal stall, close to the altar, though he watched them covertly from between his fingers, as he also memorized every detail of the building itself, under cover of bowing deep in devotions.

The two were there on the third day, as expected, but something in the squire's restlessness, and the way he kept glancing anxiously at his younger master, suggested that they might have other plans that day besides lingering at the basilica. After the last Gospel, as soon as the priest and his servers had disappeared into the sacristy, the monk who was Evaine glided down the center aisle to approach the royal stall. Javan was still kneeling beside his squire, head bent dutifully to the usual prayers following Mass, and he looked up curiously as the dark, bearded young monk bowed to the High Altar and then came to dip a knee before the royal stall.

"Your pardon for any intrusion, your Highness," Evaine murmured in her stranger's voice. "My superior asked that I give you this medal and his blessing, if I should see you here in this holy season. A soldier of the Lord should have such a patron."

As the monk held out something vaguely coinlike in shape and silvery in color, Javan extended his hand automatically. The stranger's fingers brushed the royal palm as the gift was imparted—an emphatic tingle that warned wordlessly not to react visibly—followed by the crisp, impersonal order crackling in his mind: *Go to the priest's study when I have gone, and wait.*

Stunned, Javan did not even look at the medal immediately, only closing it in his palm and bowing his head, stammering some inanity of thanks as the monk's hand moved in the promised blessing. Charlan edged closer as soon as the man had disappeared through the door leading to the sacristy and Father Boniface's study, craning his neck to get a look at what Javan held.

"What is it? What did he give you?"

Javan glanced at the medal long enough to see that it was a Saint Michael, then passed it to Charlan, using the brief contact of their hands to ready the pre-set controls he was being forced to use more and more often to distract his squire.

"It's just a Saint Michael medal," he said under his breath.

"A Saint Michael?" Charlan whispered, tilting the medal on his palm. "Now, why on earth would he want to give you that? You don't suppose he's a Michaeline?"

Javan shook his head, though he suspected that the stranger, if not a Michaeline himself, at least had been sent by one—probably Joram. "You heard him, Charlan," he whispered, planting the plausible lie. "He said a soldier of the Lord should have such a patron. If I do find a religious vocation, doesn't that make me one of God's soldiers, after a fashion?"

"I suppose," Charlan agreed. "I wonder who he was, though. Do you suppose Father Boniface knows?"

"He might," Javan replied, taking back the medal and slipping it into an inner pocket as he got to his feet. "Come on, let's ask him. We can wait in his study."

"Very well, but we can't stay long. You know how testy Earl Rhun gets when you're late for court."

"It doesn't start until noon," Javan said, as he made for the door with Charlan at his heels.

The little corridor beyond was dim and chill, only faintly lit by a rushlight set in a niche beside the sacristy door at the far end. The door to the priest's study was closer, directly to Javan's left, and he tapped at it lightly before trying the latch and then boldly entering, ignoring the dull buzz of voices in the sacristy beyond.

He had half expected to find either Joram or the stranger monk inside, but the little panelled room was deserted. A fire blazed merrily on the hearth to the right, lighting the well-scrubbed stone flags before it to a golden glow and warming the bed mounded with sleeping furs, where Father Boniface had lately slept, but the mullioned window opposite the fireplace was covered with heavy woolen drapes of a dull green-gold that filtered out almost all the daylight.

Most afternoons found Boniface perched on a stool behind the wide oak table that dominated the window side of the room, the light at his back, carefully copying one of the many valuable manuscripts he borrowed from various sources. An illuminated capital *I* adorned the sheet pinned to the tilted table top this morning, with Boniface's quills and brushes and inkpots all neatly laid out to one side. The wall to the left was lined with pigeonholes and shelves for holding manuscripts, a good many of them filled, and a high-backed oak settle was built into the center, wide enough for two people to sit. Toward this seat Javan pushed an unresisting Charlan as he closed the door behind them, exerting control as he often had before.

"Sit down and have a nap, Charlan," he murmured.

Charlan folded onto the settle and obeyed instantly, chin nodding onto his chest as he folded his arms across his waist. When the gentle buzz of his snoring began to mutter reassuringly in the little room, Javan moved quietly into the shadows at the left of the fireplace, where he could not be seen easily from the door, and flattened himself behind the out-thrust of the massive stone chimney breast and mantel. There he waited.

The firelight continued to dance, flickering patterns on the stones of the floor. In the corner directly opposite Javan, just to the right of the window, the single crimson eye of a votive light shimmered reassuringly on Father Boniface's *prie-dieu*. Other than that, nothing else moved in the room besides Javan's light breathing and Charlan's gentle snores.

After what seemed like an eternal wait but, in fact, was only a very few minutes, Father Boniface came in, looking neither left nor right and going immediately to the *prie-dieu* to kneel and bury his face in his hands, apparently oblivious to the following presence of the hooded, grey-clad monk who closed and locked the door by which they had entered. Javan thought it was the same one who had approached him in the basilica earlier, but he could not be certain because the monk kept his back to Javan as he moved quietly to Charlan, laying both hands briefly on the sleeping squire's head. When the figure finally turned, pushing back the hood from what should have been a black-bearded face, Javan was startled speechless to see that it was Evaine, her bright hair pulled back tightly, blue eyes twinkling with mirth even as she held a forefinger to her lips for silence.

"But, that's impossible!" Javan whispered, despite himself, as he stepped from his hiding place in the shadows beside the fireplace.

Shaking her head, Evaine came to take him by the shoulders, smiling all the while.

"Not impossible, merely improbable," she reassured him, staring into his eyes. "But we haven't much time, my prince. All unwittingly, you've set yourself the perfect cover, so long as you remain in Rhemuth, but I see from young Charlan yonder that your presence is expected elsewhere very soon—which means I must be more brief than I had hoped. But, come and let me show you a safe Portal."

"In *here*?" Javan whispered, as she gestured toward the panelled wall that ran between the window and fireplace walls.

Not answering verbally, Evaine went to reach around the oblivious Father Boniface, pressing at something underneath the armrest. Instantly a section of panel in the middle of the wall slid back, revealing a cubicle just large enough for two adults to stand in comfortably. Evaine backed in without hesitation, turning to hold out her hand to Javan. She slipped her arm around the prince's shoulders as he joined her, and he could feel her mind enveloping his with a soft strength that was at once reassuring and a little threatening for its strangeness—for he had never worked with her directly before.

"I'm going to risk taking you back to the sanctuary for a few minutes," she murmured in his ear, sliding a door closed in front of them with her free hand. "Don't try to learn this Portal right now; just relax and let me take you through. Can you do that without help?"

Nodding, he closed his eyes and made himself relax, leaning his head against her shoulder and pulling back his shields. He had wanted this for so long that it was hard to accept it, now that the moment was here, but he let her slip into his mind without resistance, pushing back that part of him that still tried to shrink gibbering from such contact. The touch of her other hand across his eyes pushed him deeper, reeling perilously close to the edge of unconsciousness as she reached for the energies and began to bend them to her will.

All fear left him as he suddenly realized that he *understood* what she was doing, a part of him dazzlingly aware of how and why she did what she did, a part of him exulting in the brief, stomach-churning instant of vertigo that he had come to associate with Portal Transfer. He knew where he was even before he opened his eyes, and the sight of Joram and Queron confirmed it.

Steady! her mind spoke in his, not withdrawing from the controls he had allowed to permit the jump. *Unfortunately, I've inadvertantly picked a morning when time is at a premium for you. I apologize if this seems brusque or dictatorial. I need to do a very fast strip-read and then ram home a fairly stiff briefing. If you resist at all, it may hurt you, but we need all the information you can give us, and you need everything we can tell you.*

Her one arm supported him around his shoulders, and her free hand still was laid across his brow, partially obscuring his vision, but he was aware of Queron and Joram moving in to assist her, and knew that even if he wanted to resist, he could not stand against all three of them. Besides, he had permitted Queron a deep reading, that time when Tavis brought him to the sanctuary. Either he trusted them or he didn't—and if he didn't, he might as well give it all up now.

"What do you want me to do?" he whispered, gripping tight as Queron and Joram each took one of his hands.

Relax and let yourself go even deeper than you did for me that other time, came Queron's reply, directly in his mind. *Use everything Tavis taught you, and everything you've learned since then. You're perfectly safe. We'll be right with you.*

He let himself sink in response to their encouragement, floating briefly in a tingling, euphoric state that was not at all frightening or unpleasant. But then he was a vessel being emptied, his very essence not only draining through massive holes someone had punched through his shields, but being sucked from him with increasing force, verging on real pain as the pressure grew.

Then the process reversed, so quickly that a wave of nausea threatened to fill his throat with bile, and he felt as if his head were being filled with molten lead, heavier and heavier, burning through all the orifices of his skull, permeating every fiber of his being. He was trembling as he surfaced, though control was his again, and his head felt as if the top might come right off if he moved his eyes too quickly. He groaned as he tried to focus on Queron's face, instinctively flinging his mind into the Healer's soothing, letting Queron take him briefly away from the pain, deep into Healing trance. When he came out, it was better, but he still felt a little queasy.

"A full Deryni couldn't have done better, my prince," Queron said softly, speaking aloud rather than in his mind, to spare his bruised psychic senses. "If your head still hurts in an hour or two, try to take a short nap. A good night's sleep should take care of the rest. All right?"

A little dazedly, Javan nodded, trying to sort out the new information that started sifting into his consciousness if he was not thinking about anything else.

"What about future contacts?" he murmured. "Do I bring my reports here?"

Joram shook his head. "No more written reports, if you can avoid it. They're too dangerous, if you should be caught. For regular contacts, make an excuse to see Father Boniface after Mass on a Tuesday; someone will join you shortly. Or leave that medal Evaine gave you in the Portal chamber, and someone will come the next day."

"I can't just come through?"

"No, because this site may not always be secure," Evaine replied. "Besides that, you might not be able to cover things alone at your end—and we might not always be available. We're—ah—working on several projects that may take us away from the sanctuary for a day or two at a time. No one else here knows that you can use a Portal on your own. Nor should they know."

"Oh. I hadn't thought of that."

"Evaine, you'd better take him back now," Joram murmured. "If he doesn't show up back at the castle when he's expected, someone's apt to come looking for him."

"It does get easier, son," Queron assured him, just before Evaine engulfed him in her shields once again and took him back to the study Portal.

Once they were there, she held his shields open while he learned the Portal coordinates, making sure he had them memorized before she let him go. Both Deryni senses and visual inspection through a spy hole revealed that nothing had changed in the study, and Evaine gave him a reassuring hug before letting the door slide open.

"The good Father will remember a brief conversation about a text by Saint Ruadan," she said, moving across to rummage briefly through the top row of pigeonholes. "Ah, I was sure he'd have a copy here somewhere. This is what he's shown you, and he'll put it away when you've gone. All *you* need to know, if he should later question you about this conversation, will sort itself out while you're asleep tonight."

"*Liber Sancti Ruadan*," Javan read, unrolling the top of the scroll. "As a matter of fact, we did discuss this text once. That was the same day he showed me one by someone called Leutiern." He grinned. "Poor Boniface seemed almost scandalized when he told me that Leutiern was Deryni. In fact, he's got texts by several Deryni mystics here. He's shown me a few. He used to collect them, before the *Custodes* cracked down on Deryni scholarship. He lives in mortal terror that they're going to find him out, one of these days."

"I don't suppose he's got anything by MacDara," Evaine said, heading back toward the Portal cubicle. "Or the *Liber Ricae*. That's what I really need."

Jaw dropping in surprise, Javan tossed the Ruadan scroll on the writing desk and squatted beside the range of pigeonholes closest to it, skimming a finger impatiently across the ends of the scrolls closest to the floor as he bent to read their titles.

"I never heard of that second one, but MacDara—I've seen that name. Some of these are really old. He keeps them on the bottom here, so most people won't notice the titles. Here. I don't suppose this is what you're looking for?"

He continued to scan the other scrolls as he held the MacDara manuscript for her perusal, and she glanced at it and then did a doubletake.

"Dear, gentle Lord!" Her eyes widened as she glanced through the others Javan kept producing. "Are there more of these?"

"I think so. He has some locked away, too. One by a fellow called—" The prince's eyes unfocused as he tried to recall the unfamiliar name. "I think he was a Gabrilite. Something like Dom Edwin—no, Dom Edouard." He grinned at her look of surprised excitement. "Is that important?"

"Important? Javan, these are some of the classic mystical texts of the past two centuries," she whispered, clasping the scrolls to her breast. "Tell me, does anyone else know what Boniface has here?"

"Well, not right now, I don't think."

"Oh, thank God. And can you cover the absence of these, at least while I go through them?"

"Certainly. It will be one less thing for him to worry about."

"How about getting me access to those ones he's got locked up?"

"Easy. I can get them tomorrow at this time and put them in the Portal for you to collect whenever you want."

For answer, she only gave him a radiant smile and touched his cheek in gratitude before stepping back into the Portal to pull its door shut before her. As their eyes met a final time, just before the door closed her from sight, Javan thought he might do just about anything for her, and unaccountably, for several seconds, found himself entertaining quite titillating thoughts about this most remarkable woman—who was quite old enough to be his mother!

But then the urgency of the hour seized him more strongly than the stirrings of his first adolescent infatuation, and he set himself to the tasks remaining at hand. After unlocking the door, he took up the scroll he and she had agreed should be his excuse for the morning's diversion and tapped it against his hand as he walked over to where Father Boniface still knelt. The priest startled awake as Javan tapped him lightly on the shoulder with the scroll.

"I'm sorry, Father, I just realized how late it's getting, and I'm supposed to attend court this morning. The regents will be furious if I don't show up. May I come back tomorrow?"

"Why, of course, my son," Boniface said, rising creakily from his knees. "I must have dozed off while you were reading that passage. It really isn't that boring."

"Certainly not," Javan agreed. "I've always liked Saint Ruadan. I'd like to continue our discussion tomorrow. Good God, Charlan's gone to sleep, too." He used the scroll to swat Charlan just a bit more vigorously than he had Boniface. "Wake up, man! Rhun will have your hide for letting me stay so long!"

The squire startled awake and knuckled sleep from his eyes as sheepishly as usual, not thinking it odd at all that he had dozed off after a perfectly good night's sleep. After suitable leave takings, he and his royal master were on their way back through the yard and into the inner ward, arriving in the great hall just ahead of Rhys Michael.

"Been praying again, eh, Javan?" the younger boy quipped, as they took their places on stools to the left of the throne. "You'll wear out your knees."

Rhys Michael's sarcasm bothered Javan more than usual that morning, perhaps because his head had settled into a dull, regular throbbing as he and Charlan climbed the hill to the inner ward, but he made himself only shrug and smile as everyone rose for the entrance of their royal brother.

Oddly enough, the exercise in forbearance seemed to soothe his aching head, so that, by the time court recessed for a midday repast, only a nagging vestige remained—and that all but disappeared when he had eaten. The afternoon saw Javan the model of a dutiful and biddable prince, even Regent Murdoch smiling and agreeable about Javan's performance, when they adjourned at the end of the day.

CHAPTER TWENTY-ONE

Foursquare shall it be being doubled.

—Exodus 28:16

Prince Javan's performance did not stop with the court of Gwynedd, though his greatest performances were still to come and would mostly go unappreciated by any but his Deryni allies. He was as good as his word, when it came to producing the manuscripts Evaine asked for, and laid three precious scrolls in the Portal chamber after Mass the very next day. Two more followed, a day later.

The documents were not precisely what Evaine had hoped for, but piecing together information from them and from the other sources already at her disposal put Evaine onto another line of speculation that had not occurred to her before. By the night of Good Friday, she was ready to share her findings with Joram and Queron. She gathered them in the *keeill*, after everyone in sanctuary had retired for the night, and warded the *keeill* doors against intrusion before taking them to crouch around the white-gleaming slab of the sunken altar's mensa. They watched expectantly as she undid the ties of a soft leather pouch and upended its contents onto her hand.

"This new material seems to deal with advanced warding techniques," she told them, laying out the four white and four black cubes that made a set of Wards Major. "A lot of it was veiled in allegory, as these things so often are, but I think I've isolated at least one new configuration. Now, most Deryni with any training at all know the basic spell for constructing Wards Major."

She had been moving the four white cubes into a solid square in the center, and now set the four black ones at the diagonals. "This is the starting point for it—and for half a dozen other configurations of varying complexity, the most powerful of which, as we know, can raise this altar slab to reveal the black and white cube altar that supports it."

"What we've usually called the Pillars of the Temple," Joram said.

"That's right." Without bothering to name the cubes or activate them magically, she placed her first and second fingers on the first white cube and the black one at its diagonal and switched them, then did the same with the two diagonally opposite, so that the central square ended up checkered black and white, with cubes of opposite colors at the four corners.

But when she would have gone on to the next step, Queron suddenly seized her wrist.

"Wait! Don't do that yet!"

"Why? What's wrong?"

"Just wait!"

"Queron, the cubes aren't even activated," Joram murmured, stealing a startled glance at Evaine, whose wrist Queron still held. "Nothing's going to happen."

"I know that."

Queron's voice was strained, intense, forbidding further conversation, and both Joram and Evaine fell silent, only watching as the Healer-priest continued to stare at the cubes. When, after a few more seconds, he softly exhaled and released Evaine's wrist, he looked a little sheepish, and brushed a hand self-consciously across his eyes.

"I'm sorry. I certainly hadn't expected *that* memory to surface."

"Can you tell us about it?" Evaine asked quietly.

"I—that's what I'm not sure about." He swallowed uncomfortably. "Good God, I never really thought I'd be put into a situation where I'd seriously consider violating my vows."

Joram cocked his head curiously. "Your priestly vows or the seal of the confessional?" he asked.

"Not exactly either." Queron drew a deep breath and exhaled it as fully as he could, as if steeling himself for something either unpleasant or dangerous. "This—ah—has to do with that—ah—other tradition besides Gabrilite, that we talked about, some time ago. You'll remember that I mentioned in passing that I hoped I wouldn't have to make a choice."

"You don't have to tell us," Evaine said.

"No, I think I do," Queron said. "That's just the point. Something that never quite made sense before, that was part of that earlier tradition, suddenly took on a whole different perspective as you started to move those cubes around. There was a piece of ritual that the Master used to do, several times a year, at morning meditations. We were always taught that it was symbolic—exactly what the symbol was, was never made quite clear—and I never questioned that. But—well, let me show you a part of it, and see whether it makes any sense to either of you. If I don't actually work the spell, I don't suppose I'm technically in violation of my vows—and if it doesn't mean anything to you, we can just drop the whole thing."

"Queron, this really isn't necessary," Joram began.

"Yes, it is, at least this far," Queron replied. Drawing a deep breath, he picked up the four cubes at the outer corners of the black and white square formed in the center and placed them on their opposites, forming the familiar checkerboard of a cube altar.

"Now, there's a proper ritual procedure for what I just did, of course, but the result was to end up with this configuration, which mimics the cube altar underneath this slab."

Evaine nodded. "The actual arrangement of the cubes is quite logical, of course. Father always suspected that there was an actual working that went with it, but we never found enough evidence of one to risk trying anything."

"Well, I'm not certain what the intention was," Queron said, "but what the Master used to do was to set up this configuration in the proper sequence, then recite a particular prayer while he held his hands over the checkered cube—sort of cupped, as if he were consecrating the Eucharistic elements. After a while, energy washed outward from the cube, all the way to the edge of the altar." He cocked his head thoughtfully. "Actually, I suppose I always thought the working was to purify the altar. But now that I think about it, he only ever did it on the cubical altar in our Chapter House—never the oblong one in the sanctuary—and the cubical altar was only ever used for meditation."

Evaine nodded. "I remember Rhys telling me about that altar—a cube of bluestone, wasn't it? And Father recognized it as a power nexus of some sort. In fact, he even wondered if there was some connection with the black and white altar under Grecotha."

"I wonder what Queron's Master would have done with a black and white altar," Joram mused. "And if it was only for purification, why was it never done on the regular altar?"

Raising an eyebrow, Evaine cocked her head. "Now, there's a thought—if you would agree, Queron."

"Try it on a regular altar?" Queron said.

"No, try it on a black and white altar." She patted the white slab beside the piled up cubes. "Try it right here."

Queron looked uncomfortable with the thought at first, but then his expression turned more speculative. "I wonder if I *could* do it. And what hidden meanings was I missing in my youthful ignorance? Thinking back, the symbolism was *not* just that of purification, though it was a part of it."

"I thought we were looking for a stronger warding spell," Joram said uneasily. "Besides, what you're talking about obviously was intended to be kept secret from those not of your Order."

"I can *do* a stronger warding," Evaine said, a little impatiently. "That's what I brought you here to show you. But a new purification spell might also be useful—if that's even what it is. It doesn't seem to be dangerous, in any case."

Queron nodded half reluctantly. "You're right on both counts, Joram. However, I'm not sure that hidden part of my Order even exists anymore—and we do seem to have some rather special needs. Besides that, I confess I've aroused my own curiosity as well. God, I hadn't thought about that in years." He grimaced. "I suppose I *am* still a little uneasy about working this outside the Order, but—never mind. I'm going to do it. The oaths I've exchanged with the two of you are at least as solemn as anything I swore to the Gabrilites. Let's try it."

"You're sure?" Evaine said.

"Yes, I'm sure." Deftly Queron dismantled the little cube matrix and reset the individual cubes in their original starting places, the four white ones forming a square in the center, with the four blacks set at the diagonals. He twined his fingers together and flexed them backward briefly until the knuckles cracked, then disentangled them and wiggled them briefly while he ordered his thoughts and Evaine and Joram crouched to either side of him.

"I think I'll raise the altar first," Queron murmured, poising his right hand over the cubes. "The Master always did the special working from a standing position. I don't know that it would make a difference, but I think we ought to duplicate the original conditions as much as possible."

"I agree," Evaine said, as Joram glared resigned disapproval.

"So, I'll name the components. *Prime!*" he said, touching his right forefinger to the white cube in the upper left of the square and speaking its *nomen*.

Immediately, the named cube began to glow.

"*Seconde!*"

The cube to its right also lit from within.

"*Tierce! Quarte!*"

The two white cubes below the first two also came alive, making of the four a single white square bracketed by the still unactivated black ones at the corners. Queron drew a slow, steady breath before touching the black cube at the upper left-hand corner of the larger square.

"*Quinte!*" The fifth cube began to gleam with a dark, blue-black sparkle like black opal.

"*Sixte!*" Likewise the black cube at the upper right glowed.

"*Septime! Octave!*"

As the last two cubes came alive, Queron stretched and flexed the fingers of his right hand and smiled as he exhaled softly.

"This *is* a beautifully balanced working," he breathed—and set his first two fingers on Prime and Quinte as he balanced the first *phrasa*: "*Prime et Quinte inversus!*"

All of them felt the subtle shift in the balance of energies as the two cubes changed places, intensifying as Queron moved the next two: "*Quarte et Octave inversus!*"

Next, the tricky bits, as he set his fingers on Septime and the transposed Prime.

"*Prime et Septime inversus!*"

And finally, "*Sixte et Quarte inversus!*"

What resulted was a softly glowing saltire composed of one black and one white diagonal, Might held in balance by Mercy. And carrying the operation to its conclusion would create the Pillars of the Temple, but in three dimensions, with the balance of the altar itself firmly established as the Middle Pillar, the mediating force which could facilitate even greater things.

Picking up the black Septime, now at the upper left diagonal, Queron lightly placed it on Quinte, the black cube immediately adjacent to it, at the same time speaking the *cognomen*, "*Quintus!*"

The balance was off now, and he must move quickly, lest it slip irretrievably out of reach. He steadied the energies as he picked up Quarte, now in the upper right-hand corner, and deftly stacked it on Seconde, still in its original place.

"*Sixtus!*"

More energy, more manageable now, licked up his fingers as he placed Prime on Tierce, white on white, and Sixte on Octave, black on black, with the last two *cognomena*.

"*Septimus! Octavius!*"

And the balance steadied, so that all at once the configuration *was* the Pillars of the Temple—four miniature columns, alternating black and white, forming the miniature cube. Gathering the energies, and making of himself a channel for the balanced energies of the Middle Pillar, Queron set his hand on the cube and willed it to rise. It seemed to cleave to his palm as his hand rose, and the white marble slab rose ponderously beneath it, silent save for the soft, satiny whisper of polished stone against stone, gradually revealing the four large black and white cubes that supported it, and then the four white and black cubes that supported *them*, all squared at the corners by round columns as thick as a man's upper arm.

Queron slowly got to his feet when the second tier of cubes began to appear, not relaxing until the base of the structure emerged—a slab twin to the altar top, only black, a handspan thick. When it stopped, Queron removed his hand, flexing his fingers and exhaling loudly. Evaine and Joram had also risen with the altar and looked at him expectantly from either side.

"So far, so good," Evaine murmured. "I assume you have to start again now. This is an end point, so far as anything *I* know."

Sighing again, Queron nodded, dismantling the little cube and setting up the small cubes in their original configuration, white cubes forming a solid square in the center and the black ones set at the corners.

"You're still sure you want to do this?" Joram said.

Queron nodded. "I certainly do. I know a lot more now than I did as a novice. I'm curious as to what the old Master *did* intend, when he used to do this working. I remember that it was always at the Quarters and Cross-Quarters, and the novices were encouraged to keep an all night vigil in the Lady Chapel the night before— though that wasn't required. Odd, that—because otherwise, we were rarely offered such options."

He drew another breath, as if shaking off the weight of long-ago memories, then held his hand briefly over the cubes.

"Very well. It starts the same way the other variation did, by naming the eight components. I remember that the Master never spoke the *nomena* aloud, because he thought it interfered with the proper mind-set. So I'll do as he did."

Not pausing for their reaction, he brushed his forefinger quickly over the eight cubes in the same order as before, beginning with the four white ones and then naming the four black ones. Each sparked to life as he touched it, and Evaine and Joram followed his progress easily, *Prime* through *Octave*.

"The first half of the next part also goes the same," Queron whispered. He set his first and second fingers on Prime and Quinte and intoned the familiar *cognomen* as he changed their places: "*Prime et Quinte inversus!*"

Quarte and Octave followed, their *cognomen* also almost sung. "*Quarte et Octave inversus!*"

When he had switched the second pair, they were left with a central square of black and white alternating, with a cube of the opposite color at each outer corner. And now, instead of transposing Prime with Septime and Sixte with Quarte, as he had done before, he picked up the white Prime from the upper left diagonal and set it carefully on Quinte, the upper left black cube, with a *salutus* sung in one of the eerie Gabrilite plainsong chants:

"Primus est Deus, Primus in aeternitate. Amen."

Touching his right hand to his breast, he made a profound bow to the altar, then picked up black Sixte, setting it gently on white Seconde as he sang the next *salutus*:

"Secundus est Filius, Coaeterus cum Patre. Amen."

Again he bowed profoundly before picking up black Septime to place it on Tierce.

"Tertius est Trinitas: Pater, Filius, et Spiritus Sanctus. Amen."

Another bow before picking up the final cube, Quarte, to set it on Octave and complete the checkered cube.

"Quattuor archangeli custodes quandrantibus sunt. Quattuor quadrant coram Domino uno. Amen."

The completed cube glowed with the soft, opal fire of its original components, a jewel-like miniature of the larger cubes of black and white marble that supported the white altar slab on which it rested. Queron raised his clasped hands to his lips, closing his eyes briefly as he gathered his concentration to continue, then drew his hands apart at chin level, palms turned toward one another, and began to chant.

"De profundis clamavi te, Domine: Domine, exaudi orationem mean. Adorabo te, Domine . . ."

He turned his hands over the cube as he prayed, palms cupped gently as if in blessing, fingertips slightly overlapping. All of them could feel the power gathering—a taut, tingling sensation that began at the crown of the head and quickly permeated to the toes.

"Fiat lux in aeternam. Fiat lustratio, omnium altarium Tuorum," Queron murmured. Let there be light in eternity. Let there be purification of all Thine altars . . .

Light began to glow beneath Queron's hands, emanating from the cube matrix. As he tipped his palms apart and raised his arms, light fountained upward between them—a miniature pillar of fire centered over the matrix, as thick and high as a man's forearm. He brought his hands briefly to cover his eyes as he continued to sing, then crossed them on his breast and bowed profoundly.

"Quasi columna flammae me duces, Altissime, in loca arcana

Tua . . ." Like a pillar of fire Thou shalt lead me, O Most High, into Thy secret places . . .

The pillar remained as his psalm ended, hovering in the stillness. Fearlessly Queron stretched out his right hand toward the top of the pillar, lowering it onto the flame.

"Gloria in excelsis Deo . . ."

But the flame did not appear to burn, and gave way beneath his touch. The pillar fattened as he compressed it, pooling wider and wider out from the cube matrix as his hand descended, living light washing over the surface of the altar all the way to the edges and then brimming over in a cascade of luminance that was swallowed up by the black edges of the base slab. Queron's hand touched the top of the matrix as the light reached the corners of the mensa slab—and gave at the pressure, the entire altar beginning to sink, the light continuing to glow across its top and sides.

"Sweet *Jesu*, where's it going?" Joram whispered.

"Back into the dais," came Evaine's awed reply, "though somehow, I don't think the Master's spell ever did *this*."

Queron's expression suggested that it most certainly had not, but he kept on singing the *Gloria* and the altar kept sinking—and kept sinking even when the white mensa drew level with the floor of the dais, becoming flush with the level of the dais, sinking beyond that, until even the now-kneeling Queron could no longer keep his hand on the small cube. It did not stop until the top of the mensa had sunk its height and half again below the top level of the dais, just as Queron's singing ended. Evaine and Joram were also on their knees, peering uneasily into the hole made by the altar's retreat.

"Why did it do that?" Joram murmured, as Evaine conjured handfire and sent it into the opening.

Queron gasped as the light revealed an extension to the opening, stretching back toward the north, and dropped onto his stomach to lean down for a closer look as the other two also peered down.

"There's a passageway and what might be stairs leading down!"

"I suspect we were meant to step onto the altar as it was sinking," Evaine said. "Getting down shouldn't be too difficult, but getting back up might be a problem."

Queron was already swinging his legs down into the opening, easing himself over the edge to drop lightly to the white mensa, avoiding the stacked cubes.

"I don't think I'll have any trouble bringing it back up. It concerns me more to stand on the altar, but that's obviously intended, in this case." He squatted down to peer into the side opening. "Ah, there *is* a stair—a spiral one. Anyone else coming down?"

Joram looked uneasy and muttered something about hoping there were no nasty surprises waiting, but he gave a hand to Evaine as she sat down on the edge of the opening, gathered her skirts around her, then eased down with Queron's aid. Joram followed when Queron had stepped into the stairwell, bracing the heels of his hands on the edge and avoiding the ward cubes. The only real surprise, not nasty at all, turned out to be their discovery of a small, unfinished chamber that apparently lay directly under the Portal chamber and its lobby. It was a roughly hewn room not much larger than the cells back at the sanctuary, with traces of further digging that might eventually have become other passages leading—who knew where?

"Well, it's obvious that whoever built this complex got interrupted before they could finish it," Queron said, when they had finished their perusal of the chamber. "Didn't you say that this was an Airsid complex?"

Evaine nodded. "We've occasionally come across their traces before, but I don't know a lot about them except that they're supposed to have been at least the philosophic precursors of the Varnarites."

"Who, in part, were the precursors of the Gabrilites," Queron agreed. "What I don't understand is that altar up there. When the Master—" He broke off as an odd look came across Evaine's face. "What's wrong?"

She shook her head. "Nothing's wrong. But when your Master worked the spell, you *did* say that he always did it at the bluestone altar in your chapter house?"

"That's right."

"And he did it as a meditation and ritual purification of the altar. Also correct?"

Queron nodded.

"Suppose the ritual had come down from a much earlier tradition that used a black and white cube altar rather than a bluestone one," Evaine said, "and suppose that the ritual not only purified the altar, but also operated the mechanism for opening the way to another, more secret inner sanctum."

Joram nodded emphatically. "And if the original tradition had been transmitted incompletely, as sometimes happens, no one would have been any the wiser. Or maybe the additional meaning got lost in melding the different strands of discipline that made up the Gabrilite tradition."

"That's certainly possible," Queron agreed. "But if there *was* a tradition of secret chambers under black and white altars—good God, what about the altar down in the ruins? It's right in the middle of *ancient* remains! Maybe there's another chamber under *it*. What if *that's* where the Varnarites hid their most important archives?"

An hour later, the three of them were gathered around that altar, Joram carefully clearing away debris from around its base so that it *could* sink, if their theory proved correct, while Evaine helped Queron clean off the top. They found a large triangular chunk of the shattered mensa on the floor nearby, and Queron eased it approximately back into place before setting out the ward cubes again in their starting configuration. He skimmed silently through the setting of the *nomena* and *cognomena*, and spoke the *phrasae* instead of singing them, his hands trembling a little in the light of the handfire Evaine and Joram had conjured to hover above the matrix he was erecting. Since the altar was already raised, he was able to go directly to the purification configuration.

"*Primus est Deus . . . ,*" he whispered, setting the first black cube atop the first white one.

"*Secundus est Filius . . .*"

The next white cube was set on the next black one, beside the first.

"*Tertia est Trinitas . . . Quattuor Archangeli custodes . . .*"

The last two cubes were set into place.

"*Adorabo Te, Domine . . . Fiat lux in aeternum . . .*"

Again, as he spread his hands over the matrix, light grew beneath them, flaring to a flaming pillar as he drew his hands to either side. He did not bother to sing the *Gloria*; only reached out his hand to cup the top of the pillar of fire and press it downward. And as the light dispersed at his will, spreading over the mensa and down the black and white sides, the entire altar began to sink.

CHAPTER TWENTY-TWO

*And thou shalt put it under the compass of the
altar beneath, that the net may be even in the
midst of the altar.*

—Exodus 27:5

This altar's descent was not as smooth as the one beneath the *keeill*,
but the fact that it sank at all seemed wonder enough, in that instant
when it actually began to move. They could hear the stone grate in
passage, the track doubtless clogged at least partially by the debris
of decay and destruction, but the mass sank steadily—not only to
the level of the dais floor, as they had always believed was as far as
the *keeill*'s altar would go, but slowly beyond that point, without
further wobble or tremor. As it reached the depth of a normal step,
Joram carefully stepped down onto the altar surface, careful not to
disturb the still-glowing ward cubes, and prepared to hang onto the
edges of the opening as he continued to sink—just in case it should
go farther than he wished to go.

But it halted at the expected depth, just even with his shoulders,
with a grinding jar that suggested it was not going any farther. Joram
grinned roguishly and ducked to look at the side opening he had
been watching grow, summoning his handfire down for a closer look.

"Well, well, well. This one appears to be a dog-leg stair instead
of a spiral. Are you two coming down, or do I get to go into the great
unknown all by myself? Incidentally, I think this is the way it was
supposed to work—to step onto the altar as it sank. Otherwise, I
can't imagine how anyone would get down here at all conveniently—unless they had a ladder stored somewhere, which hardly
seems like the Airsid way."

"We'll keep that in mind, next time we come," Evaine said.

She braced her hands on his shoulders as he reached up to help her down. Queron sat at the edge of the opening and swung his legs in, vaulting down with only minor assistance from Joram.

"What *I* want to know is what's at the bottom of the stair," Queron said. "Whatever it is, it *should* be a finished structure, unlike the *keeill*. This has all been here for a very long time."

Since it had been Queron's spell that let them discover the cube altar's secret, they let Queron lead the way, Evaine following the Healer and his handfire down into the narrow stairwell, Joram bringing up the rear with more light. After the stair had descended the equivalent of several storeys, turning back on itself a full three hundred sixty degrees, they found themselves emerging on a landing that opened on an area of such vast darkness that it swallowed up most of the effect of their handfire. Immediately to their right, either a corridor or another chamber once had opened off, but that way was now permanently blocked by a massive collapse of stone and rubble that also had smashed the floor immediately adjacent. Loose tiles grated and shifted slightly underfoot as Queron moved closer to inspect the blocked entryway.

"We won't get any farther in *this* direction," he said, turning back to the others. "However, there's certainly something out *there*."

He gestured into the heavier darkness as he conjured more handfire, and the others followed suit, scanning with Sight as well as with vision and hearing. The extra handfire made little difference.

"There's something straight ahead," Evaine said after a few seconds, sending a sphere of handfire lower along the ground in that direction. "It's a power source of some kind, damped but still quite potent. Is anyone else reading that?"

As both men turned their attention to that area at her bidding, her floating handfire began to disclose low steps heading upward— a dull, dusty black that drank the light, curving away to either side as circular steps leading up a dais. They moved carefully closer as she sent her light upward, finally setting foot on the first step—and faltered as the handfire was suddenly reflected back at them, bright silver flashing off the polished black side of something massive and rectangular. On it, as Evaine nudged the handfire higher with her mind, they could just make out the vague silhouette of what appeared to be a recumbent human form, its head toward their right.

"Bloody hell!" Joram muttered under his breath. "It's a tomb."

"Possibly," Queron replied, a little distractedly. "But not just *a* tomb. Someone went to a great deal of trouble over this burial. Let's have a closer look."

"A very *careful* look," Evaine added, holding back just a little as Queron ascended the first step.

Slowly, even reverently, they climbed—seven steps, as in the *keeill*—eyes fastened on the silhouette that became more and more clear as they approached. A nagging suspicion began to whisper at the edges of Evaine's mind as they came nearer, grown to a praeternatural certainty by the time she paused on the top step. Gazing across the silence of dust that had not been disturbed for centuries, she knew who it must be who lay on the bier, but an arm's length away—for bier it was, not mere tomb. The form outstretched along its length was no waxwork or stone-carved effigy but a corpse, somehow preserved.

"I will both lay me down in peace, and sleep; for Thou, Lord, only makest me dwell in safety," Queron quoted from the Psalms. He bowed low and made a curious salute to the right, toward the corpse's head, with both his hands.

"You know who it is?" Evaine whispered.

"Of course. It's Orin."

"*Orin?*" Joram gasped.

"Aye. And look at his resting place: the pillars of Might and Mercy laid on their sides to form his bier, with the four to one proportions of the ward cubes. The four black ones form the Pillar of Might, and the four white ones, the Pillar of Mercy, with Orin himself as the Middle Pillar, recumbent upon them. *This* tradition I know—as *he* would have known it, and his followers, who laid him here."

Awed, Evaine looked upon the body again, noting and now understanding why the half of the bier nearest her was black, and its opposite white. A thick layer of dust overlaid everything, dulling the top surface to a near uniform grey, but it was not only the dust that obscured the body lying there. Fragile, its colors dimmed by the dust, a fine net of multi-colored silk cord shrouded the body beneath, each knotted jointure of the netting secured with what looked to be a small *shiral* crystal drilled through the center for fastening in place.

Evaine did not touch the net, but she held one cautious hand over a section of it for a moment, then ran her palm close over a portion that trailed off the edge of the surface. The stones definitely were *shiral*, but bound into the knotted silk in some unfamiliar fashion that felt vaguely of a spell she had encountered before, though she could not fully place it.

"*Shiral* and silk?" Joram said softly, close by her left elbow.

Nodding, Evaine continued to scan, increasingly intrigued by what she read. "Aye, this is the cording lore. I know a little of it, beyond what we use for the Council binding, but most of it has been lost over the centuries. 'Tis women's magic, for the most part. This one is a preservation spell, I think—a little like something Rhys did a few times. Queron, does it feel of what Healers do, to preserve bodies?"

Carefully, as a tight-lipped Joram watched, Queron ran his Healer's hands above a section of the net covering the body's left knee.

"It's similar," the Healer finally said, "though I haven't a clue how this particular working was done. It *is* the source of the power nexus we sensed from the stairwell, and I could produce a similar effect *for a time*, but it wouldn't last anywhere near as long as this one seems to have done. And if we move the net, I can't answer for *him*."

"You really do think it's Orin?" Joram asked after a moment.

"I do."

Queron's two simple words, backed by uncompromising personal conviction, unleashed a torrent of silent speculation in both his listeners. For Orin had been a mage of legendary, even supernatural, strength and ability, the most learned of an ancient order of Deryni adepts whose wisdom had shaped Deryni esoteric thinking for nearly three hundred years. It was Orin who had known and tapped the ancient mysteries of which Camber and his children had only dipped the surface—most specifically, the author of the Protocols that had enabled Camber to take a dead man's shape and memories, and Evaine to assume the guise of someone who had never been.

And perhaps Orin had known the secret of the spell that even now held Camber bound in some state like unto death, but not that final severing of the silvery cord—a spell from which, if legend served, he might be roused and healed and saved. And now, to look upon Orin himself—

His face was covered beneath the shroud of netted *shiral* crystals by a dense, dust-laden veil of white silk, so they could not guess his features, but his raiment they could survey with wonder—a curious blending of sacred and secular, calling to mind both the familiar and the unknown. He was known to have been a tall, well-made man in life, and even in death he projected an ineffable melding of priest and prince, the dust dimming the colors but never his splendor.

Around his body, just beneath the net, lay a fine, copelike mantle made of what they first took to be some darkish, close-napped fur, its formal folds spilling back off his hands to pool softly on the bier at either side. When Evaine gently blew at the dust on one shoulder, however, the "fur" was revealed as thousands of tiny, iridescent bird feathers stitched individually to a backing of scarlet silk. It shimmered in the light of their handfire, taking on different hues every time their breath stirred the feathers again and another layer of dust was dissipated. An ankle-length tunic of fine violet wool showed through the parting of the feathered cloak, of a shade very close to that chosen by the Camberian Council for their formal robes.

"An Airsid color," Queron remarked. "Did you know that, when you chose it? And those solar crosses embroidered along the sleeve edges are Gabrilite motifs, of course—and Varnarite, before that."

Solar crosses were worked across the toes and insteps of his slippers, too—twisted gold thread on white silk, encasing long, narrow feet. Violet silk hosen disappeared under the tunic, whose hem was also stitched with gold.

It was the hands that captured their lasting interest, however, when they bent to notice closer detail—the fine-veined hands crossed on the breast in a pose denoting pious repose. A silver chain wound among the long, tapered fingers, one of which bore a band of silver engraved with dust-dulled symbols, and the chain led above the hands to a heavy silver medallion set with a coin, of a size to nestle in the circle of a man's thumb and forefinger. Evaine breathed out softly as she saw it, leaning a little on her brother's arm as she bent down for a different angle.

"Well, well, do you see what I see?"

Joram nodded and leaned closer to puff at the dust on the silver, uneasiness giving way to curiosity.

"It looks like another dower coin. In fact, it could even be the one that made the seal we copied off Jodotha's documents."

"If we're careful," Queron said, reaching in to prod cautiously at the medallion, "we may be able to get it out without disturbing anything else. I could be wrong, but it doesn't appear to be actually under the net. It may have been put here after his burial."

"Be careful," Evaine murmured, as Queron delicately grasped the medallion by the edges with his Healer's fingers and began to lift it.

Slowly the chain emerged as Queron manipulated the medallion back and forth, back and forth, freeing it from the grasp of long-dead fingers and delicate silken cords. When it was completely clear, he smiled and handed it to Joram. The younger priest blew away the dust and burnished it with a fingertip before holding it down where all three of them could see it.

"If this isn't the coin that made that seal impression, I'd say it's from the same house," he offered, after a moment. "I can't see any difference."

"And you were never able to identify it?" Queron asked.

The Michaeline shook his head. "It has to be very old. I checked all the resources we have at hand—which I'll admit are somewhat limited, these days—but it isn't any house *I've* ever heard of. Of course, if it was an Airsid House—provided, of course, that the Airsid even *had* Houses . . ."

"Ah, yes, that is by no means certain," Queron agreed, leaning closer to peer at the rim of the coin's mounting. "Could that be a hinge there, on the left, or am I seeing things?"

Scowling, Joram tried to work a thumbnail under the opposite edge. "Looks as if it could be. If so, there may be a compartment underneath. It's thick enou—ah-ha!"

With his exclamation, the coin swung out on its hinges to reveal a thin, flat circle of crystal—and under it, a small, gently curving lock of rich red hair.

Queron whistled low under his breath. "Well, well, I think this about confirms that we're dealing with a dower coin. The hair would have been cut at the owner's tonsuring or religious profession. Was Orin a redhead?"

Evaine, taking the locket from Joram, turned it over and froze. "I don't know about Orin, but *this* lady certainly was."

The miniature on the back of the medallion had been executed on a wafer-thin roundel of ivory slightly smaller than the dower coin, the detailing so fine that the woman gazing up at them seemed almost to breathe. Rich red hair framed delicate but lively looking features. The chin was pointed, the mouth firm but curved in just the suggestion of a smile. The eyes were dark, with a depth that seemed to transcend the medium of mere painter's pigment.

"Sweet *Jesu*, can this be Jodotha?" Queron whispered.

"I'd guess it is," Joram replied. "The same coin-seal appears on documents we know were hers."

"That doesn't look like a nun's habit she's wearing, though," Evaine observed, indicating the close-necked white garment in the miniature. "Nor is the unbound hair what one would expect of a religious. Not that we've ever gotten any indication that she necessarily *was* a religious, other than the dower coin. And look what she's holding. Queron, are your eyes good enough to make them out?"

Queron nodded. "That's an Alpha and Omega on the book in her left hand. And it looks like a flagon in her right. Usually, those are symbols of a deacon's function. I wonder if the Airsid ordained women."

"You mean, to the priesthood?" Joram said.

"Well, to the diaconate, at least. What's the matter, Joram? Does that shock you?"

"Well, not exactly, but—"

"Oh, come now, you should know your ecclesiastical history better than that!" Queron scolded. "What do they teach you Michaelines anyway? You *know* that the scriptures speak of us all being a royal priesthood, a holy nation."

"And a peculiar people," Joram said sourly. "We certainly are that—especially if we're going to stand around debating canon law when we've just made one of the most spectacular discoveries of our age! Isn't anyone else interested in what else we may be able to learn? That *is* why we came, isn't it?"

He scowled as he beckoned his handfire closer and bent over the shrouded face, puffing vigorously at the dust on the silk, and Queron moved closer to peer over his shoulder.

"Forgive me," he said mildly. "Can you make out any features?"

"Not much. He had a beard, though, and there appears to be a narrow gold circlet or fillet across his brow. Evaine, was he a prince of some kind?"

"Not in any worldly sense," she replied, moving around to the head of the bier. "He was of noble family, though, and there's evidence to suggest that in the Airsid tradition, a gold fillet was the mark of an adept. Look at the texture, though. It isn't a solid band at all. It's woven, probably tied behind. That would—"

Her voice cut off as she glanced up to read Queron's reaction and, instead, caught something unexpected out of the corner of her eye. She turned her head slightly to the right and froze for just an instant, a look of astonishment on her face.

"Oh, dear God!" she murmured, collapsing to her knees and clenching the locket to her lips.

Instantly Joram and Queron were scrambling around the head of the bier to reach her, both of them stumbling to a halt at her side and behind her as they saw what she had seen.

The woman lay on her right side, with her back along the cool white length of the bier. A cloud of dust-dulled red hair spilled across the black and white tiles beneath her head, tendrils trailing off the edge of the dais, and her right arm was curved under, to cushion it. Beneath her coating of dust, it was difficult to estimate how old she had been when she died, but none of them had any doubt that she was the woman in the locket.

She wore a gown of violet silk, the same shade as Orin's wool, but no jewelry save a torque of twisted gold around her throat. Her feet were bare. She lay on a mantle of scarlet that partially covered

her left shoulder, a corner drawn close under her chin with one
graceful hand, as if she had thought to shield herself from the cold
of her long sleep, here at the side of her mentor. A wand of ivory,
almost like a baton of office, nestled close along her right arm. Her
left sleeve and the part of her side that lay beside and beneath it
were stained with a darkness that showed black on the violet and
brown on the ivory when Joram cautiously beckoned his handfire
nearer.

Queron, ever the Healer, leaned forward on his hands and knees
in a fruitless attempt to see the wound more clearly, then rocked
back on his heels, still not taking his eyes from the still form.

"I take it that we're all agreed, this *is* Jodotha," he said quietly.
"Do any of the legends say how she's supposed to have died?"

Evaine shook her head. "Not precisely. Some traditions have her
involved in trying to save King Llarik's two sons—both of whom
were executed by their own father in 699. Orin was already dead by
then, of course—he was considerably older than Jodotha. Whatever
happened, I—guess she decided to come back here and die beside
him."

"But, she's supposed to have been a Healer, isn't she?" Joram
said. "If she had the strength to get back here from wherever it
happened, wouldn't she have had the strength to Heal herself?"

Queron cocked his head wistfully. "Maybe she didn't want to
Heal herself, Joram. If she was the princes' protectoress and failed
to save them, maybe she didn't want to live anymore. After all, Orin
was long dead, the princes' cause lost, the Airsid scattered—"

"Aye, I think the Airsid died with her," Evaine murmured,
clutching the locket to her breast as she slowly shook her head.
"How could things have gone so far awry? And all that knowledge,
lost . . ."

Queron nodded. "Those were dark times, especially that hundred
years or so during and after Llarik's reign—up until Bearand had just
about earned his title of saint. With all the barbarian incursions, the
failure of the Pax Romanum, the cost of the Moorish repulsion, it's
a wonder we have as much as we do. Imagine, if the great libraries
had burned, for example."

"They may, yet," Joram muttered darkly, "if Edward MacInnis
has anything to say about it. All the best parts, anyway."

"No, some of the best parts may be *here*," Evaine said, "maybe
even inside this bier. Finding the burial place of both Orin and Jodotha has to rank with the major historical discoveries of the past
two or three decades."

"Ah, but dare we use what they left?" Queron asked, glancing uneasily at Jodotha's body. "If Orin and Jodotha were half as powerful as legend suggests—

"Why, Queron, I'm surprised," Evaine said, reaching out to touch a lock of the still-bright hair. "Joram is supposed to be the cautious—oh!"

As her finger brushed the hair, the whole body began to shimmer, setting up a resonance that could be sensed but not seen. Evaine jerked back her hand in alarm, and all of them edged back from it.

But then, quietly, with no fuss at all, the body simply collapsed in on itself and went to dust. Within seconds, all that remained was a dust-coated garment of stained violet silk, an ivory wand, similarly stained, and a twisted golden torque, partially contained in a crumbling mass of faded scarlet that once had been a woolen mantle. Not even teeth or fragments of bone remained.

"Well," Queron said softly, after a moment in which all of them resumed breathing, "it would appear that at least a part of the matter has been taken out of our hands." He inched forward on his hunkers and ran steady fingers above the ivory wand, the torque of gold, then turned to smile wanly at Evaine.

"I think that these should go to you, dear lady. Oh, they're clean—but not for us men. Take them."

Solemnly, Evaine handed Jodotha's locket to Joram, then reached out and plucked the torque from the ruin of wool, blew dust from its surface, wiped it on the hem of her gown. Cleaned, the torque showed bold patterns of interlace and brilliant color, elegantly traced insets of scarlet and purple and blue and green enamel done in details so fine, she could barely make out all the lines. The solar crosses of the Gabrilites were there, but also more ancient symbols.

She polished it again against her skirt, then touched it to her lips before slipping it around her neck. The ornament gleamed like the collar of a princess, and the wand she picked up resembled a scepter. Joram offered her his hand as she made to stand, and his slight bow, begun as a gesture of lightness, changed to one profound as she took his hand and rose. None of them dared to speak until she let out a great breath and glanced at both of them.

"Well, what of Orin now?" she said. Avoiding Jodotha's dust, she moved to the head of the bier, but still on Jodotha's side. "I was serious when I suggested that some of his missing scrolls might be hidden in the bier, but I'm not anxious to start dismantling it."

"That may not be necessary," Queron said, moving with Joram to the left side again, where they would not further disturb Jodotha's remains. "The scrolls may be much closer than that. Look there, at that bulge under his left arm. He's got *something* buried with him—and it's about the right shape."

"You may be right," Evaine said, leaning down to get another angle. "We'd have to move the net to get at them, though. How safe do you suppose that would be?"

Joram, moving closer to the foot of the bier, folded his arms uneasily. "Maybe we should think about it and come back later."

"No, if the scrolls are here, we need them now," Evaine said. Coming around to the left side, she laid her wand on the floor close in the angle of the bier, then ran her hands the length of the body just above the surface of the net. Gingerly she touched one of the *shiral* crystals fastened in a portion of the net not covering the body. She could feel the energy harnessed in the crystal and its balance with the others, but that balance was very delicate. With a sigh, she raised her head and glanced at the others.

"I would say that if we disturb the net, his body is going to go to dust just the way Jodotha's did. However, I think that's *all* that will happen."

"I agree," Queron said promptly.

"Which means," Joram said slowly, "that it's a question of disturbing the dead and *maybe* getting what we came looking for, or leaving him in peace and losing whatever that is under his cloak—which we don't even know for certain is the information we need."

"That's true." Evaine sighed and began again. "Joram, I'm no more fond of disturbing the dead than you are, but if we don't do this, then we might just as well not have found him. Of course, it goes without saying that when time and circumstances permit, we'll gather the dust and reinter it properly in consecrated ground. In fact, we could mingle their dust." She reached out to touch her brother's arm. "I think she would have liked that. And somehow, I think it's fitting."

Joram, staring hard at the locket he held, closed it in his fist and nodded. "You're right. Forgive my squeamishness. I went through something like this once before, though, when I had to move Alister Cullen's body. And it didn't help that it looked like Father at the time."

No one could gainsay that. After a dozen heartbeats, Queron sighed and moved back to the head of the bier. Joram was already at the foot, tucking the Jodotha locket into the front of his cassock. Evaine remained on the left and gingerly picked up the very edge of the net where it trailed off the bier.

"If you two will lift evenly, I'll try to gather up the slack in the middle," Evaine said, as they all took hold.

As one, they lifted the fragile net, pausing several times for Evaine to free the cords net from where they had hung up on a cloak clasp, a slippered toe, one curved finger. As the net cleared the body, the last contact broken, it was as if the dust began to crawl on the body, alive in a rainbow shimmer of strangely shifting light on light.

Quickly they lifted the net clear and laid it on the floor on Evaine's side; but by the time they could straighten up, all that remained of the great Orin was a collapsing mound of moldering clothing laid out in human shape, the fabric upthrust by several lumps and bulges. Queron, boldest of them all at that point, gently moved aside the fold of feathered cloak that still covered the most suspicious bulge, then grinned widely.

"We were looking for scrolls, I believe?"

The two loosely rolled scrolls lay with a wand that was the mate to Evaine's. One was tied with a cord of royal blue, the other with violet. Evaine drew a quick breath at that, for she had read long ago of a rumored fifth, blue-bound protocol known only as the Scroll of Daring and she saw, by Joram's expression, that he also recognized the possible significance.

But, the violet-corded one?

"Could that be a *sixth* protocol," Joram whispered, glancing up at Evaine's awed face.

"I've never heard of one. But that *could* be his working notes—"

"I take it that the blue-bound one is the fifth protocol," Queron murmured. "Are you saying that the other one is the *Codex Orini*?"

"Ah, you've heard of it, too," Evaine answered, somewhat distractedly. "Yes, the blue one will be the missing fifth protocol." She picked it up carefully from its bed of dust and ruined wool and tapped it lightly before slipping off its cord, to open it and scan the first few lines.

"Ah, yes. *On Staring Patterns, Moon-Scrying, and the Blocking of Power in Those of Magical Birthright,*" she read with a growing grin. She handed the scroll to Queron with a slight bow. "Yours, I believe, for the next time you see Tavis and Sylvan."

"And the other one?" Queron urged.

"The other one—ah, yes." Almost reverently she lifted it and shook off the worst of the dust, carefully blowing more dust from the violet cord. "This one I think I'll save until later."

"A wise decision, saving it," Joram muttered. "In fact, I think I'd open it in a warded circle, if I were you."

Queron glanced at him sharply. "You sense something?"

"Not exactly. Just a feeling that—whatever is in there is very powerful. I'm not sure I even want to be around, when she opens it."

"Intuition or just natural caution?" Queron pressed.

"Perhaps a little of both. It probably doesn't mean anything." Joram glanced at the dust again, then extracted the second ivory wand. "Here's the mate to yours, Evaine. Do you think it was a magical implement, or just some kind of symbol of office?"

"Could be either—or both—or neither, though I'd guess they're symbols of office. We can certainly use them as such." She handled Joram's wand thoughtfully, then retrieved her own and compared the two, side by side, her scroll tucked under her arm. "Yes, Coadjutor wands, I think. They'll add a little of Orin and Jodotha's presence to our deliberations—which seems fitting, since we have them to thank for so much of our esoteric tradition."

"I'll concur with that," Queron agreed. "And Joram," he continued, picking Orin's ring out of the dust, "suppose you take this and keep it in trust for us. Probe it, when you have the time, and see what you can learn."

"I couldn't wear it," Joram protested, wiping his hands nervously on his cassock.

"Then, put it away," Queron said, placing the ring in Joram's hand and closing his fingers over it. "When you're ready, it will be there. Your sister isn't the only one in your family with talent, you know."

"Very well."

As Queron scanned the dust again, Joram slipped the ring into his belt pouch and looked much relieved. Queron, when he had finished, glanced at the others.

"Let's come back tomorrow or the next day to finish here," he said quietly. "We'll need a few things to do the job right. For now, it's been a very busy night, and I think we all need time to rest and to digest what we've learned."

He got no argument from either of them.

CHAPTER TWENTY-THREE

*But you shall not mock at me thus, neither will
I break the sacred oaths of my ancestors to
keep the Law, not even though you tear out
mine eyes and burn out mine entrails.*

—IV Maccabees 2:53

What remained of the night brought but fitful sleep for any of the
three Deryni. Nor might they lie abed, for Holy Saturday made early
morning demands of everyone in the sanctuary. Emotionally wrung
out from their experience and already primed with the stark, solemn
symbolism of Holy Week, all three reported bizarre dreams when
they conferred after Joram's first Mass the next morning. In addition,
Evaine found herself possessed of an inexplicable desire to see the
remains of Orin and Jodotha blessed and laid to rest as quickly as
possible.

"I don't know why it's so important; it just *is*," she said, when
pressed for a reason. Indeed, though sheer logic could support absolutely no urgency for reinterring a pair dead these nearly three
centuries, some unignorable sense beyond logic did insist that this
was a task best resolved, and quickly. Even Joram came to agree, to
his own surprise.

Sheer practicality presented its own problems, however. Logis-
tically speaking, a worse day for the task than Holy Saturday could
scarcely be imagined, even if the symbolism of descending into the
tomb was inescapable. If the Lenten season was more than usually
demanding upon the services of God's priests, then the transition
into Eastertide was doubly so; and in the small community dwelling
in the Michaeline sanctuary, any untoward absence, especially by
all three of them, would be all too obvious.

Nonetheless, they decided that a very few free hours might be squeezed out if they were careful, between the stark recitation of Prime and the more demanding rites of the night's Easter Vigil, with its blessing of the newly kindled fire and baptismal water and the lighting of the Paschal candle. Under guise of retiring for an afternoon's rest and meditation for the long night ahead, while the rest of the community did likewise, the three returned to the tomb beneath the altar under Grecotha, bearing with them a small hearth broom, an ivory coffer bound with iron, and two capacious leather satchels. The two priests prayed quietly over the dust-filled clothing for a few minutes. Then they and Evaine bent to the delicate task of sifting the remains of the two Deryni adepts from the clothing left behind.

They started with Jodotha. The wool of her mantle came to pieces in their hands, and had to be gathered into one of the satchels for later burning, but the silk gown held, so that its contents could be carefully poured and shaken into the ivory coffer. Shifting Jodotha's mantle revealed another ring where her right hand had lain, an apparent twin to the one Orin had worn. Inside, the Latin inscription confirmed her identity: *Jodotha, serva Deum.*

"Servant of the gods," Evaine translated, showing it briefly to the others before tucking the ring into an inner pocket to compare with Orin's, later on.

"Yes, but which gods?" Joram said archly.

But they had no time to speculate further just now, as the afternoon wore on toward Vespers and the demands of the night. After sweeping the rest of Jodotha's remains into the coffer, they had to start on Orin. The feathers of the cloak had been stitched to silk with silken thread, so it fared very well, but Orin's robe, being wool, had disintegrated to dusty, cobwebby-looking shreds of faded purple. These joined the remnants of Jodotha's mantle in the first satchel. They scooped the rest of the cloak's contents into the ivory coffer. His silken hose and leather slippers went into the bag with Jodotha's gown, along with the net of *shiral* crystals, carefully folded.

When all was done, Evaine set the coffer in the center of the bier, squarely on the intersection where the four center cubes met, and stood back to look at it again. Queron carried the satchels and broom, and Joram held the feathered cope across one arm. Relieved of its recent occupant, the bier's construction as a configuration of ward cubes was at last clearly apparent, the left half formed by four black cubes and the right by four white. Queron flicked a last speck of dust from one white corner, near where Orin's head had lain, then glanced quietly at the others.

"I'm struck by the fitness of a funeral bier symbolizing the Pillars of the Temple," he said after a pause. "It's such a logical extension of the cube altar configuration, I wonder that no one ever seems to have made the connection before. In fact, something comes back to me now from my days at Saint Neot's, that made no sense at the time—but then, neither did the cleansing ritual that brought us to this place."

The eyes of both his listeners turned silently upon him as he went on.

"My Order *did* know of this," he said wonderingly. "They *must* have known. They veiled it from profane eyes—and indeed, even we brethren didn't know the full significance—but the Elders of the Order *surely* must have known. I can see that now."

Joram was looking at him oddly. "They—knew about this?"

Nodding, Queron laid down his satchels and broom, moving closer again to set his hands on the corners near where Orin's head had been. "They may not have known consciously, but they knew *something*. We had a special catafalque at Saint Neot's that only was brought out when one of the Elders died. It was made of eight hollow, wooden cubes that bolted together to make a shape like this—and came apart for ease of storage and assembly, I'd always assumed. The top surfaces were plain, stained wood—yew, I think— and the sides were carved with the symbols of our Order and our Faith, as one might expect. The surfaces that butted together were blank." He ran a fingertip along the join of black and white cubes.

"But the insides of the cubes were painted, some black and some white—something I only found out when I was a very senior brother in the Gabrilites, when I was poking around in the storeroom where the cubes were kept, looking for something else. It never occurred to me to ask about it, but when they were bolted together, the cubes with the black insides would have been lined up along the left side and the white ones along the right. The significance didn't register until just now."

"You mean no one ever noticed, before that, when they were setting up the bier?" Evaine asked.

"If they did, I never heard anyone comment on it," Queron replied. "Brother Sacristan always supervised the preparations for an Elder's funeral. Not only that, I don't recall ever being asked to help assemble the bier, though the cubes must have been very heavy, and someone would have had to bring them into the church from storage. Novices and junior brethren handled most of the other preparations, but the bier was always in place when we began."

"And I'll bet that Brother Sacristan was always an Elder, correct?" Joram asked.

"Always."

"What you've been describing suggests that there may have been a—an Order within an Order," Evaine ventured, after a few seconds. "Obviously, some practices had lost at least part of their original meanings from older times—like the purification ritual—but is it possible that a very select inner Order were attempting to perpetuate old Airsid traditions?"

Queron nodded thoughtfully. "That is entirely possible. We had an advisory Council of Elders—twelve of them, headed by the Abbot." He managed a sheepish smile. "Ironic, isn't it? I was up for election as an Elder when I left to champion Saint Camber. If I'd stayed, presumably I'd know. But of course, if I'd stayed, the three of us would not now be having this conversation, would we?"

"I suggest," said Joram, beginning to unfold the feathered cloak, "that we not continue this conversation just here and now, or we'll be answering even more questions than this has raised. We should be getting back. It must be getting close to time for evening services."

Sighing, Evaine took an edge of the cloak and helped him spread its semicircular shape along the length of the bier, so that most of it was off the floor. The rounded shape of the ivory coffer bulged the cloak in the center, and Evaine touched her hand to a corner of the bier that was still exposed.

"There's just one more thing," she said softly, not looking at either of them. "This symbolism speaks to me. Not just because of its association with Orin and Jodotha, but for some other reason that I can't quite articulate just now. I want Father to rest on a bier like this, if we should fail in our attempt to bring him back—perhaps in that chamber under the *keeill*."

It was the first time she had expressed the possibility that they might *not* be able to bring him back. For her listeners, the possibility went even further.

"Evaine," Queron said quietly, "do you have some premonition?"

A little uneasily, she shook her head. "No. I simply believe in preparing for the unexpected. It shouldn't be difficult to finish the room under the *keeill*. The bier can be a wooden one, like your one for Gabrilite Elders—indeed, the only way we'll get one down there is in pieces—but I want him to rest in balance between the Pillars. We can even paint the outsides of our cubes," she added with a stiff smile.

"And what else?" Joram asked, studying her closely. "Out with it, Evaine. You haven't said it all yet."

Glancing at her now folded hands, she shook her head. "You're right. There's more. If—if I should die in the attempt—no, let me finish, Joram. I have to say this." She drew herself up straight to face them. "If I should die in the attempt, I want my body to lie beside Rhys, on another bier like this. Will you both promise me that?"

Solemnly they promised, neither of them even trying to give her assurance that of course they would be successful, and of course she would not die. After that, they knelt briefly in prayer for Orin and Jodotha, each raising his or her own silent petitions before the two priests blessed this final resting place and the three of them headed quietly back the way they had come, to greet the miracle of Easter.

Easter was celebrated all over the land in the next hours. In cathedrals and in tiny parish churches, the Easter liturgy proclaimed God's promise of salvation and life eternal for those who believed, and voices young and old raised the glad songs of praise and thanksgiving for the Divine mercy. Even Deryni were almost welcome in the churches on this most holy of days, though the Easter homilies without fail touched on the need for Deryni to amend their ways and forswear their evil powers.

In Rhemuth no less than in any other place, the Easter message rang clear, and nowhere more splendidly or with more pomp and ceremonial than in the Cathedral of Saint George. The king and his brothers were among the most august of those who celebrated in Rhemuth's newly refurbished cathedral, Javan and Rhys Michael serving Archbishop Orris at the altar while Alroy led the offertory procession, presenting the bread and wine to be consecrated.

Afterwards, there was a feast that lasted well into the early evening, replete with all the meats and sweets set aside during the penitential season of Lent. Other than Hubert, whose presence was required in Valoret at this most holy of seasons, all of the regents were present with their wives and families—even Duke Ewan, who had journeyed down from Kheldour. Alroy held a formal Easter court the next day and wore a tall crown of gold filigree set with rubies and was permitted the appearance of real authority, though at least one regent was always at his side.

The regents were planning something, though. In the month that followed, between Easter and the twins' thirteenth birthday on the twenty-fifth of May, Javan gradually became aware that it had something to do with Duke Ewan, by far the least offensive of the five.

Immediately the courts and feasts of Easter week had concluded, Ewan retired once more to his lands in the Kheldish Riding—a departure unremarkable in itself, for tacit agreement had always been that Ewan's constant presence at court was not required, it being understood that his duties as viceroy in Kheldour required his attendance there, just as Hubert's episcopal duties required his in Valoret.

This time, however, Ewan's departure seemed to spark a spate of criticism, though no one made particular comment to the duke himself to suggest that his continued presence was expected or required. No sooner was he beyond convenient recall than muted rumblings began to whisper among the remaining regents, spearheaded by Earl Murdoch, that perhaps Ewan should be asked to resign, and might be replaced by Hubert's brother Manfred—though that worthy quickly headed off to Caerrorie to inspect the progress on his new manor house, lest he be accused of campaigning for the appointment. Javan heard the gist of this discontent from Oriel—who overheard of it while attending one of Murdoch's nasty sons, who spoke all too freely under Oriel's hands while having a riding injury attended to.

Very soon, Archbishop Hubert made an unannounced visit to Rhemuth, ostensibly to satisfy himself that Javan's religious instruction was proceeding satisfactorily, but almost certainly to discuss the matter of Ewan with his fellow regents as well, for he had numerous long, intense meetings with his three cohorts before heading back to Valoret. He interviewed Javan several times during his three day stay, as if to give credence to his parochial intent in coming to Rhemuth, but the meetings were always in the presence of others, so Javan dared not use his meager hold over Hubert to increase his knowledge. The bulk of the archbishop's time was spent with the other regents.

One thing Hubert did give genuine attention to, and that was Javan's disinclination to use Bishop Alfred as a spiritual director. Hubert was wise enough not to try to force the issue, for, by definition, such direction must be a very personal matter. Nor did he take exception to Javan's study of the classics with Father Boniface. He simply wished to have closer control of what Javan was studying and thinking.

Accordingly, on the day of his departure, Hubert put his postulant prince's further spiritual guidance into the hands of two priests of the *Custodes Fidei*: Father Lior, of the Inquisitor General's office, and the local *Custodes* abbot, one Father Secorim, who were instructed to supervise personally all Javan's future religious involvement. The prince's twice-weekly sessions with Father Boniface were permitted to continue, in the very convenient study at Saint Hilary's, but daily attendance at Mass there came to an end, as the *Custodes* priests subtly began trying to mold their charge to a more biddable and compliant mind by assistance at their own Masses.

Two things only eased the pressure on Javan, during that all too-long month between Easter and his birthday: the improving weather of spring, which allowed a resumption of daily rides and other outdoor activities curtailed by the winter, and the temporary departure of Regent Rhun, who betook himself to Sheele, finally to take possession of the former Thuryn earldom. Even Murdoch absented himself for a week or so, to escort his son and new daughter-in-law to the family seat in Carthane, where the young couple would make their first home and Richard was expected gradually to take up the reins of government in his father's stead.

For a few weeks then, only Earl Tammaron, of the regents, was resident in Rhemuth, governing his young charges with rather more indulgence than his colleagues might have approved, had they been present. Under his supervision, a delighted King Alroy was permitted to hold several minor courts to hear local appeals—which both Javan and Rhys Michael were permitted to attend—but there were no other official functions during the early weeks of May. All three boys were expected to attend morning and evening prayers with the royal household as well as Mass on Sundays, to take their evening meals in the great hall with the court and, weather permitting, to spend several hours a day in the weapons yard or riding out with the master of horse—and of course, Javan had his own additional regimen set up by his *Custodes* watchdogs. But otherwise, Tammaron made few demands.

The situation should have made it much easier for Javan to pursue his own devices, gathering the intelligence information that his Deryni allies needed. But with most of the regents absent, little news came to court except through Tammaron—and he had definite ideas about what it was necessary for under-age princes to know. Javan continued to report to Father Boniface's study several times a week for "classics" studies—and often met there with one or another of the Deryni he had come to know and trust. But once he had told them of his suspicions about a shake-up coming in the Council of Regents, and the intensified scrutiny he was receiving from Hubert's *Custodes*, he had little else to pass on, other than to keep them abreast of the ongoing situation regarding the regents' captive Deryni. That, too, gave cause for serious thought.

Of the four Deryni normally at court, not counting the half dozen or so that were attached to the garrison, only Oriel was at all in evidence. Rhun and Manfred had taken Sitric and Ursin with them on campaign, and were not expected back until shortly before the twins' birthday. Javan spotted Declan Carmody occasionally, but that troubled man was still not back to full duty following his blow-up of some three months before. Javan avoided him whenever possible, lest he endanger the risky and still fragile alliance he had formed with Oriel.

As for Oriel's wife and baby daughter, Javan had been able to learn little. He did discover that the families of all the collaborators were being held in carefully guarded quarters at Rhemuth Castle. Javan had caught a glimpse of Alana d'Oriel one day, taking the air in a walled courtyard where no one else was allowed to go, but any attempt actually to speak with her or with any of the other captives was impossible. Her quarters, like those of the other men's wives, were too secure for even a Deryni-trained prince to penetrate.

Thus did the weeks after Easter pass, both Javan and his allies mainly biding their time, waiting for Pentecost. Evaine continued her research, now with both Joram and Queron to assist her with the new documents they had acquired, and the Healer-priest scoured his memory for other bits of forgotten Gabrilite tradition that might have held a double meaning, and might be useful to them now.

Physical activity there was for the Deryni, too. As a break from their academic and psychic ferreting, they set about tidying and finishing the chamber under the *keeill*. To assist with the heavy work, Evaine enlisted the aid of her four loyal men-at-arms, their memories suitably manipulated, by their own consent, to guard the place's secret. Against the day when the revival of Camber should actually be attempted, they even built a set of wooden cubes like those Queron had described, though they painted the outsides as well as the insides black or white, before assembling them in the completed sub-*keeill* chamber. The men-at-arms did *not* assist with that, no matter how effective Evaine believed her control of the men's memories to be.

Mostly, though, the three Deryni bided their time, fretting increasingly as May counted out its latter days and Pentecost loomed closer, with the expected emergence of Revan's active ministry. For even had they settled on a clear procedure for attempting to revive Camber, they dared not risk it until Revan's mission was well underway, lest the attempt claim one or all of their lives and leave the mission leaderless.

Accordingly, though they marked the feast day of the king and Prince Javan with a Mass for their continued good health and prosperity, they did not expect any particular change in Rhemuth. Nor did Javan himself, as he let Charlan help him dress for the formal birthday court, following their attendance at a solemn High Mass in the cathedral earlier in the morning.

"What kinds of gifts do you think you'll receive, your Highness?" Charlan asked, as he pulled a tunic of bright blue wool over his master's head. "I shouldn't be surprised if there's a new sword, or perhaps new trappings for the R'Kassan colt—or maybe even a proper warhorse, to use until the colt is old enough for heavy work."

Javan grinned and tugged at the cuffs of his sky blue undertunic, giving the oversleeves a shake to settle the knee-length tippets. The blue wool skimmed the lighter silk without hindrance, flaring into deep folds at the narrow hips, where Charlan knelt to fasten a belt of hammered silver plaques. The oversleeves hit at elbow length in the front, far more flamboyant than was Javan's usual wont—bright with scarlet, gold, and darker blue embroidery at their edges and all up in their lining, which was scarlet. The front of the overtunic was open to the waist, to show the high collar and embroidered front of the undertunic, all silver filigree work on the sky blue.

The shoes Javan wore, soft crimson leather with cutwork that showed discreet flashes of his black woolen hose, had been Charlan's gift to him, earlier that morning. He had not worn them to church, for the streets were too muddy to risk ruining them, but the rest of the day's festivities would all be indoor. Javan pointed his toe to admire them again as Charlan clipped a sheathed dagger to the belt of plaques.

"A new saddle would be nice," the prince avowed. "Or a new bow. I'd like to have a new bow. My old one is too light a draw anymore, especially with the longer arrows I'm using now."

He pantomimed drawing a bow and nocking the arrow to his ear, and Charlan gave the bicep of the bow arm a playful punch as he got to his feet.

"You've grown over the winter, sir," he said, picking up a comb as Javan ducked to peer into a small wall-mounted mirror and began energetically raking his fingers through his short black hair. "Here now! Let me give you a hand with that, sir. I won't have the other squires thinking I can't take proper care of my young lord. Many's the eye that will be upon you today."

"Aye, all the regents' eyes," Javan sighed, though he stood still and let Charlan comb his hair. "Maybe most of them will go away again, as soon as this is over. At least I'll be of age in another year. Then I won't have to take orders from anyone."

"Aye, but your choices will always be constrained by this," Charlan said, crowning Javan with a silver circlet embellished with crosses and garnets. "And if you should set it aside, as the regents surely intend you should do, you'll be bound by other constraints, no less compelling." Charlan cocked his fair head. "*Do* you intend to take Holy Orders, Sire?"

Looking at himself in the mirror, with the coronet shining in the wan light, Javan knew that he never could set aside his royal birthright willingly; but he dared not tell Charlan that, for Charlan could not help relaying the information right back to the regents, if asked about it.

"I couldn't do it right away, Charlan," he said honestly, not adding that he could never do it, knowing the avarice of the regents, who would remain fiercely protective of their powers and perquisites, even once Alroy and Javan were of age. "It's a very important step, and I'm very young to make so far-reaching a decision. Father Lior and Father Secorim have been most helpful, but they have also made me realize how much more I have to learn, before I could presume to announce my life's intentions. I shall continue to meditate on the matter—which means, I fear, that I must continue to drag you to my nocturnal vigils and soul-searchings, to the detriment of your sleep!"

He grinned as he said the last, giving Charlan one of his most disarming smiles, and the squire chuckled, apparently well satisfied.

"Whatever your final decision, my lord, I shall always count it my honor and privilege to have served you," he said, bending to kiss Javan's hand in renewed homage. "But for now, I think your Highness had best repair to the hall, or we shall never learn what gifts have been allotted you on your birthday."

The gift-giving portion of the afternoon began well enough, though Javan was somewhat discomfited to see all five regents present with their families, and all four of the regents' captive Deryni—though the latter kept quietly in the background, and probably were not recognized for what they were by most of the foreign dignitaries who came to pay their respects to the king and his brother on their natal day. In a procession of worthies that took more than an hour, sumptuous gifts were laid before the royal brothers, accompanied by courtly speeches and no little braggadocio. By the time they were done, Javan had received two small Kheldish carpets, a brace of fleet deerhounds from Cassan, a mound of new sleeping furs from the mountains of the Connait, a pouch of freshwater pearls from one of the princes of Howicce, and a bolt of gold-shot scarlet silk from the Hort of Orsal. Alroy received similar gifts, but in greater number or of higher quality, since he was king.

They received nothing from Torenth, but they had not expected anything, since the King of Torenth still sheltered the bastard sired by the late King Imre on his equally late sister, and supported—at least in principle—the boy's claim to the throne of Gwynedd. Eventually, the House of Haldane could expect more trouble from that quarter, for young Mark of Festil had turned thirteen just after the first of the year, and his supporters surely would press his claim as soon as they thought there was any reasonable chance of winning.

But not now, and not in the immediately forseeable future, when their own Torenthi king was hardly a year upon his throne, and still of only eighteen years himself. Arion of Torenth would not lightly support a foreign war effort when his own hands were still uncertain on the reins of government; and his young kinsman's supporters were still smarting from the defeat dealt them by a Haldane army a decade ago, when they had sought to put the boy's mother on Gwynedd's throne. No, this day brought only silence from Torenth.

And when the foreign ambassadors had finished their presentations, Alroy's vassals came forward to make similar gifts to the royal twins: pouches of golden coins and brooches and clasps of silver most cunningly wrought; falcons, hounds, racing steeds; and even the promise of a breeding to a coveted stallion owned by Lord William de Borgos, whose racing stud was unsurpassed in all the Eleven Kingdoms.

One of the most popular gifts, given to Alroy and Javan jointly by a southern baron, was a Cardounet board made of ebony and olivewood, inlaid around the edges with mother-of-pearl and semiprecious gems. The pieces, too, were carved of ebony and olivewood, painted with the appropriate livery colors, and with real gems set on the priest-kings' crowns and the miters of the two archbishops.

Even Rhys Michael cast covetous eyes at that gift, though his attention and, indeed, that of all the court, were immediately diverted when Bonner Sinclair, the young Earl of Tarleton, presented Alroy and Javan with a wicker cage containing two pairs of sharp, ebon-bright eyes surrounded by sleek brown fur.

"What are they?" Alroy asked delightedly, as the man slipped the wicker catch on the cage door and let the creatures out.

"Ferrets, Sire," Tarleton said, grinning. "They make wonderful pets, if they don't carry off all the palace treasure. They're prodigious thieves!"

The animals were a little skittish at first, and the male gave Alroy a sharp nip on the finger before running inside his tunic and finally settling in his sleeve. The other, intended for Javan, was soon scampering among the piles of gifts arrayed around the throne, filching coins and jewels, and ended up taking refuge in the lap of a delighted Rhys Michael.

"They do choose their own friends, your Highness," Lord Tarleton told Javan apologetically. "I can bring you another, if you like, though I can't guarantee she'd be partial to you."

"No, let my brother have her," Javan said a little sadly. "My studies keep me too busy for a pet anyway."

He was to regret his words a little later, for it seemed the regents had already decided he was destined for the cloister. When it came time for the regents to present their gifts, Alroy's were pointedly princely: new armor, a blunted tournament sword, a set of campaign maps of the border regions, a matched pair of boar hunting spears, and the crowning gift: a fully caparisoned warhorse the color of rich cream.

"Oh, he's magnificent! Thank you, Lord Tammaron," Alroy gasped, as the stallion was led back out of the hall.

Javan's gifts were no less sumptuous, but clearly reflected the majority of the givers' ecclesiastical hopes for the king's twin. Duke Ewan gave him the bow he had coveted—a beautiful length of handrubbed hickory, inlaid along its back with horn—but all the other gifts were far more suitable for a man long in Holy Orders than a boy of thirteen: a richly illuminated Book of Hours, a rosewood and silver crucifix worthy of a cathedral chapel, a relic of the martyred Saint Willim sealed in a crystal reliquary, and from Hubert, a starkly functional silver chalice and paten and a chasuble of creamy wool, surprisingly plain compared to the other gifts.

"I'm told these were your father's, when he was a priest at Saint Foillan's Abbey," Hubert told him, his tone hinting far more than his actual words. "When you come of age, you'll want to set up your own household, so I thought you might like these for your own use. It saves a chaplain having to bring his own," the archbishop concluded, as he laid the folded vestment over Javan's arm, as if bestowing it on a newly ordained priest.

Javan tried to look suitably moved, but he knew what Hubert was really trying to convey and he doubted his father had ever even seen the vestments and Mass vessels that Hubert piled onto his lap. After murmuring something noncommital and reasonably gracious, he handed them off to Charlan as soon as he decently could, though he felt that everyone was watching him, even when the court bard read a poem in his brother's honor.

The mood shifted almost immediately, however, and made Javan almost forget about the archbishop's latest attempt to nudge him toward a religious vocation. For Earl Murdoch, after conferring briefly with Rhun, Tammaron, and Hubert, suddenly strode to the center of the dais and bowed perfunctorily to the king.

"By your leave, Sire, now that the gifts have been presented, we have one item of business that must be completed before we adjourn for your birthday feast. Have I your leave to speak?"

Alroy signalled his assent with a nod and a half-raised hand—as if withholding it might have made any difference—but it was clear to Javan that his brother had no notion what Murdoch was going to say. Javan thought *he* did, though. The chief regent had a scroll stuck through his belt next to a serviceable-looking dagger, and he made Alroy and then his brothers another, more formal bow before taking out the scroll, though he did not unroll it yet.

"My Liege, your Highness, my lords and ladies," he said, half turning toward the hall. "I speak for my fellow regents in this matter, to acquaint you with a point of law. As some of you may recall, it was the decree of our late beloved King Cinhil, in setting up a regency council to govern his sons during their minority, that it would be the prerogative of any four of those regents to expel and replace a fifth of their number if they unanimously adjudged him to be incompatible with the majority. I regret to inform the King's Grace and this court that it has become necessary to exercise that prerogative."

All at once, Javan realized precisely where Murdoch and the others were *not* looking, as Duke Ewan eased slowly to his feet. Ewan was only thirty-seven, but he suddenly looked *old*.

"So, therefore, do we, Earl Tammaron Fitz-Arthur, Earl Rhun of Horthness, Archbishop Hubert MacInnis, and myself, Earl Murdoch of Carthane, expel from our number the noble his Grace the Duke of Claibourne, and name in his stead the Right Honorable the Earl of Culdi, Lord Manfred—."

"Murdoch, I'll kill you!" Before Murdoch could even finish, Duke Ewan was vaulting across the men and benches separating him from Murdoch, bellowing his outrage, a long highland dirk suddenly clenched in his burly fist. The weapon caught the scroll Murdoch raised instinctively in a warding-off gesture, grazing Murdoch's cheek, but Murdoch's dagger was already in his free hand, darting in to counter Ewan's next blow.

"Stop him!" Rhun shouted.

But the two were already grappling for the weapons, Ewan with murder in his eyes and Murdoch with his long arms and legs wrapped around the heavier, more experienced Ewan as they rolled over and over. Ewan's men leaped in belatedly to help him, only to be taken on by the scores of royal guardsmen who poured into the hall. Javan never quite saw clearly how it happened; only that suddenly there was blood everywhere and Ewan lay dying with several of his men, both hands pressed futilely around the bloody hilt of a long dagger buried in his gut.

A hush fell across the hall as Murdoch staggered to his feet, breathing hard, clutching a nasty gash across one bicep. Blood leaked from between his fingers and dripped on one of the newly presented Kheldish carpets as the injured regent glared an unmistakable summons for Oriel to attend him.

"But no priest for any of those!" Murdoch barked hoarsely, as two *Custodes* priests started to move among the dying men. "No grace for traitors! And you!" His uninjured arm lanced toward Declan Carmody, who was the closest other Deryni besides Oriel. "I want MacEwan broken! You see now why we removed him. He was plotting to overthrow the king. I want the names of his confederates. I want his mind ripped from him before he dies!"

"No, please. Not Declan!" Oriel whispered, catching urgently at Murdoch's sleeve. "Ask Ursin. Ask Sitric. Ask *me*! Carmody isn't well enough yet. He may crack!"

Enraged, his face purple with choler, Murdoch rounded on Oriel. "Are you defying a direct order, Healer?" he rasped. "Are you *asking* to see your wife and daughter die? That can be arranged!"

"Oriel, don't." Declan's voice was calm and controlled as he moved quite purposefully toward the writhing Ewan, waving back the other two Deryni, who had started forward in alarm. "It isn't necessary. You don't have to fight my battles for me."

A profound silence fell as he came to kneel by Ewan's side, and the duke made a vague, anguished attempt to flail his pain-wracked body beyond Declan's reach as the Deryni hand was lifted toward him, his face draining of what color remained.

Some unspoken message must have passed between them then, however, because suddenly Ewan stopped trying to squirm away and fixed his eyes on Declan's, hands falling away from the steel impaling his gut. His lips moved in silent words that might have said, *Bless you*, as Declan seized the hilt of the dagger and quickly withdrew it from the wound. In that same instant, Ewan closed his eyes and threw back his head for Declan's coup—a swift, deft slash across the throat that severed both carotid arteries and brought oblivion in an instant.

"What the—"

Before anyone could stop him, Declan drew the bloody blade hard against one of his own wrists, shifting to the other hand even as the first blood spurted, to slash deep into the other wrist. But before he could turn it on his throat and end the matter for good, the soldiers were on him, wrestling the weapon from blood-slick fingers and bearing him to the ground, instinctively trying to staunch the life-blood spurting from his wrists.

"You *dare* to defy me!" Murdoch thundered, scuttling across the hall to glare down at the wounded Deryni. "You *dare!*"

"The duke died before he could be questioned, my lord," Declan said almost dreamily, already far from his own pain. "I have not defied you. I simply choose not to live under your conditions any longer. I believe I've done too good a job for Oriel to save me," he added, flexing his slashed wrists in the blood-slick hold of his captors and grimacing. "Not that I'd let him, in any case—or that *you'd* let him, with your own wound bleeding so badly. You'll pass out, if he doesn't do something quickly, you know. You could even die."

Murdoch gritted his teeth as he sat down hard on a stool and let Oriel start tearing away the sleeve from his wound, and Archbishop Hubert came halfway between Murdoch and Declan.

"You know, of course, that suicides are condemned straight to Hell," Hubert said softly. "And *I'll* not give you absolution."

"Nor would I ask it of you," Declan whispered, letting his head lie back and relaxing in the hands of his captors. "I have *some* pride left."

"We'll see about pride, when you watch your wife and those little boys die before your eyes!" Murdoch said, stirring under Oriel's hands.

"No! I have not disobeyed!" Declan struggled to sit up, but now his captors would not let him.

"Bring them!" Murdoch ordered coldly. "And neutralize *him.*"

Merasha was coursing through Declan's system before he could even fathom his own danger, so horrified was he at what Murdoch threatened for his family. One of the *Custodes* monks was responsible, calmly wiping off a long, sharp bodkin after he had darted in to crouch by the stricken man's side and stab it into his neck.

"Th-the guards call it a 'Deryni pricker,' " Rhys Michael whispered breathily, clinging to Javan's arm in stunned disbelief and starting to shake as guards marched out to do Murdoch's bidding. "The *Custodes* invented it. B-but, Javan, they aren't *really* going to k-kill Declan's family—are they?"

For answer, Javan could only hug his younger brother closer, himself shaking, all too aware that the regent could and would do exactly what he threatened.

Nor could any entreaty swerve Murdoch from his intentions— not Alroy's nor his brothers' nor even the uneasy protests of Tammaron and a handful of the courtiers whose appearance at court had begun so lightheartedly. While the court waited for the guards' return, the drugged Declan's wrists were tightly bound to slow the bleeding, and Ursin and Sitric were also dosed with *merasha*. The heartsick Oriel was spared long enough to Heal Murdoch's wound—a procedure over which he dawdled until Hubert threatened *his* family—but then he, too, was made to submit to the drug that made further resistance impossible. Murdoch intended that all of them should witness the consequences of Declan's defiance, and would brook no possibility of further insurrections in the Deryni ranks.

Only the regents' wives were allowed to withdraw to the room behind the dais, to spare them actually witnessing what was about to happen. For the rest, the guards secured the hall to ensure that no one else shirked his or her duty to see justice done to a rebellious Deryni and his family.

Alroy said not a word after that, only sitting trembling and whey-faced on a throne that suddenly seemed like a torture chamber to him, the sharp-eyed Hubert at his side. Manfred broke up the embrace of the two younger brothers and stood by Rhys Michael, who looked as if he wished he was anywhere but where he was. Rhun guarded Javan, forbidding him to turn away. When the guards finally brought in Honoria Carmody and her two little sons, Javan felt that he was going to be sick and actually swallowed down bile, not wanting to believe Murdoch was actually going to do it.

To the undying relief of all present, Murdoch did relent a little—to the extent that the execution of those innocents was mercifully quick—bowstrings knotted swiftly around three slender necks, over almost before it began. Still, a communal gasp rippled through the court as the deed registered, capped by Declan Carmody's faint, drugged groan of anguish.

But Declan himself was to be permitted no such merciful end. An example must be made of him, to ensure that no other Deryni got ideas above his station and tried to turn against his masters. To screams which the doomed Deryni could not keep back, he was stripped and spread-eagled right on the floor before the throne, first castrated and then slowly disemboweled, his entrails dragged from his belly even as he shrieked out his agony yet could not end it. Loss of blood from his many wounds let him slip into unconsciousness before they could tear his heart, still beating, from his opened chest; and when they could not rouse him to continue their sport, they unbandaged his wrists, so that it could be claimed that the actual cause of death had been his own violence against himself. By the time they beheaded and quartered his mutilated body, Declan Carmody was long past knowing or caring.

Javan cared desperately, though. Nor would he let himself shrink from any sickening detail, filing away each crime to be charged against Murdoch when the time came, his thoughts racing the while through prayers for the dying man's soul. (Had he tried *not* to watch, Rhun would have held his head like an undisciplined infant—unspeakable liberty! But that, at least, was something over which Javan had some modicum of control.)

He was handling himself rather well, he thought, until Hubert formally announced that the dead man would not be afforded Christian burial, having died by his own hand. When the executioners' assistants began gathering up the pieces in wicker baskets to dump them into the river, Javan was finally and unashamedly sick all over Rhun's highly polished boots.

Alroy and several far older courtiers already had fainted by then—as had Oriel, for whom the lesson was really intended. And Javan was but the youngest—by no means the only—person to retch up his guts at the horror of what they had witnessed. Rhys Michael managed to keep his stomach and head under control, but had started shaking halfway through. Even now, one of the royal physicians was giving him a strong sedative and ordering him taken to his rooms.

There was no birthday feast that night, and Alroy cancelled all his appearances for three days thereafter, against all possible entreaties and wheedlings of the regents. Javan gave all his gifts to the *Custodes Fidei*, for he would not have them tainted with Declan Carmody's blood. Following his lead, his brothers also gave away their gifts—though, in fact, many of them ended up in the hands of the regents themselves. From that moment on, Javan vowed his vengeance for what had been done—and on Murdoch in particular.

CHAPTER TWENTY-FOUR

*The spirit of the Lord is upon me, because he
hath annointed me to preach . . . deliverance to
the captives.*

—Luke 4:18

The information networks that had always served the clans carried
word of Ewan's death northward with a speed almost suggestive of
Deryni magic. Less than a fortnight later, backed by his two uncles
and over a hundred armed clansmen wearing black cockades in their
bonnets, Ewan's son and heir rode into Rhemuth to claim his titles.
The show of force was real, in that his uncles, the Earls of Eastmarch
and Marley, had brought along an additional escort of fifty hand-
picked knights, but the duke himself was counted as of little real
consequence. For Graham Donal Angus MacEwan, now the Duke
of Claibourne and hereditary Viceroy of Kheldour, was an eleven-
year-old boy.

To alienate that eleven-year-old any more than he already had
been was to court disaster, however. The titles that the boy bore
were of immense consequence—so immense that the regents dared
not even consider refusing to confirm the boy in his new rank. The
holdings comprising Kheldour represented fully a quarter of the land
area of Gwynedd. The regents could ill afford to lose that land. That
young Graham was even willing to come to the capital and do public
homage and fealty for his holdings, after all that had happened, bespoke much of the good judgment of his uncles, who would be *his*
regents until he came of age—for neither Kheldour nor Gwynedd
would be the better for a split, with the threat of an eventual Festillic
reinvasion ever in the offing.

Besides that, public reaction to the manner of the old duke's death was already vocal and highly negative, even though the official accounts emphasized that Ewan *had* been trying to murder the regent Murdoch, which *could* be construed as an act of treason. However, even Murdoch finally admitted, albeit grudgingly, and only in the bosom of his fellow regents, that perhaps he had overreacted to Ewan's altogether justified anger at being so summarily dismissed. Certainly, Murdoch had failed to predict what Ewan would do, on learning of the dismissal. To attaint the son for the supposed sins of the father—and attainder was the only legal way to bar Graham from his ducal titles—was to add insult to injury and court even greater public outcry—and possibly even force the kingdom into civil war.

So young Duke Graham was permitted to assume his titles. The presence of his uncles was allowed at his recognition and swearing in, but both were warned to hold their peace, lest some angry outburst again escalate matters beyond anyone's intentions. Hence, when young Duke Graham swore his oaths, his small hands between Alroy's not much bigger ones, his uncles knelt sullenly to either side of him, each with a hand on his shoulder, since he was a minor. Hrorik of Eastmarch, the elder, said little, but his younger brother Sighere, Earl of Marley, smoldered with resentment; the borders knew quite precisely how the late duke had met his death, and would not forget. Only with notable forbearance did the two endure the ceremonies, as Graham finally was invested with the coronet, the sword, the banner, and the cauldron. But neither brothers nor grieving son had reckoned on the fact that the regents were not yet finished with the slain Duke Ewan, though his body had gone home to Kheldour many days before.

"We welcome you to this noble company, your Grace," King Alroy told his newest duke, as he had been coached. "We sympathize with your loss, for we have also lost a father not so very long ago. In light of that loss, and at so tender an age, we would inform you that we have determined to relieve you of some of the burden of this high estate."

"Sire, his Grace asks no relief from the burden he has just assumed with his coronet," Graham's Uncle Sighere said, looking very much like his own late father and namesake, the first Duke Sighere, as he stood, hand resting just a little too purposefully on the hilt of his dirk. "The Clan MacEwan is willing and able to discharge the duties set out for his Grace's grandfather, the first duke, and performed by his father, the late duke; and my brother and I have already sworn to uphold your Highness' wishes in this matter."

With a nervous glance at Earl Rhun, Alroy continued. "No one is questioning the ability of the Clan MacEwan to carry out its sworn duties, my lord of Marley," he said. "However, since Duke Graham is even younger than myself, we feel it wisest to lighten his responsibilities at this time. Accordingly, we have this day dismantled the viceregality of Kheldour into its component lordships, and we are placing these lordships under direct Crown rule." Consternation rippled through the assembly. "To assist us in that rule, we have appointed the Honorable Fane Fitz-Arthur as our Deputy Regent for Kheldour, to oversee the administration of these lands."

The highlanders roared their disapproval, battering their dirks against highland targes—for they had been forbidden to enter the court armed with broadswords—and Sighere and Hrorik made empassioned appeals for a slacking in the king's intentions—or, rather, the regents' intentions—but to no avail. Well coached by his regents and bolstered by their presence at his side, Alroy was implacable. Kheldour as a separate political entity ceased to exist from that date. Henceforth, it was to be governed as a collection of separate counties, baronies, and Graham's one duchy, all under the direct scrutiny of the Crown. Graham had best take his uncles and retainers and go home, before words were spoken or deeds done that could not be undone, to the peril of the oaths of loyalty and fealty the young duke had just sworn.

Graham and his uncles went—yet another goal accomplished in the regents' master plan to bring all of Gwynedd under their closer rule. The exercise offended Javan nearly as much as the slaughter of Ewan and the hapless Declan Carmody and his family, if in different ways. He sought out Oriel to talk about it, but the Healer was still almost physically ill over Declan's death, and the manner of it, cursing his own impotence which had allowed such an outrage to take place.

"You *know* that I could have blasted them all!" he told Javan angrily. "I'm *Deryni*, able to draw on the fires of the universe if I choose. But I did *nothing*! I stood by and let it happen, to save my own skin."

"And the lives of your family," Javan reminded him, telling him the truth, even though he, too, would rather have denied it. "Oriel, it would have been foolish to do anything else besides what you did. While you were trying to focus the fires of the universe on those who deserve to burn, their archers would have made a pincushion of you. There was nothing you could do. There was nothing *I* could do. Do you think that makes me any happier about it than you are?"

Shaking his head wearily, Oriel managed a tiny "No."

Javan sighed and laid a sympathetic hand on the Healer's shoulder. "Oriel, I need your prayers. I'm about to start something very dangerous," he murmured.

"Dangerous?" Oriel lifted his head. "What are you going to do?"

Rising, Javan moved over to the tiny window in Oriel's chamber and peered out. "I'm going to skirt a little closer to the question of Holy Orders. I've got to see that something else happens, and I may actually have to take Orders in order to justify my actions, later on. I'll confess, I don't relish the idea." He glanced back at Oriel and smiled bravely. "I do *not* have a religious vocation, despite the archbishop's most fervent prayers. And while I do have some influence over *him* these days, I haven't dared touch any of the *Custodes*. I don't think Hubert realizes what he's created. Anyway, I could end up locked away in a monastery—if I don't end up dead."

Oriel tried to talk him out of the scheme, just as Joram did during the brief meeting they managed a few days later in the little study off the basilica sanctuary. The contact had only just been possible, for Joram and the others were deep in the throes of preparing for Revan's emergence into his full ministry at Pentecost—which was precisely what Javan wanted to talk about.

"I'm going to do it, so you'd better make sure he knows ahead of time so he can plan," Javan told him, as the former Michaeline was gathering his wits on the Transfer Portal to leave, having exhausted all the arguments he could think of. "I'd rather have your blessing than defy you, Joram, but this is the only way I can see that might work. So you'd better make the most of the situation, because I won't be talked out of it."

After Joram had gone, his blessing most reluctantly given, the prince spent a brief time in prayer in the basilica, where Charlan was waiting for him, then returned to begin composing the letter to Valoret, informing the archbishop of his intention to join Hubert there for several weeks' retreat, being sick at heart over the slayings he had witnessed on his birthday. In asking for the archbishop's personal guidance in several matters of conscience, some of them having to do with important choices he must make for his future, he knew he had offered Hubert a bait that would not be refused.

Nor was it. A few days before Pentecost, permission came for the prince to depart for Valoret. The archbishop's letter made it clear that he believed he had just about won Javan over to the religious life. Black-clad and somber, Javan said and did nothing to diminish that impression as he set out for the former capital with a small escort led by Hubert's brother, the regent Manfred, who would be continuing north after delivering Javan to Valoret. Enroute, Javan drew Manfred out about religion—a subject of some indifference to

Manfred, until he recounted how his brother had decided upon a career in the church—a confidence that surprised Javan, especially when it came out that both Manfred and Hubert honestly believed that Hubert's was a genuine vocation.

He did not test that intelligence once he arrived in Valoret, however, for he did not want to engage Hubert in conversation that might trap him into making a commitment he would later regret. If possible, he preferred not to make any commitment at all, where that was concerned, though he was prepared to do whatever must be done, in order to see his plan to successful completion. Claiming the need for seclusion, to fast and pray awhile before discussing anything further, Javan promptly did just that—though what he prayed for was word of the success of Revan's mission with the Willimites. He would not consider the possibility of failure.

Manfred and his escort rode on to take possession of Cor Culdi, the other principal seat of his new earldom, now that his castle at Caerrorie was nearing completion. And that was how Lord Manfred MacInnis, Earl of Culdi and Baron of Marlor, came to be riding past the Willimite encampment on that pleasant June morning of 918, as Revan prepared to emerge from his forty days' retreat and announce his official mission. Without doubt, the very last thing Manfred expected to encounter enroute was the birth of a new religious cult.

Revan and his several partners in the subterfuge about to be set in motion had been honing their preparations for weeks, while he and a handful of his Willimite "disciples" kept seclusion on the mountaintop above the old Willimite camp. By skillful manipulation of a few selected individuals' memories, Sylvan O'Sullivan had been inserted into the master's inner circle with a sufficient past to satisfy any but the most dogged suspicion—though they were careful not to make him too much the master's favorite. That honor was reserved for the man called Brother Joachim, who had been among the first to respond to Revan's undoubted charisma and embrace his teachings, along with Flann and Geordie. These four formed the core of Revan's closest discipleship, and at least one of them was always with him.

And in the camp below, the disguised Tavis O'Neill also played out his role, his missing hand padded out with a bandage and supported by a sling, so that he attracted no undue attention. During the forty days of contemplation leading to this day, Revan had not come down from his mountain, but he occasionally had preached to selected audiences, sending his intimates down to invite chosen ones to attend him and hear his musings on what he believed his mission was to be; they were primed. Where Revan's own sheer persuasive force had not won them over, subtle manipulation by Tavis or Sylvan usually had; and a few had simply disappeared, if their subversion seemed too difficult or too unlikely for safety. Tavis was among them now, mingling with the other men and women gathering beside the river to await Revan's promised arrival, testing the feel of the day, doing his best to make certain that their star performer should have no unexpected surprises.

Nor would Revan go into battle armed only with his own resources. By his own charisma and a growing instinct for evaluating people quickly, Revan was perfecting his ability to induce dizziness and even a trancelike receptivity in some subjects on his own. Often, he could reinforce such tendencies with the power stored in his Willimite medallion. In addition, Sylvan and Tavis had taught Revan how to activate triggers previously set by one of the Deryni, to produce the illusion that it was Revan who took away the Willimite Deryni's magical powers, for those first miracles when they dared not have Sylvan too closely associated with Revan. And they would have their planted Willimite Deryni.

But would it all work outside a controlled situation? That was the question. Revan's performance this morning might well determine the entire course of his ministry; and any of a host of possible disasters could lead to all of their deaths.

"I'm ready, my friends," Revan said quietly, as he emerged from the cave where he had spent that last night in solitude.

Nearly a dozen heads turned toward him expectantly, some a little fearfully. Those who had been sitting stood. Later, several would swear that even then, a light shone from his face, though some never did see it. Bracing himself against the familiar olivewood staff, Revan picked his way down the slight slope toward them, his sandalled feet stirring the bleached wool of his robe. He wore a plain, short mantle of rusty black over that, for the spring morning was chill, and his beard and hair were still damp from his morning ablutions. He gave a faint smile as Joachim and then Sylvan and Geordie came and knelt to kiss the hem of his robe. He raised his free hand in a gesture half greeting and half blessing as the others also fell to their knees, young Flann settling rapturously at his feet.

"What will happen today, Master?" one of the Willimites asked softly. "What will you tell your children?"

Revan shook his head gently and began to move among them,

touching a hand here, an upturned face there, letting them see him, touch him, believe in him.

"Will you believe me if I say to you that I do not know?" he murmured. "The Lord God has vouchsafed to tell me I must go, but He has not said what I must say. You must trust, as I do, that all will be revealed in His time. Do you believe this?"

Weeping tears of hope and joy, a middle-aged woman wearing a tattered blue gown clasped her hands to her breast and nodded. "We do, Master. Oh, give us your blessing!"

"Not my blessing, but the blessing of the Lord," Revan replied, passing his palm above them as they bowed their heads. "Now pray with me, my children, before we go to join your brothers and sisters." He folded to his knees among them and clasped the staff before him, bowing his forehead against its gnarled smoothness.

"Lord, hear my prayer, and let my cry come unto Thee. I am not worthy to come under Your roof, so You have set me to Your work here underneath Your sky, among Your people. Give strength and guide me, Lord, as I go to do Your will, and bless all Your children who cry to You in their despair. *In nomine Patris, et Filii, et Spiritus Sancti . . .*"

"Amen," they answered, as he crossed himself and rose.

They followed him down the mountain then, humming a tuneless hymn that began as a simple chant on a higher note and then a note several steps down, harmonies intertwining as additional voices joined in. The dozen quickly became a score, then three score, four score, as they descended toward the river. By the time they approached the spit of land he had chosen for his pulpit, jutting out into a still pool in this bend of the river, there were more than a hundred of them, and the hymn had shifted spontaneously to a *Veni Sancti Spiritus*, chanted over and over on two notes.

No one followed him onto that smooth, whitely shimmering stretch of sand, though Sylvan and the half-dozen others who were his special intimates crouched in a front rank across its narrow neck, and the others came that far. The rest began filling in behind them and ringed the pool as closely as they could, settling quietly on cloaks and mantles spread in the sun. Revan turned his back to them and bowed his head as he gave them time to settle, until well over a hundred men and women were sitting expectantly around the pool, waiting.

As a profound silence spread outward over the assembled company, Revan gave them a few more minutes to let the expectation build, then slowly raised his head and thrust his staff into the sand beside him. Lifting both arms to shoulder level, palms outstretched, he threw his head back further and closed his eyes, making his body a living sigil of the crucified Christ in Whose name they expected him to speak—and for Whose forgiveness at this near-blasphemy he devoutly prayed.

"Here am I, Lord," those closest heard him whisper. "Speak, for Thy servant listens."

Nothing happened for a very long time, yet still he stood with arms outstretched and head thrown back. Strangely, no one fidgeted. After a while, his arms and then his whole body began to tremble. Then, all at once, his back arched and he fell to the ground, seemingly in convulsions. The crowd muttered at that, several coming to their knees, as did Sylvan, but he and the others would not let anyone pass.

"The Spirit comes upon him!" Brother Joachim murmured. "Let him be."

Revan lay writhing in the sand for several more minutes, moaning softly, then suddenly went limp. No one dared move. After the space of a few deeply drawn breaths, he slowly began to stir, dragging himself to his knees facing them, his eyes glazed still by some apparent glimpse of Other.

"What return shall I make unto the Lord?" he quoted softly, letting his gaze pass over and through them as he steadied both hands on the ground beside his knees. "Oh, see, taste, for the Lord is good. For He has spoken to His lowly servant and revealed a great joy, which shall be to all His people."

"What joy, Master?" they entreated him. "Is it the Word that was promised?"

Slowly, shakily, Revan got to his feet—he had lost his sandals in his thrashing—still a little dazed looking as he swept the brown eyes over them again.

"Oh, my brothers and sisters, I know not how to tell you of my vision."

"Tell us, tell us!" their cry came.

"I bring you word of a great mercy, for the cleansing of all God's people," he said tentatively. "Before, the Lord commanded me to tell you that those who walked in darkness would face a great judgment and be tried in the forge of the ages. He would burn away all imperfections and refine the dross from the pure gold, and great would be the fire and great the pain for those who must be so purified."

Revan drew himself up straighter, gaining confidence as he realized they were truly listening.

"But the Lord of Hosts, in His infinite mercy and love, has seen fit to grant His favor even to those who have walked in the uttermost darkness—even the children of darkness, called Deryni. To any of that race who do earnestly repent of their evil and renounce the darkness forever, the Lord shall give a special sign of His grace. By water shall He change those who seek His mercy earnestly, in a new baptism of water and Spirit. The water of purification shall quench all evil, as water quenches a torch, and the Lord of Hosts shall raise them up into new life, cleansed of the evil which has enslaved them."

"He would cleanse even the Deryni?" one man murmured.

"But, how can this be?" another said. "Even if a Deryni renounces his evil powers, he is still Deryni."

As the ripples of agreement spread, one of the Willimite Deryni slowly stood, wary disbelief warring with hope on his bearded face. Revan did not appear to notice him, but everyone else did.

"Do not mock me, Master," the man said quietly. "I know what I am. I have confessed it to my brethren and renounced my evil instincts, but I am what I am, and shall be until the day I die."

"And I say to you," Revan said, suddenly throwing off his mantle and striding into the water, "that the Lord now offers you the means to break from your old life and be what you would be—His dearly beloved child of earth, untainted by what you were before. He has given cleansing into my hands, and commands me to share it with any who earnestly repent. Yea, even those who have only been corrupted by contact with the evil ones may be purified, if they earnestly seek God's mercy. Do *you* seek it, Brother Gillebert?"

More consternation rippled through the throng, but Revan merely held out his hand to the Deryni who had spoken, inviting him to come forward. And because this entire opening scenario had been so tightly orchestrated, Gillebert did, slowly and haltingly, as he had been instructed to do—though he remembered it not—his eyes locked yearningly with Revan's.

"Aye, come, Brother Gillebert," Revan said softly, retreating farther into the pool, though with his hand still uplifted in summons. "Take off your shoes, for you enter holy water. Patrick and Joachim, help him, for the love of God. Come, Gillebert, and take my hand, that I may lead you to purification. All ye people, pray with me as our Brother Gillebert takes his salvation in his hands and lets God wash away his iniquity."

Gillebert was ankle deep in the water now, the awed Patrick, who was also Deryni, standing behind him with the discarded shoes clasped to his breast. Tears streaming down his cheeks, Gillebert strode farther into the water, knee deep, hip deep, seeming not to mind the cold as his hand clasped Revan's.

"Blessed be God, Who has brought you to this place," Revan said, leading him deeper, "and blessed shall you be, for trusting in His infinite mercy and love."

The water was lapping just above their waists as he stopped and turned back to face the hushed multitudes, positioning his unwitting Deryni accomplice immediately in front of him, facing his right.

"I shall immerse you fully," he said in a voice that only Gillebert could hear, clasping the man behind the neck and at the forehead, forearms braced against back and chest. "Grab onto my wrist, and keep your legs and back straight. I'll do the rest. Now, take a deep breath and hold it," he added, as he pressed the man backward.

"Be cleansed by the Holy Spirit!" he cried, tilting the man backward under the water and triggering the reactions set by Sylvan before. "May this act of faith wash away your impurities, that you may emerge to new life!"

The crowd gasped as Revan brought him to the surface and steadied him onto his feet again, water streaming from the man's hair and beard. Gillebert looked more startled than frightened, blinking and faintly disoriented as he wiped the water from his eyes.

"In mystery He comes to His children and makes them clean," Revan said, beginning to guide his subject back into shallower water. "In mystery He speaks, and His children hear."

In that instant, Gillebert gave a stifled little squeak and pressed both hands to the sides of his head, his eyes huge with awe and amazement mixed.

"It's gone!" he gasped. "My power is gone! It used to be like a little voice, constantly telling me things I did not wish to know, but it's gone! I'm clean!"

Near pandemonium broke out at that, several of the Willimites charging into the water, Deryni among them, to see for themselves. For a few minutes, as several Deryni checked Gillebert, hardly anyone noticed that Revan had dropped to his knees in the shallower water a few feet away, head bowed and hands clasped at chest level. Those who did notice assumed he was giving thanks; in fact, he was praying that no one would see through their deception.

In any case, he was ignored for several minutes while Gillebert's benefactors helped him from the water and surged around him, becoming increasingly excited as he explained and reexplained—or tried to—what he thought he had experienced. After a few minutes, several others, Sylvan cautiously among them, helped the dripping Revan back to shore, where they had spread his mantle on the warm sand. Revan came along compliantly, but did not really seem to see or hear them, the while murmuring prayers of praise to God for the favor granted.

After a few more minutes, those flocked around the still-astonished Gillebert suddenly turned and converged on Revan. Sylvan knew a moment of panic in that instant, for many of those who had sprung to Gillebert's support were not among those whom Tavis and himself had pre-conditioned to go along with the fantasy they were weaving. But it soon became apparent that they sought Revan's further ministrations and not his life.

"Cleanse us, Master!" they begged him, falling to their knees all around him on the warm, clean sand. "Free us from the curse of the Deryni. Make us new in the sight of the Lord!"

And Revan rose and reentered the water.

Thus it was that the Regent Manfred and his party came upon him later in the morning, baptizing in the chill, quiet pool in the bend of the Eirian River. His brother had warned him he might find the Willimites here, and Manfred knew vaguely who they were. But as he drew rein on a low bluff overlooking the pool, it occurred to Manfred that these people did not look at all the way he had always heard Willimites described. Down in a pool formed by a bend in the river, a bearded young man in a soggy white robe appeared to be dunking people under the water, and two long lines of people seemed to be waiting to be dunked.

"You there!" Manfred called, stabbing his whip at an amply padded individual near the edge of the crowd—a prosperous merchant, by the cut and quality of his gown—or former quality, for the bright brocade had never been meant to be immersed in water. "What the devil's going on here?"

"No devil, sire," the man said genially. "That's the Master Revan. He preaches a new baptism to free us from the Deryni."

"A new baptism?" said a chunky *Custodes* priest riding in Manfred's party.

"Well, not a baptism in the same sense as Holy Mother Church teaches, Father," the man tried to explain. "Master Revan says it's a cleansing, a—a purification. It removes the taint of having had contact with Deryni, and it even cleanses Deryni themselves! That man over there, Gillebert, is one of our Willimite brethren. I've known him for years. And he used to be a Deryni, but—"

"What do you mean, he *used* to be Deryni?" the priest broke in with a snort. "Either one is or one isn't. If that man was Deryni this morning, he's Deryni now—and I can prove it!"

"He *isn't*," the merchant said stubbornly, suddenly anxious for Revan, down in the river, as well as the closer Gillebert.

"Easy enough to solve this dispute," Manfred said, signalling with his whip for mounted soldiers to go and cut Gillebert from the rest of the crowd. "Stand back, you people," he called, for those making way for the soldiers began to rumble resentfully as they realized they were being infiltrated by armed men. "Fellow, you won't be harmed if you're not Deryni, as these folk claim. Are you the one they call Gillebert?"

One of the soldiers had Gillebert by the back of his tunic by now, and was marching the protesting man back toward Manfred.

"Come on, man. Speak up. Are you Gillebert?"

"Aye, sire, I am," he murmured, landing with a whuff as the soldier brought him before Manfred and released him with a shove, sending him sprawling to hands and knees.

"Gillebert *What?*" the priest said, swinging down from his horse and taking a long, narrow tube out of his cincture. "And is it true that you claim not to be Deryni anymore? Guards, someone get down and hold this man."

The mutterings of the small crowd gathering around them began to take on a touch of menace as two soldiers dismounted and seized the bewildered Gillebert, one of them cuffing him sharply on the side of the head while the other grabbed onto a handful of hair and twisted it.

"Answer the Father's question, sirrah!"

"I—my name is Gillebert—just Gillebert. Ow! Gillebert of Droghera!"

His eyes fastened fearfully on the tube the priest was tipping back and forth, and he squirmed a little as the man unscrewed the tube in the middle to reveal two slender needles fitted in the top half, each as long as a finger joint, and set just far enough apart that they did not touch. Something wet glistened on the steel slivers, a droplet trembling at the end.

"Gillebert of Droghera, eh?" the priest said, moving closer. "Aren't you a little far from home?"

"I—I came to join the Willimites," Gillebert babbled, grimacing as one of the soldiers wrenched his head back and to the side and the other pulled open the neck of his shirt. "Wh-what are you going to do?"

The priest smiled grimly and brought his needles closer. "If you aren't Deryni, you needn't fear. This shouldn't hurt much," he added, as he jabbed the needles into his victim's neck, just at the join of shoulder and collarbone, and Gillebert gasped.

"You have just tasted the sting of a cunning new device which we call a Deryni pricker," the priest went on. "Very shortly, we will know for certain whether you are or are not Deryni." Gillebert bit back a sob as the priest jerked out his needles and a little rivulet of blood ran down his neck. "There was *merasha* on the needles— which, if you *are* Deryni, you already know will begin to affect you very shortly in quite interesting ways."

Nodding, Gillebert slumped in his captors' arms, his voice low and despairing. "I know what *merasha* does, priest. And I *was* Deryni. But my powers are gone! Master Revan has washed me clean of that taint, I swear it! He is touched by the Spirit. He brings hope to those who have walked in darkness."

Whether or not Revan was, indeed, touched by the Spirit, it soon became clear that Gillebert of Droghera was no longer touched by *merasha*. The drug had its expected sedative effect, subduing the unfortunate Gillebert into a drowsy, compliant state, but he showed none of the other symptoms of disorientation, incoherence, or nausea univerally suffered by those of his race.

"But, can we be sure he actually *was* Deryni?" the priest asked, as the soldiers released a staggering but totally coherent Gillebert to his fellows. "And who is this latter day John the Baptist who calls himself Revan? Could it be that he himself is Deryni, and somehow has learned to take away his fellows' powers?"

"I couldn't tell you that, Father, but this man is not Deryni now, and I'm almost certain their Master Revan is not and never has been," Manfred said, signalling his soldiers to mount up, for the crowd was still uneasy and muttering and might well get nasty if they pressed their luck. "Now that I think about it, I've heard of this Revan before. They say he was a servant in the household of Rhys Thuryn and the daughter of Camber of Culdi. Gossip has it that the man believed Thuryn responsible for the death of his sweetheart and ran away, vowing to destroy Deryni. After that, he joined the Willimites and got religion. For a while, he was talking to stones up on a mountaintop—probably that one over there," he added, gesturing sourly toward a nearby peak with his whip. "More recently, my brother says he's been preaching the coming of some new pronouncement about Deryni. This is rare, though—to destroy them even as he 'saves' them from civil and religious persecution."

"I don't like it," the priest muttered. "The fellow should be taken into custody and questioned."

"From this mob?" Manfred returned. "I think I'd rather keep my head, thank you. We'll return to Valoret and tell my brother, though. He's an archbishop; let him decide what to do—and send a small army, if he does intend to take this Revan fellow away from his followers."

Hubert sent no army of any size, however, though he did decide to come to the Willimite encampment to see for himself just what Revan was doing. Because Manfred brought him the report in the evening, when he was supping with Javan, the prince also became privy to the latest news on Revan. And because Javan had been carefully building Hubert's confidence for several days, both by open conversation and more subtle persuasion, it was no particular feat to be included in the party that Hubert shortly marshalled to revisit the site on the banks of the Eirian.

Hubert, being already well informed about the progress of the quasi-Willimite cult, came rather better prepared than his brother had been, and brought Ursin O'Carroll as his personal Deryni sniffer, along with Father Lior and another experienced *Custodes* priest. They also brought a crack troop of Hubert's episcopal cavalry, just in case Revan's growing numbers of disciples took exception to their archbishop's investigations.

CHAPTER TWENTY-FIVE

Then they that gladly received his word were
baptized.

—Acts 2:41

Three days after Pentecost, Javan drew rein with Archbishop Hubert
at the top of the bluff overlooking the pool where the prophet Revan
held daily court. The day was warm and fine. Javan's plain black
attire, suggestive of a junior cleric, made him all but invisible in
the archbishop's entourage. Father Lior, of the *Custodes Fidei*, rode
at Hubert's other side, and the Deryni sniffer Ursin O'Carroll was
among the twenty *Equites Custodium* knights that Hubert had
brought for a show of strength. Several more priests and other attendants rounded out the party, befitting Hubert's rank. Though the
throngs seated on the banks around the pool recognized their archbishop immediately, and reacted with suspicion to the presence of
the armed men at his back, they did not recognize Javan—for who
would have expected the presence of a prince of the blood, disguised
as a cleric?

Javan hoped Revan did. He would, if Joram had warned him as
Javan asked. Javan had told the Michaeline all about the scenario
he had worked out, if he actually got the chance to do what he
planned. All morning he had been calculating the risks, as the archbishop's party drew nearer and nearer the confrontation point,
knowing that he could never anticipate *all* of them. And yet, the
possible gains were inestimable. He hoped Revan *did* know—and
Sylvan and Tavis. It would be extremely difficult if they did not,
and far more dangerous.

Javan tried not to appear too interested as he scanned the scene below them, searching for his Deryni allies. Revan had been preaching as they approached, and paused briefly as his audience murmured in faint hostility, raising a hand to quiet them before going on.

"I do not presume to understand why the Lord has chosen me, the most lowly of His servants, to make His will known to you in this peculiar fashion. But chosen me He has, as many here can attest. And I come to proclaim His mercy to all who will humble themselves before the baptism of purification. Whether ye be Deryni or only tainted by their darkness, the Lord commands me to offer His grace to all who truly repent of their wickedness and would enter the cleansing waters. Now pray with me, my brothers and sisters, that hearts may be moved to guide feet toward His salvation."

"A dangerous message," Father Lior murmured aside to Hubert, as Revan sank to his knees to lead the assembly in prayer. "Were he to be brought before a heresy tribunal, no one would think twice if he were found guilty and sentenced to burn."

"Aye." Hubert nodded. "At very least, he skirts the edges of blasphemy, preaching a second baptism for the exorcism of Deryni evil. Yet even in his error, he does us a service, for he *does* preach that the Deryni are evil. Even better does he serve our cause if what he does is real."

"You think he does work miracles, then?" Lior asked, clearly disapproving.

Hubert smiled, a prim, self-righteous pursing of the tiny, rosebud lips. "Whether they are miracles or not, dear Lior, I neither know nor care. But if he does make Deryni no longer what they were, then who am I to stand in his way?"

"*If*, your Grace," Lior murmured. "Such an important little word."

"My thought, precisely. Ursin?"

Javan held his breath as the Deryni sullenly kneed his horse closer.

"Aye, your Grace."

"Ursin, what think you of yon preacher? Do *you* think that Master Revan has been given some miraculous power to wash a Deryni clean of what he is?"

Masking an uneasiness that only Javan seemed able to sense, Ursin shrugged. "I would not presume to consider myself qualified in matters of faith, your Grace."

"Ah, no. Of course you would not. Well, do you think him Deryni, then? Or can he have discovered some fatal defect of your race which enables him to strip you of your power?"

Before Ursin could reply, Lior snorted. "It's all an illusion. The man has some odd charisma, and people want to believe that they've been cleansed of the Deryni taint—so they *are*, so far as they or anyone else is concerned. After all, we don't actually know of any confirmed Deryni who have been 'purified,' now do we?"

"Hmmm, my brother Manfred seemed to think that Gillebert of Droghera had been Deryni, and was no more."

"But based only on hearsay, your Grace," Lior countered. "I say it's all a colossal hoax."

"Indeed, it may well be," Hubert agreed, thoughtfully stroking his multiple chins. "On the other hand, it occurs to me that we have the means to test this Revan even now, with someone we *know* is Deryni."

Ursin's head snapped around to stare at the archbishop in disbe-lief. "Surely you're not proposing that I should go down for this—*baptism*," he whispered.

Javan, praying that Hubert meant to do precisely that, could hardly believe that no one heard his heart pounding.

"Why not?" Hubert said. "If he's a fraud, who better to unmask him? And if he isn't—which seems at least possible—then you, too, will be 'delivered.' "

"And will that save me, I wonder?" Ursin said bitterly. "If I am no longer of any use to you, will I end like Declan Carmody's family, coughing out my life against a knotted bowstring?"

Hubert studied the ends of the reins in his gloved hands. "You *could* end it like Carmody himself, if you prefer," he said coolly. "But, be of good cheer. If this Revan is real, and you *should* become 'merely human,' do you think I would not rejoice? I am your spiritual father, Ursin. Your salvation is my dearest concern."

Grimacing, Ursin glanced down at the prophet, now entering the water with several of his disciples, as several more began shepherd-ing the faithful into orderly lines to await his ministrations.

"Perchance my lack of faith comes from my wretchedness," he muttered softly. "A Deryni must expect nothing better."

Father Lior bristled at the unmistakable mockery in Ursin's tone, and Javan dreaded the possible consequences, but Hubert only chuckled softly.

"I really don't care whether you believe me or not, my dear Ursin, so long as you do as you're told. Now, pretend to be one of the faith-ful and go down to the 'Master,' if you value even your wretched-ness—and that of your family. Captain Ramsay, please accompany him—and you will no doubt wish to 'purify' yourself as well, after such prolonged contact with a Deryni."

Ramsay's expression suggested that he wished no such thing, but he was a good soldier and would obey orders. He saluted briskly before dismounting and handing off his horse to another of the officers, pausing to divest himself of helmet, sword, brigandine, and boots.

"Come, Ursin, we must not keep Master Revan waiting," Hubert urged, when Ursin did not immediately follow suit. "And do not disappoint me, Ursin. You know how I hate disappointments."

Though still reluctant, Ursin knew better than to argue further. Sighing resignedly, he swung down from his horse and took off his mantle, belt, and boots, handing them to a sour-faced soldier who approached with the stripped Ramsay. The sun shone brightly on their bare heads as they started down the hillside, Ramsay all but shepherding Ursin with a hand under his elbow, and Javan wondered whether the Deryni's fears really were well-founded. Surely Hubert would not discard Ursin so lightly, once he was no longer of use. Not even Hubert could be that heartless. And what *would* happen to Ursin's family, if Ursin was discarded?

But, no time to worry about Hubert now. For better or for worse, Ursin O'Carroll was about to become an official example of Revan's supposed power. Javan prayed that if it all went wrong, the end would be quick, both for Ursin and his family, but meanwhile Ramsay and the captive Deryni were wading into the pool. Along with the rest, Javan watched anxiously as the two were met by several of Revan's disciples—one of them Sylvan, he suddenly realized!— and were deftly shunted into different lines, Ursin in the one Sylvan had charge of. The two would still come to Revan in succession, but Ramsay would come first. And Ursin, who was expecting something to happen when Revan tilted him under the water, would *not* be expecting an assault to come from Sylvan. Perhaps Sylvan had already worked his magic!

All unaware, the Deryni sniffer stood beside the Healer as another Willimite led the reluctant Ramsay forward to receive purification at Revan's hands. As Revan set a hand on the man's shoulder and spoke to him quietly, and the man ducked his head self-consciously at some question Revan asked, Javan realized that Sylvan had casually turned his gaze up to the bluff where the episcopal party watched, and thought he caught just a hint of acknowledgment from Sylvan, just before the Healer returned his attention to Revan.

"Receive purification, ye who would repent of past corruption," Revan said, laying Ramsay back into the water against his arm, his other hand pressing the forehead under the water. "Arise a new man, washed clean in the grace of the Lord of Hosts."

Ramsay sputtered and wobbled a bit as Revan brought him to

his feet, but looked immensely relieved as his Willimite guide began leading him back toward the shore. He quite forgot to look for his charge. Ursin, unaware that he was already blocked and controlled, never faltered as Sylvan led him to stand before Revan, who clasped his hands prayerfully at his breast before lightly laying them on Ursin's arm.

"Rejoice and pray with me, my brothers and sisters, for I perceive that another actual Deryni has come to beg the Lord's mercy. His Grace the Lord Archbishop has seen fit to send us his own Deryni, in the hopes that he might be cleansed of his evil. Look, there sits his Grace to witness this great blessing."

The stir and whisper of the multitude turning to look at Hubert and his party covered whatever Revan said next—which annoyed Hubert greatly, for he had hoped not to have attention called to his presence—but apparently the prophet had only asked Ursin's name, which Ursin gave.

"Then, take my hand and believe that the Lord will make you clean, Brother Ursin," Revan said, clasping the Deryni's head between his hands and laying him back in the water. "Come, Holy Spirit, and purify the heart of this child of darkness, that he may know light. In the name of the Father, and of the Son, and of the Holy Spirit," he concluded, as he raised Ursin up.

Ursin coughed and sputtered as he got his feet under him, drying his face on a cloth that one of the other disciples handed him. He staggered a little then, as the totality of his loss hit him, so that Revan had to steady him with a hand under his elbow. Javan could see him nodding at something Revan said, and kissing Revan's hand before passing beyond him to emerge from the water while the next man faced the Master, but his face was white as he rejoined Ramsay, and he kept passing a hand over his eyes, as if trying to push aside a veil.

It took him several minutes to make his way slowly back up to the bluff where Hubert waited, and Javan could see the dread in his eyes as he came, dripping and pasty-faced. Hubert and Lior had dismounted, and the *Custodes* priest was readying one of the Deryni prickers as Ursin approached. Javan and the others of Hubert's party remained mounted. Ursin appeared dazed and hardly even flinched when Lior stuck him in the back of the hand with the pricker, just as he knelt to kiss Hubert's ring. Hubert's hand on his shoulder kept him on his knees.

"What happened, Ursin?"

The man shook his head. "Your Grace, I don't know what came over me," he whispered, lifting stunned, desperate eyes toward the archbishop. "He—he *must* be a miracle-worker. When he took my hand, I—got dizzy. I felt a sudden warmth come over me, and my senses reeled as I fell back into the water. It was like—like being wrapped in a rainbow for just an instant, and then a moment of— not really *pain*, but a—a wrenching feeling."

"And then?" Hubert urged.

"I—I'm not sure. I think I—passed out for a few seconds. Because the next thing I knew, I was standing up again and someone was helping me wipe my face—and my—my powers were gone!"

"How do you feel now?"

Ursin managed a wry, bitter grimace. "Bereft. Blind."

"Not—disoriented?"

Ursin swallowed hard. "No, your Grace."

Hubert glanced past him at Lior, who was curiously examining his needle and vial. "Is it possible he's shamming?"

"If he is, he's shamming *no* reaction, which I've always been given to understand is impossible for Deryni," Lior murmured, coming around to peer under one of Ursin's eyelids. "I don't understand it. He's reacting like a human."

"Dose him again," Hubert ordered.

"He could pass out."

"I didn't ask for a medical opinion; I gave an order."

"Very good, your Grace."

Javan could not tell whether Lior approved or not—not that it mattered much, for Lior was the regents' tool, and would do what he was told. The priest showed no emotion as he dipped his instrument into the vial of *merasha* again, then jabbed it hard into the muscles of Ursin's left forearm. Ursin gave a little gasp and tensed, sinking back on his heels with a sob when Lior had pulled the needles out, but all of them knew that the dose was not yet deadly, even for a Deryni—though a third might be. Hubert fidgeted impatiently as they waited for the drug to have its effect, but all that happened was that Ursin soon began to weave on his knees. His eyes, when Lior tilted his chin toward the sun, were wide and dilated, but even to Javan's unpracticed observation, Ursin appeared to be feeling no effect beyond the sedative action expected of a human. Ursin himself looked amazed, for he surely knew what the effect of even a single dose of *merasha* ordinarily would have been.

"It's impossible, and yet—where's Captain Ramsay?" Lior suddenly seemed to remember that the guard captain had gone down with Ursin. "What did you experience, man? Did this Revan—do anything odd?"

Ramsay blinked once or twice, apparently having trouble with his recall. "I—he asked me my name," he said tentatively. "I told him, and then he asked if I wanted to be purified from my contacts with Deryni."

"And you said?"

Ramsay's expression said that he thought that quite the most ridiculous question he had heard in some time. "His Grace told me to say that I did, so that's what I said, Father."

"Don't be impertinent," Hubert warned. "Did he immerse you then?"

"Aye, your Grace."

"And what happened then? Spill it, man. What did he do to you?"

"I—he—he pushed me back under the water," Ramsay murmured, gazing unseeing past Hubert as he made himself remember. "It was a falling sensation, as you might expect, and I felt the water close over my face like a tomb. It wasn't cold, though. It was warm, and I was safe. And I—think, if he'd kept me under very long, I would have breathed in the water without a struggle—but he brought me up before I could do it. I felt light-headed as I came to the surface, like—like something *had* happened. But I don't know what it was," he added lamely, as his eyes flicked back to Hubert's face. "I swear I don't, your Grace."

"Hmmm, the man obviously commands a certain magnetism, your Grace," Lior said, after a few seconds. "I think he may be very dangerous."

Hubert nodded thoughtfully. "Yes, but mostly to Deryni, perhaps. I wonder."

For the first time, Javan dared to speak up.

"Your Grace, have you considered that God may well be presenting you with a unique opportunity?" he said quietly.

"Eh, what's that?"

"Well, you want to eliminate the Deryni, don't you?"

"Of course."

"Well, isn't it far better to let God do it, so that you don't have their blood on your hands?"

Hubert bristled. "The Deryni slain so far have been criminals whose eradication was ordered by temporal as well as ecclesiastical authority, for sedition and treason against the Crown as much as any disobedience of Holy Mother Church. There is no blood on my hands."

Raising one hand in a gesture of forbearance, Javan shook his head. "No, you don't understand, your Grace. I never said there was—yet," he said, personally allowing as how little Giesele MacLean and Declan's wife and sons were just as dead, for having no blood shed. "But here you have an unrivaled opportunity to let someone else be the agent of Deryni destruction, so that you can't possibly be blamed. If a new prophet has come along who can elimi-nate the Deryni and make the people see it as a positive thing, with-out the killing, isn't that what would most please a God Who seeks out His sheep who have strayed, and Who rejoices when the prodigal returns home?"

Lior looked doubtful, but Hubert clearly was thinking about what Javan had said.

"What harm can it do, just to try it for a while?" Javan urged. "It certainly can't hurt for humans to go through his little ritual, if they believe they'll be better people for it—and he may catch quite a few Deryni in the net. With a little encouragement, he might catch even more. *And*," he gave the word extra emphasis, "if he later became troublesome, he could still be eliminated, discredited. Fa-ther Lior has already suggested a heresy tribunal as just one possibility."

"That is, perhaps, true," Hubert allowed.

"Of course it's true. All he needs right now is a bit of semiofficial support for what he's doing—even the vaguest confirmation that receiving his 'purification' is a desirable thing—for humans as well as Deryni. And someone important needs to set an example for the humans. *You* couldn't do it, of course, because it all really is on the shaky fringe of orthodoxy, but I have an excellent notion who could."

Even as Javan's intention started to register, he was squeezing his horse forward, already past the guards who might have tried to seize his bridle.

"Your Highness, no!"

"I know what I'm doing, your Grace," Javan called, pulling up to pivot his mount on its haunches. "It's so simple, it's beautiful. I'll give you a full report after I've seen him."

Red-faced, Hubert started after him a few steps. "Javan, this is madness! You don't know what he might do to you. By the obedience you owe me, come back at once!"

"Tell those men to stay where they are!" Javan snapped, stabbing a warning finger in the direction of guards who had started forward to try to stop him. "If anyone lays a hand on my royal person, I'll see him hang! This is a matter of conscience, between the arch-bishop and myself."

As the guards pulled up in confusion, Javan minced his horse slightly across the hillside, farther from the guards, but no farther from Hubert, who was fuming.

"And what says your conscience about this willful disobedience?" Hubert said harshly. "Whatever are you *thinking*? Or *are* you thinking?"

"I am thinking that I'm in my fourteenth year, your Grace, and nearly a man," Javan said quietly. "I am thinking that I'm a prince of the blood, whose example can influence a great many people, in ways that mere decrees never would. I am thinking that if I were to endorse that man down there, many people might go to him who otherwise would not have the courage, and that this might save more bloodshed. And as a man whose father was a priest, and who has been considering the priesthood for himself, this is a service I could do *right now*, years before I could actually become a priest—a service that might be pleasing in the eyes of God."

"And just what do you intend?" Hubert demanded, a bit less emphatically, after a taut moment of consideration.

"Why, my entire line has been tainted by contact with the Deryni," Javan replied, keeping a straight face only with an effort. "Surely you agree. If one of the royal family presents himself for purification from that taint, who will not follow?—Deryni as well as humans!"

He did not give Hubert time to think further on that argument. Turning his horse's head, he urged it down the hillside, ignoring the archbishop's halfhearted continuing protestations and praying he had not gone too far. The crowd parted before him as he drew nearer the water, his identity finally registering. Revan had been busily baptizing during Javan's exchange with the archbishop, but everything came to a halt as the prince's horse splashed into the water fetlock deep and Javan reined it in. The prince swept back his hood fully onto his shoulders so they could all get a good look at him, his eyes meeting and locking with the prophet's. It was the first time he and Revan had met face to face.

"You preach an interesting message, Brother Revan," he said quietly, as the crowd hushed all around him. He could sense Hubert and his entourage easing down the hillside, but he did not turn to see their progress. "I wonder, is it equally valid for princes as for these good folk?"

As he swept his free hand over the assembly, Revan came a little into shallower water, flanked by Sylvan and Brother Joachim.

"The Prince Javan Haldane," Revan said quietly, making him a slight bow, right hand to breast. "Yes, Sire, my message is for all who would truly repent of their past and give themselves into God's merciful cleansing."

Javan backed the big palfrey a few steps so that it no longer stood in the water, noting that Hubert and his minions had halted, apparently abandoning their threat to interrupt what he was about to do.

"It will take a great deal of cleansing, I fear," he said, returning his full attention to Revan. "The Deryni have touched all my family for many years. Can God wash that away?"

"Why, what can God *not* do, your Highness? The Scriptures tell us that all things are in His power. And He welcomes all his sheep back into His fold."

Javan forced a bitter laugh. "I fear I am a black sheep, Brother Revan. Nor is this pool deep enough to wash the taint from me."

"In this case, your Highness," Revan countered, "the efficacy of the cleansing depends not upon the depth of the water but upon the strength of the cleaning agent."

"*You*, Brother Revan?"

Smiling, Revan fell to his knees, shaking his head. "Not I, my prince, but the Lord of Hosts, to Whom be all glory forever and ever." He lifted his eyes and his arms heavenward, praying for his subject.

"Lord, hear your servant, who yearns to bring this gentle prince to the purification You have promised. Move his heart to repentance, and his soul to acceptance of this wondrous gift which You offer. Give him the courage to shake off the evil which has enslaved him—"

As Revan prayed on, Javan let himself be wrapped up in it, regretting the hypocrisy of what he was doing, but confident of the necessity. After a few seconds, he bowed his head, letting his shoulders gradually slump as if in resignation. And though the tears he conjured were for the friends he had lost in the past months, they would serve as tears of softening and contrition to observers.

"—I command no one, I compel no one, but the Lord of Hosts shall do all these things—"

After a while, increasingly lulled by Revan's prayer, Javan allowed a faint sob to escape his throat and swung a leg over his horse's back, letting himself slip to the ground. His fumbling attempt to unlace his boots was soon assisted by several pairs of willing if hesitant hands, and someone else took his mantle and belt as he stepped out of the boots and began limping into the water toward Revan.

"The Lord's name be praised, for He brings His servant to be blessed," Revan said, shifting from prayer to preaching again as he rose to acknowledge Javan. "May the Lord bless you in this hour of repentance. May He stretch forth His hand and lead you to purification."

He held out his hand as Javan approached, and Javan could feel a very real magnetism in the guileless brown eyes as the prophet backed into deeper water, drawing Javan with him like a moth to flame. A part of him wondered how Tavis and the others had done that.

"Blessed be your feet, which have brought you to this place," Revan murmured, pausing when the water had reached his waist and waiting for Javan. He laid his left arm around Javan's shoulders as the prince reached him, tears streaming down both their faces now, and raised his right hand in blessing above Javan's head.

"O Thou Holy Spirit, descend upon this Thy servant, Javan Haldane, and cleanse him of any evil." As he laid his hand on Javan's forehead and pressed him backward, vertigo came with the physical sensation of sinking beneath the water, and Javan could not read anything but a cool, rippling sensation that would have been shields in a Deryni. He did not know what it was in the human Revan.

Reassurance came through too, though, and a confirmation that all was going as it should. He also thought he caught a little of the comfortable abandonment that Ramsay had reported—a lassitude that made him disinclined to resist the soothing rainbow colors that flashed and swirled behind his closed eyelids—part of the overlay that Tavis and Sylvan had set up, he knew, but it was no less effective for him knowing its source. He sensed that Revan was still speaking, but he could not hear the words, and hardly cared what they were in any case.

Not until he was being raised up again, the water streaming off him from head to waist and slicking his raven hair back off his face, did he return totally to his senses. It was Sylvan who handed him a towel with a slight bow, and the other Willimite who began leading him slowly toward the shore.

"Blessed be the Lord, blessed be His Holy Name," Revan intoned, his voice following Javan from the water. And Javan, as he stepped onto grass and someone laid his mantle on his shoulders, gathered its folds close under his chin and turned to look back. Revan had followed him knee-deep into the shallows, and made him a slight bow as Javan's eyes met his.

"Go with God, my prince, and find your peace."

Nodding, Javan started to turn away, then turned back and fell to both his knees, head bowed.

"Give me your blessing, I pray, Brother, to speed me on my way."

"Not my blessing, but the blessing of the Lord of Hosts," Revan said, raising both his hands. "The Lord bless and keep you. The Lord give you peace and rest, and the certainty that you will be with Him, at the day of reckoning. May He forgive you your sins, and bless you, and be gracious unto you, and cleanse you of that which troubles you. In the Name of the Father, and of the Son, and of the Holy Spirit, Amen."

To Javan's dismay, the multitudes crowded around to kiss *his* hand then, before forming new lines to go into the water to receive purification at Revan's hands. And one man who came down from the slope opposite where Hubert watched and waited was a prize indeed—Lord Torcuill de la Marche, a Deryni who had served Javan's father. The once striking Torcuill looked terrible and nearly fell from his horse as he drew rein at the bottom of the hill and dismounted.

The crowd rumbled dangerously, for he was the first Deryni from outside their ranks to come to their attention. They had not known of Ursin's identity, and the few Willimite Deryni had long ago denounced their powers.

"Your Highness, is it true?" Torcuill murmured, staggering to within a few yards of Javan, desperation and hope writ harsh across his face. "I've been riding for days."

Playing out his necessary part, Javan drew his mantle more closely around him and stood a little straighter.

"I know you," he said coolly. "You're Deryni. I remember you from court, before my father died. Is *what* true?"

"That Master Revan can redeem me." His voice breaking with emotion, Torcuill collapsed at Javan's feet, clutching at an edge of his mantle. "Oh, God, I hate what I am!" he sobbed. "It's cost me— *everything*. My—my wife, my children, my lands—everything I spent a lifetime working for. I tried to save them, but a—mob found us. They killed theeeem," he wailed. "My wife and all my pretty bairns. They're dead, can't you see? Oh God, what's to become of me? I want to blot it out! I want to rip it all from my memory!"

Even knowing it was all an act, Javan could not help but be moved. His hands were trembling from more than the chill of being wet as he lifted his eyes to Revan, who had waded out of the water as Torcuill poured out his grief. Dripping, the prophet knelt on the grass beside Torcuill and stroked a gentle hand across his brow.

"What is your name, my brother?" he whispered, slipping his hand to the man's shoulder as Torcuill sat back on his heels to look at him uncertainly.

"Torcuill de la Marche," the Deryni replied.

"Torcuill," Revan repeated. "And do you truly mean what you say, dear Torcuill? Do you earnestly entreat the Lord to wash you clean of your iniquity and make you pure?"

Awed, Torcuill blinked a little dazedly at Revan, then nodded.

"Praise be to God, who has brought you to this place," Revan breathed. "Torcuill de la Marche, I believe you have found what you seek, if you will but take it. If you truly repent of your past life and are determined to set it aside forever, the Lord can give you purification. Yes, and forgetfulness of what you were, if you desire it. Will you take His peace?"

Breathing hard, taking Revan's hand as if it were a lifeline, Torcuill nodded. "What must I do?"

"Come with me," Revan whispered, rising to tug at Torcuill's hand. "Come into the cleansing waters with me, and the Lord shall give you peace. This is His promise to His children, Torcuill. Believe it, and you shall be redeemed."

Trembling, Torcuill rose. Weeping, he followed Revan into the water, Sylvan and Joachim plunging after to steady him at first as the two waded deeper, deeper. Javan, sensing movement on the hillside behind them, knew that Hubert was taking the bait, coming down to see the miracle for himself. He sank to his knees to watch Revan do his work, aware that the rest of the multitude were also kneeling all around him, hampering Hubert's progress.

Sylvan and the Willimite remained in the shallows as Revan led his subject into chest-deep water and set his arm behind Torcuill's back, bowing their heads over folded hands as the prophet laid his right hand across the Deryni's forehead and lowered him into the water. Javan could not hear him clearly, but the words did not matter anyway. Both Torcuill and Revan had already set their stage with exacting perfection. By the time a dazed Torcuill was wading out of the water, assisted by one of the Willimites, many of the others watching around Javan had started toward the lines forming up again. And Hubert and Father Lior were striding through the throng like avenging angels, their guards clearing a path before them, directly to Javan.

"Arrest that man!" Hubert ordered, pointing past Javan at Torcuill, emerging from the water. "I know him, and I'll have him hanged. He's a notorious Deryni."

"Arrest him for being born Deryni, your Grace?" Javan said, as the guards laid hands on the bemused Torcuill and dragged him unresisting before Hubert. "He is Deryni no longer. The Master Revan has washed away his past."

"Yes, yes, and confession and absolution wash away a man's past, too, but he still must make restitution for what he has done."

"And what has Lord Torcuill done besides what you would have everyone of his race to do?" Javan retorted. "Can you not recognize when your prayers have been answered, Archbishop? Torcuill de la Marche is no longer Deryni. Test him, if you doubt it."

"I shall do precisely that," Hubert said between clenched teeth, motioning Lior forward with his Deryni pricker.

But all their testing revealed no chink in the illusion just fabricated. Twice Torcuill was dosed with *merasha*, only to slip into a drowsy, compliant state, apparently remembering little of his past life.

"But, he *was* Deryni," Hubert murmured, as Lior gave him a shrug signifying that nothing more could be done. "I *know* he was Deryni. That's why he was removed from the royal council."

"And well did you rid us of him," Javan agreed, lying through his teeth. "But now a better way has been presented to rid us of the Deryni—and to save them as well. And is not your mandate as archbishop the cure of souls?"

"I'll not be instructed in my duties by a boy, even if he *is* a prince," Hubert muttered between clenched teeth. "You go too far, Javan."

"I apologize if I have offended your Grace," Javan murmured, making a contrite little bow. "But I *know* it must be better to save lives than to take them. Surely you cannot argue that, your Grace."

"Hmmm, we shall see," Hubert replied. "And we shall speak more of this later."

"Of course, your Grace. But in the meantime, I suggest you satisfy yourself that there's nothing Deryni about Master Revan and let's be gone—because if you try to take him, you'll have to deal with all these people. I wouldn't count our chances too high, if you threaten their prophet. He *has power*, your Grace. I've felt it. And it isn't Deryni power."

He was hoping that the faint challenge would make Hubert decline to test Revan with *merasha*, if only because it put the drug that much closer to himself, but Hubert became most adamant on that point.

"I don't intend to use force unless it's absolutely necessary," Hubert said, as two guards waded out to request Revan's presence. "If he's legitimate, he won't mind being given a clean bill of health where Deryni are concerned. And if this *is* some Deryni trick, we'll know that, too."

But Revan approached compliantly enough, giving Hubert courteous greeting and kneeling to kiss his ring in token of filial obedience as a son of the Church.

"I am honored to meet your Grace," Revan murmured. "I am likewise honored that you thought to lend your presence to this gathering. The people are heartened to see their archbishop acknowledging the wonder it has been my good fortune to bring. And the participation of their prince has won all their hearts."

Hubert snorted, somewhat disarmed by the acclamation. "I don't presume to understand all of this, though further inquiries will be made, you can be certain. And I shan't attempt to take you into custody here. Your followers might not like it."

"No, your Grace, they would not, though they would permit it if I told them to do so."

"I see." Hubert sniffed. "I shall ask you point-blank, then. Are you Deryni?"

"Of course not, your Grace," Revan said with a smile. "In my younger, more foolish days, I served a Deryni household, but all that is behind me now. Does the good Father Lior wish to test my veracity? I understand that the most holy *Custodes Fidei* are quite adept at unmasking secret Deryni."

Hubert laughed a harsh, mirthless laugh. "Do you think that will prevent me having you tested, simply because you have raised the point first? I assure you, it will not. Father Lior?"

At the snap of his fingers, Lior was at his side, readying his *merasha*. Smiling slightly, Revan held out his hand, hardly flinching when Lior jammed the charged needles deep into his palm. As Lior pulled the needles out and mixed a few additional drops of the drug with the blood on the upturned palm, Revan merely smiled wistfully and shook his head.

"You honor me, Father, by giving me a wound like in kind but not degree to Our Lord's wounds. But I truly am not worthy of this honor. I am not fit to tie the lachets of His sandals. Truly, I am but the humble messenger, bringing God's promise to these who have walked in darkness." He jerked his chin in the direction of the still captive Torcuill. "One need not be *of* the Dark to sense the Dark and seek to light it."

By now it was obvious that Lior would get no reaction from his drug. With a snort, Hubert slapped away the hand of one of the guards supporting Revan on his knees before him.

"Oh, get away and let him be. I don't know what he is, but he isn't Deryni. Maybe he *is* sent by God to cleanse us of the Deryni curse. I don't know. You men, bring the horses down. I'm tired of this place. And his Highness and I have some unfinished business when we return to Valoret."

CHAPTER TWENTY-SIX

*I was not in safety, neither had I rest, neither
was I quiet; yet trouble came.*

—Job 3:26

Javan's knees were nearly numb from kneeling, but he knew he must
not stand or even shift position. He had been kneeling in near darkness for the best part of an hour now, in the tiny, windowless chamber that the archbishop usually reserved for disciplining errant
monks. The starkly functional *prie-dieu* faced away from the door.
Not only was its kneeler unpadded, but the surface was carved with
crosses whose imprint would remain on a penitent's throbbing knees
for hours after the actual penance had been endured. Just above eye
level on the whitewashed wall, a painted Christ writhed on a painted
cross, bloody and nearly lifesized, suffering horribly—a Christ with
no pity to spare for a lowly miscreant awaiting judgment.

Javan had heard of the little room, but he had never seen it before
tonight. Actually, he supposed he was lucky Hubert had sent him
here instead of to one of the abbey dungeons. He could feel the
archbishop's presence behind him, dark and threatening. A single
torch near the door cast the shadow of the episcopal chair on the
wall before him. It also cast the shadow of Hubert himself, as he
rose and came to stand directly behind Javan, toying with the whip
of knotted cords piously called the "little discipline."

"You defied me in public, Javan," the archbishop finally said,
speaking for the first time since entering the room. His voice was
deceptively mild. "I can overlook many lapses, for you are yet young,
but I cannot overlook open and public defiance, especially in a situation which might have become dangerous to your person."

Trying to keep from shivering, for he would *not* show weakness in front of the enemy, Javan kept his head ducked in an attitude of contrition and thrust his crossed arms further into the sleeve openings of his thin black robe. His bare feet ached from the cold, especially his twisted foot, and he wondered whether he would fall, the first time he tried to stand up. Just walking here had been hard enough, without his special boot.

Actually, he suspected that was probably all part of the plan. Javan had known from the start that he would have to pay the price for his performance by the river. He had crossed Hubert inexcusably. Though Hubert dared do no serious physical harm to a prince of the blood, abundant options existed for princely discipline, all of them distinctly unpleasant—and Javan had no doubt that the archbishop would exercise one of the more disagreeable of his options. Other than to place Javan in the charge of two grim and silent *Custodes* monks for the ride back to Valoret, Hubert had not spoken to him since leaving the river. It was the monks who had brought him to the little chamber, after seeing that he changed from his still damp cleric's attire into the traditional garment of a penitent. He could sense them lurking just outside the door.

"Javan, I speak to you now, not as one of your regents but as your archbishop," Hubert said after a heavy sigh. "When you asked to come to Valoret and make a religious retreat, you may have forgotten that you placed yourself under my rule and the rule of this House. The fact that you are not yet in Holy Orders absolves you from the traditional vows of poverty and chastity, but not from obedience. When I allowed you to accompany me to the Willimite encampment, it was with the understanding that you recognized that. I did *not* expect you to defy me in public, regardless of whether I later came to accept the possible merit of your arguments. It is for that open defiance that you are kneeling here now and for which you must be punished. Do you understand?"

Swallowing miserably, Javan bobbed his head in assent. "Yes, your Grace."

"And do you understand why this wicked, willful behavior cannot be tolerated?"

"Yes, your Grace."

"*Why* can it not be tolerated?"

"Because you are archbishop, and my spiritual father, your Grace," Javan murmured, saying what he knew Hubert had to hear before they could wind this uncomfortable business to a speedy end. "But—may I say something, your Grace?"

"If it honestly pertains to this discussion, yes. However, I hope you don't intend to offer an excuse for what you did."

"Not an excuse—no, your Grace. But an explanation, if I may."

"Very well."

Javan drew a deep breath, calling upon all the eloquence at his command.

"First of all, I beg pardon for any offense my behavior may have given. I truly did not set out to defy you. Had our discussion been able to take place in private, I feel certain you would have seen my argument as disagreement rather than defiance. You have taught me to examine my conscience, your Grace, and in conscience, I felt that I *had* to do what I did. But I see how my public conduct of the matter appeared to challenge your authority. I am sorry for that, and I deserve whatever just punishment you see fit to impose."

Hubert snorted, but it was a resigned, almost indulgent snort rather than one of total disbelief. "And *why* did you feel you *had* to do it?" he demanded. "What colossal arrogance makes you think that your evaluation of the situation was necessarily superior to mine?"

"Because I'm *tired* of all the killing!" Javan blurted, half turning to face Hubert, to the agony of his shifting knees. "Your Grace, I don't know how much more I can take! I try to be a proper prince and endure what I must, for the sake of my rank, but how much can that rank demand? How many more helpless men must I see drawn and quartered, their families coldly killed—"

"You will endure what you must," Hubert said stonily, setting the end of his whip against Javan's chin to turn his face back to the bloody *Christus*. "Like Him, you will endure what is set before you. You will drain your cup to its dregs, because you are a prince and may someday stand in the stead of God, either as a priest or even as your brother the king does now. And it is not for you to determine, at your young and tender age, what you will or will not endure. Do I make myself clear?"

Tears welling in his eyes despite his will to the contrary, Javan nodded jerkily.

"*Do—I—make—myself—clear?*" Hubert repeated, with each word rapping Javan smartly on the shoulder with the end of the whip.

Sinking back dejectedly on his heels, no longer worrying about his knees, Javan managed to murmur, "Yes, your Grace."

"Excellent. I am delighted that we understand one another. Now." Hubert took in a deep breath and sighed. "There is the matter of penitence. I am satisfied that you understand your error and that you are contrite. Accordingly, I forgive you—with the understanding that you will not allow this to happen again. We shall speak later of the implications of what you have done. Abbot Secorim will be dining with me this evening, and I expect you to join us. In the meantime, however, there is the matter of a suitable punishment for your behavior. Do you have any suggestions?"

Javan shook his head.

"Very well, then. First of all, because you have confessed your fault readily, without trying to deny your guilt, I shall do you the courtesy of treating you as a man instead of a wayward boy. Accordingly, I shall *not* turn you over my knee and thrash you."

Javan allowed himself the faintest sigh of relief at that reprieve.

"However," the archbishop went on, "since your offense was against my authority as archbishop, when you owed me obedience as a retreatant under my roof, I suggest that the penalty be assigned as if you were a lay brother living under the rule of this House. If one of my monks had committed this offense, the penalty would be twenty lashes, administered by two of his brethren." Javan started as the thongs of the "little discipline" were flicked lightly over his shoulder. "It can draw blood, but you will not be scarred. Do you accept this punishment?"

Javan swallowed, but he gave a nod. He had feared far worse.

"I accept it, your Grace," he murmured.

"Then you will signify your acceptance by kissing the 'discipline,' " Hubert said, shoving the handle of the whip under Javan's nose. "The appropriate verbal response is, *'Deo gratias.'* "

"*Deo gratias,*" Javan murmured obediently, ducking his head to comply, trying not to notice the smooth gleam of the knots in the leather thongs.

"So be it. And may God sustain you in your repentance and aid you to bear manfully the penalty you have invoked by your transgression," Hubert murmured, withdrawing the whip and using it to trace a cross over Javan's head. "*In Nomine Patris, et Filii, et Spiritus Sancti, Amen.*"

"Amen," Javan whispered, before Hubert had to prompt him.

"Very good. I'll leave you for a while, then, to prepare yourself," Hubert said. "When the brothers come in, you will stand. They will ask your forgiveness, which you will give. You will then strip to the waist and kneel, upright and with your arms outstretched in imitation of Our Saviour, on Whose example of suffering you will meditate while the penance is carried out. The brothers chastising you have many years experience disciplining young monks and will attempt to gauge their strokes by what they believe you should be able to endure without crying out. If you *do* cry out, an extra lash will be added for each occurrence. Please try to ensure that this will not be necessary."

He was gone before Javan could try to assure him that such would be uppermost in his mind. The soft snick of the door closing made his empty stomach churn, and he wondered how long he had before the monks came in. As he eased off his knees to stand, he gasped with the sharp pain of circulation suddenly returning. Steadying himself against the kneeler's armrest to spare his lame foot, he bent to massage first one knee and then the other as he flexed them in turn. Hubert had said that the "discipline" would not scar him, but what about his knees? The pain was fierce as circulation returned—and went completely numb as someone knocked softly at the door and then the latch lifted.

Chilled, Javan stood straighter and watched as the two *Custodes* monks entered, the taller one carrying a bucket with two short handles protruding from it. Their hoods were up, and the torchlight behind them, so he could not see their faces, but he sensed they were not the same ones who had brought him here. A sharp whiff of vinegar twitched at his nostrils as the one put down the bucket and both of them knelt.

"Pray, forgive us, your Highness, for what we must do for the good of your soul," the shorter one murmured.

Javan nodded, his voice catching a little in his throat. "I—forgive you right readily," he managed to whisper.

He could not quite seem to manage the fastening at the neck of his robe, however, and had to let the taller man help him. Opened, the upper part of the garment fell in loose folds around his waist, girt in by the plain rope cincture tied around his waist, leaving his upper body exposed.

"Lift the edge of your robe a little before you kneel, your Highness," the man murmured, guiding him to face the *prie-dieu* and the fresco beyond. "The sharper discomfort in your knees will help keep your mind off your back."

Surprised, Javan did as he was bidden, wincing a little as he lowered himself onto the carved wood—though at least it was a familiar pain. The pungent tang of vinegar was much stronger as he heard the men taking their whips out of the bucket, and it made the bile rise up in his throat.

"Brace yourself against the armrest before you raise your arms," the monk advised again, now behind him, "and bite on this." A hand thrust something brown and flat in front of his mouth—a thick piece of leather, he realized, as he bit down.

"Now let us all recite a silent *Pater Noster*," the other monk said quietly. "And afterward, let each stroke of the little discipline drive your error from you, that you may be sanctified in the mercy of the Lord our God."

Javan prayed the prayer as he had never prayed it before, arms outstretched and head held steady, focusing on the lettering painted above the suffering Christ's head—*INRI*, picked out in a ruddy gold that glowed in the torchlight. He must have prayed it faster than the monks, for it seemed forever before the first stroke snapped across his back, more startling and wet than painful. The second was no worse, but the third stung like nettles, and the fourth began to burn. After a few more, he became increasingly thankful he had the piece of leather to bite on. By the time they reached the halfway point, he only hoped he could hang on.

For the second ten, he could only endure, impaled on his own will not to cry out, his arms trembling as if he hung on a cross in truth, like the man on the Tree before him, though he uttered not a sound. He lost count before they finished, and was only aware that it was over when he heard them putting the whips back into the bucket.

"Well stood, lad," the short monk murmured beside his left ear. "You can put your arms down now—though I'd advise you to keep a good bite on that bit of leather."

His arms were trembling so badly, he could not think what the man meant; but when he had been guided to rest his hands on the armrest in front of him, he found out. He gasped as the other monk sponged cold vinegar over his back, the acidic liquid burning in each weal. He wondered whether he was bleeding, though he could not tell with the vinegar running down his back.

The pain abated a little from the treatment, though, and he was able to stop his trembling as the short monk helped him draw his robe back over his shoulders and stand.

"You're a credit to your house, my prince," the monk said quietly. "I've known grown men to cry out from less than we gave you."

Javan winced as he straightened his knees, still leaning hard on the *prie-dieu*, not looking at the man. "I'm surprised you didn't keep on until I *did* cry out. Wasn't that the whole purpose?"

"Only to a certain point," the man said frankly. "The true purpose was to test your self-control, to bring you right to the brink, but not break you. The penalty should be sharp enough to hurt a great deal, to the very edge of what one can bear, to impress the seriousness of one's error, but not enough to humiliate or do permanent harm. You'll remember this lesson, I think—and the fact that you tested yourself beyond what you thought your limits were. That builds character rather than tearing it down."

"We'll take you to your squire now, your Highness," the taller man said. "He'll help you bathe and dress. His Grace is expecting you in less than an hour."

Several hours later, long after the final course had been cleared away by silent, obliging monks, Javan remained a reluctant guest at Hubert's table. He could not have said, afterward, what he had eaten, but it lay in his stomach like lead—a condition not helped by the fact that the room was far too warm. Furthermore, Hubert had seated him closest to the fire—normally an act of solicitude to an honored guest, but one which tonight only made Javan more aware of the state of his back. According to Charlan, some of the weals criss-crossing the royal back probably would show bruising by morning, but the squire assured him that there was no blood. Indeed, he had commended the skill of the monks who carried out the punishment.

"You're lucky those monks knew *exactly* what they were doing, your Highness," Charlan allowed, as he gently bathed the weals, dried them, and then applied a soothing ointment. "I don't suppose you have much experience with such things—princes don't get thrashed the way squires do—but this really doesn't look too bad. If you wouldn't mind a little friendly advice from someone who's survived a few thrashings, I'd suggest that you wear soft shirts, sleep on your stomach for the next few nights, and choose stools to sit on rather than chairs."

The first had already been laid out with the starkly plain black tunic and hose they had decided was politic for the evening; the second was a necessity to be tested later that night; and the third turned out not to be a choice that must be made. Hubert had provided a stool at the place designated at table, but otherwise made no allusion to what had happened earlier in the evening. Javan could not tell whether Secorim knew or not, though the abbot surely must have received reports, both from his men present at the riverside and from the two who had carried out the punishment. While they supped, neither abbot nor archbishop spoke of any but the most inconsequential of subjects, and Javan spoke hardly at all.

After supper, however, as Hubert poured strong red wine for all three of them, Javan knew that further avoidance of the afternoon's events was going to be impossible—and it was becoming equally impossible to ignore his back. Soft as his old shirt was, next to his skin, he could feel the linen sticking to his flesh—from sweat, he was sure, but he kept imagining it was blood. Seeing the bloodred wine in the cup Hubert set before him did not improve his state of mind.

"So," Hubert said, sitting back with his elbows on the arms of his chair, a fine silver goblet cupped between his two hands. "Why don't you tell Father Secorim what you know of this Master Revan, and why you feel that the new baptism he preaches does not present a threat to Mother Church."

Javan cupped his hands around his own goblet, considering very carefully before he spoke. He had barely tasted his wine, for fear of loosening his tongue too much—he *knew* it was strong. Still, the temptation was great to drain it and ask for more—anything to numb the burning ache of his back.

"It's—difficult to know where to begin, Father Secorim," he said after a slight pause. "I like to think I've studied a great deal, but I'm not a theologian. Nonetheless, I have always been taught that our God is a loving and merciful God, Who cannot bear to see His children suffer."

"He is also a just God, your Highness," Secorim replied, "and He will not suffer the wicked to go unpunished."

Javan let himself give a nod, thinking quickly. "Of course not. But I was always taught that when a sinner repents—when he turns away from his sins and resolves to amend his life and return to the community of God's people—God forgives. The Shepherd rejoices at finding His lost sheep and returning it to the fold. The Father welcomes His prodigal son and takes him back into His embrace. Nowhere in the sacred writings can I find a passage that says the Shepherd slaughters His returned sheep, or that the Father slays His son."

"Ah, but the Scriptures give us numerous examples of the wicked being brought to the fire at the Day of Judgment," Secorim said. "Surely you do not intend so weak an argument in defense of the Deryni."

Javan sighed, doing his best to show distaste at the very notion. "I am not defending Deryni, Father. But perhaps there's another way to bring in these lost sheep besides slaughtering them. If they can be made to turn from their former lives—if, indeed, they no longer have the *ability* to return to their former lives—is this not better than the slaughter? I don't know if I can bear to see another helpless man butchered—or, worse, women and children put to death, simply because of what they are."

"And you believe that this Master Revan offers an alternative, even though he preaches a sacrament contrary to the teachings of Holy Mother Church?"

"I don't think he means it as a sacrament, Father," Javan said, thinking fast, "and certainly not a substitute for sacramental baptism. It's a—a purification, a specific purification for a specific purpose."

"Ah, so he purports to purify those who come to him," Secorim said, nodding shrewdly. "And by what authority does he claim to do this? *Not* by the authority of the Church, I hasten to point out."

Javan glanced at the cup between his hands, all too aware of the trap Secorim was laying. "Father, he doesn't just *claim* to do it," he said, glossing over the dangerous question of authority. "If what he does were only a token act, with no effect on the recipient, one might charge him with blasphemy, for presuming to offer a grace whose efficacy cannot be proven.

"However, he *does* purify Deryni. He washes away their past and gives them a new beginning, free of their accursed powers. That's *provable*, Father—and far more objectively than most of the 'official' sacraments."

Secorim looked shocked, but Hubert only signalled with his hand for the abbot not to interfere.

"I see I shall have to instruct you further on the nature of true sacraments," the archbishop murmured, "but, go on. Tell Father Secorim of your 'proof.' "

Javan chanced a quick glance at Hubert before returning his attention to Secorim, trying to decide just how upset Hubert actually was about the sacramental question. Well, he could sort that out later. He had already denied any claim to be a theologian.

"Very well, your Grace," he murmured, settling on another approach with Secorim. "Father, today your monks tested two known Deryni with *merasha*. Neither showed any effect beyond the drowsiness I'm told usually affects humans. Unless you no longer consider *merasha* a reliable method for detecting Deryni—a thought which I, personally, find quite appalling—we must concede that a change has occurred—the very change for which all of us, I believe, have been praying: that God will strip the Deryni of their powers and turn them back to His paths."

"I do not pray for a conversion of the Deryni," Secorim muttered through clenched teeth. "I pray for their destruction!"

"And I pray for deliverance from their influence!" Javan retorted, knowing he must defuse *that* line of hatred immediately, or all was lost. "I pray for deliverance, and today my prayer was answered."

Secorim snorted derisively. "How, *answered*?"

Trembling with the strain, his back afire with the pain of his scourging, Javan made himself push his cup away and clasp his hands on the table before him.

"Father, I am not greatly learned in theology, but I know what I saw and experienced, and what my conscience tells me," he said softly. "I don't know the source of Master Revan's authority to preach what he does, but I can tell you that something happened out there today. I went down there wanting to believe him, but prepared to resist him with all my might, if his words seemed false.

"But they weren't false," he went on, looking Secorim in the eyes and daring to extend his fledgling powers just a little. "If I'd *hoped* this might be a way to stop the wanton killing when I went down there, I *knew* it was right when I spoke to him face to face.

"Father, my family has been touched by the Deryni more than anyone else. But when I went down to Master Revan, and he led me into the water, I could feel the taint melting away. When he immersed me, it was like—like being wrapped in sunlight that swirled all around me, into every part of me, and washed away all the years of pollution." He cocked his head at Secorim. "They can't harm me anymore, Father. For the first time in my life, I'm free of them. But I don't wish them any harm. On the contrary, if Master Revan can save them from themselves—why, what a blessing! Isn't that what the Church wants? To bring her lost sheep back to the fold?"

Secorim snorted, breaking the faint spell Javan had been weaving by taking a large gulp of wine. "Hubert, I'm amazed," he muttered, after he had swallowed. "You really want to make a priest out of *this*?"

As Javan bristled, only barely holding his anger in check at the insult, Hubert cocked a wry smile and put his own goblet down. "Peace, Secorim. Prince Javan is young and sometimes does not realize the full implications of what he says. In one respect, however, I am inclined to agree. Putting the purely theological arguments aside for a moment, let us talk about expediency. If, as we have always maintained, the Deryni are evil and must be destroyed, then a means must be found to accomplish this. We have stopped short of wholesale slaughter, at least in part, because of the public outcry it causes, when women and children are killed along with their menfolk.

"But if the destruction of the Deryni can be brought about in a manner not offensive to those who abhor physical slaughter, by the Deryni themselves—then, is not the same end accomplished? As Prince Javan himself pointed out, before taking matters into his own hands at the Willimite camp, God desires the return of all His sheep to their proper folds. Perhaps later, some of the folds will be found to be slaughter-pens—but that is for the future."

Secorim chuckled unpleasantly at that, lifting his cup to Hubert in enlightened assent, and Javan felt his stomach churn, though he kept his eyes carefully averted and his hands clasped between his knees. His Deryni allies had considered the danger that Hubert outlined. Javan had hoped it would not occur to Hubert—at least not so soon. For the cold facts were that anyone known to have been Deryni before would be as helpless as any mere human, if taken after being blocked—*more* helpless, if the Church decided that only fire, and not water, could totally expiate a Deryni's guilt.

But given a few years to disperse and relocate, with no way for new associates to prove that a person once had been Deryni, many of that race would find their way to places of safety. It was a risk that Joram and Evaine and the others were prepared to take—and to take on behalf of others of their race—if only Revan's mission could find acceptance, even for a few months or years.

Much of that acceptance depended upon Javan's performance, however; and knowing that, he put on the sort of face he knew Secorim and Hubert must see.

"You are too quick for me, your Grace," he murmured. "These are aspects I hadn't considered. But for now, why not wait and see what this Revan does, since he *is* eliminating Deryni? Watch him, by all means. Retest him, if you still believe he's some kind of new Deryni, or if his message changes in ways you don't like. You can always bring him in, later on."

"The notion *is* tempting," Hubert agreed.

"I see," Secorim said. "Just let him continue this charade of illicit baptism, possibly endangering the souls of those who are *not* Deryni?"

Hubert made a thoughtful noise as he sipped at his wine. "Hmmm, I doubt there's any immediate danger, my dear Secorim. Javan has already pointed out in an earlier discussion that if what Revan does *is* ineffectual, no harm is done. And meanwhile, it soothes public sensibilities—which will be all the more outraged, if eventually he is found to be a fraud."

The possibility of exactly that eventuality haunted Javan for the rest of the conversation, numbing him to much further participation. He hoped Hubert would take it for fatigue and the pain of his back. Later, after Secorim had left them to return to his own quarters, Javan realized abruptly that Hubert was pondering what to do about his suddenly independent young prince.

"If I had any sense at all, I'd lock you away on bread and water for a week or two, just to be certain my message of earlier this evening got through," he said, studying Javan shrewdly. "You're beginning to think for yourself—which can be dangerous in an extra prince."

Chilled, Javan slipped to his knees before the archbishop, wondering if he dared use his powers to ease the situation. He had never tried it before with Hubert fully conscious.

"If—if you think I should go into retreat, I'll do it, and gladly, your Grace," he whispered. "You have given me much to think upon—and I truly deserved your discipline."

As he sank back on his heels, pretending to sniffle back tears and bending to bring the hem of Hubert's cassock to his lips, he could sense the archbishop preening and relaxing a little. Now, if Hubert would only do what he usually did . . .

"There, there, dear boy, you need not abase yourself before me," Hubert murmured, letting his hand drop to rest negligently on Javan's bowed head. "I am your spiritual father, and I do what I do only for your welfare."

Then, sleep—for my welfare, Javan commanded silently, reaching out with his mind to caress the controls that would make Hubert obey. *Sleep, and remember nothing of this . . .*

Within seconds, the ringed hand slipped from his head—and was as quickly grasped, to maintain the physical contact—and Hubert was snoring softly, his head tipped against the high back of his chair. Easing himself back to his knees, watching Hubert carefully all the while, Javan enclosed the hand in both of his, then bowed his head to lay his cheek slowly against the wrist—so that anyone entering unexpectedly would see nothing amiss at first glance. Then, more stealthily than he had ever done before, he eased into the fringes of Hubert's mind.

He could not bear to maintain the contact for long. Brushing Hubert's mind was like skimming scum from a midden. The shadows he glimpsed churning just below the edge of consciousness were ugly and often frightening—but with little bearing on his immediate aim.

So. Perhaps Prince Javan is coming around at last, he set in Hubert's mind. *For a while, I feared it might take forever, but I believe we may finally have weaned him from any remaining softness he once had for the Deryni—and this odd Revan person is at least partially to blame. Disturbingly unorthodox, this Revan— and I probably ought to get rid of him before he gets out of hand— but he does seem to be playing into our hands for now.*

So I think I'll let him operate for a while longer, just to see what he'll do—and keep a very close watch on him. Time enough, later on, to crush him if he becomes inconvenient.

In the meantime, there's my puzzling little prince. I feel certain Javan will be ours entirely, one day, but for now—yes, patience is the best policy. He will come to accept the religious life, if I do not press him. A royal bishop could be a powerful tool, indeed.

Javan was nearly retching from the prolonged close contact, by the time he had finished, but he made himself linger yet a while longer to set certain other compulsions and tidy the few remaining loose ends, making certain Hubert would have no inkling that the doctored thoughts were not entirely his own. As he let Hubert regain consciousness, he allowed himself the luxury of sinking back to the floor, still clutching Hubert's hand, weeping with relief rather than the despair he seemed to display.

"Oh, how can you bear to have me nearby, your Grace?" he sobbed. "I repaid your trust with defiance. I was ungrateful and willful."

"There, there, my son, do not weep. I know what a difficult day this has been for you," Hubert murmured, never thinking to wonder how his hand had gotten from Javan's head into his grasp. "Indeed, it has been altogether too long and difficult—and perhaps I was overharsh. You *are* still but a boy—yet, you withstood your penance like a man. I *am* proud."

Trembling, for his back hurt abominably from the strain of bending the way he was, Javan made a visible show of trying to get himself under better control.

"I beg you, your Grace, do not send me away in disgrace like some errant schoolboy. I—I have so much to learn—and I would learn it at your feet. Give me leave to stay here and study in Valoret, I pray you."

"To study in Valoret, eh?" Hubert murmured. "Why, do I detect a desire to taste the religious life more fully?"

"Well, I—I *should* like to explore that possibility, your Grace. But I'm not ready to make any vows yet—"

"Not permanent ones, no. Of course not. You're far too young. But perhaps you would like to live here as a lay brother for a year or two. Oh, not as an ordinary serving brother, but as a—ah—a 'pre-seminarian.' I shall supervise your studies myself. I *would* wish you to take temporary vows, however. It's customary among the lay brethren, even at your age—well, at fourteen, though we shan't quibble about less than a year. In any case, temporary vows can easily be dispensed, if—if you should be needed at the capital."

Javan swallowed, chilled by the thought of taking vows—even temporary ones—but aware that this was one concession he probably would have to make. He tried not to think about being needed at the capital, for that would mean that his brother the king was dead.

"Would—would I still be able to go back to Rhemuth to see my brothers?" he asked—a far more important question, at this point, if he was to keep himself informed of Alroy's welfare, in particular. "We've never been apart for very long, and I fear I should miss them very much."

"Of course you would, my son," Hubert murmured, lifting his hand to stroke Javan's head benignly. "And of course you may go back, as often as you like—provided you give me ample notice. Let us say, a month."

"A month?"

"Why, Javan, a month is not a long time in an abbey. If you truly wish to try the religious life, even on this limited basis, then you must conform to the rule that all the other brethren follow. That rule does not allow for whims, though it can bend in the face of advance planning. Besides, we would not wish to interrupt your formal course of study, now would we?"

"N-no, your Grace." At least the formal education would always stand him in good stead.

"Good, then. I'll make the arrangements. I shall need to consult with the other regents, of course, but I don't think they should object. Oh, and you do understand that we'll have to postpone your actual vows until Lammastide, when the ban is lifted on ordinations and the like, but that's only for a few weeks. I shouldn't want anything to be construed as irregular about your vocation, later on—*if* it transpires that you are, indeed, called as you begin to think you are," the archbishop added with a self-righteous smile. "You can certainly begin your studies and informal observance of the Rule before then—from tomorrow, if you like."

Thanking God for the temporary reprieve from the vows, at least, Javan bowed his head in acceptance. "Thank you, your Grace. May I have a few days in solitary retreat, to meditate on it?"

"Of course you may, my boy!"

Hubert insisted that they pray together in his oratory after that. It was only for a few minutes, but it seemed like hours. All the time they knelt there, Javan had to fight the urge to dart onto the Portal and flee—anywhere, so long as it was away from Hubert. And he had just condemned himself to possibly years in Hubert's daily company, putting on a pious charade, playing a very, very dangerous game.

But it was for a very high purpose, and he knew it. His Deryni allies could no longer gain access to the regents; Javan could. True, his access would be to only one of the regents, but Hubert would be challenge enough for the next few years. The very notion of trying to influence Murdoch or Rhun was unthinkable, this early in the game. Tempering the archbishop's religious fanaticism, even a little, would not be easy, and must be done with a subtlety and wit that Javan dared not dream he had yet, but after tonight he was convinced that it was at least within the realm of possibility, and could make a major difference in whether Deryni survived at all in the next few years.

He must also spend these next few years learning everything he could about the cold, soulless world of politics in which he would have to move, if he ever became king. He had decided he could do that best from the safety of the cloister. Joram and Evaine would be furious when they found out what he had done, for taking even temporary vows placed him that much closer to the day when Hubert might just lock him away in some distant monastery against his will—one more inconvenient prince eliminated, just as they might eliminate poor Alroy, though Alroy might only escape through death.

Still, it was something he had to try. Just as he had needed to try with Revan, to give their plan the best possible chance of succeeding. It had been worth the pain and humiliation of the "little discipline," if it had won Revan a little more time—which it appeared to have done.

Every muscle in Javan's body ached by the time Hubert at last released him, and he nearly wept with the pain when Charlan peeled the linen of his shirt away from his back and bade him lie on his stomach so his weals could be dressed. The ointment the squire used this time was different, and cooled and soothed as it lulled Javan to the very edge of sleep. He became aware, just before he drifted into drugged unconsciousness, that someone besides Charlan had been ministering to his back.

The brush of the other's mind was like a mother's caress, accepting and reassuring, and he felt tears of relief stinging his eyes as he surrendered to that other's touch.

CHAPTER TWENTY-SEVEN

*And the vision of all is become unto you as the
words of a book that is sealed.*

—Isaiah 29:11

"Ah, you should have seen him!" an elated Ansel MacRorie crowed,
as he and Jesse MacGregor burst into the Camberian Council chamber three days later. "What a magnificent prince! I know you were
set against it, Joram, but he may have outguessed us all. It was a
triumph! The people loved him for what he did. Now hundreds are
flocking to hear Revan preach and receive his new baptism. Jesse
and I counted at least a dozen Deryni, just the two days we were
there, didn't we, Jesse?"

The grinning Jesse tossed a dusty pair of saddlebags onto the floor
behind his chair, chuckling good-naturedly as he and Ansel took
their places to either side of Saint Camber's Siege in the north, still
empty and likely to remain so as long as Tavis remained with Revan
in the field.

"Aye, and you'll be proud of your Trurill men, Lady Evaine,"
Jesse said. "Your lads have been spiriting the converts away almost
as quickly as they're dunked, to get them sent off to safe places."

Evaine did not look up, and Joram glanced first at Queron and
then at Niallan, the oldest but most junior member of the Council,
nodding for the latter to proceed.

"How about Torcuill de la Marche?" Niallan asked quietly.
"When Sylvan reported, that first night, he said the *Custodes*
drugged him with *merasha* but got no reaction. Did our men get
him away?"

Ansel nodded, suddenly subdued, suddenly aware that something was not right. "Aye. There was no question of being able to restore him first—he probably would've gone into convulsions with that much *merasha* in him—but—what's wrong? What else have you found out that we don't know about? It was a triumph, at least while we were there. Don't tell me that the bloody regents—"

"The 'bloody regents' haven't exactly done anything," Queron said quietly. "Not this time. Well, *one* of them has," he conceded. "It's going to be all right—I think—but, what were you saying about Prince Javan's triumph? I wonder if you have any idea what it cost him."

Stunned, the two youngest members exchanged glances, then returned their attention to Joram, looking to him for explanation.

"Well?" Ansel asked. "Are you going to tell us?"

Joram fixed a stony gaze on his hands folded on the table before him. "Why don't you ask Evaine? She saw him."

"*She saw him?*" Ansel repeated, as if unable to believe what he had just heard. "How? Where?" he demanded. "Were you there at the river, too? If you were, were Jesse and I just risking our lives for nothing?"

"*Stop it!*" Evaine cried. "I do not have to answer to you, and no, I was not at the river!"

"Ah, but you do have to answer to them," Joram said. "You're still a part of this Council, and you have to answer to all of us. Tell them where you saw him—and then try to justify your totally irresponsible action."

"Joram, I will not be bullied in public, simply because you're my brother! I had good reason for what I did—and as it turned out, it's a good thing I went ahead, or we should never have known about Javan."

"*What* about Javan?" Ansel demanded. "He's all right, isn't he? God, they haven't *killed* him?"

"Nothing so dramatic," Queron murmured, trying to make peace. "You're aware, though, that he and the archbishop had words, before Javan went down to Revan."

"Yes, of course. But we thought everything was all right, when Hubert came down, afterwards, and let Torcuill and Revan go."

Jesse shifted impatiently. "Let Lady Evaine tell it. What happened to the prince?"

"He will be staying at Valoret for the next several years," Evaine said calmly, "as a lay brother attached to the *Custodes Fidei*."

"What?" Ansel blurted.

"It was largely his choice," Evaine said sharply. "Apparently, our good archbishop was most upset not by Javan's argument but that he did it in public. He found this doubly intolerable in that Javan owed him simple obedience, as a retreatant living under his spiritual direction. Accordingly, he gave Javan the option of accepting the same discipline meted out to lay brethren living under the rule of the abbey: twenty strokes of the 'little discipline.' It's a—"

"I *know* what it is!" Ansel retorted, fuming. "You're saying that Hubert had a royal prince *whipped*, like some—"

"*He's all right*," Evaine said, cutting him off. "They didn't even draw blood. The men who administered the penance knew *exactly* what they were doing. It's a common enough penance, in the monasteries."

"That much is true, at least," Joram muttered. "Scourging is not that unusual."

Ansel snorted. "If it isn't that unusual, then why are *you* so angry about it?"

"He's angry because *I* went to Valoret and found out about it," Evaine retorted, toying with the ring she now wore on her right forefinger—Jodotha's ring. "He's angry because I took another shape to do it and then went through the Portal in Hubert's oratory. I concede that it was dangerous."

Ansel, whose elder brother had died with another man's shape upon him—a shape-change set by Evaine and the slain Rhys—sat back abruptly, all the fight suddenly gone out of him. Jesse, who had heard about the procedure but had no firsthand knowledge of it, pursed his lips silently.

"It was a shape I've used before," Evaine continued lamely, after a moment. "A young monk I call 'Brother John.' He started out as a Michaeline, but I've made him a *Custos* now. He was just another of his Order in the archbishop's palace—and certainly, no one would expect a *Custos* to be Deryni."

"Yes, but through the *archbishop's* Portal?" Jesse breathed.

"Javan was the first of us bold enough to use it," Evaine said. "I suspect he will continue to do so, when and as he can. As for my own use—well, after Sylvan's report of the incident at the river, I was reasonably certain that the episcopal bedchamber would not be occupied until quite late. I went through the Portal there and listened in on part of a conversation between Javan, Hubert, and the head of the *Custodes* in the next room. I read the rest of it from Javan's memory later on, unbeknownst to him. In all, though I acknowledge that our prince will be walking a very narrow edge of constant danger, I think he's made a prudent decision, under the circumstances. Staying at Valoret for the next few years, learning everything he can—and strengthening his influence over Hubert—

I think he'll be able to do far more than most young men his age to help our cause.

"And believe me, he *is* a man. Make no mistake. Not only did I hear him handling Hubert and Secorim; I saw his back, after Hubert finally let him go to bed. I also questioned one of the monks who administered punishment, who seems sympathetic. Javan didn't cry out once."

Ansel snorted. "That won't last forever—not once he's really under Hubert's thumb. Hubert will break him, given time."

"No, I think Javan may break Hubert, given time," Evaine said, smiling slightly for the first time. "He set some interesting suggestions, after Secorim had left. He doesn't dare make any drastic changes, for fear the other regents will notice and investigate—just as we don't—but he's setting the stage for his own ease, and the easing of Revan's situation. A time will come, I have no doubt, when he'll have gone as far as he dares—but meanwhile, at least a few more of our people will have had a chance to survive."

Ansel chuckled unpleasantly. "Maybe he'll dare to go further than you think. Just suppose, for example, that the archbishop should meet with a small accident."

"For God's sake, Ansel!" Niallan blurted. "You're talking murder. He's still a thirteen-year-old boy."

Ansel snorted, pushing back his chair. "Aunt Evaine just said he was a man. Besides that, he's a prince. And he *has* killed before."

"In self-defense, yes," Evaine said coolly. "But I won't ask him to murder. Besides, if anything were to happen to Hubert, after Javan specifically asked to be taken under his roof, they'd be at him with Deryni sniffers, *merasha*—you name it!"

"Which is also why *I* haven't simply gone through the Portal while Hubert's asleep and squeezed his fat neck in two," Joram told Ansel. "Few things would give me greater pleasure, but few things are also almost guaranteed to make things worse, not only for Javan but for our people."

"But—we can't just do nothing!" Jesse cried.

"We *aren't* doing 'nothing,' " Evaine said. "Javan is doing something, and Revan is doing something. *All* of us are doing something, Jesse—even if it's mainly waiting, just now. So—try to have a little patience," she finished lamely, gesturing vaguely with her hands. "We're *all* doing the best we can."

"You were hard on young Jesse, earlier," Queron told her, when he found her several hours later, poring listlessly over the stacks of parchments and the few artifacts they had brought out of Orin's tomb. "What's wrong? Couldn't you sleep?"

Sighing as she shook her head, Evaine picked up Orin's ring and slipped it onto one of the ivory wands. She wore its mate on her right forefinger, as she had since the night they found it. The rings shimmered in the candlelight as she held the wand horizontally and set Orin's spinning, silver purring silkily against polished ivory.

"No. I don't know what's wrong, Queron. I'm beginning to feel a little uneasy. I—*know*—that I'm on the verge of finding out what I need to know, but for the first time in my life, my power frightens me. It could kill me—not to mention you and Joram. My children could be motherless as well as fatherless. And we might not even succeed. We could give up our lives for nothing."

Queron shrugged and, with a sad, gentle smile, sat down across from her. "You're the only one who can decide whether the risk is acceptable, Evaine. If you say it is, we're with you. If you say no, then it's over, finished. *I* won't push you. And God knows, Joram won't."

Nodding, Evaine let the ring slide off the wand and onto the table beside the candle, continuing to turn the ivory staff idly in her hands. "I wish it were that simple. If I could put *him* out of my mind, perhaps it would be. But I can't." She glanced over at the shrouded form which was her father's body.

"I have to do it for *him*, Queron, don't you see? Even if I can't bring him back, but only release him, I must do it."

"He *chose* to do what he did, Evaine, knowing what the outcome might be. And I don't think he'd want you to sacrifice yourself—"

"Don't talk to me of sacrifice!" she snapped. "*He* is the one who made the sacrifice, in the hope that I might be able to bring him back to finish his work. If I can't—well, could *you* condemn your own father to be locked in a helpless body, walled up in a tomb, for all eternity? That isn't an empty shell over there, Queron." She pointed at the body with the wand. "*Rhys'* body is an empty shell. I can't change that, but I accept it. Oh, Tavis put a preservation spell on it, so it isn't rotting, but Rhys isn't in it, and he never will be again. Nor would I put his soul back in that body, even if I could, because that phase of his existence is over, finished. Besides, there's a part of Rhys that's always with me—that will always be with me, until I'm also finished with *my* body and he and I are totally at one again."

"And Camber *isn't* with you?" Queron asked quietly.

"Not in the same way—no. It's both weaker and more intense. At times, he seems very, very near. But there's a—a fog that I can't pierce. It isn't like the veil that separates the worlds. God knows, I've at least glimpsed past that from time to time. What separates Father is—different. That's all I know to call it. And the answer is in one of these scrolls—I'm sure of it. I just haven't yet found the key."

Queron smiled gently, setting his Healer's hand lightly across her wrist. "Why don't you get some sleep, Evaine? You're exhausted. How long have you slept since you saw Prince Javan?"

"Not enough," she whispered, covering his hand with hers and smiling. "But I'm not quite ready to go to bed just yet, and I don't want you pulling any of your Healer's wiles to try to make me! Remember, I was married to a Healer."

"Yes, and he was a far finer Healer than I'll ever be, no matter how long I live. Tell me, do you intend to reread *all* the scrolls again tonight?"

"I'm sorry, Queron." She glanced down at her lap, ashamed of her outburst. "No, of course not. I just wanted to check a couple of passages."

"Half an hour's worth?" Queron ventured.

"No more than that, I promise."

"Very well." Sighing, Queron patted her hand over his, then rose. "Sleep well, when you do sleep. And remember—half an hour."

"Half an hour," she agreed.

She gazed distractedly into the candle beside her for several minutes after he had gone, finally letting her attention wander back to the stack of scrolls lying on the table before her. Most were still in their protective leather tubes, the colored cords around them coded to their names: the Protocols of Orin. She felt certain the answer had to be here, somewhere, but in which one?

Not the Green, for that dealt with Healing. Not the very basic and important Vermillion, with its careful instructions for scrying, setting Wards, constructing Portals. The Yellow was equally unlikely, though it dealt with spells connected with the dead: taking a dead man's shape, reading the memories of one recently dead, and assimilating the memories of same. But Camber was not dead; she was certain of that.

The Royal Blue, then—the volume to which she had most recently gained access. But while that had been of help to Queron in instructing Tavis and Sylvan on further intricacies of the power-blocking procedure, neither that nor the material on staring patterns and moon-scrying seemed to be applicable.

That left the Black Protocol, then, whose advice they had used numerous times for placing another shape on the dead—but again,

Camber was not dead. By the same argument, the procedure for reanimating the dead would be equally useless—though at least that topic touched closer to the mark than any other they had found. The other subject of the Black Protocol concerned calling up creatures—a practice fraught with dangers to the operator as well as the object of the creatures' attentions, and one which Evaine had never pursued.

Sighing, Evaine opened the Black Protocol long enough to skim over its table of contents again, then pushed it aside and pulled out the last possibility: the *Codex Orini*. She had held high hopes for this one, guessing that it might contain some of Orin's working notes—as, indeed, it did, except that the material seemed to deal only with meditation, and the difficult and little known esoteric discipline sometimes referred to as the Conversation of the Holy Guardian Angel. It was a subject which, under any other circumstances, would have commanded her keen interest and further study—her father would have rejoiced at the find—but unfortunately, it seemed to have little if any bearing on the problem at hand.

The Conversation of the Holy Guardian Angel is one of the most noble and worthy ambitions of the dedicated Servant of the Light, she read, for perhaps the sixth or eighth time since retrieving the scroll. *The committed Seeker who perseveres in the quest for this most sacred of contacts with the Spirit will touch the secrets of the functioning of the Universe, gaining inestimable grace in that growth toward union with the Godhead which is the goal of all enlightened and evolving beings.*

Sighing, Evaine let the scroll curl back on itself and close, rubbing weary hands across her face. The temptation to enter the quest that Orin outlined held great allure, but she must not let herself be distracted from her mission. She *must* find a way to reverse the spell that bound her father between life and death.

Pushing aside the rolled scrolls, the wands, the medallion and ring they had taken from Orin's body, and the torque Jodotha had worn, she rose and moved to the bier where Camber's body lay. They had draped the net of *shiral* crystals over his lower body, but they had not activated it. Blinking back tears, Evaine laid her right hand over his—the fine, aristocratic hands curved just—so—at waist level, as if cupping something precious, that must not be spilled.

His flesh was cool beneath her touch, but never as cold as she expected. Even when they recovered him from the snow, beside the slain Jebediah, he had not been really cold. Both she and Joram had been too numb with grief to notice it at the time, or perhaps attributed it to the recency of death, but they had noticed it since. Its reality haunted both of them, a continuing reminder that it was *not* death that bound him, but something else—something that, with care and love and, perhaps, sacrifice, might be reversed to bring him back to carry on his work.

"I'll do whatever I must," she whispered to him, searching the calm, expressionless face with tear-dimmed eyes. "I'll try to bring you back—or release you, if that's what's meant to be—but you've got to help me. I can't do it by myself."

After a few minutes, when she got no more response than she had all the other times she had talked to him this way, she sank to her knees and then to a cramped sitting position beside the bier, letting her hand trail down the side to catch in the net of *shiral*. The crystals were cool against her cheek as she leaned her head against the net-covered side of the bier. After a little while, she slept—and dreamed.

She seemed to be standing in sunlight, on some vast, windswept plateau high above the world. The sky was closer here, but the air was no less sweet. The warm, comforting smells of growing things surrounded her—dew-kissed grass and nodding grain and flowers and sun-warmed soil—and she gloried in the miracle of life, of love, lifting her palms heavenward in wordless, joyful thanksgiving as she twirled and threw back her head to drink the blessing of the sunlight, laughing.

The twirling brought a heady, gladsome giddiness that stayed with her as a profound sense of peace when she stopped. The peace persisted as she lowered her eyes to the horizon, intensified as her eyes picked out movement, awe catching in her throat as she made out an approaching shape.

Across a grass-fragrant carpet spangled with tiny white and yellow flowers, a noble form advanced toward her, indistinctly robed in a greenish shimmer of rainbow and sunlight that did not declare the being either male or female. Softly curling hair the color of ripe chestnuts, tumbling shoulder-long, framed a face of such indescribable beauty and strength that Evaine wept to see it. The being halted a few strides beyond reach, gazed at her sympathetically for several seconds, then drew its hands apart, one above the other, to let a shower of palm-sized silvery rings pour from one to the other in a sweet, musical trill of chiming metal that seemed to echo the ringing of tiny, silvery bells.

But, what does it mean? she was conscious of thinking, a part of her observing from outside the dream.

Again, the being parted its hands before her, raining silvery rings from one hand to the other—and again, and again, until her senses pulsed to the music of their ringing and she fell to her knees, one hand pressed to her reeling head while the other lifted half in warding off and half in entreaty.

Show me again. I don't understand, she pleaded. *What is it you want of me?*

With an expression of infinite patience, the being parted its hands once more, starting the shower of rings all over again—only this time, the rings seemed to interlock like a chain, still chiming musically into the lower hand, but linked still when the upper hand lifted the topmost of them, stretching and releasing, stretching and releasing. Three times the being repeated this mysterious action, then closed the pile of rings between its hands and held them out to her.

Trembling, daring to trust, Evaine lifted her hands to accept what was offered, cupping her palms to receive it, putting all thought of possible consequences from her mind. The touch of those otherworldly hands was cool, but what they laid in her right hand seared like fire. She gasped and jerked back her hand, jolting from sleep to consciousness in less than a heartbeat, opening her eyes to the very real, thumb-sized imprint of something circular on her right palm—and the metallic tinkle of something bouncing on the floor and rolling.

She was after it by its sound, pouncing on it like a cat on a mouse, before it could come to rest. It was Jodotha's ring, she discovered, to her surprise, as she held it to the meager candlelight and then conjured handfire to stare at it in amazement. But the ring had been on her hand; she could still see its indentation around her right forefinger.

But she could also see another indentation on her right palm—a stark white circle that was not the mark of pressure, but something else—more like the burn she remembered from her dream, except that there was no pain. And it fit the ring exactly.

Thoughtful, Evaine sat back against the side of the bier and turned the ring over and over in her fingers, studying the tiny crosses and other symbols engraved around the outside—noticing, for the first time, that there were odd, irregular marks along the edge of the ring.

Curious. Now, why had she never seen those marks before? And what did the dream mean? Silver rings. She closed her eyes to conjure up the images again.

Silver rings, strung in a chain. Silver rings, interlocking. Rings. More than one ring. Jodotha's ring and—

Orin's! Her eyes popped open as she remembered the other ring, that had been there all along. Orin's ring, twin to the one in her hand. As she scrambled to her feet, to stagger back to the work table, she knew that she would find markings on the edge of Orin's ring, too. Again, she could not think why none of them had ever noticed before.

Holding the pair of them to the light, she saw that she was right. There *were* markings on the edge of Orin's ring! And held thus, beside Jodotha's smaller one, she knew that the rings would interlock—not linked, like the rings in her dream, but one inside the other, a perfect match!

Trying to stop her hands' shaking, she turned the two circles in the light, trying to decide which way they went. When matched correctly, she now had no doubt that the marks on the edges of the rings would line up to form writing of some sort—and that she would only have one chance to make the match. If she got them wrong way round, the marks would disappear—and who knew what might be necessary to bring them back to try again.

But the rings provided no visual clues. The symbols carved around the outsides of the bands were similar, but no direct match—all of the symbols present, but in different order. Nor could she gain any insight from trying to match the markings on the edges, without being able to put the rings together.

Very well, then. She would have to rely on something besides visual evidence. Some clue in the rings themselves, perhaps. Maybe—something to do with polarities—a not unlikely possibility, given the balance inherent in nearly every example she had found of the sort of magic that Orin and Jodotha favored.

Polarities. Opposites. Positive and negative. Black and white. Left and right. Male and female . . .

Nodding to herself, Evaine shifted the rings' positions, taking Orin's ring in her right hand and Jodotha's in her left, weighing more than physical substance, settling into a cool, dispassionate meditative state.

Polarities. Hold Orin's ring unmoving and feel its orientation. Project into its structure and sense the balance of the individual who had worn it.

She closed her eyes to sense it better, eliminating mere physical sight, which knew nothing of the ultimate balances.

Now hold that first balance and concentrate on Jodotha's ring. Different. Balanced in its own way, but different. The same, but different. Turning the second ring in her fingers, she knew they would only match one way.

Turn it like a coin—crowns or shields? One way was right, the other was not. If Orin's was the shield, should Jodotha's match, as shield, or complement, as crown? Where was the balance point? How did they balance? Crown . . . shield . . .

And suddenly, the two were balanced—an unshakable certitude. Inhaling deeply, she opened her eyes and let the breath out slowly, gazing at the two rings resting on her palms. Then, without further hesitation, she picked up the smaller, lighter circlet of Jodotha's ring and placed it on top of Orin's, prodding it gently with her forefinger to make it nest inside the larger band. Their union made no sound, but she felt the faint snick of the one seating in the other, and she slid them both onto the table and then onto the edge of the *Codex Orini*, where the silver would show up better against the creamy parchment. The marks on the edges of the rings were still visible, and as she slowly turned the outer ring against the inner, the marks became letters, spelling out four words in Latin.

Domine, fac me vitrum. Lord, make me a glass . . .

Turning the rings over, she found the rest of the words on the other edges. . . . *ut tibi incendam.* That I may burn for Thee.

"Make me a glass, that I may burn for Thee," she murmured, puzzling over the words. "A glass . . ."

She looked back at the interlocked rings, lying on the edge of the *Codex*, then looked more closely at how the space inside the circle suddenly seemed to have taken on a purplish hue.

"No, not a glass. A lens!" she exclaimed, pushing the rings over part of one of the lines of writing—and grinning as new writing appeared *between* the lines penned in mere ink. "A lens, by God! A lens!"

As she scrambled to unroll the scroll to its beginning, she slid the rings to the space between the first two lines. The writing that appeared was Orin's fine, distinctive hand—and remained, a glowing, fiery red, as she passed the ring between the lines.

"And it burns!" she whispered to herself, appreciating the wit. "Of course!"

She hardly knew whether to laugh or cry as the sense of the words emerged in translation, from that ancient, mystical language taught her by her father, so many years before—the language that now, perhaps, would enable her to release him from the magic that bound him so near and yet so far.

To the Reader who will have advanced thus far, my fraternal greetings across the unknown years, for we be brethren in this great

Work. But only if thy need be great must thou proceed beyond this point, for the knowledge I leave in these words is of most solemn import, and of great danger, both to the operator and to the object of attention. For I would share with thee the secret of preserving life even beyond death—and perhaps, if thou art daring indeed, of bringing life back out of death . . .

CHAPTER TWENTY-EIGHT

I shall not sit as a widow, neither shall I
know the loss of children.

—Isaiah 47:8

The full impact of the words did not register in the first reading or even in the second. Indeed, Evaine's most immediate concern became the necessity to preserve the words so arduously gained. She spent the next hour copying what she read through the lens of the joined rings, fearful lest the words fade before their sense could be fully grasped. Her fear was justified, for by dawn the words had faded utterly from between the lines of the *Codex Orini*. Nor could she call them back, no matter how she manipulated the rings.

But by then, she had her fair copy and could pore over it at her leisure—though the sense of the words troubled her, the more she studied their implications. Accordingly, she never showed the complete transcription to Joram and Queron. Instead, she wrote out an expurgated version for their guidance and then destroyed the original—which mattered little, since she had committed the entire thing to memory. And *that* she shuttered away from all but the most rigorous and insistent of retrieval methods that her brother and Queron might be tempted to try.

That did not keep them from asking questions, though, when she finally presented the draft and her outline of the procedure for the working she proposed.

"This is intriguing material, but what's the source?" Queron asked. "Much of it is fairly straightforward, but some, I've never even heard of, much less seen done."

"You have what you'll need," she said, not looking at him.

"What she means," said Joram, "is that we have what *she* thinks we'll need. You've censored the Orin material, haven't you?" he said accusingly. "This isn't the entire document. What is it that you don't want us to know?"

"It doesn't matter," she murmured, looking past them at nothing. "It's enough that one of us has to worry."

Nor would she let them draw her out about it further.

They would not be ready to try the working for many weeks, in any case—for it was *working* and not mere spell which was required to undo what Camber had set, that cold day in January. The preparations went beyond the mere provision of a physical setting in which to perform the rite. The operators themselves must prepare, with a period of fasting and meditation.

And always thought must be given to the possibility of failure and the mortal peril to those who failed. In fact, she believed that Joram and Queron faced little real danger; *she* was the one most at risk. Nor did death itself hold any personal terror for Evaine, with husband and firstborn already gone before her. If she did die, what she would regret the most was not seeing her other children grow up.

But to bring her father back to carry on his work—how many other people's children might not live to grow up if she did not follow through with what she had begun and risk that death?

Which brought her back to the question of Camber himself. If they did *not* succeed in reviving him—whether he remained in his present state or merely passed into true death—the survival of his cult as saint must be ensured. Queron, who had founded a religious order on the promulgation of that cult, did not need convincing. Miracles had occurred, whether or not Camber's body had been assumed into heaven before his canonization, and many, many people, both human and Deryni, looked to the quandam saint as a source of hope and inspiration.

Joram was less certain, though he finally admitted that the survival of the cult of Saint Camber underground could only reinforce what Revan was doing out in the countryside to save Deryni.

"It's all based on a lie, though!" he protested, late one night in July, when Evaine and Queron had almost worn him down. "Saint Camber, Revan's baptisms—they're all lies."

"So, I should point out, is the persecution of Deryni!" Queron answered. "You don't exterminate an entire people, just because a few of them have misused their powers over the years, Joram. If that were true, and justice were to be done, then the human population should be exterminated, too!"

"There are some who should!" Joram said stubbornly.

"Aye, and there are Deryni who deserved exactly what *they* got. But judgment must be made on an individual basis—which the regents seem increasingly unwilling to do. Because of that, we have to do something to even the odds. Giving people the hope and inspiration of Saint Camber, or blocking the powers of some of our people so they can get away—these are ways of doing that, without taking more innocent life. If ever we were to begin taking indiscriminate reprisals, we'd be no better than our persecutors."

"Who believe that we're devils or in league with devils," Joram murmured, bowing his head over clasped hands. "Sometimes, Queron, it's all I can do to celebrate Mass—wondering if perhaps Hubert and his minions are right. Maybe we *do* contaminate everything we touch. Maybe a Deryni *isn't* fit to be a priest. Maybe I'm deluding myself to think I'm worthy even to *try* to make a difference."

"None of us are worthy, Joram," Evaine said quietly. "But worthy or not, *someone* has to rise to the situation and say, 'Enough'—and then carry through with action that might, conceivably, make a difference. At least we're *trying*—which is more than a lot of our people out there, who have given up hope. What harm can it do, at least to *pretend* that Father is a saint? There have been saints before, and will be again, whose sanctity rests on far slimmer evidence. You've probably prayed to a few of them yourself."

Eventually, though Joram steadfastly refused to state that he thought his father actually *was* a saint, he agreed to carry on as if Camber *were*, and gave his promise to support the cult of Saint Camber, if they did not succeed in reversing Camber's spell. In a testament written and rewritten many times in the days that followed, Joram carefully reiterated the story he had first conceived for the convocation that ultimately proclaimed Camber's sainthood: that he, Joram MacRorie, and not heavenly agencies, had removed his father's body from its resting place in the vaults at Caerrorie and hidden it away—which did not detract in the least from the miracles and visitations ascribed to the saint at his canonization. Indeed, Joram confessed, over the years he had come to believe that his father might truly have been a saint. In affirmation of that growing belief, Joram planned to retrieve his father's remains from their present resting place and entrust their keeping and veneration to appropriate pious persons who would faithfully guard and promulgate the high principles for which Camber MacRorie had lived and died.

It was a telling and powerful statement, and would all but guarantee the resurgence of the Saint Camber cult, once released beyond the circle of the three of them who knew the literal facts of the situation. Even when it was written, Joram remained uncertain about the advisability of releasing it, and drew comfort from the realization that it would *not* be released without further consideration, unless none of them survived the attempt to bring Camber back—a possibility Joram counted highly unlikely. In case the unlikely occurred, however, Joram sealed his testament with a stasis spell keyed to Niallan, whom they all had agreed should try to hold the Council together if none of them returned, placing it with similarly sealed testaments prepared by Evaine and Queron.

For Evaine, those days of planning and preparation were a time of double strain, for in case *she* did not survive, she must make personal provisions of a different kind than those required by the two priests. She spent as much time with her children as she could spare, knowing that she must make every minute count, just in case she did not return from that dark journey, near unto death itself, where she must seek her father.

Mornings she spent with Rhysel—not eight until November, but already a scholar and wise beyond her years, as Revan had pointed out, what seemed like years before—a Revan then not yet what they had made of him. Daily they read and discussed the poetry and other writings that Camber had shared with Evaine at the same age. Sometimes Evaine included Bishop Dermot, whose background in the classics approached her own. Perhaps Dermot would take on Rhysel's further education, if Evaine did not return.

Then there was Tieg, who would need more specialized teachers before too long—Tieg, the precocious four-year-old with such awesome gifts of Healing and the ability to strip his people of their power. As Evaine played at "bears" with her surviving son, she wondered what would happen to him if she could not be there to see that his education was carried out as it should be. There were no more *scholae* for the training of Healers.

And finally, there was little Jerusha, the baby whom Evaine might never even really know. Like her father and her brother, Jerusha would be a Healer of breathtaking potential—and perhaps she, too, carried the blocking talent already evidenced by her brother. But at eight months, she was still a laughing, happy baby, sitting up strongly and starting to stand, wide-eyed and amazed at the world she was discovering—and already, she thought that Fiona MacLean, and not Evaine, was her mother.

"She adores you," Evaine whispered, as she watched the infant settle into sleep in her little cot, a tiny hand clasped around two of Fiona's fingers. "If she never saw me again, she would never even miss me."

"Nonsense! *You're* her mother." Fiona looked at her strangely. "Evaine, what's wrong? You look like someone who *doesn't* expect to be seen again."

"I'm sorry. I suppose I'm just tired."

"No, it's more than that," Fiona said. "Something's been troubling you for weeks. I kept meaning to ask you, but—you're not ill, are you?"

"No, I'm fine."

"Well, you don't look fine," Fiona fretted, disengaging her fingers from the grasp of the now sleeping Jerusha. "You look like walking death sometimes. You've lost weight, there are circles under your eyes—I thought you'd start getting some proper rest, once Revan was safely established."

"Fiona, please don't lecture me. Joram lectures me, and Queron lectures me—"

"And a lot of good it does, I can see," the younger woman retorted. "But if you want to work yourself into an early grave, don't mind me. It's none of my business. I'm only the one who takes care of your children. Why should you talk to *me* about what's bothering you?"

Tears stinging unbidden in her eyes, Evaine turned her face away. "Forgive me," she whispered. "You, of all people, have a right to know as much as I dare tell. There's—someone very precious to our cause, who's locked away. Getting him out will be very, very difficult and very dangerous."

"And you might not come back," Fiona murmured, sitting down, stunned. "Oh, Evaine, I didn't know."

"How could you? I've gone to extraordinary lengths to keep it secret. And please don't ask who it is, because I can't tell you that."

"I promise."

"In any case, it isn't the threat of death that concerns me. It's the possibility that my children will be left orphans. When I think about that, I—"

She buried her face in her hands, trying not to break down entirely—a resolve not helped by the embrace of Fiona's arms around her shoulders.

"Oh, Evaine, dearest sister, please don't cry," Fiona whispered, stroking the golden hair as Evaine let the tears come. "Oh, I'm not as gifted or as highly trained as you are, so I can't offer any direct help with—whatever it is you have to do. But I know you wouldn't even be thinking about doing this—whatever it is—if you didn't believe it was terribly important. I *will* promise to be a mother to your children, though, if—if you don't come back. You don't even need to ask."

"I know that," Evaine whispered, "but thank you for reassuring me. God knows, I don't *want* to leave them, but—oh, Fiona, if you only knew how important this is."

"But, I do know. You've just told me," Fiona murmured, hugging her close and stroking the golden hair. "Hush now. Everything will be fine."

The days passed, and preparations intensified, both physical and spiritual. Dietary restrictions had been in force among the three for all the previous month, to purify their bodies for the demands of the Work now scheduled for the first of August. Now, as July counted out its final days, Evaine added periods of actual fasting to their preparations, along with a gradually increasing regimen of meditation designed to focus the concentration.

One remaining task she postponed almost until the end, and that was to see Javan one last time. She did not tell Joram or Queron, for fear they would forbid it. Nor did she put on another guise, lest the extra exertion sap her strength for the more important working, now but two days away. She was already short on sleep, for sleep deprivation was said to sharpen the adept's perceptions during the actual working.

She chose the hour of Vespers, when Hubert was unlikely to be in his quarters but Javan *might* be. Though she had left him no memory of her previous visit, she had planted the inclination to use the archbishop's oratory whenever possible, in hopes of just such an eventual contact. As hoped, she sensed the prince's sole presence as she came through the Portal. He was kneeling at the *prie-dieu* with his head bowed over his folded hands, all but invisible in black tunic and hose. He had been deep in meditation, and looked up with a start as he suddenly sensed the Portal activity.

"*Jesu*, you shouldn't be here!" Javan breathed, as she turned back her hood to let him see her face.

"Why, didn't you hope one of us would come?" Evaine whispered, smiling as she crouched down to face him, eye to eye.

"But, it's dangerous!"

"Ah, and what you're doing is *not* dangerous, eh?" she countered.

"What do you mean?"

Evaine smiled sympathetically and laid her hand on his forearm. "I believe that you asked Hubert to let you stay in Valoret, did you not?"

"Who told you that?" Javan demanded, aghast.

"I believe you also agreed to take vows."

"*Temporary* vows!"

"Vows, nonetheless. Which may not be that bad a thing," she added, holding up a hand to stop his argument. "In fact, you've probably arranged one of the safest places possible for these next few years, while you're still so vulnerable. And if you really live the spirit of those vows, putting aside the personality of the man to whom you must swear them, you should find these years a time of great personal growth and insight. But you must still be very, very careful."

He sat back on his heels, resentment warring with pleasure at seeing her. "I know what I'm doing."

"I'm sure you do. Just try to be sure that Hubert doesn't. I gather that you *have* taken steps."

He looked away, suddenly uncomfortably aware just how slender his influence over Hubert was. "I've made a few—ah—adjustments. I can't do too much, though, or someone will notice, even if *he* doesn't."

"Precisely what I told the others." She smiled. "Well, you don't need me to lecture you. When will it happen?"

"Two days hence, in the afternoon," Javan murmured, hanging his head. "I—how did you know?"

"I was listening, there by the door, when you asked him."

"You were right there, and I never realized?" Javan whispered, shocked. "But, how—"

"Hush. When Sylvan reported on Revan that night, he warned us that you and Hubert had exchanged hot words. It followed that he would take you to task—probably as soon as he got you back to Valoret. I took a chance that he'd be late turning in, regardless of how he chose to deal with your little flash of independence. It was only a stroke of luck that made him choose to do it right here in his apartments."

"Well, it wasn't *all* done right here," Javan replied, lowering his eyes. "I suppose you know about the little room Hubert has, up in one of the towers—the *disciplinarium*?"

She gave him a grim nod. "I also know about the scourging you took, if that's what you're asking—and that you endured it as bravely as any of us could have done. You must be very careful, though. Once you are bound to Hubert by vows, even temporary ones, he will be quite within his rights to deal with future transgressions even more harshly. I *think* that your rank will always spare you your life, unless you go totally beyond the bounds of common sense—but he might make you wish you could die."

"He wouldn't dare!"

"Unfortunately, I think there is little that Hubert MacInnis would *not* dare. But, we're wasting valuable time. He will be returning soon, and I have something important to say to you. I—have a task to perform. As fate would have it, I must do it the same afternoon you make your vows. So, since I cannot be with you, I ask that you pray for me, Javan—and pray to the blessed Camber, my father, to aid us both in what we must do."

"What—what are you going to do?" Javan dared to whisper. "It sounds dangerous."

"No more dangerous, in its way, than what you are doing." She smiled. "But we all must serve as best we can. Please don't ask me more."

"Very well." He inclined his head in assent. "Will I—see you again, soon?"

"If it is within my power, you have my word on it, my prince. And if I cannot come, someone else will. We shall not abandon you."

He felt tears welling in his eyes, and he had to look away to keep from crying.

"Are you going to die?"

"Eventually we all die, Javan."

Javan had all he could do to keep from shouting at her. Biting back his fear and anger, he made his fists ball in his lap until he could feel the nails cutting into his palms.

"*I know that!*" he whispered, daring to meet her eyes. "And *you* know that isn't what I asked. This thing you have to do—could you die from it?"

He saw her own tears glittering, just before she looked down.

"Yes. That's one of the reasons I came to you tonight."

"To say good-bye?"

"Yes," she whispered. "And to give you certain knowledge that you may need, if I—can't be with you in the future. If you should become king."

Her words hit him like a fist in his gut, calling up confused half memories of the night his father had died. They had not wanted him to remember any of it, but he and Tavis had dredged up fragments—enough to know that magic had been worked upon him and his brothers—his father's magic, Deryni magic.

And if he did become king eventually, the magic would be his, too. Part of it was his already, to all their great surprise. He was gasping open-mouthed as he came forward on his knees to stare at her, his hands squeezing the armrest of the *prie-dieu* in a death grip.

"What happened to me, the night my father died?" he whispered. He had asked the question so many times before, he could hardly believe she might finally answer it. But her grave, solemn expression promised that this time would be different.

"I mayn't give you conscious recall, but I *will* set the knowledge in place, to be triggered if you need it," she said, setting her hands on his shoulders. "This also will be less gentle than I would have wished for you—but unfortunately, we haven't the luxury of time for subtlety. I daren't risk being interrupted by Hubert."

"I understand," he whispered. His eyes never wavered from hers. "Just do what you have to. I'm not afraid."

"No." She smiled. "You are one of the bravest young men I know. Relax and open to me now. And remember to pray for me."

He nodded wordlessly and closed his eyes as her hands slipped up to his temples. He tried to obey her instructions, but his eyes were stinging with tears, and he could not seem to clear his thoughts.

Peace, my prince, she whispered in his mind. *If we should not meet again in this life, remember what we have fought for—you and I and Tavis and Rhys and all the others—and do your best to help the Light triumph.*

I will—I promise! he managed to form the words in his mind.

God bless and keep you, my prince. Now go deeper yet, and take the knowledge of your destiny.

She rammed the knowledge home then, knowing that she hurt him, but unable to temper the force of her sending, lest she not have time to finish—for Hubert would return very soon. Javan passed out before she had made more than a start—which was as well, since it freed her to go even faster, without worrying over whether she hurt him.

She blocked his memory then of all but her request for his prayers, knowing that at least she had given him a chance, if he had to take a throne alone one day, without Deryni support. She left him slumped over the *prie-dieu* with the memory of a dream that she had come, brushing a last, fond kiss to his downy cheek before leaving him to the footsteps that approached through the archbishop's outer chamber.

Her awareness of his prayers would help her endure what she had to do, and reminded her of yet another reason it might be necessary to offer up her life—whether or not that offering was accepted.

CHAPTER TWENTY-NINE

Seek Him that maketh the seven stars and
Orion, and turneth the shadow of death into
morning.

—Amos 5:9

Javan woke with a nagging headache on the appointed day, exhausted by dreams that he could not recall and light-headed with hunger, for Hubert had prescribed a strict fast of bread and water only for the three days leading up to his profession. Charlan was not due to rouse him for nearly an hour, but he could neither retrieve the dreams nor go back to sleep. He thought one of the dreams might have been about the Lady Evaine, but he could not define more than a vague sense of foreboding. To appease his anxiety, he decided to pray for her. Charlan found him a little while later, kneeling beside the bed in his nightshirt, head bowed over his folded arms, and marked it as evidence of humility before the step he was about to take.

"Beg pardon, your Highness," the squire said hesitantly. "I apologize for the intrusion, but it's time to dress for Mass. You must be very moved by what you are about to do."

Javan looked up blearily, not bothering to correct Charlan's misapprehension, since he knew it would go straight to the archbishop as soon as Charlan left, and would reinforce what he wanted Hubert to think.

He would miss the squire—if not his apologetic spying for the archbishop. Charlan would be leaving his service today, for lay brethren, even royal ones, were not permitted servants. They had already said their good-byes. Charlan was being transferred to the king's household—though with luck, he could continue to visit Javan once

a month to report on affairs at court. It was a stipulation the archbishop had agreed to readily enough, in exchange for Javan's promise
to try the religious life, but Javan did not know how long the arrangement would last, once he was under vows.

But he must not waste precious energy worrying about that just
now. He had enough to concern him, wondering whether Hubert
might try to put something over on him during the ceremony of
profession—some innocent-seeming phrase inserted into the vows,
for example, that later might be used to try to bind him more permanently. He thought not, but he knew he could never fully trust
Hubert, no matter how closely he believed himself to be in control—
and his controls just now were not nearly as close as he would like.

He dressed carefully for the archbishop's early Mass, affecting an
air of thoughtful detachment as he donned a layman's attire for
perhaps the last time. He was not required to serve this morning,
since he would be a central figure in the afternoon's ceremony, so
during the Mass he had time to pursue his own meditations while
others made the appropriate responses. Charlan, kneeling beside
him for the last time, was very, very quiet. Javan found himself
thinking about Saint Camber, and wondered whether the Deryni
saint ever deigned to extend his protection to humans.

He hoped so, for he sorely needed protection of some sort, to
keep him from being swallowed up by the situation he himself was
about to allow. The thought of devoting a few years to God at this
stage of his life did not distress him in the least, for he was practical
as well as reasonably pious and recognized the advantages of the
intensive training he would receive during that time.

But he must not let Hubert and the others force or trick him into
making it permanent. His brother Alroy had not looked good at all,
the last time Javan saw him, and might well die before he got an
heir—an heir who would be the regents' puppet from the start, to
the detriment of all Gwynedd.

Better that Alroy should die without issue than play into the
regents' hands by giving them a new king—for Javan felt sure that
his brother would not last long, once the regents had themselves a
new prince in the direct line. He wondered whether they had already
picked out the royal bride—and whether Alroy and Rhys Michael
would attend this afternoon. He had asked that they be present, even
though the ceremony was a semiprivate one; he had sent the invitation himself, along with an expurgated account of his reasons
for taking vows.

But one could never be certain whether letters got through or
how they might be altered in transit. The regents were all too clever

and devious. He would not put anything past them, if it served their purposes.

The sacring bells of the Consecration called him back from his mental wanderings, and he made himself concentrate on the rest of the Mass in a more seemly fashion. He noticed, as first the Host and then the Cup were elevated—and as he had begun to notice some weeks ago—that a faint shimmer seemed to surround each. He wondered whether Hubert or any of the others could see it, too—though he doubted it. Someday, if he ever got the chance, he thought he might ask Father Joram about it. It seemed like the sort of thing that a Deryni might see—though the question of why he himself should see it did not occur to him.

Meanwhile, the familiar magic of the Sacrament gave him scant comfort this morning, for Hubert passed him by for Communion. He would not be permitted to receive again until he had been confessed and professed, later this afternoon. He felt cold and empty when he rose to leave the chapel, for he had not begun the day without Communion for many a week now.

Nor was he allowed any further ease after Mass was over. Hubert paused on his way out to bless him, before going on as usual to break his fast with the brethren of the *Custodes Fidei*, but Javan was not invited to accompany him this morning. Nor did Charlan linger, after bobbing self-consciously and a little moist-eyed to kiss the royal hand a final time as squire to prince. Instead, two monks Javan had never seen before came to conduct him silently to a close, narrow chamber where a barber monk trimmed his hair in the short, pudding-bowl shape affected by most clergy. He would receive the tonsure later, during the ceremony of actual profession—something Javan found vaguely disturbing, though Hubert had assured him that tonsuring was symbolic only, and did not bind him irrevocably to the religious state.

He was taken to another room after that, windowless and lit only by a few rushlights set in pottery dishes, where steam lazed upward from behind a heavy woolen curtain of grey a shade darker than the room's stone walls—the ritual bath required of all postulants making their first profession. As a purification, a symbol of washing away one's past, Javan supposed it was not dissimilar to what Revan was preaching down by the river, though Hubert would be appalled if he knew Javan had even thought of the comparison.

More conventionally, Javan recalled that candidates for knighthood underwent a similar purification the night before their dubbing, for similar reasons, and told himself that this was little different. He would *be* a knight, but owing allegiance to the Light rather than any earthly overlord—though he must pay lip service to his archbishop, at least for now.

As he had been coached beforehand, he bowed and murmured, "Deo gratias," when one of the monks drew aside the curtain and indicated that he should enter and disrobe. The cubicle beyond was close and humid, lit by one rather puny rushlight set high in a niche in the corner. The bath was wooden and round, its ironbound edge reaching nearly to his waist, steam billowing energetically from the water's surface. Javan stripped quickly when the curtain had fallen, glad to be rid of the high-necked black tunic and hose, which he folded neatly on a three-legged stool. He could find no towel or replacement garb, but supposed those would be provided at the appropriate time.

Only setting aside his special supportive boot gave him any particular pang of regret—though Hubert had assured him he might have it back tomorrow. The archbishop knew that walking without its support was an awkward and painful process, but insisted that even a prince must go unshod to his profession. Javan teetered a little unsteadily on the lame foot as he climbed into the wooden tub, wincing as he lowered himself into the steaming water—hotter by half than he would have wished on this balmy August morning. Trying not to think about it, he ducked under the water several times, riffling through his shorn hair to rinse away the loose clippings from his barbering. Between dunkings, he was vaguely aware of footsteps outside the curtains and doors opening and closing. He tried not to think about that, either.

Hubert had said he would have the best part of an hour for the ritual bath, but he was ready to get out in half that time. As he climbed out, dripping, he was not surprised to find that someone had exchanged his secular clothing for a rough-napped towel and a thin, ankle-length black robe, similar to the one he had worn to the disciplinarium. He hoped they would not be repeating that little excursion as a part of the profession. And not only was there no girdle to knot around his waist this time, he noted, as he began toweling himself dry, but there were not even any undergarments.

He shivered as he pulled on the robe, knowing it was all calculated to produce anxiety, to make the postulant feel stripped down to the barest essentials—and annoyed with himself because the intention was working. He found a comb hanging on a nail on the wall, and used it to slick his shorn hair into some semblance of clerical decorum, though he had no mirror to inspect his handiwork.

Shortly, two different monks returned for him. The air outside was cool compared to the bath chamber, and he felt it as a chilling draft across his bare nape and down the neck of his thin, billowing robe, as they led him hobbling from the room on bare feet. In another small, close room, an anonymous priest waited behind a screen woven of rushes and thin wooden laths to hear his confession. The voice that greeted him in the name of God and invited him to confess his sins was not that of Hubert or Secorim or any of the *Custodes* clergy that he recognized, but he had no doubt that the man *was* a member of that Order—and Javan firmly believed that *Custodes* priests would violate the seal of the confessional without a second thought, if they deemed it for the good of the Order.

So Javan turned his thoughts to the common failings he had rehearsed ahead of time—a general confession that would astonish no one and implicate no one. Easing his weight off his lame foot, he knelt beside a grille set in the screen and bowed his head, crossing himself as he spoke the ritual phrases.

"Bless me, Father, for I have sinned. It has been a day since my last confession, and I have committed no conscious sin since then. But because I am about to take holy vows, I desire to make a general confession covering my life. These are my sins."

Three others sought shriving that morning as well—not as preparation for holy orders, for two were priests themselves, but as fortification against the dangers they might encounter in the hours ahead. Joram and Queron confessed one another, in the still, early morning hours before heading off to make their final preparations, but Evaine sought out Bishop Niallan, after the sanctuary's morning Mass. Like Javan, she did not confide all to her confessor, even though she knew that this priest would keep the confessional's seal even unto death. Still, she did tell him more than she had dared confide to Joram and Queron.

"I have lied to Joram and Queron, Father," she whispered, focusing on one end of the purple stole set around his shoulders. "I have told them there is but little danger in a mission I must perform. But if I told them the truth, they would not let me go—and I must."

Niallan nodded slowly, his steel-grey eyes shuttered and unreadable. They were sitting in Niallan's cell, on the edge of his cot, with Wards set round the little room for privacy.

"This danger," Niallan ventured, sounding her out with consummate skill. "Is it to you alone, or does it involve them as well?"

"There is some small danger to them as well, but they know the risk and are willing to accept it. My risk is far greater."

"And *you* are prepared to accept *that* risk?"

"I am, Father." She looked up at him with bright blue eyes. "I must. And if a sacrifice is required, then I must make that, too. Is it wrong to insist that I be free to make this choice?"

Niallan was looking at her strangely, a taut foreboding playing about the lines around his mouth, and for an instant Evaine was not sure of him.

"You obviously have thought long and carefully about this," he said, after a troubled pause.

"Yes, Father. And I have begged that this cup not be placed before me. But if it is presented, then I must drink it to the dregs."

"And must your children drink it, too, if you should perish in this venture?"

"That is the hardest part of all," she whispered, looking away. "To know that my children may become orphans because of my actions. And yet, I still must take that risk. I've—made arrangements, if I should not return." She handed him a sealed parchment packet. "Fiona will see to my little ones and be a better mother to them than I could be, if I decided not to dare what my heart tells me I must. But only I can do this other thing. Do you understand, Niallan?"

After a moment, he closed his eyes and nodded, laying his hand over her folded ones, his bishop's ring burning like a beacon between them. "Not entirely, child, but it's clear that you have powerful reasons for what you are doing. I—will not question you further, for I sense a power at work here which far transcends anything I might call into play." He glanced up at her with a sad wistfulness. "Will you at least allow me to pray for you?"

"Aye, of course," she said with a faint, tremulous smile. "And there is one other favor you can do for me as well."

"Anything that is within my power, dear child."

"You can give me the Last Anointing and Viaticum, in case my journey takes me—beyond where either of us would have me go. It would give me great comfort."

Niallan winced as if she had struck him a physical blow, but after a few heartbeats he gave a stiff nod.

"If you truly desire it, of course I will do it. You should be aware, however, that Joram and Queron may sense it. The mark of such sacraments is often discernable to priests of their caliber."

"They have their own concerns this morning, Father," she whispered, thinking of the preparations already in progress. "By the time it might become apparent to them, it will be too late to stop me from what I must do."

"Very well, then. If you'll wait here, I'll fetch the oils and a pyx from the chapel."

She slipped to her knees when he had gone out, bowing her head over folded hands to pray.

At noon precisely, monks came to conduct Prince Javan Haldane to the chapel of the *Custodes Fidei*. He had spent the previous hour on his knees in the *disciplinarium*, reciting the *Pater nosters* and other prayers assigned by his confessor. Fortunately, his general confession had not required more physical penance. The monks who came to collect him pulled a second robe of nubbly white wool over his head and set a new, lighted beeswax candle in his hand before leading him out into the corridors of the archbishop's palace.

Javan was very conscious of his limp, and felt very young and very small as he made his painful way down the stairs to approach the open chapel door. The *Custodes* had taken over a former refectory for their chapel—vaulted and windowless, stark and austere in decor, but easily large enough to hold the score of priests, knights, and serving brothers of the Order who waited to witness his profession. Instead of a crucifix, the wall above the altar bore a huge fresco of the Christ as *Pantocrator*, the Creator of All, royally enthroned and crowned as He would appear at the end of time, to judge the world. Strategic touches of gold leaf made the dark, hypnotic eyes seem to stare directly at Javan, standing all the way outside the chapel door. The book of the Gospels lay open in His left hand, showing the Alpha and the Omega, even as His right hand was raised in blessing—or in judgment. Javan had seen this *Christos* before, and doubted he could expect much compassion from those who served Him.

Two knights of the Order stood to attention at either side of the opened door, silent and expressionless in their black brigandines, the scarlet-lined mantles of the Order flung back on their shoulders. Inside, black-cassocked *Custodes* brethren lined the center aisle down which Javan must pass, all of them girt with the double cincture of Haldane crimson and gold which he, too, would shortly wear; all with short, hooded capes lined with crimson, the haloed lion badge of the Order bright on their shoulders.

Paulin of Ramos, the Order's Vicar General, was waiting at the end of that aisle, flanked by his Inquisitor General on the one side and by Father Secorim, the abbot of this particular *Custodes* chapter, on the other. Paulin's staff glittered in the candlelight, the sword in the lion's paw catching the fire in a lance of light, reminding

Javan again of the power this man now held over so many innocent people. To the left, Archbishop Hubert lent the weight of his presence and approval to this gathering, coped and mitered as he observed from a thronelike chair. Javan was trembling by the time he had passed through that gauntlet of men he knew sworn to destroy the people he held most dear in the world, and he had to be helped back to his feet after making his genuflection at the foot of the altar steps.

"Javan Jashan Urien Haldane." Paulin spoke the name like a judge reading a death sentence, pointing the head of the staff at him like an accusatory finger of deadly steel. "What would you of the *Ordo Custodum Fidei*?"

Dry-throated, his heart pounding in his chest, Javan managed a reasonably competent liturgical bow, right hand pressed to his breast as he held his candle aloft in his left hand.

"God aiding me, Father General," he said steadily, "I would try my vocation in this House."

In that same moment, as a sworn enemy of Deryni came to take a candle from the hand of a prince with burgeoning Deryni powers, a Deryni sorceress paused at the foot of the dais steps leading up to a bier formed of four black and four white cubes. It was not the wooden one that she, Joram, and Queron had constructed beneath the *keeill*, but the more strongly evocative one where Orin had lain. They had decided, only days before, that their working should not be attempted so close within the confines of the Camberian Council, lest those keeping the watch for Sylvan and Tavis detect their activity. In addition, this chamber provided a safe and suitable place for their subject to rest in the future, if today's work should not succeed.

The three of them had brought Camber's body down the night before, laying it on the bier under the net of *shiral* crystals. They had set Wards around it. Joram and Queron had returned to make the rest of the physical preparations early this morning, freeing Evaine in these last hours to compose herself for the working.

Joram turned to gaze down at her as she hesitated, Queron also coming to the edge of the dais to meet her. The Healer had donned his Gabrilite robes of white for the occasion, with the green of one of Rhys' old Healer's mantles thrown around his shoulders to provide a visual link for Evaine. Joram wore his formal Michaeline robes—deep blue cassock and mantle, the white sash of his knighthood, and the knotted scarlet girdle that was also the mark of a Michaeline. His father's sword hung at his side. Beyond them, just visible in the light of the plain white tapers set at the quarters of the dais circle, Evaine could see the gleaming length of the black side of the bier, only a vague smudge of lighter shadow above it hinting at its precious burden.

"You're sure you want to go through with this?" Joram said, as she started up the steps, lifting the skirts of her gown of dusty black.

The slate was cold beneath her bare feet, and the marble of the black and white checkered dais floor colder still. She did not answer Joram, only going to gaze down almost reverently at the body laid out on the bier. The net of *shiral* crystals had been removed. A white drape covered his loins, but otherwise he was naked. They had taken off his Michaeline habit, to give Queron immediate access to the wounds that had brought him to the edge of death and would kill him yet, if not tended as soon as he was revived—*if* he could be revived. The wounds looked fresh, even after this long, but there was no blood. Turning her gaze to his face, serene and composed within its frame of silver-gilt hair, Evaine could almost believe he only slept. And his hands—the hands were still cupped in that odd, static attitude close above his heart, as if to keep something precious from slipping away.

"The gash along his hip *looks* the worst," Queron said, coming to stand quietly at her elbow and gesturing toward it with his hand. "The thigh wound was more serious, though. He lost a great deal of blood from that one. I'll have to go very deep to repair it, and I'll have to work very quickly. The other wounds are reasonably superficial, but the aggregate blood loss was staggering. If this were any ordinary sort of case, I'd have liked a second Healer present," he added wistfully.

Evaine grimaced to see the wounds, but she had seen them before, when she helped Joram wash and lay him out for burial. Seeing them afresh, though, she wondered whether Queron *would* be able to save him, even if she did manage to bring him back.

"I can do it," he murmured, answering the question she dared not ask. "You just worry about your part. Or—*don't* worry. Just do what you know you have to do. When it's over, I'll put *you* back together, too, if you overextend."

Joram's snort said what *he* thought of that notion, but he turned away before Evaine could see his face. Drawing a slow, steadying breath, she lifted her head to the shadowed ceiling overhead, forcing her doubts back beyond conscious concern, then exhaled softly, balance restored. She wore Jodotha's torque around her neck, and felt its weight across her throat as she looked back at them.

"*None* of us is going to overextend," she said briskly. "We'll take things one step at a time, as usual. I believe it's customary to ward the circle first. We'll begin by centering."

She would work from the South when they began the actual ritual, for she must face the Northern gate to Call him back. But for now, she moved to the East, where a censer released faint wisps of an incense that tugged at the senses, its undertone just slightly different from the usual liturgical blend. Queron moved to the East as well, for he would keep his watch at the head of the bier, ready to work his Healer's magic at the appropriate time. The aspergillum he handed her was a tuft of evergreen bound to a handle of myrtlewood, stuck in a small silver bucket of holy water. Joram, taking up his station in the West, removed his sheathed sword from his belt and laid it on the floor at the foot of the bier, standing then to balance Queron. He would not look at Evaine, though, and kept his eyes averted until she had turned to face the East, the aspergillum held across her heart.

"Terribilis est locus iste," she said in a low voice, after a moment. *"Hic domus Dei est, et porta caeli . . ."* Terrible is this place; it is the house of God, and the gate of Heaven, and it shall be called the court of God.

"Amen," Queron replied, Joram joining in just behind him.

After inscribing a cross in the air before her with the aspergillum, Evaine turned to her right and began tracing the first circle with holy water, chanting the ancient words as she moved.

"Asperges me, Domine, hyssopo, et mundabor; lavabis me, et super nivem dealbabor . . ." Sprinkle me, O Lord, with hyssop, and I shall be purified; wash me, and I shall be whiter than snow . . .

She kept her eyes half closed as she walked the circle, feeling the familiar energies start to build. Peace settled upon her like a mantle as she marked the confines of the circle with the tracery of holy water, serenity shimmering like a fog in the trail of droplets she left, surging heavenward at each quarter, where she paused to salute.

By the time she completed her circuit, she was as centered as she had ever been, totally detached from her former fear. She knew Queron sensed it as she sprinkled him; she could see it in his eyes as he made her a deep bow before taking the aspergillum to sprinkle her in turn.

Drop down, ye dew from heaven . . . The words whispered in her mind, a further blessing from Queron, who actually understood a little of what she must go through, without even being told. His tranquillity accompanied her as she went to Joram, who bowed his head dutifully to receive the purification, arms crossed on his breast, no longer presenting anything but centered harmony.

Turning to her father's body was harder, but she kept her thoughts centered on her purpose as she sprinkled the recumbent form with holy water in the form of a cross. Nor did she linger to look at him before returning to the East to put aside the aspergillum. Queron was tipping more incense into the thurible as she moved on to her place in the South, and she bowed her head and crossed her hands on her breast as he began the second casting of the circle, billowing clouds of sweet-smelling smoke following him and hanging on the air.

"*Dirigatur, Domine, oratio mea, sicut incensum, in conspectu tuo . . .*" Welcome as incense smoke let my prayer rise up before thee, Lord; when I lift up my hands, be it as acceptable as the evening sacrifice . . .

Incense of a stronger sort and concentration tickled at Javan's nostrils as he knelt before Paulin of Ramos and Father Secorim. Paulin had taken his candle and set it on the altar. Admonished as to the duties and responsibilities of a cleric, as well as the privileges, Javan was now to receive the tonsure. It would not be the full tonsure of one entering major orders—and indeed, those taking vows as lay brethren were not even required to be tonsured—but Hubert and Secorim had decided that the symbolism was important, and Paulin had concurred.

"You have come of your own free will to make this commitment," Paulin told him, reading from a great book that one of his monks held—a statement which was not precisely true, but Javan knew he had no other real choice just now. "Because the next years will be a time of testing your vocation, which is as yet unformed and untrained," Paulin went on, "it is meet and right that you should set yourself apart from the world and its distractions. Donning the garment of humility is a symbol of this setting apart, as is the putting aside of your secular attire. In further token of your commitment to this path you have freely chosen, we cut a lock of your hair, as an outward symbol of the sacrifice of a part of your very body in pledge of fidelity to God's work."

Javan closed his eyes as the Vicar General took up a pair of golden shears from a tray another monk brought him. He could hardly bear Paulin's touch, gathering what felt like a monstrous hank of hair from his crown. He forced himself not to flinch as the shears snipped close to the scalp in a solid, metallic snick.

In fact, the lock was no bigger around than a man's thumb. Javan caught just a glimpse of it before Paulin laid it in a small silver bowl held by one of his monks and continued with an exhortation to prayer, forcing Javan to bow his head.

"O Lord, strengthen Thy servant Javan in his resolve, that he may be a worthy aspirant to the high vocation for which Thou callest him . . ."

The circle glowed around the dais where Evaine waited, as she also prayed that God might strengthen her in her resolve. Joram had traced the third and final circle with the sword, setting the spell in place with brisk Michaeline thoroughness, and the dome of the circle's protection arched above their heads in a shimmering violet span, proof against any force wielded by mere mortals—even Deryni ones.

Now the formal Wards must be set, calling upon the protection of those great archangelic beings who ruled the elemental forces. They had agreed that Queron and Joram should make the actual invocations, leaving Evaine free to embellish on the images they conjured and to integrate them into her own protective and supportive framework. She faced the East from where she stood, extending her senses to note and savor every nuance of power summoned, as Queron began, lifting his arms to the East to conjure golden handfire and send it streaking into the flame of the eastern ward candle as he called the Guardian of Air.

"Behold the Mystery of Air—even Raphael, the life-giving One, veiled in the wings of wind and storm. Come, mighty Raphael, and grace us with thy presence and protection!"

Evaine could not see the great Presence suddenly looming behind the eastern candle, but It was there. Her mind filled in the details of convention—the pale hair lifting on the breeze that likewise stirred half-transparent draperies of palest gold and cream and yellow, pressing them close around a slender yet powerful form, lithe and straight as a willow wand. Raphael looked nothing like that, of course, having no true physical form. Nonetheless, she inclined her head in salute to what the image meant to *her*, before turning to the south, aware of Joram circling the bier deosil to come and stand beside her facing South.

"Behold the Mystery of Fire—even Michael, the consecrating One, veiled in the flames of all that is eternal," Joram said, following the pattern that Queron had set and sending conjured handfire to glow crimson and orange in the southern ward candle. "Come, mighty Michael, and grace us with thy presence and protection!"

Evaine had an impression of fiery wings, though they shed no physical light or heat, and built up the rest of the image for herself—the tall, stern visage, flaming hair surging from the discipline of a fillet of ruddy gold; golden body armor, finely scaled like salamander skin; the flaming sword, echoing the one on the Michaeline badge on Joram's mantle. Ah, she knew Michael very well.

Saluting him, she and Joram turned to face the West, where Queron now strode to call up bluish-green handfire, sending it forth from between his palms like a streak of comet fire.

"Behold the Mystery of Water—even Gabriel, the purifying One, veiled in the coolness of the seas and lakes and summer rain. Come, mighty Gabriel, and grace us with thy presence and protection!"

She locked on the image of Gabriel almost immediately—pale blues and greens and dappled lavenders, ever-shifting, winged like the others but glistening with running water, as if constantly emerging from a sunlit waterfall. She gave profound salute to Gabriel, who was also the Herald of the Blessed Virgin, and breathed a prayer for special intercession.

Joram left her and moved to the North. The icy imagery of snow-encrusted pools came to mind as Evaine turned her concentration Northward—not the warm sparkle of sunlit showers—for she had long since guessed that her ultimate business must be with the harsh Lord of Earth rather than the Lady's mercy.

"Behold, the Mystery of Earth," Joram whispered, a slight tremor in his voice betraying *his* recognition of that requirement, as he conjured the green fire that signified that quarter. "Even Uriel, the Stabilizing One, veiled in the gems and caverns of the deepest places, who callest all at last to the Nether Shore. Come, mighty Uriel, and grace us with thy presence and protection!"

Thunder brooded beyond the northern light, and the very air within the circle took on a heavy, charged, oppressive quality that tasted faintly of sulphur. Evaine caught a faint impression of a shifting, green-black mantle, iridescent as a magpie's wings, but Uriel declined to show a face. He was out there, though; she could feel it. And she would have to deal with him—as she had always known she would.

The hands she had crossed on her breast were trembling as she turned back to the East and bowed in final salute, completing the circle, and she had to press the top one hard over the one beneath, willing her heart to slow to its previous measured rhythm. She drew several deep breaths to calm herself, knowing the others were waiting for her to continue, and drew renewed strength and determination from the time-honored phrases that doubtless had been spoken in this very chamber for who knew how many years.

"We stand outside time, in a place not of earth," she said, knowing that it was true. "As our ancestors before us bade, we join together and are one."

She could feel the others binding into the link, making it so, and knew the further strengthening of that bond as Joram began the ancient invocation.

"By Thy blessed Evangelists, Matthew, Mark, Luke, and John; by all Thy Holy Angels; by all Powers of Light and Shadow, we call Thee to guard and defend us from all perils, O Most High."

"Thus it is and has ever been," Queron continued. "Thus it will be for all times to come. *Per omnia saecula saeculorum.*"

The great *Amen* that they raised in affirmation of that prayer set the seal on their coming together, resonating with the strength and unity of their combined will, and the crosses they traced upon their breasts became as armor, proof against all but the Will of God Himself. Secure in that knowledge, Evaine raised her arms to her two compatriots, speaking the words of the *exortio* as a personal affirmation of their intent.

"Now we are met. Now we are one. Regard the Ancient Ways. We shall not walk this Path again. So be it."

"So be it!" they replied, saluting her with right hands to hearts.

In response, Evaine crossed her hands on her breast and bowed to them before settling quietly on the little stool they had set for her in the south, fetching from beneath it a worn leather pouch containing ward cubes that had been her father's. These she upended into her lap as Queron moved into position at the head of the bier, his open hands resting lightly to either side of Camber's quicksilver hair, already settling into Healer's trance.

While Evaine separated the cubes, white in her right hand and black in her left, Joram withdrew to stand just to the left and inside of the light marking the northern quarter, hands resting quietly now on the quillons of a sword he had borne under similar circumstances many years before, the night a king died—ready to open a gate, as he had that other time, and probably with little more knowledge or awareness of what might happen when he did. Evaine pushed down a tiny twinge of remorse as she glanced up at him—dear, gentle, stubborn Joram, trusting her, even though he did not approve or understand—and prayed that he would not think too harshly of her after it was over. Standing there in the flickering light of the ward candles and the glow from the arch of the circle, his pale head bent over his folded hands, he looked very much like the man lying on the bier.

She made a tiny pillar of the black cubes then, stacking them in the center of a black square diagonally to the left of the one on which her left foot rested. The four white cubes she placed on the white square diagonally to her right. She drew a deep breath as she straightened, setting her hands on the tops of her thighs and holding the breath for a few heartbeats before letting it out slowly.

So. Before her was a glyph of what she had to do, childish in its simplicity—a symbolic rendering of the task for which all the rest had been but prologue, carefully crafted to bring her to this moment.

For by the power of her will alone, and for the sake of the man who had trained her to use that power of will, she now must make of those tiny, symbolic pillars the very real and solid Pillars of the Temple—the temple of the Inner Mysteries, whose corridors communicated with Divinity Itself and life and death, at levels only rarely given to mortals still bound by physical form.

Between these Pillars she must pass, in a very real sense, and even beyond the Purple Veil itself, if she had any hope of bringing that man back.

CHAPTER THIRTY

*Where is Uriel the angel, who came unto me at
the first? for he hath caused me to fall into
many trances.*

—II Esdras 10:28

Smothering darkness enveloped Javan briefly as he knelt at the feet
of the Vicar General of the *Custodes Fidei*. It was only the hooded
black scapular of the Order being pulled over his head, but it felt
like a pillow, choking off his breath.

"Receive this vesture of our Order as a shield and a protection
against the wiles of the wicked ones," Paulin intoned—by which
Javan knew he meant the Deryni. "Thus, if thou art steadfast against
the enemies of God, thou mayest change it one day for a robe of
glory."

Robe of glory, indeed! As Secorim joined Paulin to free his head,
adjusting the hood to lie smoothly down his back, Javan thought of
little Giesele MacLean. That hapless innocent surely wore a robe
of glory now, safe and secure in the hands of God, but she had been
murdered by men who espoused the same dark purposes as the *Custodes*. And if Archbishop Hubert, watching so sanctimoniously from
his episcopal throne, had *not* had a hand in her death, he certainly
had been responsible for the deaths of other Deryni, and for founding
the *Custodes*.

Javan hated the stiff, crimson-lined scapular of the Order, though
at least it bore only the moline cross of a lay brother on the left
breast, and not the full *Custodes* achievement of the haloed lion.
Yet he was committing himself to wear it daily, indefinitely—and
there was worse to come. Later in the ceremony, after he had made
his vows, he would receive the braided cincture of crimson and gold

to hold the scapular in place, symbolic of the binding of those vows. He hated that even more, because it profaned the colors of his House by what the *Custodes* stood for.

Before that indignity, however, came the prostration and litany—and before that, he realized, as someone put the silver bowl with his lock of hair in his hands, he must make an even more personal offering on the altar of the *Custodes*. Paulin and Secorim stepped apart to give him access, and Javan rose shakily, a hand steadying him under one elbow.

"*Introibo ad altare Dei,*" the assembled *Custodes* sang. I will go up to the altar of God, to God Who gives joy to my youth.

But there was no joy in Javan Haldane as he mounted the altar steps that afternoon. The painted eyes of the Pantocrator seemed to pierce him through the heart as he made his genuflection, and he wondered, not for the first time, how the *Custodes* managed to justify the atrocities they committed in His Name. Asking Him, he lifted the bowl briefly in his two hands, as he had been coached, bowing his head slightly in acknowledgment of whatever Higher Force there was that transcended the narrowness that the *Custodes'* God allowed. His prayer, as he set his offering on the altar, was simple: *Deliver me, O Lord, from mine enemies, and make me worthy to serve Thee.*

He kept those words in his mind and heart as he backed haltingly down the steps again, awkward on his lame foot, to prostrate himself where he had knelt before, arms outstretched in the attitude of crucifixion—a further offering of himself for the True God's use. After a long, long moment, when he could only hear the beating of his own heart, a choir began to chant an invocation to the Holy Spirit, and he let their words take him deep into his own meditation.

Closing her eyes, Evaine, too, set herself to sinking deeper and deeper into trance—controlling breathing, centering energies, slowly beginning to build the requisite images on the inner planes. In her mind's eye, she could see all as it was—the tiny cubes stacked where the great Pillars must rise; the bier beyond them, black-polished side reflecting her own image, pale face and hands and feet suspended against a reddish glow that was the Southern Ward, sitting straight and erect like some slumbering goddess of earlier times.

Atop the bier, the pale outline of her father's body seemed to float like a sea-borne wraith, the white drape across his middle spilling almost to the floor on her side. Queron was a cool, silvery pillar of strength and power standing at the head, energy already flaring around his head and Healer's hands—quiescent, ready. Beyond them, the shadow of Joram's head and shoulders, sober in Michaeline blue, loomed against the blacker background of the North. And *there* lay the challenge, beyond the Northern Gate. *There* lay the One she must face, if she hoped to bring her father back to the land of the living.

Drawing a deep breath and settling even deeper into the Otherness requisite for these sorts of workings, Evaine returned her attention to the Pillars, seeing them swell and grow, pushing toward the ceiling—certainly to the limits of the circle—stabilizing as the circle contained them. In the shadow world to which she now turned her concentration, she knew the Pillars to be as substantial as the floor under her feet, solid with a power which transcended the mere time and space of the physical world. A mist seemed to have intensified between the Pillars, even as the Pillars themselves solidified, and she stood up in her astral form to look more closely, rising out of the body that sat so quietly behind her.

Queron apparently sensed the movement, for he came physically to stand behind her physical body, laying his Healer's hands on her shoulders and linking with her physical functions to make sure she remembered to breathe, her heart to beat. She watched him curiously for several seconds, a part of her aware that she had never, ever been so deep before, even when she used to work with Rhys.

Then she turned around and saw the Figure standing just beyond the Pillars. A faint breeze seemed to stir gossamer robes of citrine, olive, russet, and black, and just a hint of towering opalescent wings, lifting softly curling locks of titian hair around an achingly beautiful face. She thought it might be the angel of her dream of the rings, though she could not be sure. She did not remember the eyes being so intense—a yellowish, grass-green, like peridots, seeing through to her very soul.

Respect and honor to thee, Shining One, and to the One Whom thou servest, Evaine breathed, daring to give the being salute, right hand to breast, as she would hail one of the Quarter Lords.

The being inclined its head in acceptance of the salute, apparently taking no offense, but not speaking, either. Instead of rings this time, the graceful hands held two silver cups. As one was raised and tipped above the other, the contents poured out in an unending, light-shimmering cascade of all the colors of creation, filling and spilling around the being's feet in a pool of living luminescence that neither grew nor diminished.

Thou showest me rainbows, Evaine said. *The symbol of God's promise that He should never again destroy the world by water.*

Indeed, the being spoke in her mind. *By water doth He bring the world salvation, both by holy baptism and by the rite which serves to save thy people. The one is for all to cherish, by many outward faiths, in many different forms; the other shall be of but a little duration, but shall save many.*

Revan's mission is but short-lived, then? Evaine questioned, sorrow blunting her hope. *More innocents must perish at the hands of the Blind?*

The Blind, too, shall see—one day, the being replied. *Thy work shall not have been in vain, nor the sacrifices made by thee and thine. Thy soul's mate awaits thee, when thine earthly tasks are done. Thou hast served well. Naught further is required of thee.*

For just an instant, Rhys seemed to stand before her, as real as anything in the chamber, looking as he had in their younger days, green-clad and laughing, his Healer's hands held out to her in love and pride. She raised a hand to touch him, but he melted away before her eyes. And in that instant, the impact of the angel's *other* words set her gasping.

No! Something further is required! Why dost thou tempt me from the task I came to do? She gestured toward the body on the bier, visible *through* the being. *My work will not be done until he is free!*

The being looked a bit bemused by that, cocking its beautiful head wistfully as it brought the cups to breast level, still standing in a pool of iridescence.

Thy quest is known to me, Child of Earth, the being said, after a slight pause. *And I know whom thou seekest. Where he doth dwell, thou canst not go.*

Do you hold him, then? Evaine dared to ask.

Not I, Child of Earth, but he is held.

May I see him, then?

That favor is not mine to grant.

Then, will you let me pass?

The risk is great to mortals—even those of thy race.

I know the risk! You gave me the keys to read it for myself! Evaine cried. *But, he is mortal, too, and I know he is not wholly free.*

He chose his fate, the being replied.

Aye, without knowing fully what he chose. Let me free him! Holding him serves no purpose.

For a long moment, the being simply gazed into Evaine's eyes, the beautiful face clouded with an expression of incredible compassion. The depth of that gaze reached into her very soul, stripping away all subterfuge, laying bare all strengths and failings. When Evaine thought she could bear it no longer—though pulling away was unthinkable—the peridot eyes shifted to the cups.

Instinctively Evaine held out her hands as the cups tilted toward her, catching at a weightless froth of cobweb-fragile stuff as it billowed over her hands. Gradually it solidified into a silklike strip like a scarf or stole that would not settle down to any one color. It trailed nearly to the ground from both her hands, both burning and chilling, at the same time, and she sought the being's eyes in question.

Take this token as a sign that thou hast passed this portal with my blessings, the being said. *Thou must seek a higher One than I, and thou must be prepared to give whatever price is asked. Thou shalt have but one chance. To falter is to perish utterly, along with him and those who aid thee. To persevere may also cost thy life and the lives of others, if thou hast not the strength to do what must be done. Thou alone canst attempt this thing, but thou shalt not suffer alone, if thou failest. Dost thou understand?*

Nodding, Evaine clutched the rainbow to her bosom, fearing for Joram and Queron now, though her own fear was gone utterly.

I understand, she whispered. *What must I do?*

For answer, the being merely smiled sadly and backed between the Pillars, to vanish in a shrinking point of light.

Very well. She had her answer. As she had suspected all along, she must pass between the twin Pillars of Severity and Mercy, making of her own body and soul the Middle Pillar of Equilibrium. Only in perfect harmony, in perfect balance, might she dare to essay the crossing to that Higher One to whom her guide had alluded. Only in perfect equilibrium might she hope to gain audience with the Force that held her father balanced between the worlds.

She cast the rainbow over her hair like a veil as she prepared to step between the Pillars. Mist lay just beyond, but she paid it no heed as she set the balances. The fog was cold and close as she took a first step and then a second, and a brief moment of vertigo clutched at her stomach, but it passed quickly. For a moment she could make out nothing. But then the fog began to melt away in strips and she could see.

She seemed to stand at the edge of a vast, open plain beneath a star-clogged sky. Frost made the very air crackle, and crunched beneath her bare feet, but she did not feel the cold. Far on the horizon before her, something darker blotted out the stars. It grew larger as she started walking toward it, and her feet seemed to grow heavier with every step she took.

Gradually, the shape became a massive trilithon, two great, upright stones supporting a third. The space beneath the capstone reminded her of the niches in the *keeill*, and she wondered whether its builders might have drawn their inspiration from just such a vision as she now was experiencing. As she drew nearer, her feet felt as if each new step was trying to shift the Earth itself, until she realized she was drawing near to the very Gate of Earth.

And beyond the Gate of Earth lay the realm of the Archangel of Earth, the mighty Uriel, whose provenance was not only the mountains and caverns and craggy cliffs but the bounty of growing things, and the cycle of death and rebirth, of flesh as well as vegetation—even the bringer of life to a close, and transition, and the bringer at last to the Nether Shore, where souls passed to their judgment. It was Uriel she must face—Uriel, declining to manifest when they set the Wards, waiting for her to cross into *his* territory.

She would oblige, then—for was this not what she had come to do, to discover the Force that bound her father's soul and bargain for his release? The opening beneath the trilithon was the entrance to that other realm. She breathed a last prayer for courage as she crossed her hands on her breast and stepped inside. Closing her eyes then, for she knew the Angel would not communicate by sight or sound, she opened her mind to stillness and waited.

Pressure. Power. A swooping, stifling sensation, as if buried inside living rock, constricting, restraining—and then—limbo. She did not struggle through any of it, only opening herself to the rhythm of the earth, riding its tides, passively attentive.

After a time, a query formed in her mind. How dared she come here? What good could she hope to gain? He whom she sought was well enough content where he was, though more constrained than he might have been, had he been able to wield the energies correctly. He had not passed over to the Nether Shore, into true death, but neither was he entirely free to walk upon the earth. Nor would he wish to return as mere mortal, having tasted the potential of his present state, constrained though it was by his blunder and limited to only occasional forays back across the great Divide.

Ponderously, Evaine tried to comprehend, only gradually coming to fathom just what her father had done. His spell had worked—to a point. Camber had bypassed Death, but only at a terrible cost. In exchange for the freedom to move occasionally between the worlds, continuing in spirit the work no longer possible in his damaged body, he had forfeited, at least for a time, the awesome ecstacy of union with the All High. Had he been more canny with his spellbinding, he might have won both, at once free to come and go in the Sacred Presence and to walk in both worlds as God's agent and emissary.

But Camber had not fully understood the spell he wove, in that moment of imminent death. Death had not bound him, no. But he was bound, nonetheless. By the fierce exercise of his extraordinary will, he had sometimes been able to break through to the world and make his presence felt, but those times were rare indeed, and costly on a level only comprehensible to those who have glimpsed the Face of God—or been denied that glimpse. And until the balance should be set right, by the selfless sacrifice of someone willing to pay in potent coin, that Face might remain forever hidden from Camber Kyriell MacRorie.

Evaine lingered hardly at all over her decision. She had guessed for some time that it would come to this. Bringing Camber back to life clearly was out of the question, and mere death would but set him back on the Wheel, to start again in another incarnation without benefit of any of the wisdom gained so dearly in this life—no insurmountable calamity for so advanced a soul as Camber, but a most untimely loss for human and Derynikind just now, whose cause he had served so faithfully and so long.

So she must release him to that joyful purpose beyond life, in which great adepts chose their work and eschewed the Great Return in preference for specialized assignments, teaching mankind to grow in the likeness of God. For herself, the choice would mean death of the body, for mortal flesh could not sustain the outpouring of energy she must make to send *him* on into that next dimension; but she had known the sacrifice was likely. Others had gone fearlessly unto death; so would she.

And there would be Rhys, waiting for her when her work was done, and her beloved Aidan—and other friends and partners in the Great Dance who had also fallen in the cause of the Light. It was not an ignoble end. Nor was it even an end at all.

Humbly she laid her decision before the One who had granted her a hearing. In peace, she came to know how it must be done. All in centeredness, she willed herself back into her body, imparting the information to Queron in the same thought with which she forbade him to try to stop her. The Healer's hands trembled on her shoulders, but he did not raise his head, only helping her maintain her deeply centered state as she opened her eyes upon the physical world once more and made herself look at her brother.

"I'm ready, Joram," she said softly, her love for him welling up in her breast as he looked up at her with a start. "Open a gate to the North, and we'll be done with it. Remember the night that Cinhil died. This once, please don't argue. Just do it—for me."

The color drained from his face as she rose, Queron's arm still around her shoulders, and walked slowly to the near side of her father's bier, passing easily between the Pillars this time—the Pillars that only *looked* like stacks of tiny cubes of ivory and ebon. Somehow she knew that Queron had not made the same passage, though physically he still supported her on her right.

Joram did not argue, either. He had opened his mouth as if to speak, but then he only closed it and bowed his head over his sword, shifting his right hand to its hilt as he turned to face the North. A moment he paused, the sword extended diagonally across his body with the point resting at the edge of the circle, where the shimmering dome met the edge of the dais. Then he slowly drew the blade upwards and across, sweeping down to his right, cutting an arching doorway in the very fabric of the circle. A darker darkness yawned outside, and then a gust of wind carried a flurry of dead leaves into the circle—altogether real and substantial!

Joram looked stunned at that, but still he made no protest, only backing reluctantly to the left, clear of the opening, to sink to one knee. He braced the sword against the upraised one and leaned his cheek against the hilt, but he would not turn his face toward her. He would be expecting Camber to pass beyond the circle. She hoped he would not be too angry when she went on instead.

Smiling, Evaine turned back to her father, bidding Queron withdraw with a grateful caress of mind to mind. He inclined his head in acceptance before stepping back from the bier, his hands at his sides, no longer even making pretense that he intended to try to heal Camber's wounds. She sensed Joram's tension at the movement, but he did not turn around—a mercy for which she blessed him.

Gathering all of her love and hope and power, she laid her hands on her father's hands, surrounding the cupped curve, molding her own hands to fit his, easing the curve apart. At the same time, she eased her mind into the pattern of the spell he had woven, seeking the binding, touching a flicker of his awareness of what she was doing, reassuring him that her choice was freely made, in an ultimate service of their cause and of her love for him.

You shall go on, and I shall go on, in separate paths for the present, but ultimately to meet in the Light, she told him. *It is meet. It is fitting. You have your work, and I have mine. I love you, Father, but there is another man waiting for me, and he and I have been parted for far too long.*

She would not allow his protest, for she sensed that other's coming, outside the circle—and that Other, familiar now, Who waited as *he* had done before, when a king passed by. It was time. She was ready.

Closing her eyes, she let herself settle even deeper into concentration, reaching for the energies she now knew how to tap—searching out that other power nexus, close beneath his heart, where all his binding to this physical plane was centered. It was simple, really. All she had to do, to make the balance right, was to reach out with her mind, just—so.

She let herself become a living channel as the power began to flow, bidding it funnel through her hands and into *him*, building and building, *pushing* the energy as the speed and pressure of the flow increased, even though she knew she did irreparable damage to a body of mere flesh. She felt no pain at all. She drew power from the Warding energies, from the reservoirs of the cubes beneath his body, from the very depths of her own lifeforce—and beyond. The completion was sudden and profound, like a deep organ note sounding through her entire body, or a gong left reverberating on the silence after blessing.

For just an instant, she gained one final sensory impression: an overwhelming visual image of her father, all his wounds healed and a semblance of youth restored, opening his eyes to smile up at her in love, compassion, understanding, even forgiveness and gratitude for the inestimable price she had paid for his release.

Then he was simply gone, and she was turning her face to the gateway in the circle, where a dearly beloved man with unruly red hair and laughter in his amber eyes beckoned to her with one outstretched hand, a giggling nine-year-old perched precariously astride the green-mantled shoulders. She gave no further thought to the body she left behind, as it collapsed softly into Queron's arms like a spent set of sails. She had eyes only for the man, the boy—and then the great Light that beckoned from beyond the shadows as she passed outside, caught up in a flutter of green-black wings.

Joram did not see her go, too intent on her fainting body to turn his Sight outward, but Queron Saw. It was the last thing he saw with eyes or Sight for three days, and a sight he would remember until his dying day.

The Heirs of Saint Camber

INDEX OF CHARACTERS[1]

AARON, Brother—Queron's alias among the Willimites.

ADRIAN MacLean, Lord—grandson of Camber's sister Aislinn and father of Camber Allin (called "Camlin"); killed with Rhys' and Evaine's son Aidan and others at Trurill, by the regents' men. (*)

AGNES Murdoch, Lady—eighteen-year-old daughter of Murdoch of Carthane, wed to the Regent Rhun.

AIDAN Thuryn—deceased eldest son of Rhys and Evaine; mistaken for Camlin MacLean at Trurill and killed by the regents' men, age 10. (*)

AILIN MacGregor, Bishop—*see MacGregor, Bishop Ailin.*

AIRSID, The—an ancient Deryni fellowship, origin pre-500 AD. (*)

AISLINN MacRorie MacLean, Lady—late sister of Camber, who died at Trurill; dowager Countess of Kierney and mother of Iain, the present earl. (*)

ALANA d'Oriel—wife of the captive Healer Oriel.

ALBERTUS, Lord—Grand Master of the *Equites Custodum Fidei*; as Peter Sinclair, former Earl of Tarleton, was present with Rhun at the sack of St. Neot's; brother of Paulin of Ramos.

ALFRED of Woodbourne, Bishop—Auxiliary Bishop of Rhemuth; formerly confessor to King Cinhil.

ALISTER Cullen, Bishop—Deryni former Vicar General of the Order of Saint Michael; Bishop of Grecotha and Chancellor of Gwynedd under King Cinhil; briefly, Archbishop of Valoret & Primate of All Gwynedd; alternate identity of Camber; a founding member of the Camberian Council.

---

[1] A (*) indicates a character mentioned only in passing, possibly deceased.

ALROY Bearand Brion Haldane, King—age 12; under-age King of Gwynedd; elder twin of Javan.

ALOYSIUS, Father—a canon priest at Valoret Cathedral.

AMBERT Quinnell of Cassan, Prince—client prince of Cassan, northwest of Gwynedd; father-in-law of Fane Fitz-Arthur, Tammaron's heir. (*)

ANNE Quinnell, Princess—daughter of Prince Ambert of Cassan and wife of Fane Fitz-Arthur. (*)

ANSCOM of Trevas, Archbishop—deceased Deryni Primate of Gwynedd. (*)

ANSEL Irial MacRorie, Lord—age 18; younger son of the slain Cathan; grandson of Camber.

ARIELLA of Festil, Princess—slain elder sister of the late King Imre and mother of his son, Mark. (*)

ARION of Torenth, King—age 18; newly crowned King of Torenth. (*)

AURELIAN, Dom—a young Gabrilite Healer who took refuge with Gregory at Trevalga.

BONIFACE, Father—a priest at Saint Hilary's Basilica in Rhemuth; calligrapher and illuminator.

BONNER Sinclair, Lord—Earl of Tarleton; nineteen-year-old son of Peter Sinclair, the former Earl of Tarleton (later Lord Albertus, Grand Master of the *Equites Custodum Fidei*); nephew of Bishop Paulin.

BURTON, Father—a priest of the *Custodes Fidei*.

CAMBER Kyriell MacRorie, Saint—former Earl of Culdi; father of Joram and Evaine; canonized as Saint Camber in 906; sainthood rescinded by Council of Ramos in 917.

CAMLIN MacLean, Lord—age 11; son of the slain Adrian MacLean, Master of Kierney, whose rightful heir he is; survived crucifixion at the hands of the regents' soldiers at Trurill; aka Camber Allin MacLean.

CATHAN Drummond—age 8; son of Elinor and Jamie Drummond.

CATHAN MacRorie—slain elder son of Camber, father of Ansel and the deceased Davin. (*)

CHARLAN—Javan's new squire.

CINHIL Donal Ifor Haldane, King—late King of Gwynedd (reigned 904–917); father of Alroy, Javan, and Rhys Michael. (*)

CONCANNON, Father Marcus—*see Marcus Concannon, Father.*

CONNOR—a guard at Valoret Castle in the service of the regents.

CRONIN, Brother—Abbot of St. Mary's in the Hills.

CULLEN, Bishop Alister—*see Alister Cullen*.

CUSTODES FIDEI—the Guardians of the Faith; religious Order founded by Paulin of Ramos to reform ecclesiastical education in Gwynedd for the exclusion of Deryni.

DAVET Nevan, Bishop—deceased itinerant bishop. (*)

DECLAN Carmody—Deryni in service of the regents; one of the two Deryni in chains with Rhun at sack of St. Neot's; wife and two small sons held hostage for his good behavior.

DERMOT O'Beirne, Bishop—exiled and outlawed human Bishop of Cashien.

DERYNI (Der-in-ee)—racial group gifted with paranormal/supernatural powers and abilities.

DESCANTOR, Bishop Kai—*see Kai Descantor, Bishop*.

DUALTA Jarriot, Lord—a Michaeline knight. (*)

DRUMMOND—*see Cathan, Elinor, Jamie, and Michaela Drummond*.

EDOUARD, Dom—Deryni author of *Haut Arcanum*. (*)

EDWARD MacInnis of Arnham, Bishop—twenty-year-old son of Earl Manfred, and nephew to Archbishop Hubert; Bishop of Grecotha after Alister Cullen.

ELINOR MacRorie Drummond, Lady—widow of Cathan MacRorie and mother of Ansel and Davin by him; wife of Jamie Drummond, by whom she bore Michaela and Cathan.

EMRYS, Dom—renowned Gabrilite adept and Healer; Abbot of St. Neot's; slain there while closing the Portal. (*)

EQUITES CUSTODUM FIDEI—Knights of the Guardians of the Faith; military arm of the *Custodes Fidei*; given the infamous "Benediction of the Sword" which absolves from malicide.

ERCON, a Saint—elder brother of St. Willim; martyred during his attempt to find his brother's murderers; patron of the Little Brothers of Saint Ercon, founded by Paulin of Ramos. (*)

ERENA—Willimite disciple whose sick child was "cured" by Revan and Queron. (*)

ESTELLAN MacInnis, Lady—new Countess of Culdi; Manfred's wife.

EVAINE MacRorie Thuryn, Lady—Deryni adept daughter of Camber; sister of Joram; widow of Rhys Thuryn; a founding member of the Camberian Council.

EWAN, Duke—Duke of Claibourne and Viceroy of Kheldour; one of young King Alroy's five regents; son of Sighere, Gwynedd's first duke.

FANE Fitz-Arthur, Lord—eldest son of Earl Tammaron and husband of the Heiress of Cassan.

FITZ-ARTHUR—see *Fane, Nieve,* and *Tammaron.*

FIONA MacLean—younger sister of the slain Adrian MacLean and granddaughter of Camber's sister Aislinn.

FLANN—a Willimite disciple of Revan.

GABRILITES—priests and Healers of the Order of Saint Gabriel, an all-Deryni esoteric brotherhood founded in 745 and based at Saint Neot's Abbey until 917, when the Order was suppressed and many of its brethren slain; especially noted for the training of Healers.

GEOFFREY MacLean, Lord—late younger brother of Iain and father of Richeldis and Giesele. (*)

GEORDIE—a Willimite reformed Deryni and disciple of Revan.

GIESELE MacLean—age 12; niece of Iain, Earl of Kierney.

GILLEBERT—a Willimite reformed Deryni.

GRAHAM MacEwan, Lord—eleven-year-old son and heir of Ewan, Duke of Claibourne.

GREGORY of Ebor, Lord—Deryni Earl of Ebor and an original member of the Camberian Council; father of Jesse.

GUAIRE of Arliss, Lord—former aide to Alister Cullen and a founding member of the Servants of Saint Camber. (*)

HALDANE—surname of the royal House of Gwynedd.

HONORIA Carmody—wife of the Healer Declan Carmody.

HOWICCAN, Pargan—classic Deryni lyric poet. (*)

HRORIK of Eastmarch, Lord—Earl of Eastmarch; younger brother of Regent Ewan and uncle of Graham.

HUBERT MacInnis, Archbishop—Primate of Gwynedd, Archbishop of Valoret, and one of young King Alroy's five regents; younger brother of Earl Manfred and uncle of Bishop Edward.

IAIN MacLean, Lord—Earl of Kierney; father of the slain Adrian MacLean; nephew of Camber. (*)

IMRE, King—fifth and last Festillic King of Gwynedd (reigned 900–904); father of Mark of Festil, by his sister Ariella. (*)

IVER MacInnis—son of Manfred; marries Lady Richeldis MacLean.

JAFFRAY, Archbishop—slain Deryni Archbishop of Valoret. (*)

JAMIE Drummond, Lord—grand-nephew of Camber and second husband to the widowed Elinor; father of Michaela and Cathan.

JAVAN Jashan Urien Haldane, Prince—age 12; younger twin brother of King Alroy; born with club foot.

JEBEDIAH of Alcara, Lord—slain Deryni Grand Master of the

Order of Saint Michael; a founding member of the Camberian Council. (*)

JERUSHA Evaine Thuryn—infant daughter of Evaine and Rhys; a future Healer.

JESSE MacGregor, Lord—Deryni Master of Ebor; eldest son and heir of Earl Gregory; becomes a member of the Camberian Council.

JOACHIM, Brother—Revan's chief Willimite disciple.

JODOTHA of Carnedd—Deryni adept and disciple of the Great Orin. (*)

JOHN, Brother—an alias of Evaine.

JOKAL of Tyndour—a Deryni Healer-poet. (*)

JORAM MacRorie, Father—youngest son of Camber; brother of Evaine; priest and knight of the Order of Saint Michael; a founding member of the Camberian Council.

JOREVIN of Cashel—a Deryni adept-author. (*)

JURIS, Dom—a fugitive Gabrilite Healer temporarily in Bishop Niallan's household.

KAI Descantor, Bishop—Deryni itinerant bishop who died destroying the Portal in Valoret Cathedral's sacristy. (*)

KENRIC, Dom—a fugitive Gabrilite temporarily in Bishop Niallan's household.

KINEVAN, Dom Queron—see Queron Kinevan, Dom.

KITRON—Deryni author of *Principia Magica*. (*)

KYRIELL—Camber's name in religion. (*)

LEUTIERN—a Deryni adept-author. (*)

LIOR, Father—a priest of the *Custodes Fidei*; assistant to the Inquisitor General.

LIRIN Udaut, Lady—twelve-year-old daughter of the Constable of Gwynedd and bride of Richard Murdoch.

MacDARA, Eamonn—a Mearan Deryni poet, author of "The Ghosting of Ardal L'Estrange." (*)

MacGREGOR, Bishop Ailin—Hubert's Auxiliary Bishop at Valoret.

MacINNIS—see Edward, Hubert, and Manfred MacInnis.

MacLEAN—see Adrian, Aislinn, Camlin, Fiona, Geoffrey, Giesele, Iain, Mairi, and Richeldis.

MacRORIE—surname of Camber's family; see Ansel, Camber, Cathan, Davin, Evaine, and Joram MacRorie.

MAIRI MacLean, Lady—widow of Adrian and mother of Camlin.

MANFRED MacInnis, Lord—new Earl of Culdi and later a Regent of

Gwynedd; elder brother of Archbishop Hubert and father of Bishop Edward.

MARCUS Concannon, Father—Chancellor General of the *Custodes Fidei*, in charge of all seminaries and other institutions of education in Gwynedd.

MARK of Festil, Prince—posthumous son of Imre and Ariella and carrier of the Festillic line after his parents' deaths. (*)

MICHAELA Drummond—age 10; daughter of Elinor and Jamie.

MICHAELINES—priests, knights, and lay brothers of the Order of Saint Michael, a militant fighting and teaching Order, predominantly Deryni, formed during the reign of King Bearand Haldane to hold the Anvil of the Lord against Moorish incursions and defend the sea-lanes; suppressed under the Regency of King Alroy.

MURDOCH of Carthane, Lord—Earl of Carthane and one of young King Alroy's five regents.

NEVAN, Bishop Davet—*see Davet Nevan, Bishop.*

NIALLAN Trey, Bishop—outlawed Deryni Bishop of Dhassa; later, a member of the Camberian Council.

NICARET—Deryni widow engaged as a wet nurse for Evaine's infant daughter Jerusha. (*)

NIEVE Fitz-Arthur, Lady—Tammaron's countess and mother of four sons by him; widow of the late Earl of Tarleton, by whom she bore Peter (later known as Lord Albertus) and Paulin (of Ramos).

NORRIS—a guard at Valoret, in Rhun's service.

O'BEIRNE, Bishop Dermot—*see Dermot O'Beirne, Bishop.*

O'NEILL, Lord Tavis—*see Tavis O'Neill, Lord.*

ORDO VERBI DEI—Order of the Word of God.

ORDO VOX DEI—Order of the Voice of God.

ORIEL, Master—a Healer in the regents' service, particularly Hubert and Tammaron; wife and infant daughter held hostage for his good behavior.

ORIN—Deryni adept and mystic; author of the *Protocols of Orin*, a collection of scrolls containing extremely potent spells of Deryni magic. (*)

ORISS, Archbishop Robert—Archbishop of Rhemuth; former Vicar General of the *Ordo Verbi Dei.*

PARGAN Howiccan—*see Howiccan, Pargan.*

PATRICK, Brother—one of Revan's reformed Deryni Willimite disciples.

PAULIN (Sinclair) of Ramos, Bishop—younger son of the Earl of Tarleton and stepson of Earl Tammaron; founder of the Little Brothers of Saint Ercon (912), a teaching order; first bishop of newly formed See of Stavenham, which office he resigns to found the *Custodes Fidei.*

QUERON Kinevan, Dom—former Gabrilite Healer-priest and founder of the Servants of Saint Camber; later, a member of the Camberian Council.

RADAN, Sir—a weapons master at Rhemuth Castle.

RAMSAY, Captain—one of Hubert's men "baptized" by Revan.

REVAN—lame former tutor to Rhys and Evaine's children; kingpin in the Camberian Council's attempt to save Deryni by blocking their Deryni powers.

RHUN of Horthness, Lord—called The Ruthless; Earl of Sheele and one of young King Alroy's five regents.

RHYS MICHAEL Alister Haldane, Prince—youngest surviving son of King Cinhil, age 10.

RHYS Malachy Thuryn, Lord—deceased Deryni physician and Healer; husband to Evaine, father of Rhysel, Tieg, and Jerusha; a founding member of the Camberian Council. (*)

RHYSEL Joscelyn Thuryn—eight-year-old daughter of Evaine and Rhys.

RICHELDIS MacLean—age 13; niece of Iain, Earl of Kierney.

RICKART, Dom—Gabrilite household Healer to Bishop Niallan.

ROBERT Oriss, Archbishop—*see Oriss, Archbishop Robert.*

RONDEL, Sir—a knight in Lord Manfred's service.

RUADAN of Dhassa—Deryni author of the *Liber Sancti Ruadan.* (*)

SECORIM, Father—Abbot of the Valoret chapter of the *Custodes Fidei.*

SERAFIN, Brother—Inquisitor General of the *Custodes Fidei.*

SIGHERE, Lord—Earl of Marley; uncle of Graham MacEwan.

SINCLAIR—surname of the Earls of Tarleton.

SITRIC—Rhun's second pet Deryni.

STEPHEN, Father—a priest at Valoret Catheral.

SULIEN of R'Kassi—ancient Deryni adept; author of *Annales.* (*)

SYLVAN O'Sullivan—battle-surgeon/Healer in Gregory's household.

TAMMARON Fitz-Arthur, Earl—Chancellor of Gwynedd; one of young King Alroy's five regents.

TAVIS O'Neill—former Healer to Prince Javan, with ability to block Deryni powers; later, member of the Camberian Council.

THURYN—surname of Rhys; *see Aidan, Evaine, Jerusha, Rhys, Rhysel,* and *Tieg.*

TIEG Joram Thuryn—age 3; Healer-son of Rhys and Evaine.

TIERNAN, Brother—a monk at St. Mary's in the Hills.

TORCUILL de la Marche, Lord—Deryni baron dismissed from royal council post by regents.

TREY, Bishop Niallan—*see Niallan Trey, Bishop.*

UDAUT, Lord—Constable of Gwynedd.

URSIN O'Carroll—Manfred's pet Deryni; former classmate of Tavis, and a failed Healer.

VARNARITES—Deryni adepts and scholars who founded a proto-university at Grecotha, late 7th-early 8th century; the Gabrilite Order broke off pre-745.

WILLIAM, Saint—child martyr to Deryni ill use; patron saint of the Willimite movement; younger brother of Saint Ercon.

WILLIAM de Borgos, Lord—proprietor of the finest racing stud in the Eleven Kingdoms. (*)

WILLIMITES—anti-Deryni terrorist group sworn to punish Deryni who escape justice through normal channels; mostly suppressed in 904 under King Imre, but resurging during the latter reign of King Cinhil as a fundamentalist religious sect bent on forcing Deryni to renounce their evil powers and take up a life of penance.

INDEX OF PLACES

ALL SAINTS' CATHEDRAL—seat of the Archbishop of Valoret, Primate of All Gwynedd.

ARNHAM—birthplace of Bishop Edward MacInnis.

CAERRORIE—Camber's principal residence as Earl of Culdi, a few hours' ride northeast of Valoret; now the seat of Manfred MacInnis, the new Earl of Culdi.

CARTHANE—Murdoch's earldom.

CASHIEN—episcopal See formerly held by Bishop Dermot O'Beirne.

CASSAN—petty princedom ruled by Prince Ambert Quinnell.

CLAIBOURNE—principal city of Old Kheldour; title of Ewan, Duke of Claibourne.

CONNAIT, The—barbarian kingdom to the west, famous for its mercenaries.

COR CULDI—hereditary ancestral seat of the Earls of Culdi, near the city of Culdi, on the Gwynedd-Meara border.

DHASSA—free holy city in the Lendour Mountains; seat of the Bishop of Dhassa, who is politically neutral, by tradition.

DOLBAN—site of the mother house of the Servants of Saint Camber, destroyed late 917.

EASTMARCH—earldom held by Hrorik, middle son of Duke Sighere of Kheldour.

EBOR—earldom north of Valoret, held by Gregory.

GRECOTHA—university city, site of the Varnarite School; seat of the Bishop of Grecotha.

GWYNEDD—central of the Eleven Kingdoms and hub of Haldane power since 645, when the first Haldane High King began to unify the area; seat of the Festillic Dynasty, 822–904; restored to the Haldane line in 904 with the accession of Cinhil Haldane.

HORTHNESS—Barony of Rhun the Ruthless.

HOWICCE—kingdom to the southwest of Gwynedd; loosely allied with Llannedd.

KHELDISH RIDING—viceregality broken off Kheldour after its annexation by Duke Sighere and King Cinhil in 906.

KHELDOUR—small kingdom north of Gwynedd, famous for textiles and carpets.

KIERNEY—earldom north of Culdi, loosely linked to the Crown of Gwynedd.

LLANNEDD—kingdom southwest of Gwynedd; loosely allied with Howicce.

MARLEY—small earldom carved out of Eastmarch for Sighere, youngest son of Duke Sighere.

MARLOR—barony of Manfred MacInnis.

MEARA—kingdom/princedom northwest of Gwynedd; nominally a vassal state of Gwynedd.

PORTEE—site of a long-vanished Healers' schola.

RAMOS—abbey town southwest of Valoret; birthplace of Paulin Sinclair; the Council of Ramos convened here in the winter of 917/918.

RHEMUTH—ancient capital of Gwynedd under the Haldanes; abandoned during the Festillic Interregnum; restored under Cinhil and Alroy.

RHENDALL—lake region north of Gwynedd; territorial title given to the heir of the Duke of Claibourne.

SAINT MARY'S IN THE HILLS—isolated monastery in the highlands above Culdi where Joram and Evaine took refuge.

SAINT NEOT'S ABBEY—stronghold of the Order of Saint Gabriel the Archangel, an all-Deryni esoteric order specializing in Healer's training; in the Lendour highlands; destroyed by troops led by the Regent Rhun on Christmas Eve, 917.

SHEELE—Rhys and Evaine's manor house north of Valoret; later, seat of the Earldom of Sheele.

STAVENHAM—episcopal See held briefly by Paulin of Ramos before founding the *Custodes Fidei*.

TARLEVILLE—Earl Tammaron's estate on the Eirian River, several days' ride north of Rhemuth.

TEMPLUM ARCHANGELORUM—long destroyed abbey with ancient esoteric antecedents, location unspecified.

TORENTH—kingdom to the east of Gwynedd; origin of the Festillic line, a cadet branch of the Torenthi royal House; ruled by King Arion.

TREVALGA—Earl Gregory's new estate in the Connait.

TRURILL—castle of Lord Adrian MacLean, Master of Kierney; sacked by regents' forces winter 917/918.

VALORET—Festillic capital of Gwynedd, 822–904.

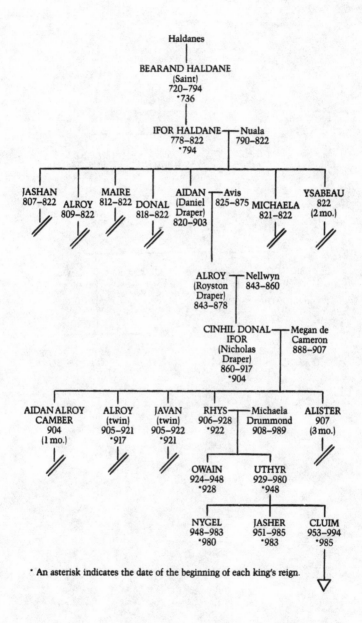

Haldanes

BEARAND HALDANE
(Saint)
720–794
*736

IFOR HALDANE —— Nuala
778–822   790–822
*794

JASHAN   MAIRE   AIDAN — Avis   YSABEAU
807–822 ALROY 812–822 DONAL (Daniel 825–875 MICHAELA   822
        809–822   818–822 Draper)   821–822   (2 mo.)
                                 820–903

ALROY —— Nellwyn
(Royston 843–860
Draper)
843–878

CINHIL DONAL —— Megan de
IFOR   Cameron
(Nicholas   888–907
Draper)
860–917
*904

AIDAN ALROY   ALROY   JAVAN   RHYS —— Michaela   ALISTER
CAMBER   (twin)   (twin)   906–928 Drummond   907
904   905–921   905–922 *922   908–989   (3 mo.)
(1 mo.)   *917   *921

OWAIN   UTHYR
924–948   929–980
*928   *948

NYGEL   JASHER   CLUIM
948–983   951–985   953–994
*980   *983   *985

* An asterisk indicates the date of the beginning of each king's reign.

381

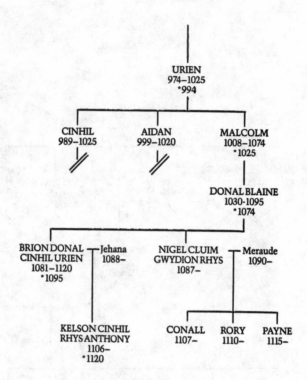

APPENDIX IV

THE FESTILLIC KINGS OF GWYNEDD AND THEIR DESCENDANTS

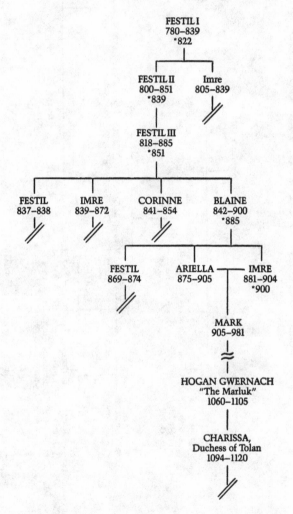

* An asterisk indicates the date of the beginning of each king's reign.

APPENDIX V

PARTIAL LINEAGE OF THE MacRORIES

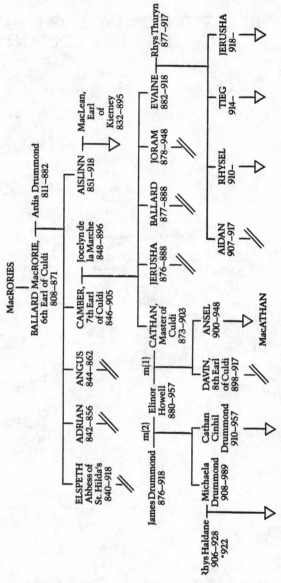

An asterisk indicates the date of the beginning of each king's reign.

ABOUT THE AUTHOR

Katherine Kurtz was born in Coral Gables, Florida, during a hurricane and has led a whirlwind existence ever since. She holds a Bachelor of Science degree in chemistry from the University of Miami, Florida, and a Master of Arts degree in English history from UCLA. She studied medicine before deciding that she would rather write, and is an Ericksonian-trained hypnotist. Her scholarly background also includes extensive research in religious history, magical systems, and other esoteric subjects.

Katherine Kurtz's literary works include the well-known Deryni, Camber, and Kelson Trilogies of fantasy fiction, an occult thriller set in WWII England, and a number of Deryni-related short stories. At least three more trilogies are planned in the Deryni universe, and several additional mainstream thrillers are also currently in development.

Ms. Kurtz recently moved to Ireland, where she lives with her husband and son.